A Modest Proposal

THE BUTTERFLY BOX 1

A Modest Proposal

THE BUTTERFLY BOX 1

a novel

Michele Ashman Bell

Covenant Communications, Inc.

To all the mothers who've stood in dressings rooms with their crying daughters because it was so difficult to find a modest dress for a formal dance. You are not alone.

This book is for you.

Chapter One

Lost in thought, Lauryn Alexander drew several final, sweeping lines on the evening gown she was sketching, then held it out to look at the completed picture.

Before boarding the flight from New York City to Las Vegas, she'd noticed a classic movie magazine with a picture of Ginger Rogers on the cover. The structured bodice and long, flowing silk of the gown Ginger had been wearing inspired Lauryn, and she couldn't wait to get seated on the plane so she could pull out her sketchbook and get the image down on paper.

Not that it would matter. The sketch would end up in her file with all the others she'd drawn, along with her frustration. But that didn't stop her from creating elegant gowns, at least on paper.

"Excuse me, miss," the woman next to Lauryn said. "That's a beautiful drawing. Are you a designer?"

Lauryn smiled at the woman who was probably in her mid-fifties. Her chic haircut and classy knit suit spoke of wealth and sophistication.

She's probably wearing a St. John, Lauryn thought. St. John suits were thousands of dollars, and nothing was more beautiful than the fabric and fit of a St. John. Lauryn became aware of her own clean-cut khakis that she was wearing with the button-front trench coat she had designed herself.

"Yes, I am," Lauryn answered. "I design for Jacqueline Yvonne."

"Jacqueline Yvonne!" the woman exclaimed. "I should have known. I love Jacqueline Yvonne's career and evening wear collections."

This time it took effort for Lauryn to smile. "Oh, yes. Well, I design outerwear," she admitted reluctantly. Not that she wasn't one of the best outerwear designers in the city. It was just that her dream was to design beautiful dresses and gowns, not what women wore over them.

"Outerwear . . . I see. Like coats and jackets," the woman said.

Lauryn nodded. She loved working for Jacqueline Yvonne; Jacqueline was like a second mother to her. In fact, she'd been a better mother to Lauryn than her own mother, but Jacqueline just didn't seem to believe in her enough to give her a chance to design the kinds of clothes she wanted to design.

"Deary, I think you ought to show Ms. Yvonne what you've done here. It's quite beautiful."

"Well, thank you," Lauryn replied. The woman didn't know that Lauryn had taken many of her designs to Jacqueline, who always assured her that her day would come, but Lauryn was losing patience. She'd designed outerwear for nearly eight years, and with each passing year, Lauryn felt her dream slipping away faster than last year's fashions. She felt tired and upset to find herself at a dead end.

"In fact," the woman held up a finger, "I need a gown for a business conference in Zurich in a few months; have you ever considered doing custom designs? I have quite a few friends I could refer to you, besides myself."

Lauryn couldn't believe her ears. "I have done a few custom designs, and I'd love to do more."

"Why don't you give me your card, and I'll give you a call when I get back to the city."

Praying she still had some of her business cards, Lauryn fished through her bag until she found the little container. There were three cards inside.

"Here you go," Lauryn said, handing two of them to the woman.

"Lauryn Alexander," the woman said, reading out loud from the card. "It's wonderful to meet you, Ms. Alexander. I'm Caroline Nottingham." She held out a perfectly manicured hand clad in a diamond ring the size of a small walnut.

"It's so nice to meet you, Ms. Nottingham. Please, call me Lauryn." The two women shook hands.

"And please, call me Caroline." She tucked the cards into her purse, then turned to Lauryn. "You know, deary, I have a feeling you will get your big break soon. I have an eye for fashion, and I don't think someone with your talent can be ignored much longer. Just don't give up on your dream. After my husband died, I was left with a lot of debt and no resources. Now I own a multimillion-dollar business. Perhaps you've heard of my hotel chain, Nottingham Plaza Hotels."

Lauryn's mouth dropped open. "You're *that* Nottingham?"

Caroline smiled. "Yes, dear. And I know what the power of positive thinking can do." The gracious woman took Lauryn's hand in hers. "Lauryn, dream big and work hard. You can achieve anything if you want it badly enough."

Lauryn felt the fire of inspiration burn inside of her. What an incredible woman.

"I believe in you," Caroline said. "You have the talent, but the greatest talent in the world doesn't achieve greatness; it's the hard work that does it."

"You should write a book!" Lauryn exclaimed.

"Funny you should say so. I actually am in the process of doing just that. In fact, you'll never guess who's agreed to write the foreword for me."

"Who?"

"Oprah."

"Caroline, that's incredible."

"It *is* incredible. I grew up in a poor area of Pittsburgh with a drunken father and a mother who held down two jobs and did ironing at home. My biggest goal back then was to finish high school, then get a job waitressing, like most of the other women in my neighborhood. And now look at me."

Lauryn nodded, awestruck by the woman.

"I did well in school, and I was smart enough to recognize an opportunity when it came my way. I was offered a scholarship at a community college and decided to give it a try. That was my ticket out. I'm a strong advocate of education. Many of today's youth don't realize that's the key that unlocks the door of opportunity."

"So that's what did it for you?"

"Absolutely. I finished college with a business degree and found a job at a Marriott Hotel in New York. That's where I met my William."

"Your husband?"

Caroline nodded with a faraway look in her eyes. "William was a musician. He played the violin for many of the shows on Broadway. He had a wonderful career in music. He passed away nearly ten years ago after a long battle with colon cancer."

"I'm so sorry," Lauryn said.

"So am I. A day doesn't go by that I don't miss him." Caroline looked down at the plain gold wedding band she still wore on her finger. "He was the kindest man I've ever known. Are you married?"

Lauryn had to stop herself from bursting out laughing. "No," she answered, not bothering to explain how difficult the dating scene was for her, a twenty-nine-year-old LDS girl in New York City.

"Make sure you marry someone who is kind. Your marriage will be a blessing in your life if you do."

"I will." She thought about her own father, who was also a kind person. But it hadn't helped him to be kind when he was married to Lauryn's mother. No one could have made a marriage work with her. "So," Lauryn asked, "how did you become a hotel magnate?"

"I learned everything about the business that I could. William's work gave him many opportunities to travel, so I gathered ideas from each of the hotels we stayed in, many of them in Europe. We weren't able to have children, so I threw myself into my work. If I regret anything it would be that we got wrapped up in our careers and didn't adopt children, especially now that I'm alone. I have my friends and a sister I see occasionally, but it's not the same."

Caroline's thoughts seemed to drift for a moment. Lauryn noticed the hint of sadness in her eyes.

"Sorry, dear," Caroline said. "I guess we all have to learn things the hard way when it comes to life."

Lauryn couldn't have agreed more. Lately that seemed to be the only way she learned anything.

"Anyway, something else I've learned is that you have to be ready when an opportunity presents itself. I had left Marriott by the time William died, so I was beside myself trying to figure out what to do. I loved my husband, but he left me with some bad investments to deal with on my own. Then, almost out of nowhere, while visiting my sister in Florida, I stumbled across a hotel for sale—a beautiful Victorian structure with an amazing view of the ocean. I was ready for a change of scenery, so I got a business loan and took the greatest leap of faith I've ever taken in my life."

"Were you scared?"

"Nearly to death!" Caroline said. "But it turned out to be the best leap I've ever made, and it led to acquiring another hotel, and then another. My philosophy was to give all my guests the same experience I wanted to have when I stayed at a hotel."

"That's fascinating. You've done this all yourself?"

"Well, I've had wonderful help along the way. A lot of the people I'd met during my years in the hotel industry came to work for me; people I knew I could trust and had the same ideals I had. I also like to think that my William has helped me a little, too."

Lauryn smiled. "I'm sure he has."

"So," Caroline said, returning her smile, "you wouldn't mind designing a dress for me?"

"It would be my pleasure. What are you thinking?"

Caroline described the dress she had in mind—something black, sophisticated, and elegant.

"I'll be gone for ten days on business," Caroline told her. "But when I get back to the city we can meet again and talk some more."

"I'll have a sketch and some sample fabrics for you," Lauryn said. "I already have some ideas."

"Thank you, my dear. You've made this a very enjoyable flight. I usually fly first-class, but this was a last-minute arrangement, and I had to take what was left. I've been spoiled. I'm sure you can imagine."

Lauryn couldn't imagine. She'd never flown first-class.

"So," Caroline asked, "are you on your way to something wonderful?"

"I'm going to meet friends in Las Vegas for the weekend."

"That sounds fun."

"It will be! They're friends from high school. We try to meet every year to catch up on each other's lives. We're very close, even though none of us live by each other anymore."

"I think that's wonderful! A weekend of shopping."

"And eating and laughing. We do a lot of that."

"And gambling."

"None of us are into the whole casino scene."

Caroline nodded. "I see." Then she shook her head. "Actually, I don't see. Why go to Vegas if you don't gamble?"

"It was just a central location for everyone. I found a great flight deal, and the others are in California and Utah. It just worked out. But like I said, we're not really into the whole Vegas strip thing, either."

"That's very wise of you. I simply abhor gambling. Part of the debt my husband left me was a result of gambling. A waste of time and money, if you ask me."

"I agree."

The flight attendant announced their descent into Las Vegas. Lauryn was amazed at how quickly the flight had gone by.

Lauryn and Caroline exited the plane together, then Caroline paused before saying good-bye.

"Thank you for making that such an enjoyable trip," Caroline told Lauryn.

"It was enjoyable for me too; you've been an inspiration."

Caroline reached for Lauryn's hand and gave it a squeeze. "Listen, deary, if I can do it, anyone can. You just have to keep your eye on your goal, be ready when those opportunities come your way, then work like crazy to make it all happen. You can do it. I see a little bit of myself in you."

"Thank you, Caroline. I hope so."

"I'll give you a call when I get home. I'll be spending more and more time in Europe. I'm opening a new hotel in Zurich. Maybe you can come and stay sometime. My treat."

"That would be wonderful!" Lauryn exclaimed.

Caroline gave her a brief hug and air-kissed her on each cheek. "Ta-ta, deary, we'll talk soon," she said, then wheeled away her Gucci carry-on bag to catch her connecting flight.

Lauryn watched as Caroline hurried out of sight, then shook her head in awe. What a woman! So accomplished, so genuine.

She walked through the airport, mulling over the conversation she'd had with Caroline. With her thirtieth birthday looming ahead of her, Lauryn decided it was time to take a good look at her life and quit settling for the routine, monotonous existence she'd been living. She wanted the next decade of her life to be one of changes and new challenges.

Excitement bubbled up inside her. Somehow she was going to make her dreams come true. No one was going to do it for her. She refused to live another decade only to look back and wonder what she'd done with the last ten years.

Squaring her shoulders and lifting her chin, she snatched her luggage off the conveyor belt and dropped it to the floor next to her. Things were going to be different starting today!

With a resolve to think positively and visualize her dreams, she headed for the entrance to hail a taxi to the hotel. She wasn't exactly sure what had happened on that flight, but something felt tremendously different inside of her. And it felt wonderful!

Chapter Two

Lauryn slowly opened the door to the hotel room and braced herself for a bombardment of hugs. She didn't have to wait long. As soon as she popped her head in the door, her friend Andrea sprang from the bed and threw her arms around Lauryn.

"Hey, Andie, so good to see you," Lauryn said, trying to hide her concern.

Lauryn was surprised at how little of her friend there was to hug. In high school, Andrea had been a bit chubby, but her infectious laugh and fun-loving personality made her a beautiful girl, inside and out. Yet she had never believed she was beautiful. Her weight struggles were a huge issue she still battled, except now she was on the other end of the scale.

"Look at you!" Andrea exclaimed, reaching up and lifting one of Lauryn's shoulder-length, honey-blond curls. "What a great haircut! You look more incredible each time I see you."

"Thanks," Lauryn said, searching for words to return the compliment. Andrea's bleach-blond hair was pulled into a tight ponytail, accentuating her overly thin face. "I'd give anything to have your tan."

"I just got back from presenting at a fitness convention in Hawaii. We filmed some segments of my infomercial there, too. It was great."

"I can't wait to hear about it." Before Lauryn could say any more she was caught in a hug by her friend Chloe.

"Hey, sweetie," Chloe said. "It's so good to see you."

"You too." Lauryn smiled at Chloe, who bubbled over with her usual enthusiasm. "How are Roger and the girls?"

"Wonderful as ever. Roger found a new job working for a clean videos store. He does the editing."

"He takes out all the bad stuff?"

"Yeah. Isn't that great? There's so much unnecessary stuff in most movies. He just edits it out."

"Do you worry about him being exposed to all that?"

"Roger?" Chloe laughed. "Are you kidding? He's the guy who doesn't even watch TV because of all the bad stuff on it. He doesn't even like me to get catalogs in the mail from Victoria's Secret or any store that carries bikinis and skimpy clothes. He's very careful about what he's exposed to."

Lauryn nodded. Roger was very stalwart when it came to gospel standards. "How's the new salon?"

"Great," Chloe said. "I'm so blessed to be able to work out of my home and stay with my girls."

Chloe's dream had always been to have her own hair salon. In high school, Chloe was constantly experimenting with her hair color. Even now Lauryn couldn't remember its natural tone. Lauryn was thrilled for her friend. She had never seen Chloe without a smile and a twinkle in her eye. Her small, five-foot-three frame embodied the most effervescent personality of anyone Lauryn had ever known. Even when things were bad, Chloe managed to find a positive side to them. Lauryn loved Chloe with all her heart but wondered if one day Chloe was going to snap because of all the emotion she held in. No one could be happy all the time, could they?

"Come on, Chloe, don't hog Lauryn all night." Emma stepped up with a smile and hugged her friend.

As happy as Lauryn was to see Emma, she pulled back with a look of concern. "How are you, Em? Have you heard anything from him?"

"Nothing," Emma said. She'd just gone through a painful divorce with a man she'd been married to for barely two years. "He wouldn't admit it, but I think he had someone else."

Lauryn looked into Emma's dark eyes. As much as Emma tried, she'd never been able to hide the sadness behind her eyes. "So, what are you doing? You said something about looking for a new job."

"I haven't found anything yet. I feel like a bird over the ocean. I can't find anywhere to land," Emma said. "I've come close a few times, but then the job falls through. I wish I would've finished college. It seems like every good job requires a degree."

"It's not too late, you know," Lauryn told her.

"Ugh! Go back to college?" Emma rolled her eyes. "You know how they say the first time you marry for love, the second time for money? That's what I need, a rich husband. Love isn't all it's cracked up to be."

"I'll take education over men any day," Lauryn's friend Jocelyn said, giving Lauryn a hug. "It's great to see you. How was your flight?"

Lauryn considered Jocelyn the natural beauty of the group. She had a long, elegant neck and dark brown hair that added to the regal manner in which she moved. But for such a beautiful girl, Lauryn couldn't understand why Jocelyn always dressed so plainly. Her hair was always pulled back, and Lauryn hadn't seen her in makeup since high school.

"It was actually incredible. I met the most fascinating woman. I'll have to tell you about her," Lauryn replied.

"I'm starving," Chloe exclaimed. "When can we eat?"

"I'm hungry too," Emma added. "I've been craving Cheesecake Factory ever since I knew we were coming. Can we please eat there sometime?"

"Why not right now?" Chloe said. "That sounds good to me."

"Works for me," Lauryn said.

"Whatever you guys want is good for me," Jocelyn added. "What about you, Andie?"

"Oh . . . sure," Andie replied. "I love Cheesecake Factory."

Emma and Lauryn exchanged glances. They were both worried about Andie's diminishing frame.

* * *

That night in their room, the girls changed into comfy clothes, then gathered on the two king-size beds. There was also a rollaway, which Emma graciously offered to sleep on. They could easily afford two or more rooms, but they wanted to sleep in the same room. That way they could stay up late and talk, then fall asleep when they got tired. Lauryn always remembered to bring earplugs since Chloe had a tendency to snore.

Each of them contributed to the candy pile, and they also munched on Cheetos and barbecue-flavored Pringles, courtesy of Emma, the junk-food junkie of the group.

"So, this is probably the best time to do the Butterfly Box," Emma said as she placed a cloth-wrapped bundle in front of them. "I do have to say that being keeper of the box this last year has proven to be interesting. Of course, I wouldn't have gotten through the divorce without each of you helping me, so maybe the box did make a difference. I gained an annoying ten pounds too, but that could be attributed more to my addiction to french fries and chocolate than anything. All I can say is, may the recipient this year have better luck with men than I had and not gain weight while the box is in her possession."

Based on Emma's last comment, Lauryn thought of Andrea. She could stand to gain a few pounds. She hadn't taken more than two bites of her salad at dinner.

Chloe placed her hand on the cloth over the box and said in a quiet tone, "Every year when this box comes out I am filled with emotion. It represents so much." She cleared her throat, then blinked her eyes a few times and gave the others a smile. "Sorry."

Jocelyn slid an arm around Chloe's shoulders and gave her a hug. "That's okay. I feel the same way."

"I'll never forget when you came up with the idea to start the Butterfly Box after Ava's funeral," Emma said to Jocelyn. "It was exactly what we needed at the time."

Ava had been an important part of their group of friends. None of them had completely gotten over her unexpected death.

"The idea really came while we were at Lauryn's pageant," Jocelyn said.

"Don't remind me," Lauryn said with a groan. "I was hoping by now you all would have forgotten about it."

"Why do you want to forget about it? That pageant changed the course of your life," Emma reminded her.

"That's right, Lauryn. Who knows where you'd be today if you hadn't done that pageant," Chloe added.

"Ava was the one who talked me into doing it," Lauryn said.

"That doesn't surprise me," Chloe said. "She could talk anyone into anything."

"Remember that time she talked me into getting my hair cut like Jennifer Anniston's and I ended up with a mullet!" Emma exclaimed. "That was by far the worst experience of my life. And I've had some pretty rotten experiences."

The others tried not to laugh, but their efforts were in vain.

"I told you to let me cut it, but you didn't trust me," Chloe said.

"After you fried Lauryn's hair and it all fell out, do you blame me?" Emma countered.

Chloe's mouth fell open.

Lauryn decided not to get in the middle of the discussion, although her hair had been a pretty horrific sight for a good month.

"That was my brother's fault. He was supposed to set the timer on the stove. How was I supposed to know he set it for two hours instead of twenty minutes?"

"All right, all right," Jocelyn finally interrupted, "this is totally off the subject. We were talking about the Butterfly Box and Lauryn's pageant."

"I'll never forget the day Mrs. Sanderson asked me to be in the pageant," Lauryn said. "Ava was there with me . . ."

* * *

April, 1995—Dixie High School

"Lauryn, wait up!" Ava called as Lauryn raced down the hall to the home economics department. "Where are you going?"

"Mrs. Sanderson said she needed to see me after school."

"Why?" Ava asked, shifting her hot-pink purse to the other shoulder. "I'm not sure. I already handed in my project."

"Me too, even though I didn't get mine half done. I hate sewing. I don't know why we have to learn how to sew anyway. No one sews anymore." Ava ran her hand through her long, blond hair.

"I actually enjoy sewing a lot," Lauryn said. "I love the creative process."

Ava looked at her with her piercing blue eyes in a way that made Lauryn feel like she'd suddenly started talking in Chinese.

"I do," Lauryn said, shrugging her shoulders. "Call me crazy."

"You're crazy," Ava said as they turned the corner. "Speaking of crazy, did you talk to Jocelyn today?"

"Yeah, her mother took off again. This time for a couple of weeks with her boyfriend."

"I'd invite her to my house, but my grandma just came to live with us."

"I'd invite her to my house, but she's probably better off alone than with my mother."

Lauryn didn't know whose mother was worse, hers or Jocelyn's. Even though her parents were still married, she wondered how her dad put up with her mom's yelling, outrageous spending habits, and antagonistic attitude toward the gospel.

They arrived at the home economics room. Lauryn reached to open the door.

"Wait!" Ava exclaimed. "I probably shouldn't go in there. She'll bug me about my sewing project."

"She hasn't even started grading them. Come in with me, just in case I'm in trouble or something."

"You, in trouble!" Ava scoffed. "The only time you go to the principal's office is to pick up awards."

"That's not true. I've been there for other stuff," Lauryn said.

"Like what?"

"I don't know . . . meetings."

Ava rolled her eyes and shook her head, then reached for the doorknob. "Face it, Lauryn, you and I are total opposites."

"Maybe that's why we get along so well."

Ava laughed. "Yeah, maybe so."

"Girls, come in," Mrs. Sanderson said as she got up from her desk.

"Hi, Mrs. Sanderson," Lauryn said. "You wanted to see me?"

"Yes, Lauryn. There's something I wanted to talk to you about. Hello, Ava. I was happy to see you turned in your project. Have you had a chance to find that assignment you left in your friend's locker?"

"Uh, not yet. But I'll look again tomorrow," Ava answered with a noncommittal toss of her head.

"Well, Lauryn, you're probably wondering why I asked you to come and see me."

Lauryn nodded.

"I received a notice from an organization looking for young women who are talented, involved in their community, and who have good grades. I thought it might be something you would be interested in. It's a scholarship organization looking for girls such as yourself to participate in their program."

Lauryn had already sent out several scholarship applications but hadn't heard back from any of them yet. Her parents both worked and said they would help her out with school, but she wanted to earn her own way and go to the school of her choice.

"What do I have to do?"

"It's called the Miss Young American pageant."

"A pageant? Like a beauty pageant? No way!" Lauryn stepped back and was ready to run from the room. "I would never be caught dead doing a beauty pageant."

"It's not a beauty pageant," Mrs. Sanderson assured her. "You are judged on academics, talent, community service, fitness, and interview. I'm sure it helps if you are pretty. And that's no problem for you. You've got everything they're looking for, Lauryn. I think it would be good for you."

Lauryn shook her head and said, "I don't have time for something like that. I'm too busy with my schoolwork. I'm sure my grades aren't good enough for the pageant anyway."

"Your grades are excellent, Lauryn, and your ACT score was superior. I already gave the pageant director your name. She's going to call

you. Just think about it. You can tell her no if you want, but the winner gets five thousand dollars, and even the attendants get scholarship money."

"I don't even have—"

"Just think about it. It would be a good experience for you. Who knows, it may open a few doors, too."

* * *

Lauryn nearly broke her back trying to kick herself for agreeing to be a part of the pageant. Her friends had helped her shop for the wardrobe she'd need for the competition. She managed to find a cute swimsuit and an outfit to wear for the interview with the judges, but there wasn't a decent dress in town she could wear for an evening gown.

Five days later, Lauryn stared at the designer gown hanging on the doorjamb going into her bedroom and felt anger rise up inside of her. Her mother had promised she would get a modest evening gown while she was in New York on business, and this was what she had come up with? It was just one more sign that her mother didn't support her standards.

The fabric was beautiful, a soft turquoise chiffon over matching turquoise satin. It had a fitted bodice with a small spaghetti strap on either side. The same layered fabric comprised the rest of the gown, which was fitted through the waist, then flared out at the bottom with a short train in the back. The top was beaded and had sparkling crystals sewn generously on the front and back. It was breathtaking and, Lauryn guessed, extremely expensive.

Fingering the fabric as if she were touching a rare, priceless garment, Lauryn noticed the name on the tag. Jacqueline Yvonne. Lauryn gasped. She'd just read an article about Jacqueline Yvonne while working on an assignment for home economics. Jacqueline Yvonne was one of the newest designers to take New York by storm. Lauryn had expected the woman to be from Paris or somewhere in Europe, but she was from a small town in Montana. The article hadn't been very flattering, focusing on some of the mistakes Ms. Yvonne had made while working her way to the top.

The problem was, it didn't matter if this were the most expensive, fancy-shmancy dress this side of Milan; she couldn't wear it. And the pageant was only two days away.

She fell onto her bed in a heap and pulled a pillow over her head. Why had she agreed to do this stupid pageant? Why? Why? Why?

She was bound to get one of the other scholarships she'd applied for, based on her grades alone. The money from this pageant probably wouldn't help that much anyway.

But it was too late to back out now.

The phone beside her bed rang. She was tempted not to answer, but she rolled over with a groan and glumly said, "Hello."

"Wow, glad to hear from you too." It was her friend Jace. They'd become friends during ninth grade when they were study partners in biology, and they had stayed friends all through high school. Even though she had her girlfriends, there was something special about her relationship with Jace. In a way, he was like her best friend, the person she could talk to about anything.

"Sorry, Jace," Lauryn said. "I'm just totally regretting this whole pageant thing."

"Wait a minute. I thought everything was going well."

"It's my mom. She got me an evening gown."

"Gee, how horrible of her," he said.

"You don't understand," Lauryn vented. "There's no way I can wear the dress."

"What's wrong with it?"

"It's just not something I'd wear. For starters, it has spaghetti straps. I could never be comfortable in it."

"Why can't you fix it?"

"The dress probably cost six or seven hundred dollars. I can't just go chopping it to pieces."

"Why not? Isn't that better than not using it at all?"

"I don't—"

The front door opened and Lauryn's parents came inside, both of them talking—no, her father was talking, her mother was yelling. The door slammed shut, and Lauryn's mother continued her high-pitched tirade into the kitchen.

"It's my money and I can do what I want with it!" Lauryn's mother sounded like a child who didn't want to share her toys.

"I understand that; I'm just trying to say that with our other debts, right now may not be the best time to buy something like that." Her father tried to remain calm.

"You never let me do anything I want! Why did I ever marry such a penny-pinching fool in the first place?"

Lauryn covered her opposite ear with her hand and squeezed her eyes shut.

"What's going on?" Jace asked.

"My parents are home. They're having another fight."

"Sorry. They sure do fight a lot."

"I know. I hate it," she said, her voice gravelly with emotion.

"You want me to come over and get you? We could go get some burgers."

"No." She swallowed to clear her throat. "I'm okay."

"I'm coming over right now," he said, not taking no for an answer. "I'll be there in five minutes."

She appreciated his thoughtfulness. She really didn't want to stay home. "Thanks, Jace."

Her mother had stomped up the stairs to her room and slammed that door too.

Lauryn watched for Jace to pull up in front, then ran outside, not bothering to leave a note. Her mom wouldn't miss her anyway.

* * *

"Lauryn!" Ava's voice called out over the noise of the Frostop.

Lauryn looked up and saw her two friends Ava and Jocelyn rushing toward her.

They both gave her a hug and scooted into the booth between her and Jace. Lauryn thought she noticed a trace of disappointment in Jace's light blue eyes as he moved to the other end of the booth. Ava immediately picked up a handful of fries without asking and dunked them in fry sauce.

"What are you two doing here?" Ava asked with her mouth full.

"I needed to get out of the house, so Jace offered to take me for burgers. What are you guys doing?"

"Cruising for hot boys," Ava answered.

Jocelyn's mouth dropped open, and her face flushed red. "No, we're not!"

"Maybe you aren't, but I am. Do you have any hot friends, Jace?"

Jace's eyes bulged. "I don't know."

"He wouldn't know if his own friends are hot," Jocelyn told Ava.

"Why not? We know which girls are and which girls aren't," Ava defended herself. "Besides, now that I think about it, I've only seen you hang out with that Middleton kid, what's his name . . . Tommy? Timmy?"

"It's Tony," Jace told her. "He's got a girlfriend."

"Who?"

"Natalie Watson."

"What? Natalie Watson has a boyfriend? How does a loser like that get a boyfriend?" Ava nearly yelled.

"Shhh, someone might hear you," Jocelyn whispered, dipping her chin and shielding her face with her hand.

Ava was one of Lauryn's best friends, but she had to admit that Ava could be a little snotty, especially to kids who weren't exactly popular at school. It didn't help that Ava was a cheerleader and had been voted homecoming queen. A fact she often reminded them of.

"I'm sorry, but I should have a boyfriend before someone like her!" Ava exclaimed.

Jocelyn's face was still buried in her hands.

Ava reached for Lauryn's root beer and took a long drink.

"That's a pretty sweater, Jocelyn," Lauryn said, trying to change the subject.

Before Jocelyn could answer, Ava said, "That's mine. I let her borrow it because I wasn't going to let her wear another one of her grandma's sweaters."

Jocelyn's face registered both embarrassment and pain.

"I'm sorry, but with the right clothes, Joss, you could be the hottest girl at school. You are gorgeous. You just hide it under your frumpy clothes."

"I like how Jocelyn dresses," Lauryn said in her friend's defense. "It's unique."

Jocelyn's sense of style may have been a little outdated, but Ava's *style was extreme in a different way. Today she was wearing a tight T-shirt that barely covered her midriff and short, cutoff jeans.*

"*Whatever,*" Ava said, unaware that she might have hurt Jocelyn's feelings. "*Hey, what's that?*" She reached over and snatched Lauryn's paper napkin before Lauryn could stop her.

"*I was just sketching some ideas for my evening gown. I need to make some alterations.*"

"*Wow, this is good. Even on a napkin. Did you make this dress?*"

"*No, my mom bought it for me, but I have to make some changes before the pageant.*"

"*Cool,*" Ava said. Her attention was drawn to the front door and the large group of people coming inside, but seeing no one of interest, she quickly turned back to Lauryn.

"*I thought Emma was working tonight,*" she said. "*We wanted some free food.*"

"*Looks like you're getting some anyway,*" Jace said.

"*Oh, yeah,*" Ava laughed and looked at the onion ring in her hand. "*Sorry, hope you didn't want that.*"

"*No, that's fine. I'm full,*" Jace said.

"*I shouldn't eat much anyway,*" Lauryn told them.

Jocelyn looked at the sketch on the napkin. "*I like the changes you're making to the dress.*"

"*I think it looks better without the cap sleeve,*" Ava said. "*You are so totally lucky to have a mom that would buy you such an awesome dress.*"

Lauryn didn't answer.

Jace threw his wadded-up napkin on the table. "*I need to get going. I still have a paper to write for history. Did you get yours done, Lauryn?*"

"*I finished this afternoon,*" she said. "*It wasn't too bad.*"

"*You were smart to start early.*" Jace scooted out of the booth. "*You ready to go?*"

"*Sure. I need to go tackle that dress. But I'd rather write a history paper.*"

"*Hey, write mine and I'll figure out something for your dress,*" Jace said, flashing his dimpled smile.

"*Yeah, right! I can see it now. You'd probably staple some fabric on or use duct tape to make sleeves. I think I'll pass.*"

Jace feigned offense. "Gee, I guess you didn't see how my project in sewing class turned out. Mrs. Sanderson said mine was the best out of all the guys."

"Mrs. Sanderson told me you were the only boy who finished out of the whole class," Lauryn told him.

"That's beside the point," he objected.

"Well, if that shirt you made is so fabulous, why don't you ever wear it to school?" Lauryn asked.

"I wouldn't be caught dead in that shirt," he replied honestly.

"My point exactly!" Lauryn said.

"Let's go find Emma," Ava said to Jocelyn as she took one last bite of Jace's onion ring. "If she's not working, maybe she's home." Then her expression froze. "Wait a minute . . . don't look now, but I see some seriously good-looking college boys over there by the salad bar."

Jocelyn turned to look, but Ava hissed, "Don't look!"

Jocelyn flipped her head back around.

"Jace," Ava said, "can you tell if they're looking at us?"

"I'm not going to check out guys for you," Jace told her.

"Just look!" Ava ordered.

"All right, all right."

There was silence while Jace scanned the group and the three girls tried to act casual. Jace watched as a younger boy he knew from junior high walked past the table where the guys were seated. One of the older boys purposely stuck his foot out and tripped the boy, causing his tray full of food to splatter across the floor. The entire table of guys roared with laughter.

"Well?" Ava demanded.

"Those guys look like trouble. You should stay away from them," Jace told her.

"Whatever, Jace. Just tell us, are they looking at us?"

"Not anymore. Their food just arrived."

Ava looked disappointed for a moment, then her eyes lit up. "Wait, I have an idea. Come on, Jocelyn." She grabbed her friend's hand and pulled her to her feet.

Lauryn could tell Jocelyn wasn't excited about whatever Ava had planned, but Jocelyn wasn't good at sticking up for herself. Especially when it came to strong-willed Ava.

"See you guys later," Lauryn said, watching as Ava dragged Jocelyn to an empty table near the college boys.

Jace watched them as well, shaking his head slowly, a disapproving look on his face.

"What?" Lauryn asked.

He shrugged. "Ava seems desperate."

"She's boy crazy," Lauryn told him.

"What's the difference?"

Lauryn opened her mouth to answer but had no explanation. "Not much, I guess."

"Why is she like that?"

This was something Lauryn had wondered herself. "I think it's partly that she likes the attention she gets from boys. I don't really know. Her dad is the bishop of the ward, and her mom's in the Relief Society presidency and stuff, but Ava doesn't really seem very religious. I don't get it."

Jace's gaze traveled away from Lauryn's face.

"What are you looking at?" she asked.

"Ava. She just walked over to the table of those college boys."

"No way." Lauryn flipped around to see Ava putting on the charm, twisting a piece of hair around one finger and tilting her head as she flirted. She watched long enough for Ava to turn and wave Jocelyn over. The boys pulled two extra chairs up to the table for the girls to sit down.

"She sure works fast," Jace said.

"Whatever Ava wants, Ava gets," Lauryn said. Ava had a way of manipulating and scheming to get whatever she wanted. And sometimes it didn't matter who she stepped on to get it. Lauryn loved Ava. They'd been friends since grade school, but Ava had changed as they'd gotten older, and Lauryn wasn't sure about some of the choices Ava was making.

"I hope she knows what she's getting both of them into." Jace's concern alarmed her.

"You really think those guys look like trouble?"

"I guess they'll be fine. It's just burgers."

Lauryn looked at the table of guys again. One of them had his arm around Ava. "Yeah, just burgers."

But Lauryn couldn't help the feeling of concern that lingered long after they left the Frostop.

Chapter Three

"High school seems so long ago," Emma said, reaching for a bag of candy. "It's hard to believe Ava's been gone twelve years."

"It's true," Chloe said. "At least Ava lived her life like every day was her last day on earth."

Emma ripped open a bag of Reese's peanut butter cups with her teeth, then dumped the contents on the bed in front of everyone. "This might sound rude, but I have to admit, as much as I loved Ava, she sure used to get me in a lot of trouble."

"Me too," Andrea said. "I was grounded more than once because she wouldn't let me go home on time. I know she didn't mean to get me in trouble, but she didn't seem to have much respect for authority. But it was hard to resist her, because she was so much fun to hang out with."

"I laughed so hard with her I almost wet my pants," Chloe said. "I miss her so much, don't you, Joss?"

Jocelyn seemed to be lost in thought until Chloe asked her a direct question.

"Huh?"

"You probably miss Ava a lot. You were such good friends before you went to help your grandma our junior year."

"Oh . . . yeah . . ." Jocelyn said. "It's never been the same without her."

Lauryn detected a strange tone in Jocelyn's voice but wasn't sure what it was, like she had something on her mind and was distracted.

"I think it's time to open the Butterfly Box," Andrea said.

"Me too," Emma agreed.

There was an undercurrent of anticipation as Emma pulled back the cloth to reveal a large jewelry box made of porcelain and encrusted with gold. Slowly, she unfastened the latch and opened the lid. Even though the ceremony was the same each year, it was a part of who they were, a connection to what had brought them closer together as friends in the first place.

"There it is," Chloe said breathlessly. She reached forward and lifted an object out of the box: a sparkling tiara.

Lauryn hated that she'd put that thing in there. It should have gone to DI along with the rest of her junk. But the other girls loved it and loved to relive the story.

"When you won that crown, it was like a fairytale," Emma said.

"So true," Chloe agreed. "I think every one of us felt like we were up there with you. You represented the everyday girls—girls like us—not the polished, pageant girl who isn't real."

"Do you still remember how you felt that night?" Chloe asked.

Lauryn nodded. Even though it was over ten years ago, she remembered the pageant almost as if it were yesterday. It really had changed her life. In more ways than one.

* * *

The Pageant

Stress filled Lauryn's chest, compressing her heart and lungs, making her feel light-headed and nauseated.

She needed to leave for the pageant, but her parents were too busy fighting, and she didn't dare interrupt them to ask them to take her.

With shaky fingers, she picked up the phone, dialed, and prayed Jace would answer.

"Hey there, Miss Young American," he said brightly.

The sound of his voice uncorked her emotions, and she started to cry.

"Are you okay? What's going on?"

"I need, um . . . a ride. My parents are fighting again."

"Oh man! What's their deal? They can't give you one day?" The anger in his voice helped quell her emotions. It felt good to have someone share her feelings, someone who empathized with her, even though he didn't know what it was like to have feuding parents.

"Do you have time? Can you take me? I need help with all the stuff I have to bring or I'd just do it alone."

"No, no, don't go alone. I wanted to get there early for a good seat anyway. I can bring some homework to do while I'm waiting for the pageant to start."

She swallowed as fresh tears threatened; this time his kindness was the cause. "Thanks."

"I'll be right there. Don't worry; it's all going to be okay."

"I can't wait until I graduate and go away to college," she said.

"All the more reason to win this pageant so you can have money to use to go away to college. Give me just a minute to change and I'll be over to get you."

Somehow she needed to calm down and get her focus back, and the only way she knew how was to pray. Deep in her heart, she'd developed a strong love for her Father in Heaven. She felt close to Him because He was really the only parent who seemed to care enough to always be there for her. He had never let her down, and she knew He never would.

* * *

Lauryn peeked through a crack in the curtains and watched as each of the girls walked out and strutted across the stage. She shivered, her arms and legs covered in goose bumps. She wasn't cold, just nervous. She tried to visualize herself walking across the stage in her lime-green swimsuit in front of the judges and audience, but the thought caused her stomach to flip upside down. All the confidence she'd gained earlier during the interview portion of the competition was gone. She'd felt so good after her fifteen-minute interview. The judges had smiled at her and put her immediately at ease. Their questions pertained mostly to her bio sheet and personal interests. The rapport she'd felt with the judges during the interview had given her a sense of accomplishment, like maybe she'd actually done well, and they'd been impressed by her answers.

Her interaction with the other contestants wasn't nearly as positive. Several times she caught them pointing at her, whispering and snickering behind their hands. Obviously her choices of outfits for the competition were all wrong. With Jace's mom's help, she'd done the best she could. Her evening gown had turned out okay, but just in case, she'd brought her red, junior prom formal. And she was glad she had. She wanted to fit in and look like all the other girls, so she'd decided to wear the red gown instead. Her mother would be mad, but she didn't care.

"Contestant number thirteen, you're next."

It didn't help that she'd gotten the jinxed number of the competition either. It wouldn't surprise her if when she walked out on stage a black cat crossed her path and she passed underneath a ladder. Why not? Everything else had gone wrong.

"Take your time, smile, and try not to be nervous," the woman advised before Lauryn walked onto the stage. "You look beautiful."

"Thanks," Lauryn answered, knowing that the woman was just being nice. She probably said that to all the girls.

Even though all the others wore two-piece swimsuits, Lauryn didn't care. She'd have even less confidence with her stomach exposed and no support on top.

"Go!" the woman said.

Plastering a smile on her face and holding in her stomach, Lauryn walked onto the stage, trying to stay steady in her high-heeled shoes.

Relax, she told herself. Take your time.

She'd dreaded the interview, and it had gone well. She'd dreaded doing her talent, and it had gone even better than she'd expected. She just needed to get through the swimsuit and evening gown portions and then she could put on her sweats and go to the Frostop for a bacon cheeseburger, large fries, and a chocolate milkshake.

Feeling the tension fade from her neck and shoulders, Lauryn surprised herself by relaxing and even having fun, which was made possible by the fact that they were playing one of her favorite dance songs. Suddenly, instead of modeling a swimsuit, she felt as though she were up on stage at a dance performance, projecting her personality to the audience. Instead of walking fast like the other girls, she took her time, making sure she smiled at the audience as well as the judges.

As she struck the last pose, she gave one final smile, then strode off the stage, ready to do a roundoff back handspring because it was over.

"Lauryn, that was great," the woman at the curtain said as Lauryn came off the stage. It wasn't hard to tell that she was surprised by Lauryn's stage presence.

"Thanks."

"Hurry and change into your evening gown. And good luck!"

Lauryn smiled her appreciation for the encouragement and rushed to her dressing room to prepare for the final portion of the competition. Her mouth watered just thinking about the cheeseburger waiting for her when it was over.

All the girls were spread out in six different dressing rooms. Hers was empty when she arrived, and she was glad. She didn't appreciate the disapproving glances of the other girls who shared the space with her.

Anxious to change out of her swimsuit, she reached the cubicle where her clothes hung and stopped dead in her tracks. A gasp escaped her as she stared at the slashes in the fabric of her red evening gown.

"Can I help you with anything?" one of the hostesses asked as she entered the room. "I'm great with zip—"

"I think someone doesn't like me," Lauryn said, holding up the dress.

"This is a disaster! First of all, who did this? And second of all, you have to go on in a few minutes."

"Actually . . ." Lauryn hesitated. "I have another dress I can wear." She'd have to wear the designer gown she had stowed away in the black garment bag hanging behind the red dress. It was just one more thing for the girls to make fun of.

Lauryn slid into the silky fabric, then the hostess zipped it up.

"Turn and let me see," the hostess said.

Slowly, Lauryn turned around.

The woman's jaw dropped.

Lauryn's heart skipped a beat. Did the dress look that bad?

"That dress is amazing!" the hostess exclaimed.

With a nervous laugh, Lauryn rested her hand on her racing heart. "I was so worried. It's not like the other girls' dresses."

"No, it's not," the hostess said. "It's better. How did you find such a beautiful dress with sleeves?"

Reluctant to admit it, Lauryn said, "I sewed the sleeves and remodeled the top myself."

The woman's eyes opened wide. "You did? I can't even tell."

"I'm glad. I've been so worried. I'm not really a pageant girl. I just want this pageant over so I can go get some fast food with my friends."

"Sweetie, you need to know the judges really like you. You may not be a pageant girl, but you have a good chance of winning."

Lauryn didn't believe her. It was the hostesses' job to build up the girls and help them feel confident.

"Now, I need to go tell the pageant director what happened to your dress," the hostess said. "This has never happened before. She might have a nervous breakdown. She's already got enough to worry about."

"I don't know how we'll ever find out who did it," Lauryn said. "Maybe we should just wait until after."

The hostess looked at her, then smiled. "You know, whoever did it is not expecting you to have this dress as a backup. This might be the best revenge after all."

Last call was sounded for the contestants to come to the stage for the evening gown competition.

"That's me," Lauryn said, placing both hands on her nauseated stomach.

"You look beautiful, Lauryn. I'll be cheering for you. I'd love to see you win."

"Thank you," Lauryn said, giving the woman a hug.

"In fact, I want to walk out with you so I can see the look on the girls' faces. Maybe the one with the most shocked expression is our culprit."

Lauryn giggled. Whoever did the damage certainly would be surprised when they saw Lauryn's evening gown.

While a special community service award was presented, the contestants lined up offstage for the final phase of the competition. Lauryn and her hostess watched each girl's reaction as Lauryn found her place in line. Many of the girls' faces registered surprise, but no one looked guilty. Lauryn had no idea which one would have done it.

Soft music began to play, and it was time for the girls to begin modeling their dresses. Lauryn watched anxiously through a crack in the curtains as the first girl went out on stage. She said a quick prayer for help that she would get through it with dignity.

She squinted at the glare of lights and tried to look out in the audience to see her parents or friends or Jace, but it was too dark to see. It was better that way. If she knew how big the audience really was, she'd be even more terrified to go out onstage.

The woman at the curtain nodded, signaling Lauryn that she was next.

The hostess gave Lauryn's hand a squeeze and wished her good luck.

Lauryn had noticed that as the other girls had modeled their evening gowns, they didn't hold their poses and didn't look up beyond the row of judges. Just like she'd done in swimsuit, Lauryn decided that she was going to take her time and try to connect with the people on the back row of the auditorium.

On cue, Lauryn walked out onto the stage, feeling like she was floating on air. She kept her pace slow and made her turns deliberate and commanding. She made sure to smile at the judges, but she also lifted her eyes and engaged the members of the audience, even though they were just a sea of darkness to her. They were out there, and she wanted them to know she knew it.

The fabric of her skirt lifted and billowed, flowing and swirling as she turned. The Swarovski crystals sewn generously on the bodice of the dress caught the stage lights and glittered with star-like brilliance.

The moment was hers and she embraced it. She didn't care that someone had shredded her other gown or that the other girls thought she had no business even being in the pageant. She felt like a million dollars and wanted to let everyone in that giant room know she felt that way.

Thunderous applause accompanied her offstage. Her hostess grabbed her and nearly knocked her over with her hug.

"You were unbelievable!" the woman whispered.

Lauryn and her hostess went out in the hallway leading to the dressing rooms and then erupted with excitement.

"I know this is completely wrong of me, but I don't care. After what you've been through, you deserve to know. When you walked onto the

stage, most of the girls just stood there with their mouths hanging open. A few were trying to figure out how many pageants you'd done, because you knew how to model so well. And a couple said they wished they would have worn a dress like yours, because yours was more sophisticated and glamorous than theirs. I also have a pretty good idea who might have done this. I'm going to check their changing area right now to see if I can find any evidence. No matter what, I think you deserve to win."

Humbled by the praise, Lauryn managed to thank the hostess before she joined the rest of the contestants in the wings, ready to go onstage for the announcement of the winners.

All twenty-six contestants were called onstage and stood in a large semicircle as they waited anxiously while the preliminary awards were given. The first award was for fitness. The next award was for most photogenic.

"And for interview, the award goes to . . ." The girls held their breath. "Lauryn Alexander."

Lauryn heard screams in the audience and knew it was her friends.

With shock and delight, she walked to the center of the stage and accepted her award.

The next award was for talent.

"And for evening gown, the award goes to . . ." The announcer paused for dramatic effect. "Lauryn Alexander."

Again, screams erupted in the audience.

Lauryn nearly laughed with disbelief as she walked to the center of the stage. How ironic for her, out of all the contestants, to win the evening gown award.

Then the long-awaited moment arrived.

Second runner-up was given to the girl everyone, including the girl herself, thought would win. She'd already done several other teen pageants and was by far the most "pageant polished." Her smile, as she walked to the front of the stage, was rimmed with an edge of anger.

The first runner-up was a girl who had won the talent award for her amazing operatic rendition of "Think of Me" from Phantom of the Opera.

The auditorium was completely quiet as the final announcement was made.

Lauryn glanced at the girls standing on her left and on her right, trying to guess which one of them would win.

The girl next to her grabbed her free hand and gave it a squeeze. All the girls were holding hands.

The announcer paused. Someone in the audience yelled, "Hurry up," and the audience laughed.

"Your next Miss Young American is . . . contestant number thirteen, Lauryn Alexander!"

Several seconds passed before it sank in. She knew it had to be right, because everyone was looking at her.

Numbly, on wobbly legs, she walked to the front of the stage.

Last year's winner met her with an embrace and congratulated her. Then she attempted to pin a crown on Lauryn's head.

Still in shock, Lauryn shut her eyes as bobby pins were shoved into her hair to secure the crown, an object she'd never thought would ever adorn her.

Once the crown was in place, Lauryn stood tall and looked directly at the judges to make sure they weren't frantically comparing notes to see if a mistake had been made. But they all smiled at her while they applauded.

She dipped her chin and said, "Thank you," hoping to convey her appreciation for their confidence in her.

"You need to take your walk," the past winner whispered.

"My walk?" Lauryn said. Then she remembered that in rehearsal they'd shown the girls what to do in case they won, something she hadn't paid attention to, since she hadn't anticipated winning.

Hoping she did it right, she walked to the right side of the stage, waving at the audience, then she walked to the left side, waving and smiling until her cheeks began to hurt. When she got back to the center of the stage, she was mobbed by the other contestants.

Her hostess finally got to hug her, and the two shared a moment of triumph.

"I'm so happy for you," the hostess told her.

"Thank you. I appreciated your vote of confidence," Lauryn replied.

The other contestants faded back as a photographer began to request pictures of all the winners.

Out of the corner of her eye, Lauryn saw her friends and her mom waiting to congratulate her. And there was Jace in the background with his wide, dimpled smile. He'd predicted she would win, and he was gloating.

As soon as the pictures were done, the woman in charge of the pageant gave Lauryn an envelope with information inside.

"I'm Shelby Reynolds. I'll be working with you on appearances and media events."

There were appearances and media events? Lauryn hadn't listened to any of the information regarding the person who won the pageant.

"Hang onto this and call me in the morning. I'd like to schedule you for some appearances and do an article on you for the local newspaper."

"Okay," Lauryn said, feeling overwhelmed. She paused a moment, ready to tell Shelby about her other evening gown, then she changed her mind. She didn't need to anymore. Whoever had done it realized that in the end it hadn't helped at all. In fact, it might have been the thing that made the difference in her winning.

"It looks like you have quite a fan club waiting to congratulate you," Shelby said. "We'll talk in the morning."

Lauryn turned toward her friends, and they rushed to her, nearly knocking her to the ground.

Chloe and Andrea were the first to hug her. At least she thought it was Chloe.

"What happened to you?" Lauryn asked.

"Oh, this?" Chloe pulled at a lock of brittle, white hair. "Remember when I left the highlighting solution on your hair too long?"

Lauryn remembered all too well. "I hope it grows out fast."

"Me too."

Emma interrupted them. "Just think, Lauryn, you almost didn't go through with this."

"She owes it all to us," Andrea said, slipping an arm around Chloe's shoulder.

"It's true," Lauryn said. "I don't know why, but you guys really thought I could do this."

"Hey, that's what friends are for," Andrea said.

"Plus," Ava piped up, *"having a famous, beauty-pageant-winning friend is bound to help us attract some very cute guys, right?"*

Emma agreed wholeheartedly.

"Congratulations," Jocelyn said, ignoring them and giving Lauryn a hug. *"I'm so proud of you."*

Lauryn had detected a note of sadness in Jocelyn lately. Something was wrong—she seemed different, even more withdrawn—but now wasn't the time to talk about it.

Ava, dressed in a sleeveless top and miniskirt, was next to hug her.

"Way to go. I guess modest really is hottest!"

They both laughed, because Ava had encouraged her to wear a two-piece swimsuit and an immodest evening gown. Lauryn always wished some of her friends would be more careful in how they dressed. Ava was exactly the type of girl her mother wished she'd be. But her mother didn't hear all the things guys said about some of her friends because of the tight, revealing clothes they wore. Of course, even though Lauryn took great pains to not draw attention to her body, boys talked about her anyway, so maybe it was a losing battle. Still, why encourage them?

"Are we still meeting at the Frostop?" Ava asked, flipping a thick strand of long, blond hair back and slinging her purse over her shoulder.

"I've been on a diet all week. I'm totally bagging it tonight to help celebrate," Andrea declared.

"I'll be there as soon as I can get out of here," Lauryn told them.

"Okay, we'll see you in a bit then. Hurry!" Ava said. *"We have to celebrate!"*

"I will. I'm starving," Lauryn said.

"Wear your crown," Emma called. *"We want to show you off!"*

Lauryn gave them a fake pageant wave, and they all laughed.

She turned and found her mother waiting to give her a hug.

"Oh, hi, Mom."

Her mother gave her a smile.

"So, what do you think about all of this?" she asked her mom.

Her mom stepped forward and stiffly wrapped one arm around Lauryn. *"I knew you had it in you all along,"* she said unconvincingly.

She took a moment to examine the alterations Lauryn had made to the dress.

Lauryn braced herself for her mother's criticism.

"Who did this for you?" her mother said, fingering one of the sleeves. "They actually did a pretty good job. Of course, I like the dress better the way it was, but this doesn't look too bad."

"I did it," Lauryn told her.

"You!" Her mother looked more closely at the handwork. "You must have had some help."

"I did have some help from Jace's mom, but I do know how to sew."

"I guess I never realized how good you were." Her mother gave her an approving nod. "I'm just glad you finally realized something."

"Realized what?"

"That you're beautiful and can have more in your life. Attention, opportunity, fame, even fortune if you want it. All the things I wish I could have had at your age." Her mother reached up and touched the crown. "Things I've had to work very hard for in my life."

Lauryn looked at her mom, astounded by how different they were and by how much her mother didn't know about her. It wasn't about glory and attention. It never had been. She didn't even like the attention. It felt good to win, but that wasn't why she'd done the pageant. In fact, she doubted she would ever do another one. She was thrilled for the scholarship money and for the recognition for her accomplishments and hard work, but that was it.

"Where's Dad?" Lauryn asked, looking over her mother's shoulder.

"Uh, well." Her mother swallowed uncomfortably. "He wasn't able to make it."

"What? He didn't even come?"

"We sort of had an argument before I came, and he got pretty upset." Her mother's gaze shifted around the room, avoiding eye contact with Lauryn. "He won't be home when you get there."

"Where did he go?"

"He . . ." Her mom paused. "Well, there's simply no easy way to tell you. He moved out. I'm sorry, honey. I don't mean to spoil this for you."

"He moved out? Tonight?" Lauryn's gaze slipped over to Jace, who'd been standing by, overhearing the entire conversation. His

expression fell, and compassion filled his eyes as tears filled Lauryn's.

"I'm sorry, honey. We can talk more when you get home. Try not to let him ruin your moment. This is all about you right now."

In her own bizarre way, her mother thought she was helping, but she really wasn't. In fact, it was all her mother's fault that her dad had left.

"I'm sure you have a lot of questions," her mother said, which in Lauryn's opinion was the understatement of the millennium. "I can tell you all about it when you get home."

Lauryn nodded feebly, unable to comprehend the magnitude of the destruction her mother's bomb had just created.

After her mother walked away, Lauryn turned to Jace, who reached out for her. She accepted his hug but fought to keep her tears at bay. She could cry later. But not here, not now.

"I'm so sorry," he said.

Lauryn nodded, afraid to speak.

"I can stay and help you get all your stuff."

She nodded again and whispered, "Thanks."

Another woman approached, and Lauryn quickly composed herself. Jace took several steps back to give her some space.

"Hello, Lauryn," the woman said, extending her hand.

Lauryn looked at the woman, recognizing her as one of the judges. She looked highly fashionable in her brown silk jacket and pencil skirt.

"I wanted to congratulate you. You did a wonderful job. You're a very accomplished and beautiful young woman."

"Thank you. I'm sorry, I don't know your name." She hadn't really heard who the judges were or where they'd come from.

"Of course, I apologize. My name is Jacqueline Yvonne."

Lauryn gasped, aspirating saliva. She began to cough.

"Are you all right?" Ms. Yvonne asked.

Lauryn nodded but felt like dying of embarrassment. She coughed a few more times to finally clear her throat. "I didn't know you were one of the judges."

"The director, Cassandra Thomas, and I went to college together. She knew I was on my way to Las Vegas for my spring show, so she asked me to judge."

"It's such an honor to meet you," Lauryn said. Then she got sick to her stomach. She was wearing one of Ms. Yvonne's dresses. And she'd altered it!

"Thank you. And I was quite surprised to see you in one of my dresses." Ms. Yvonne gave her dress a scrutinizing look. "It is one of my dresses, isn't it?"

"Oh, yes. I just, um . . . well, I wasn't comfortable . . ." Lauryn stopped talking before she made it worse.

"My dear, it wasn't designed for a young girl, but you look outstanding in that dress. I like what you did and the way you've altered it so it looks more appropriate for a girl your age," Ms. Yvonne complimented.

"Thank you. I have a hard time finding clothes that fit right and cover me."

"I wish more girls had your desire to cover themselves. There are too many who want to dress like movie stars and rock stars, and it really isn't becoming for girls their age."

"I know. I would love to design modest prom dresses for teens. I want to study fashion design."

Ms. Yvonne's expression lit up. "How wonderful. I have a feeling you would turn the industry upside down." She opened her purse and pulled out a small book.

"Here," she said, handing her business card to Lauryn. "This has my private number at work and my cell phone number. When you get into college we can talk about having you come to New York to do an internship."

"Are you serious? You really think I could be like you?" Lauryn exclaimed.

"Are you serious?" Ms. Yvonne echoed. "I'm a small-town girl from Montana. If I can do it, anyone can. Besides, the way you handled yourself in that interview and carried yourself onstage, I think you have a very bright future ahead of you."

"Thank you so much, Ms. Yvonne. Meeting you is even better than winning this crown."

Jacqueline smiled, then paused in thought. "A crown is good, but you'll find that the joy that comes from winning a crown will fade in time. Remember, Lauryn, all that glitters isn't gold."

Lauryn thought for a moment about what Ms. Yvonne had said.

"Do you understand what I mean?" the woman asked.

"I think so. Do you mean that things aren't always as they appear?"

"Exactly. There are many glittery things in life . . . fame, fortune, power. But pursuing those things alone usually brings heartache. I've learned that the hard way, but luckily I figured it out before I suffered heartache. Nothing is more important than my family, my friends, and my beliefs. As long as I keep those things at the forefront, the rest of my life seems to turn out all right. Does that make sense?"

"It sure does. Thank you. I'll remember what you said."

"I hope so. Learn from my mistakes. Heaven knows I've made enough for both of us. And when you do dumb things like I have, years later they all show up in newspapers and magazines."

"I read that recent article about you," Lauryn said.

"That's what I'm talking about," Ms. Yvonne said, shaking her head. "I was hoping no one would see that."

"I was surprised to learn you weren't from France or somewhere in Europe. Your name sounds so European."

"Darling, that's not my real name. If you had a name like mine, you'd change yours too."

"What is your name?"

"Margaret Crump."

Lauryn tried not to show her surprise.

"Can you see yourself wearing a Margaret Crump original?" Ms. Yvonne asked her.

Lauryn couldn't help giggling. The stylish woman in front of her with chin-length, black hair and straight bangs across her forehead, dramatic makeup, and rhinestone-studded glasses looked nothing like a Margaret Crump.

"You just have to learn how to create your own signature look, your trademark. You must be unique!"

Nodding with understanding, Lauryn tried to memorize every word the woman was saying.

"You keep that card," Ms. Yvonne said. "I've got a plane to catch, so I've got to go, but I expect to hear from you in a few years."

"You can count on it!"

Lauryn watched the woman walk away, thrilled with the conversation they'd just had. She then turned to find Jace standing by the curtains, waiting patiently for her.

"Did you hear that?" she asked him.

"Most of it. Did she just give you her card?"

"Yes! She wants me to call her. And she liked what I did to her dress. Imagine, having Jacqueline Yvonne here as a judge."

"I'm happy for you, Lauryn. You deserve something good," he said.

Jace surprised Lauryn by wrapping his arms around her and squeezing her tight. With his face close to hers, he whispered, "You look beautiful tonight." Lauryn could feel his breath on her ear. Her stomach suddenly flipped upside down, and her face felt hot.

He held her a moment longer then pulled back and with a dimpled smile said, "Let's go. I'm starving."

With a laugh that came out strangely high-pitched, Lauryn agreed. Her heart melted as she walked backstage with Jace. He'd helped her through these last few weeks without complaint. And now, with her parents' breakup, she knew she would lean on him, and her other friends, even more. "I'm so glad you're my friend. I don't know what I'd do without you."

"You'd be left hauling all this pageant junk alone," Jace said, changing the serious tone of their conversation.

Lauryn smiled appreciatively. She was ready to get out of her high heels and into her tennis shoes and jeans. And she was ready for all the junk food she could eat!

More than anything, she wished she didn't have to go home. If anyone should have left, it should have been her mother. Lauryn's father was a wonderful, loving man.

She pushed the emotion aside, ready to bury it in french fries. She could deal with it later. Much later.

Chapter Four

"I still can't believe I even did that pageant," Lauryn said as Chloe placed the tiara back in the box.

Even though the girls knew every object in the Butterfly Box, the contents still caused memories of the past to surface. And remembering Ava always brought tears.

"What do you think Ava would be doing now, if she hadn't died?" Chloe asked, helping herself to a piece of candy.

"She'd be a movie star," Emma said without a doubt.

"Do you think she would have made it?" Lauryn asked.

Emma nodded. "I do."

"Me too," Andrea added. "She never gave up on what she wanted."

"And she was ruthless about it," Emma said. "I mean that in a good way."

"She was ruthless, wasn't she," Lauryn said, remembering how it felt to get one of Ava's direct hits. Sometimes they were very painful, even though she declared she was "just being honest."

"Only Ava could get away with talking to people like she did," Andrea said.

"It used to bother me a little," Chloe shared. "She used to hurt my feelings at times, but she was flat out rude to some kids. Even teachers."

Lauryn noticed that Jocelyn wasn't contributing to the conversation. Jocelyn didn't say bad things about anyone. It made Lauryn feel a little guilty, especially since Ava was gone now.

"You know, I heard that the case of Ava's death still isn't closed," Andrea said. "My brother is on the St. George police force, and he said they still don't think the crash was accidental."

"I didn't know that," Emma said. "I thought that case was closed years ago."

"He said they recently reenacted the crash, and whatever they found out raised more questions," Andrea answered.

"I hated that day. I still have nightmares," Chloe said.

"Me too," Lauryn said. "Sometimes I relive it, trying to figure out what went wrong. It just doesn't make sense how it happened. It really doesn't."

* * *

Graduation Day—May 29, 1996

"We did it," Ava shouted, holding her diploma high above her head. "We're done with this crazy place!" She began to twirl around and say in a singsong voice, "I won't miss the teachers, I won't miss the lunch-room, I won't miss the tardy bell . . ." One of their classmates, Herbie Finke, walked by as she was doing her version of a victory song and dance. "And I won't miss Herbie," she said directly to him.

Emma and Andrea burst out laughing, Chloe wasn't paying attention, Jocelyn looked horrified, and Lauryn was embarrassed.

Herbie looked at all of them, his gaze penetrating.

He'd been with them all through junior high and high school. Of course, Emma and Ava had tormented him, even delighted in teasing Herbie and any of the other misfits in their school. Lauryn was embarrassed by her friends' behavior. She attempted to apologize, but he quickly bent his head, looked away, and lost himself in the crowd.

"Ava, why did you do that?" Lauryn asked her.

"Do what?" Ava was still dancing a little jig.

"Say that to Herbie?"

"Who cares about creepy Herbie Finke or any of these other kids. We never have to see them again if we don't want!"

Lauryn thought that many of the kids probably felt the same way about Ava—grateful they'd never see her again.

Chloe slipped her arm around Jocelyn's waist and gave her a hug. "I'm so glad you got to come back for the last half of the year. It wouldn't have been the same to graduate without you."

The summer after their junior year, while Lauryn was busy doing parades and appearances as Miss Young American and the other girls were spending time working and hanging out at the pool, Jocelyn had gone to Seattle to live with her ailing grandmother. Her grandma couldn't afford to go to an assisted living center, but she also couldn't live alone. Jocelyn's mother wasn't open to the idea of having her grandmother live with them, so Jocelyn had given up her summer and part of her senior year of high school to help. She'd told them that even though it meant missing part of her senior year, she'd been glad to get away from her mother and live with her grandmother, who was actually the only loving parent figure in her life.

Lauryn had noticed that Jocelyn seemed different when she came back in January—more grown up, more serious, and more content with who she was. She still liked to hang out with all of them, but when Emma and Ava went boy hunting, Jocelyn passed, staying with Andrea, Chloe, and Lauryn instead. She'd even changed her style while she was gone. She still wasn't about trendy fashions, but her clothes were more up-to-date and typical for a teenage girl. She also had a nice haircut with a few soft highlights. The other thing Lauryn noticed was that school had become much more important to her, and she was driven to go to college and get an education. Instead of becoming a waitress like her mother, she was determined to become a school teacher.

"I have an idea," Ava said. "Let's go over by the D and get a group picture taken."

The giant letter D that stood for Dixie High School was positioned near the podium. Curtains on either side of it created a dramatic effect so that after each graduate received their diploma, they walked through the letter, signifying their entrance into the future.

The girls made their way through the crowd of graduates, family, friends, and faculty. It was congested, but the group wouldn't be denied.

A different group of kids from the theater department was already occupying the D, so the girls waited their turn.

"These guys are so annoying," Ava said. "I'm so not going to miss any of these people."

"Will you stop saying that," Lauryn told her. "You will be back for reunions."

"No, I won't. I'll be in Hollywood making movies and walking down the red carpet to accept my awards."

Lauryn thought that Ava certainly was dramatic enough to be a movie star. But she wasn't sure Ava could handle a lifestyle like that. Lately, Ava and Emma did things together that they didn't tell the other girls about. Things Lauryn wasn't sure she wanted to know about.

She was afraid that after high school they would all go their separate ways and never see each other again. Everything was changing. In a way, that was good. But it was also scary.

The best change for Lauryn was her acceptance to BYU that fall. She just had to endure three more months at home, and then she'd be gone. With her father gone, life at home had become almost unbearable. Her mother had no trouble getting back into the dating world, and Lauryn hated having to meet all the men her mother brought home. Her mother also didn't bother hiding some of the habits she'd kept hidden from Lauryn in the past, like smoking and drinking. The whole situation was more than uncomfortable; it was destructive, and Lauryn couldn't wait to get away from her mother and the home environment she'd created.

"Finally," Ava announced loudly as the other group finished their pictures. "We need someone to take our picture so we can all be in it."

They all looked around.

"There's Jace," Lauryn said. "He'll do it."

Jace was talking to Mr. Barton, the math teacher. Jace had been the Sterling Scholar in math for their school and the state. Lauryn had been the Sterling Scholar in Family and Consumer Sciences. Jace even had an academic scholarship to BYU. Lauryn was excited that they would be there at the same time. She felt relieved knowing Jace would be nearby, even if it was just for a year before he left on his mission.

Andrea had also been accepted to BYU, but Chloe's grades weren't good enough. Chloe and Jocelyn were thinking about going to UVSC so they could all live together in Provo. Emma wasn't sure what she was going to do yet, and Ava, well, Ava was off to Hollywood.

"Hello, Lauryn," Mr. Barton said. "Congratulations on graduating with high honors."

"Thank you, Mr. Barton."

"You kids have a good summer. Come and see me sometime when you're in town," he told them. "I'd like to hear how college is going."

After Mr. Barton left, Lauryn asked Jace to take their picture.

The girls posed in front of the D with Ava in the middle, of course. Jace counted to three and snapped their picture. He had to do it five more times, since everyone had given him their camera.

"Okay, Jace," Lauryn said after he clicked the last picture, "let's get one of just you and me." She grabbed Jace's hand and pulled him up the stairs. They put their arms around each other's shoulders, each giving the other a visible set of donkey ears.

After the picture, Jace turned to Lauryn. "I'm sad this is ending," he said with a serious expression.

Lauryn smiled quizzically. "Nothing's ending, Jace. Don't forget, we'll both be at BYU this fall."

"I know," he said as he gently brushed a curl behind her shoulder. "I guess I'm just afraid it won't be the same."

Lauryn looked at Jace and thought she saw something in his eyes she hadn't noticed before.

"Hello," Ava interrupted. "Earth to Lauryn and Jace. Hurry up and get down from there. I want a video of me walking through the D."

Ava's parents had given her a video camera for graduation, a gift that went along with the whole Hollywood theme. She showed Jace how to work the camera, then went to take her place behind the curtain.

"Ready?" Jace asked.

"I'm ready," Ava replied.

"Action!" Jace joked.

Ava walked slowly through the D, pausing to wave and blow kisses like a celebrity. Then she continued waving as she walked down the three stairs like a movie star at a premiere.

"What a nut," Andrea said to the other girls. "You know, she really is beautiful enough to be a movie star."

"Hold it, Ava," Emma said. "Let me take your picture right there."

Ava struck a pose with her hand lifted and a lovely smile on her face.

The camera clicked. "All right," Ava said as she grabbed her cap. "Let's party!" She threw her cap high in the air.

* * *

All the girls but Ava crowded into Emma's 1987 Honda Civic. High school was a thing of the past, and they planned to celebrate by packing as much fun as they could into one night. Their first stop was the senior dance at the St. George Country Club's outdoor tennis courts. Ava was driving her Mitsubishi Eclipse just ahead of the other girls. In her words, she didn't want to be "stuck at some lame high school dance in case something better came up."

With the windows rolled down and Emma's radio blasting, the girls sang along to Montell Jordan's new hit, "This Is How We Do It," and the Civic bounced as they sped down the highway.

Suddenly Emma switched off the radio dial.

"Hey, turn it back on, Emma," Andrea called from the backseat.

"You guys, look at Ava. What's she doing?" Emma pointed ahead to Ava's Eclipse, which was swerving dangerously close to the shoulder with the hazard lights blinking.

"Do you think she wants us to pull over?" Chloe asked.

"I don't know. She's going really fast." Emma pushed down harder on the gas to keep up with Ava.

They were approaching seventy miles per hour. Ava continued to swerve recklessly, just missing a fifty-five-mile-per-hour sign post.

"I'm scared, Emma." Andrea gripped the back of the seat. "Make her stop."

It was on the next swerve that Ava overcorrected and lost control of the car. Her friends watched helplessly as the Eclipse hit the shoulder, flew into the air, flipped twice, and came to a rest—a smoking wreck in the dark field.

* * *

The last thing Lauryn wanted to do was see Ava's body inside the casket, but she knew she'd regret it if she didn't. So she took her place in line with her friends, all of them still in shock at losing their friend so suddenly.

Standing in line and holding hands, the five friends waited their turn to see Ava one last time before she was buried. No one spoke; words seemed useless.

Andrea was the first to look at Ava. Emma held a steady arm around her as she joined Andrea, and together they cried. Fresh tears streamed from Lauryn's red eyes and ran down her cheeks as she watched them. The painfully tight ache in her stomach had become familiar over the last few days. She couldn't imagine it would ever subside.

Jocelyn was next to look at Ava. With quiet dignity, Jocelyn dabbed at her eyes, then reached out and gently touched Ava's hair with her finger. Out of the six friends, Jocelyn and Ava had had the least in common, but they were still loyal to each other. No one could make Jocelyn laugh like Ava.

Chloe stared down at Ava for a long time, then she leaned over and slipped her hand behind Ava's head, cradling it in her hand. She held on to the body for several seconds, sobbing into Ava's shoulder. Lauryn didn't know what to do. Finally, with Jocelyn's help, they pulled Chloe back. Chloe buried her head in Jocelyn's shoulder, and together they walked away from the casket.

Lauryn slowly approached the casket, her arms folded tightly across her chest. Seeing Ava's flawless face caused Andrea's words to echo through Lauryn's mind: "You know, she really is beautiful enough to be a movie star." Lauryn stifled a sob as she thought of how Ava's dreams had been cut short. Through all her years of Primary, Sunday School, Young Women, and seminary, Lauryn had learned about the plan of salvation and the revelations regarding life after death. There was peace in knowing the plan and understanding that they would see Ava again. But the sting of death was still so painful, and it was hard not to wonder why this had happened to someone so young and full of life.

There were a lot of theories and even more speculation about what had happened, but the incident was still considered a horrible accident. The moment Ava's car had hit the shoulder, Emma had screeched to a stop, and Lauryn and the girls had jumped from Emma's car and run toward the wreckage. They had yelled for Ava, but there had been no answer. Somehow Lauryn had known that Ava was gone, even before the paramedics arrived. But why couldn't she seem to stop the question running through her head: why was Ava driving so recklessly?

Lauryn tentatively reached out her hand and took hold of Ava's. The cold stiffness of her friend's body sent a chill down Lauryn's spine, but she took a shaky breath, bent low, and gently kissed Ava's forehead, a single tear falling into Ava's long, blond hair.

As she walked away from the casket, Lauryn was overwhelmed with the precious and fleeting nature of life. And she vowed to never take life for granted again.

* * *

"Even though it was over ten years ago, sometimes at night, I think about Ava and what she's doing," Emma said. "I wonder if she's happy."

"I still think about her, too," Jocelyn said. "I'm sure she's happy."

Emma's skeptical expression prompted Jocelyn to continue.

"On my mission, the message of the plan of salvation was probably the one most people appreciated. Everyone wonders where they came from and where they will go after they die. I told people about Ava and about my grandmother. I can't explain it, but there are times when they feel close to me."

Emma's skeptical expression turned to a mocking smile. "Oh, really?"

Jocelyn didn't flinch. "Yes, really. Especially my grandmother."

Not one to force her opinions on others, Jocelyn surprised everyone by speaking so boldly. Lauryn liked seeing this side of Jocelyn.

"Have any of the rest of you felt Ava close to you?" Jocelyn asked.

Andrea and Chloe looked at each other. They shrugged and answered that they hadn't.

All eyes were on Lauryn.

"Yeah," she said. "Actually, I have."

Emma's eyes opened wide.

"I'm not saying I had a visitation or anything, but the last time I was in Salt Lake, I was able to go to general conference. The Mormon Tabernacle Choir sang this song and . . ." Lauryn looked down for a moment to clear the catch in her throat.

"Lauryn? What happened?" Chloe asked.

"I can't really explain it. I mean, it was just so out of the blue. Ava had been on my mind a lot. And like you, Emma, I was wondering what Ava was doing."

"And?" Emma asked impatiently.

"And, I listened to this song—"

"What song was it?" Andrea asked.

"It was 'Our Savior's Love,'" Lauryn answered. "There's a part that says, 'Our Savior's love Shines like the sun with perfect light, As from above it breaks thru clouds of strife. Lighting our way, it leads us back into his sight, Where we may stay to share eternal life.' I got this feeling, not like a voice or even words in my mind, but an understanding in my heart, like a confirmation of something I already knew, that Ava was in heaven, and that she was happy and that God loved her, like He loves us."

Chloe wiped at her eyes. Andrea nodded. Jocelyn reached for Lauryn's hand and gave it a squeeze. Emma looked down.

"I've had a lot of inner peace from that experience. Not only about Ava, but everything. I mean, it was kind of confusing growing up with one parent supportive about going to church and the other parent totally against it. I felt a lot of love, not just for Ava, but for myself. I really needed it."

Emma looked up at her, the skepticism back in her expression. Lauryn noticed it right off. "You too, Emma," she said, feeling the same boldness that Jocelyn had displayed. "I know Ava is happy. And I know God loves you."

"He sure has a funny way of showing it," Emma said. "I mean, would it be so hard to give me a break, let something good happen to me once in a while?"

"You know, Emma," Jocelyn said. "I used to envy you so much when we were growing up. You had a mom and a dad who loved each other and loved you. You were like the ideal family. They cared about where you went and when you would be home and who you were with. You all went to church as a family; you probably even had family prayer and family home evening."

Emma gave an annoyed sigh and shrugged. "Yeah."

"No one made me go to church," Jocelyn said. "I went because it was the only place I could go to feel love and support and peace. I didn't get that at school, and I sure as heck didn't get it at home. Church was the one place where I felt safe and secure. My testimony was all I had, and believe me, it got me through some pretty hard stuff growing up. Actually," she said thoughtfully, "it still does. That's the difference between us. When something bad happens I look to Heavenly Father to get me through. You look to Him to blame."

Awkward silence followed Jocelyn's words. Lauryn believed every word and knew that Emma needed to hear those words as well, but it wasn't like Jocelyn to be so bold, and Emma didn't always receive criticism well.

No one spoke, and Lauryn searched for something to say to break the silence.

Suddenly, Jocelyn's cell phone buzzed.

Jocelyn looked at the display on her phone, "Excuse me. I've gotta take this call."

Jocelyn left the hotel room to talk out on the balcony.

"She's right, you know," Emma said, not looking at any of them. "I do exactly what she said."

"Don't be hard on yourself," Chloe said. "We're all doing the best we can."

"No," Emma replied. "I know better. I've just made some bad choices in my life. Dumb choices that I wish I could take back."

"We all have," Andrea told her. Lauryn noticed tears welling up in Andrea's eyes and wondered how there could be so much she didn't know about her best friends.

Emma shut her eyes. "I don't even know how I got where I am. One tiny bad choice made it easier to keep making more and more bad choices. Temptations can be wrapped in very pretty packages."

"All that glitters isn't gold," Chloe said.

"It's true," Emma said. "It's so true."

"I think you need the box again this year," Andrea said to Emma.

"Oh, no. I'll be okay. As much as I hate to say it, Jocelyn is right. I've been telling myself that I need to make some changes in my life. She basically told me what I already know. It's just so hard to admit it," Emma said.

"I think you're doing a pretty awesome job," Lauryn said.

Emma smiled at her. "Thanks."

"Please don't think you're the only one who's made mistakes," Lauryn told her.

"Yeah," Andrea said, reaching for Emma's hand. "When it comes to dumb mistakes, I could be the poster girl. I struggle with stuff every day."

"Me too," Chloe said.

All three looked at her with disbelief. Chloe had always been the most perfect of any of them. She was kind, service minded, active in the Church, and never said a bad word about anyone. Lauryn thought Chloe was as close to becoming a saint as humanly possible.

"It's true. You guys don't know me as well as you think," she insisted.

Emma smiled at her, then at the other girls. "Thanks everyone. I knew I could count on you."

The door opened and Jocelyn walked inside. She looked anxiously at the four girls sitting on the beds.

"Everything okay?" Lauryn asked.

Jocelyn nodded. "It was my grandma's attorney."

"Really? I thought your grandma passed away," Andrea said.

"She did. She left me some property in Seattle."

"Wow! Does that mean you're a rich heiress?" Andrea asked.

"No, that means I owe back taxes. I have to come up with almost a thousand dollars by the end of the month." Jocelyn plopped down on the bed. "Luckily I have some savings I can use. I was hoping to buy a new car; my Honda's got 170,000 miles on it."

"Let's hope it lives to see 200,000," Lauryn said.

"I think I know who needs the Butterfly Box," Emma said.

"I'll be fine," Jocelyn said. "Hector and I will be fine."

"Hector?" Chloe asked.

"My car. My school class named my car because I'm always complaining about it breaking down. One day one of the children told me that my car reminds him of his Uncle Hector, because he never works either."

All the girls burst into laughter.

"From then on, my car was Hector," Jocelyn said. "So the Butterfly Box needs to go with someone else. Now," Jocelyn said, putting her phone on silent, "just as it began the night after Ava's funeral, I think it's time for the Butterfly Box ceremony."

* * *

The First Butterfly Box Ceremony

After Ava's funeral, the five remaining friends met at Jocelyn's house to comfort each other and somehow process the fact that Ava was really gone. The girls sat together on Jocelyn's bed in silence, all of them still red-eyed from recent tears. Lauryn wondered how long the emptiness inside would last.

Finally, Jocelyn spoke. "I've been thinking about something Lauryn told me, and well . . . I have an idea."

All eyes turned to Lauryn, who shook her head and shrugged. She had no idea what Jocelyn was talking about.

"Do you remember how last year after your pageant that lady talked to you—that judge?" Jocelyn asked.

"Yeah, I remember."

"She said something to you that you told me. It's helped me a lot this past year." Jocelyn spoke softly, keeping the tone in the room quiet and reverent.

"What did I say?" Lauryn questioned.

"You told me that all that glitters isn't gold."

Lauryn nodded. "I remember."

"I think we've learned the meaning of this since Ava died. I mean really, is there any material thing you wouldn't give up to have Ava back?"

They all shook their heads.

"Nothing is as important as the people we love and the things we believe. I know we don't get all that spiritual when we're together, but I've been thinking a lot about this lately. I've learned some important lessons this last year. I think we're really lucky to have each other. And now here we are, going off to college, and things are going to change." Her voice cracked. She stopped and cleared her throat before she went on. *"I just don't want us to lose track of each other."*

Chloe wiped at a tear on her cheek and tucked a strand of brownish-green hair behind her ear. She'd tried to bleach her hair, but something had gone wrong, so to correct the overprocessed blond, she tried dying it dark brown. Her hair had come out a sickening mossy green color. She had an appointment with a specialist but hadn't been able to get in before the funeral. *"I've been thinking about this too. You are like the best friends ever. I couldn't have made it through high school without you. We have to promise to stay in touch."*

The others nodded. All of them were teary eyed.

"Well," Jocelyn continued, *"that's what my idea is all about—a way to not only help keep us in touch, but also to help us support each other. I want us to stay connected—even when we all live far away from each other."*

The girls watched as Jocelyn reached under the bed and pulled out a large object wrapped in cloth. She set the bundle in the center of the bed.

"What is that?" Emma asked.

"My grandma gave me this while I was living with her. It's probably the most important thing she owns." Jocelyn tenderly pulled back the cloth to reveal a large, wooden box, octagon shaped, sitting on carved lion's claws. Inlaid on the cover was a beautiful jade butterfly.

"Wow," Chloe whispered as she gently ran her finger along the box's ornate edge.

"It's beautiful," Lauryn added.

"It's quite valuable," Jocelyn explained. *"Its made out of rosewood and comes from China."*

The other girls took turns examining the box and running their fingers over the smooth jade butterfly on the lid.

"Mmm, smells good," Chloe said, picking up the box and taking a deep breath.

"My grandma's best friend growing up was Chinese. She gave her this box because butterflies carved in jade symbolize change, love, and joy," Jocelyn said.

"It's so beautfiul!" Chloe said, taking another whiff of the box.

"Grandma told me that the Chinese believe the movement of the butterfly can teach you not to take things so seriously. Butterflies have taste sensors on their front legs, so they experience life through motion, like dancing and walking."

"That is so awesome!" Andrea exclaimed. "I've always loved butterflies."

Jocelyn turned the box over and read from a brass plate. "Legend has it that whispering a wish to a butterfly, then releasing it to carry the wish to the heavens, will make the wish come true."

"I really love that," Lauryn said.

Jocelyn nodded solemnly. "Me too. I mean, I don't go around whispering to butterflies and stuff, but my grandma explained to me that all change was good, even if it doesn't seem like it at the time. She told me that change is what life is made of, and it's necessary for us to grow and accomplish things."

"I believe that," Chloe said. "But sometimes it is really hard. Like losing Ava. That sure has changed things for me."

"That's why I brought this out. We're all at a point in our lives, with graduation and college, that things are going to change . . ." Jocelyn put her fingertips on the lid of the box.

"I wish they didn't have to," Chloe said.

"I couldn't stand another day of high school," Emma complained.

"Ugh!" Lauryn said. "I'm glad to be out of high school too, but I'm not ready to grow up."

"I won't miss being teased all the time," Andrea said.

"Or gym class," Emma added.

"Or school lunch!" Lauryn said.

All at once they began sharing which item on the school lunch menu was the worst. Soggy french fries was the consensus.

"Anyway," Jocelyn said, trying to get back to the point of why they were together, "I hope you don't think this is stupid. But when my grandma gave it to me, she told me that it had been given to her by a

friend. Inside, her friend had put a bunch of little things that were special to their friendship. She told my grandma that it would bring her good luck and keep her safe. So, I just thought . . ."

They all waited for her to go on.

"What, Jocelyn. Just tell us," Emma coaxed.

"It might sound kind of silly, but I thought each of us could put something significant in the box that has to do with our friendship, to keep us safe and bring us good luck."

Lauryn reached over and patted Jocelyn on the knee. "I don't think that's silly. I love the idea."

"You do?" Jocelyn asked.

"Yeah, I do. And I think we should pass the box around among us. Each time we get together, just like this."

"Every year!" Andrea exclaimed, getting excited. "Let's try to get together every year."

"Yeah! Even if we get married and have jobs and kids and stuff, we have to get together," Chloe agreed.

"What do you think, Emma?" Lauryn asked.

Emma hadn't really said anything. She stayed quiet for a moment. Then she nodded. "It's a great idea. We've helped each other through a lot of stuff, and I don't think life is going to get any easier as we get older."

"We'll always be there for each other, right?" Chloe added.

They all agreed.

"We should have a name for ourselves," Andrea said.

"Like a club?" Emma asked with distaste.

"I like that idea," Lauryn said. "But what?"

They threw out some ideas, all of which Emma hated.

"It should have something to do with the box," Andrea offered. "That's kind of the symbol of our group."

"How about 'Butterfly Bunch?'" Chloe offered.

Emma pulled a face. "Please tell me you aren't serious."

Chloe's mouth dropped open in offense.

"What is a group of butterflies called anyway?" Andrea asked.

"We talked about this in science one time," Lauryn said. "Mr. Moody gave us an assignment to find out."

"And?" Emma asked.

"Basically a group of butterflies is called just that, a 'group.' But, there are some other accepted names. Another is a flutter of butterflies."

"That's cute!" Chloe said excitedly.

Emma's look of distaste shot down Chloe's enthusiasm in a flash.

Lauryn was thoughtful for a moment. "Why don't we just use Butterfly Girls? It really does kind of describe us."

Andrea nodded. "I like it."

"So do I," Jocelyn added.

Emma thought about it for a moment. "Yeah, I guess that's okay. Better than Butterfly Bunch or Flutter Girls."

"Chloe?" Lauryn asked.

Chloe looked around at all the girls, then said, "I love it."

"So Butterfly Girls it is," Lauryn said "And we'll have Butterfly Girls reunions every year on the anniversary of Ava's death. That way we can always keep her a part of us."

Jocelyn smiled. She glanced around at the other girls with a look of satisfaction.

Emma noticed her expression. "Now what?"

"Let's go get our stuff and meet back here in an hour," Jocelyn suggested.

"Okay. We could get pizza and watch a movie, too," Andrea suggested. "I don't want to be alone tonight.

"Me either," Chloe said.

"It's still hard to believe she's gone," Emma added.

Andrea looked toward the door to Jocelyn's room. "I still kind of expect her to come flying through the door with some crazy idea for us to do."

Chloe chuckled softly. "Yeah, me too. That whole accident seems like a dream."

"Do you guys really think it was an accident?" Emma tossed out.

"What do you mean?" Lauryn asked, wondering if Emma's thoughts were similar to her own.

"I mean . . ." She paused and looked at each of them. "We were following Ava for like five miles and everything was fine. Then out of the blue she started speeding up and swerving all over the road. I just don't see why she was driving like that. And why did she put on her *hazard lights? She must have known something was wrong."*

"The police said something may have malfunctioned in her car," Andrea said.

"It just seems too coincidental that it happened when she was driving alone," Emma said.

"I've thought that, too," Lauryn added quietly. *"Ava always wanted to ride all together before. She said it was more fun that way."* The five girls looked at each other, none of them knowing the answer.

Chapter Five

"Thanks for the food," Lauryn told Jace as he pulled in front of Jocelyn's house to drop her off. Jace was leaving the next day to go out of town for a few weeks on a family vacation.

"Hey, did you get an announcement for Tracy Cuthbert's wedding?"

"What?" Lauryn nearly choked on her gum. "Tracy's getting married?"

"Yes, to her missionary. He got home in May."

"Whoa!" Lauryn said. "That's crazy. She's crazy. Why would she get married so young?"

"I guess they thought it was right. They are getting married in the temple," he told her.

"I'm glad to hear that. Still, she's barely out of high school. She hasn't had a chance to go to college or see the world. I'm totally not getting married until I've done everything I possibly want to do."

"That doesn't make sense," Jace said. "How can you ever do everything you've possibly wanted to do? No one can ever do that."

"Well, you know what I mean. I want to travel and live in other countries. I want to get an education and have a career. After that I'll get married."

"It sounds like you think your life will be over if you get married." Jace smiled. "What if you meet someone incredible and you are willing to give it all up for him?"

"No one could make me feel that way. I just don't think marriage and a family at a young age is right for everyone. At least not for me."

"Your parents really did a number on you, didn't they?" he observed.

She couldn't take offense at his comment, because he'd helped her through a lot of family crises. Still, in her opinion, those experiences validated her feelings. "What do you mean? What's wrong with me wanting to live my life first?"

"It doesn't sound like much fun if you have to live your life alone."

"I won't be alone," she said. "I have friends. And I have you. You'll hang out with me."

"Not if I get married after my mission," he told her.

"What if you don't? What if you don't find a girl you want to marry? I guess that means you can hang out with me until you do."

"Gee, thanks," he said. Then he laughed. "Watch, you will be the one who finds someone and gets married while I'm on my mission, and I will still be single at forty."

Lauryn laughed. "Jace, you're way too cool and cute to be single that long."

He tilted his head and looked at her intently.

"What?" Had she said something wrong? "I just meant that there's nothing wrong with you to keep you from getting married."

"Gosh, thanks."

"I didn't mean it like that," she said.

"So how old do you want to be when you get married?" Jace asked.

"I don't know, not over thirty."

His eyes opened wide. "Really? That old?"

"It's not that old," she said.

"All the good guys will be taken by then."

"I guess that's the chance I have to take." She was thoughtful for a moment. "You don't really think that's true, do you?"

"What do I know?" he said. "I'm sure that won't happen."

"What if we both get to thirty and we're not married?" she asked him.

"Then . . ." Jace glanced out the window, then looked back at Lauryn, his clear blue eyes meeting hers. "We'll get married."

Lauryn's stomach flipped and her face got hot just like it had when Jace hugged her after the pageant. She looked back at him, not knowing what to say.

Jace quickly shifted his gaze back out the window. He shrugged. Then, lightening the mood, he said, "We're better than nothing."

She chuckled nervously. "At least we know we get along and would have fun together."

"We wouldn't have to fight about where to eat out or which movies to see. We have a lot in common."

"That's true." Jace understood her better than she understood herself sometimes. And he was right. Her parents' example had totally scared her about getting married. At least with Jace she'd be married to her best friend.

"Let's make a deal then," he said. "If on June first of the year we both turn thirty we're not married, let's meet somewhere, and I'll propose to you. But you have to say yes."

Lauryn smiled at the twinkle in his eye.

"Okay." She played along. "I promise. I'll be in St. George then because that's when we'll be holding the Butterfly Girls reunion. Where should we meet?"

"How about in front of the St. George Temple at noon?"

"By the steps?" she asked.

"Yes. Between the two sets of steps that lead to the front doors."

"Okay, sounds good to me. Maybe we can go in and get sealed right then."

"Sure. Why not? By that age, no one would blame us or probably care," he said.

"I'm sure my parents wouldn't. My mom doesn't even want me to get married in the temple."

"That just doesn't make any sense at all. That's the only place we'd get married, right?"

"Right," she agreed. "But there is one small problem I foresee."

"Oh, you foresee a problem?" he said, mocking her use of the word foresee.

"Yeah. You'll be married within six months after you get home from your mission because I know you're going to meet Miss Perfect-BYU-co-ed at your BYU ward, and she'll send you cookies and love notes on your mission, and you'll get home and get married and live in student housing and have six children before you graduate from college. And even after six kids, she'll still have the body of a supermodel and you'll graduate top of your class and get an amazing job offer, and your

children will be the best behaved at sacrament meeting and not even throw Cheerios on the floor."

Jace looked at her, his brow lined with worry.

"What?"

"How long have you been thinking about this?"

"About what?" she asked, unsure what he was talking about.

"My life? Six kids? Are you crazy? I suppose you already have the names of my six children chosen for me?"

"Actually, I have," she teased. "You two will be the type to use Book of Mormon names: Nephi, Sam . . . I think we'll skip Laman and Lemuel, you know, just to be safe. Sariah for a girl. Maybe Abish for another girl. Then Benjamin and Moroni would be nice."

"You're nuts." He shook his head. "Maybe I don't want to make this deal with you. If you're this nuts now, how much nuttier will you be at thirty?"

She raised her eyebrows several times. "Guess you'll just have to stay single so you can find out, eh?"

"Tempting offer. I'll take you up on it if absolutely nothing better comes along."

"Okay." She opened the car door. "But it will be your loss! I'm sure I'll be quite a catch at thirty. I don't do much sun tanning, so I won't be wrinkly and pruny. I floss every night, so my teeth should be good, too. Yep, quite a prize I'll be."

"Now you sound like Yoda."

"Worth waiting for I am." She struck a pose that looked more spastic than alluring.

"Good-bye, Lauryn." Jace laughed as he put the car in gear.

"Bring me back something from the beach—a seashell or a starfish or something."

He nodded and waved.

"Or cool flip-flops, or a fun purse!" she hollered as he pulled away.

She watched him drive off and waved until he turned the corner and was out of sight.

Funny, *she thought.* I always thought it'd be more exciting when I got proposed to.

* * *

Lauryn knocked on the front door, and Jocelyn let her in. She was the last to arrive. With candles lit around the room and a stick of jasmine incense burning, the first official Butterfly Girls ceremony began. They wanted to make it memorable and meaningful. This was the night they would create the legacy of the rosewood box that was going to tie them together forever.

An undercurrent of excitement ran through the five girls. They looked at each other as if they held an important secret between them. And in a way they did. The contents of the box would be known only to them. No one else. They had decided that each of them would place an object in the box that represented them personally, then an object that represented the group as a whole. The box would then be passed to one of them to guard and protect. The contents of the box would bring its bearer good luck and keep her safe until the next Butterfly Girls ceremony in exactly one year.

"Who's first?" Emma asked.

Chloe looked to her right and then to her left, then to Lauryn, who was sitting across from her. "I'll go first. I should go first because I have one of the most important items to put in the box."

The wattage of the undercurrent rose. The girls shivered and giggled with excitement.

"Okay." Chloe pulled out a silk bag and opened the top. "First, I brought something personal, but it's also something for the group." She put her hand in the bag and pulled it out, her fist closed tightly over the object. She then turned her hand over and slowly unfolded her fingers.

"The rhinestone hair clippie!" Andrea exclaimed. "I love that clippie."

"I know!" Chloe matched Andrea's enthusiasm. "At one time or another, everyone has worn this clippie to a dance or on a special date. And since it is so glittery, I thought it was perfect for our Butterfly Box."

The other girls nodded their approval. The clippie was indeed a perfect item for the box.

"I'll put it in there on one condition, though."

"What's that?" Emma asked her.

"*That I can take it out to wear to my wedding someday,*" *Chloe requested.*

"*Of course, Chloe,*" *Jocelyn said.* "*That would be neat if you wore it.*"

"*What's your other item?*" *Emma asked.*

"*Do you guys mind if I do it last? I think you'll understand why when you see it,*" *Chloe explained.*

Emma shrugged. "*Sure, why not. I'll go next.*" *From behind her she pulled out a tightly folded T-shirt. She shook it open, and they all laughed.*

"*Your bungee-jumping shirt,*" *Lauryn said.* "*Oh my gosh, I remember that like it was yesterday.*"

"*That was one of the most memorable days in my life,*" *she said.* "*Without you guys there, I never would have jumped. I wanted to do it so bad, but I was so scared.*"

"*So Ava went with you,*" *Andrea remembered.* "*That was a very cool day. We all jumped.*"

"*And some of us threw up,*" *Chloe said, pulling a face of disgust.* "*I can never eat nachos again.*"

They all laughed.

"*Anyway, it takes a lot of space, but it's so important because it reminds me of how powerful the support we give each other really is.*"

"*What else did you bring?*" *Andrea asked.*

Emma pulled an envelope from behind her back and held it for everyone to see. "*I also want to add something that is timeless. It captures a moment we can never have again.*"

From the envelope, she pulled out a picture of all of them, with Ava, standing in front of the D *on graduation night.*

They all grew silent as fresh tears surfaced and a wave of pain and loss engulfed them.

"*We'll never forget Ava.*" *Emma continued.* "*She always lived life to the fullest and dared to dream bigger than anyone I know. I am going to try to be more like that.*"

"*Me too,*" *Chloe said, wiping a tear from her cheek.*

Jocelyn, you're next." *Emma sniffed and reached over to grab a tissue from Jocelyn's desk.*

Jocelyn swallowed, then nodded her head as if trying to gather strength.

"*Well, first I want to put this inside.*" *She pulled a necklace made of boondoggle string and colored beads out of her pocket and placed it inside the box.*

"*Is that what I think it is?*" *Lauryn reached over and pulled the necklace back out and looked at it for a moment.* "*It is. I haven't seen this since—*"

"*Girls camp!*" *Andrea finished for her.* "*Do you remember that?*"

"*I got so homesick that first night,*" *Lauryn said.* "*The leaders almost took me home because I was being such a baby.*"

"*I was homesick, too,*" *Andrea said.* "*I just never said so because I didn't want them to fuss over me like they did you.*"

"*Thanks! It would have been nice not to be the only one crying that night.*"

"*Sorry,*" *Andrea defended.* "*I waited until everyone was asleep before I cried.*"

"*I was happy to be away from home,*" *Jocelyn said.* "*I cried when it was over and I had to go back.*"

"*Remember the snipe hunt?*" *Chloe said, a giggle erupting, causing the other girls to laugh.*

"*And Ava's dramatic scene when the snipe bit her?*" *Emma reminded them.*

"*She had the leaders convinced something had bitten her,*" *Chloe managed to say through her giggles.* "*The fake blood really worked.*"

"*It was cool her sister warned her about the snipe hunt for the first-year girls. She really turned the joke on them,*" *Andrea said.*

"*Your ward had a lot of crazy things happen that year,*" *Emma said.* "*Wasn't it your ward that had the bear break into the food tent? And you guys had the canoe tip over in that freezing water.*"

"*I was in that canoe,*" *Lauryn said.* "*I thought I was dead, trying to swim to shore in that melted snow they called water.*"

"*That was scary,*" *Andrea remembered.* "*I kept wishing I could go out and help you, but there was nothing I could do. I just had to stand and watch. And pray. I prayed like crazy.*"

Lauryn put the necklace back in the box. "*That's a good thing to put in there,*" *Lauryn said.* "*We all need to pray for each other.*"

"*That's good; I like that,*" *Chloe said.*

"What's your other thing, Jocelyn?" Lauryn asked.

"I hope it's okay, but it's something very personal that I'd like to keep private."

Chloe's face registered surprise. "You don't want to share it with us?"

"Not now. Maybe someday."

Lauryn nodded. "I'm okay with that. We probably all have a few private things we haven't shared with each other, right?"

The other girls agreed, even Chloe. "So it shows that we love and support each other unconditionally. We don't have to know everything about each other."

Jocelyn smiled her thanks to Lauryn. Then she reached forward and placed in the Butterfly Box a small box sealed with a piece of tape.

"Okay, then, let's move on," Emma said, eyeing the small, sealed box. "Lauryn?"

"Oh, yeah. Well . . ." Lauryn brought out a bag. "First, I hope there's room, because I want to put this in." She pulled her crown out of the bag.

Chloe clapped, and Andrea released a resounding "Yes!"

Emma and Jocelyn chuckled. "You sure you can part with that thing?" Emma asked.

"Gladly," Lauryn said. "Still, I have to be honest, it has a lot of meaning for me, because I never would have done that pageant without support from my friends." She glanced around the circle at each of them. "I think that each of us is a princess, and that's what I want this to represent."

"I love it!" Chloe said. "Can I try it on one more time?"

"Sure." Lauryn handed her the crown. Chloe put it on her head and smiled regally, waving like a beauty queen. "It just does something to you to have this on your head," she said.

She handed the crown back to Lauryn, who put it in the box.

"The other thing I brought was this." She pulled out a video. "I hope there's room."

"Sabrina!" Jocelyn exclaimed. "Our most favorite movie ever."

It was true. Many a sleepover had been spent watching Sabrina, starring Audrey Hepburn. The movie was the reason Ava had decided on a career in acting. Her goal was to be the next Audrey Hepburn, even though *out of all the girls in the group, it was Jocelyn who was a dead ringer for Audrey with her big eyes, dark hair, long neck, and gentle manner.*

"We have to have that movie in there," Jocelyn said. "Let's watch it first. One more time."

"Sure." Lauryn gave permission. "After we're done with this, let's pop popcorn and watch it."

Andrea was next. "Don't laugh, but I'm going to put something very important to me inside there." She held up her bottle of hand sanitizer.

Lauryn laughed. "You are never without this stuff," she said. "You must have five or six of these."

"In her locker, in her purse, in her car, in her backpack," Chloe listed.

"In my car, in my locker, and even at my house," Emma added.

"That is definitely you," Jocelyn said. "And in a weird way, it can represent something else we want to share as a group."

"What's that?" Andrea asked with confusion.

"Protection. We need to watch out for each other and stand by each other," Jocelyn said. "That's what friends do."

Lauryn smiled. "I like that. It's perfect."

"The other thing I brought is this." Andrea held up a bag of Tootsie Roll Midgies, the one candy every one of them loved.

The rest of them laughed and begged for a few of the candies before she put the bag inside.

"I know they will get hard as rocks, but we can replace them each year or something," Andrea said.

"Great idea!" Chloe snitched another candy out of the bag.

"Hey! Leave some for me to put in the box."

"Sorry. I haven't had one of these for days." Chloe popped the chocolate treat into her mouth.

"That's it," Emma said. Then she remembered. "No, wait." She looked at Chloe. "You had something else?"

"Yeah, I do," Chloe answered. "It's something that will keep a little part of Ava with us always."

She held up a baggie. Inside was a snippet of blond hair.

Emma's mouth dropped open.

"You didn't," Andrea said.

"Is that what I think it is?" Lauryn asked.

"Yep! I cut her hair while she was in her coffin, I mean, casket," Chloe announced.

"Chloe!" Jocelyn gasped.

"Hey, no one saw me," Chloe said. "Besides, I wanted to have something to remember her by."

She passed the baggie around so each of them could look at it.

"It's so weird to think this was hers," Lauryn said.

"Yeah." Andrea took it and examined it, then handed it to Emma, who quickly passed it to Jocelyn.

"I'm glad you got this," Jocelyn said, handing it back to Chloe. "It's perfect for our box."

"If not a little morbid," Emma added. "I can't believe you cut that while you were at the viewing."

"Ava didn't care," Chloe told her.

"Very funny." Emma rolled her eyes.

With reverence, Chloe carefully placed the baggie of hair on top of everything else in the box.

"I hope it shuts," Lauryn said, looking at the bulging contents.

"It will," Jocelyn assured her. "And I'll lock it, too."

The reverent tone stayed with them as the lid was slowly lowered. Then, Jocelyn inserted the key, turned it, and pulled it out.

"There," she said. "The Butterfly Box is complete. Each year, when we get together on June fifth, we'll open the box and remind ourselves of our motto, that not all that glitters is gold and that change is good."

They all nodded.

"I love you guys," Emma said.

They all shared hugs and expressed their love for each other.

"I'm so glad we're living close when we go to school," Chloe said. "If we were all going different directions, I totally couldn't do this."

"Actually, there are a lot of kids from school going to UVSC and BYU," Andrea said. "In fact, isn't Jace going to BYU too?"

"Uh, Jace?" Lauryn said, a little embarrassed, as the mention of his name reminded her of her recent conversation with him.

"Yeah, you know, Jace. You've only known him for three years now," Emma said sarcastically.

"Yeah, um, he's going to BYU. Why?" Lauryn responded quickly.

Jocelyn's forehead wrinkled. *"Lauryn, is something up with Jace?"*

Chloe suddenly lit up like a Christmas tree. *"I knew it! You two finally figured out that you're totally in love with each other, didn't you!"*

Lauryn's mouth dropped open, ready to protest, but nothing came out.

Andrea gasped. *"Is it true? Did you guys kiss?"*

"No!" Lauryn finally blurted out to stop the madness. *"No, we haven't kissed or decided we're in love. It was nothing like that."*

"What was nothing like that?" Chloe insisted. *"Come on, you have to tell us."*

Lauryn wasn't sure what to tell them. It was just a silly conversation with Jace. There was no meaning behind it. He would never make it to thirty still single.

"Lauryn?" Emma coaxed.

"Just tell us," Andrea begged. *"I'm dying to know."*

Lauryn looked at Jocelyn for help, but Jocelyn just shrugged. *"Sorry, I'm curious, too. I've always thought Jace would be a great boyfriend for you."*

"Okay, okay," Lauryn said, holding up both hands to stop the interrogation. *"I'll tell you just because what you're all assuming is much worse than anything that's going on."*

"Aha! So there is something going on," Chloe announced like Sherlock Holmes.

"No, nothing is going on. We just talked about getting married—"

"What?!" Chloe shrieked.

"No way," Andrea said breathlessly.

"No, not like that," Lauryn said. *"Oh, my gosh, will you guys mellow out and just listen? I don't know how we got on the subject, but I told him I don't want to get married until I've done everything I possibly ever want to do. And we decided . . ."* She looked at Chloe, who was practically passing out with the possibilities of what might come out of Lauryn's mouth next. *"That if by the age of thirty we both aren't married, then . . ."*

"Then what?" Andrea clenched her fists and got to her knees. *"Then what?!"*

"Then we will meet . . ." She didn't want to go on. It was too crazy to admit.

"Just tell us!" Emma exploded.

"You guys are impossible!" Lauryn said. "Okay, I'll tell you. First, Chloe, will you please take a breath?"

Chloe's hands were clapped over her mouth. Andrea tapped the back of her head to snap her out of her state of shock.

After Chloe resumed some form of normalcy, Lauryn continued. "Okay, really, this is nothing. It's just silly and won't even happen, but Jace and I agreed that if we both aren't married by the time we turn thirty, on June first we'll meet at noon in front of the St. George Temple and . . ."

"And?" Jocelyn prodded.

"And I don't know. I guess we'll see if we want to get married."

"That is amazing!" Chloe said. "You have like, like . . . like a marriage guarantee. You are the luckiest person I know. And Jace is totally the best guy around. I mean, look at what a great friend he's been to you through high school. Gosh, there was a time I thought about going after him myself."

"Chloe!" Andrea exclaimed. "That is cardinal rule number one: never go after a friend's boyfriend."

"But he's not technically Lauryn's boyfriend, right Lauryn?" Chloe defended.

"No, of course not," Lauryn said, unsure of why she was suddenly feeling protective of Jace. "If you want to like him, you should." She said the words, but her heart was protesting each syllable that came out of her mouth.

"See," Chloe said. "I just think he's a big sweetheart, that's all. But he's too focused on school and getting ready for his mission I bet."

Lauryn shrugged. She wasn't sure how Jace would react to knowing Chloe liked him. She wasn't sure how she was reacting herself. If she didn't want him, she shouldn't stand in the way of letting someone else have him. Especially one of her best friends.

With a change of attitude she said, "I could talk to him, Chloe. He's going out of town for a couple of weeks, but when he gets back I'd be happy to see if he's interested too."

"Would you?" Chloe asked excitedly as she bounced up and down. Then she stopped. "But isn't that like dating your fiancé?"

"No way!" Lauryn responded. "We were just kidding around. He's completely available."

Chloe clapped her hands. "Good. I get first dibs then."

"Okay then," Lauryn told her. "I'll talk to him."

She pushed aside her territorial feelings and smiled at her friend. It was silly to care if Jace dated anyone else, especially Chloe, who really was as sweet, cute, and fun as a girl could be. Jace would be lucky to date Chloe.

"Okay," Lauryn said one more time for her own sake. Jace and Chloe could date. Absolutely. She didn't care.

Or did she?

* * *

The five women wiped at their eyes, sniffling and laughing.

"You'd think this wouldn't happen after so many years of doing this," Andrea said. "I mean, we know what's in the box."

"Maybe we need to take a new approach," Emma said. "Maybe we should bury the box."

"NO!" the other four exclaimed.

"The memories are hard, but I don't want to forget them," Jocelyn said.

"Me neither," Lauryn added.

"I feel close to Ava when we do this."

"I was just kidding," Emma said with exasperation.

"I'm hungry," Jocelyn said. "Should we have some pizza delivered?"

"Sounds good to me," Lauryn said.

"Me too," Chloe said. "Roger can't eat cheese because of his lactose intolerance, so we never get pizza."

Truth be known, none of them felt like Roger deserved such a wonderful wife. Chloe was the one with the steady income and a solid testimony. He seemed to ride on her coattails most of the time.

They'd gotten married in May after their second year of college, just before Lauryn left for her summer internship at a fashion design institute in Milan. She'd even designed Chloe's wedding gown.

It was also the summer Jocelyn left on her mission to Jamaica.

While Jocelyn had been busy growing spiritually, Emma had been falling away from the Church, waiting tables at a truck-stop restaurant and meeting a biker who was tattooed, pierced, and filthy mouthed.

The others had watched as Emma's church attendance dwindled and she slowly became more negative and sarcastic.

Emma wasn't the only one who'd changed, though. After Chloe's wedding, Andrea had taken a job as a receptionist at a health club. With the help of a personal trainer, she'd begun working out and following a strict diet. She'd gotten down to one hundred and ten pounds on her five-foot-three frame and began teaching yoga lessons.

The problem was, she continued to lose weight, dipping below one hundred. As much as they worried for Emma's spiritual health, they worried just as much for Andrea's physical health.

Lauryn looked around at her friends and felt a surge of love, along with an overwhelming sense of concern for Emma's lack of faith and testimony, Andrea's eating disorder, and Jocelyn's financial challenges. And then there was Chloe, who acted like she was sitting on top of a rainbow, but for some reason Lauryn felt there was a very dark cloud behind that colorful facade.

And as their reunion ended, Lauryn wondered just where they'd all be a year from now. After years of designing outerwear for Jacqueline Yvonne, it was difficult for Lauryn to imagine she'd ever find a way out of the rut she was in. But as she settled back in her airplane seat and watched the Las Vegas desert disappear beneath her, the words of Caroline Nottingham echoed through her mind, *Keep your eye on your goal, be ready when those opportunities come your way, then work like crazy to make it all happen. You can do it.* Lauryn didn't know what, and she didn't know how, but she felt some big changes were about to happen.

Chapter Six

"Excuse me, Lauryn?" The new assistant came into Lauryn's office with a youthful bounce to her step. Lauryn remembered when she had still walked like that.

"Yes, Natasha." Lauryn looked up from her design and stretched her neck to one side. She'd been working furiously to get some designs completed for the spring line.

"Ms. Yvonne asked me to come pick up your sketches."

Don't kill the messenger, Lauryn reminded herself. Jacqueline had moved up the deadline for all of the spring line's designs without discussing it with the departments involved. Lauryn was usually ahead of her deadlines, but this year she was struggling for inspiration. She'd been designing outerwear too long. The newness was gone.

"Could you please tell Jacqueline I'll have them on her desk by five?" Lauryn said, reining in her frustration. "I'm almost done."

"I don't know if she'll like that. She's leaving at two."

Lauryn shut her eyes and prayed for strength. Instead, she felt her head start to throb.

"All right then," she said evenly. "I'll have them there before she leaves."

"Or I can come back and get them," Natasha said. "It's no problem."

"Thank you, but I'll take them to Jacqueline. I need to talk to her anyway."

"Okay," Natasha said. "Just holler if you change your mind."

The girl bounced out of the room, and Lauryn yanked her top drawer open and pulled out a giant-sized bottle of pain reliever.

Throwing down two capsules with a big gulp of water, Lauryn returned to her design. She knew she had to pay her dues before she could really do the kind of designs she loved. But how many more seasons did she have to endure before she had paid in full?

* * *

"Excuse me, Mr. Molnar," the young man said over the intercom. "There's a phone call from Roxanne Dupree. She's calling about the new Nicole Kidman movie."

"Tell her I am in a very important meeting!" Laszlo Molnar snapped.

"Yes, sir. Sorry, sir." The administrative assistant apologized and quickly hung up.

Laszlo looked at the man sitting across the desk from him, and they both began laughing.

"Roxanne Dupree is a powerful woman," Jerome-Leon Vincent reminded him.

"She just thinks she's powerful; we are the ones with the power. She wants me to wardrobe Ms. Kidman; therefore, she is at my mercy," Laszlo replied in his thick Hungarian accent. "Now, JL, where were we?" Laszlo thought for a moment. "Oh, yes, we were discussing Ralph Lauren's fall line. I've never seen anything more hideous in my life. Do you need a drink?"

"No, thank you. I'm going to dinner shortly," JL replied. The man leaned back in his chair with his hands behind his head. He crossed one leg over his knee, revealing a beige, alligator-skin dress shoe. "Ralph's line lacked creativity, style, and freshness. Everything he showed has already been done, either by himself or one of us!"

"Exactly. This is what we are seeing over and over and over. Nothing new. Nothing fresh. It's as if we're watching reruns from the last thirty years of fashion. This industry is in a rut I tell you!"

"But Laszlo," JL said as he smiled resignedly. "We too are slaves to the industry. You are designing clothes for one of the most powerful women in Hollywood for her new movie. That is the dream of any designer. You will make millions. But, my friend, I feel I must warn you."

Laszlo looked at JL with alarm. "Warn me? Of what?"

"I assume you haven't read the article about you in *Women's Fashion Review.*" JL looked at Laszlo with a quizzical eye.

"Another article? They can't get enough of me, can they?" he chortled, taking a long drink from his glass. He clanked it down on his desk. "So, what do they have to say this time? Certainly they can't be clamoring about the spring line yet."

"Actually, no. They reported on a completely different aspect of your designing."

"Really?" Laszlo got up from his chair and walked to the window, planting his feet wide and surveying the view like a king overlooking his kingdom.

"Yes, the report wasn't exactly flattering to your image."

Laszlo spun on his heel and glared at JL. "How so?"

"They claimed that when you lost your title as designer of the year, you began the downhill slide of your career and that the only thing new that has come out of your design house was the new letterhead on your stationery."

"What!" bellowed Laszlo, tossing his glass onto the desk and sloshing the contents across the polished glass. "Who wrote that?"

He turned to his phone and hit a button.

"Yes, Mr. Molnar."

"Get me a copy of that article in *Women's Fashion Review!*"

"I have it right here, Mr. Molnar."

"THEN BRING IT TO ME!"

A microsecond later the young man flew into the office carrying a computer printout.

Mr. Molnar nearly took off the assistant's hand as he grabbed the article.

The assistant beelined it out of the office like a prisoner escaping the lion's den.

"STOP!"

The assistant froze in position.

"Did Roxanne Dupree say what she wanted?"

The assistant's eyes doubled in size.

"Well?"

The assistant's gaze slipped to JL, his eyes pleading for help, then he looked at Mr. Molnar again.

"She . . . uh, said that . . ." He cleared his throat.

"Well, come on, spit it out."

"She called to tell you they've decided to go with another designer for the movie."

Laszlo's face turned red as his lips pursed together in an angry line.

Scrunching the paper in his hand with a choking grip, he shook with anger, growled, then hurled the paper across the room.

JL and the assistant watched and waited, the assistant poised to make a mad dash for the exit if Laszlo came toward him.

"Which designer?" Laszlo asked in a low, menacing tone.

"Excuse me, sir?" the assistant dared to ask.

"I said . . . WHICH DESIGNER!"

"I believe she said . . ." The assistant hesitated, his expression fearful. "I think it was Jacqueline Yvonne."

"I knew it!" Laszlo shrieked. "That woman is out to destroy me!" Then he looked at his friend and his assistant. "But not if I destroy her first!"

"Laszlo, listen. It's not that bad," JL said coolly. "You can recover from this. Your spring collection will be a benchmark in fashion. You will soon win back the hearts of the press and your devoted followers."

Laszlo slammed his hands onto his desk. "You're absolutely right, but," he said thoughtfully, making a teepee with his hands and tapping his fingertips together, "just to make sure . . . I have a plan."

"Now Laszlo, there's no need—"

"Yes, there is. I'm not about to let that woman drive the final nail in my coffin. She's already responsible for enough nails as it is."

"I wouldn't worry about Jacqueline Yvonne," JL replied. "She's a designer of a different sort. While you're busy changing the world of fashion, she's helping young designers break into the industry."

JL's Blackberry buzzed, and he quickly checked his incoming messages. "My driver is downstairs. I must go."

Deep in thought, Laszlo didn't acknowledge him.

"Laszlo, I must go." JL stood and swung his gray, cashmere jacket over one arm. "This will all blow over. You just need to let the dust from this article settle. Besides, it's not like you're well known for your kindness and generosity. People know how eccentric you are. They expect this kind of behavior from you."

Laszlo thought about the words for a moment. Then he snatched up the article and read a few lines.

"Why would this Bernice Thomas write such an article? Doesn't she realize how powerful I am?" Laszlo challenged.

"She did nothing but tell the truth. Perhaps you shouldn't give her so much to write about. Did you not throw your drink at a waiter and insult the president's wife because of her wardrobe?"

"Yes, but the president's wife does wear clothes that look like they're from the Salvation Army. Am I supposed to lie when they ask me what I think about the way she dresses?"

"It's not above you," JL reminded him.

"True," Laszlo agreed. "Still, someone needs to help the First Lady. So I offered."

JL snorted. "You insulted her, and *then* you offered."

"She should be thrilled I would offer," Laszlo said.

"I must leave," JL repeated. The assistant, who still hadn't been dismissed, looked at JL from a shadowed corner of the office, terrified at the thought of being alone with Mr. Molnar. "I wouldn't worry about the article or Jacqueline Yvonne," JL said. "Just focus on your spring line. That will redeem you."

Laszlo's eyes opened wide with realization. "Yes! That's exactly what I need."

JL looked unsure on what he'd said that sparked Laszlo's reaction.

"I like what you just said," Laszlo said thoughtfully as he rubbed his chin.

"About what?" JL asked.

"I need to redeem myself, and I think I know exactly what to do."

"You do?" JL asked.

"Yes, and it's the perfect way to settle the score with that woman!"

"Which one?" JL checked his watch.

"Jacqueline Yvonne."

"Laszlo, it is time to let it go. Jacqueline Yvonne has done everything possible to make it up to you. It wasn't even her fault, and you know that," JL insisted.

"She destroyed my spring show in Milan with that ridiculous notion of rejecting models for her show who were 'too thin.' The media ate me alive! Especially when the Association of Fashion Designers of Spain followed suit and banished thin models from the Madrid Fashion Week. It was a catastrophe!"

"Jacqueline Yvonne was merely making an effort to use fashion as a way to project a positive body image for women!" JL said in defense.

"But the public expects them to look emaciated! You're not telling me you agree?"

"No, of course not," JL answered. "In fact, I was lucky that since my show was a few weeks later I was able to secure enough models. Still, it also nearly cost me the show."

"There you go. We have every reason to teach her a lesson. And I know exactly what to do. And, even though I don't care about that ridiculous Designer of the Year award, I want it back. I held that title for five years, and Jacqueline took that away from me too. Yes, this could be perfect!" He rubbed his hands together in anticipation.

JL laughed and shook his head. "What are you up to?"

"Leave it all up to me. I have a plan."

"You always do, Laszlo. You always do."

* * *

Lauryn made her deadline for outerwear for the spring line with only minutes to spare. She felt good about her designs and knew they would bring a lot of business to Jacqueline Yvonne's design house. But even that success didn't quite give her the fulfillment she wanted from her job. Her specialties were gowns and evening wear. She had hundreds of sketches filed away with a dream that someday she'd see them on a runway. She hadn't gone to Milan to study or graduate top of her class at Parsons School of Design just to design jackets and coats.

Leaning back in her chair, Lauryn stretched her arms overhead and let the tension ease from her neck. Droplets of May rain spattered on her small office window.

"Great," she said out loud. She'd planned on walking to her apartment, but if it was raining she'd have to take a taxi. Oh well, it was getting dark. She shouldn't be walking home this late at night anyway.

Getting up from her chair, she walked to the window and looked out at the taxi-lined street below and the circles of colorful umbrellas flowing along the sidewalk like flower petals in a stream.

She sighed. Having her sketches turned in earlier than planned was actually a blessing in disguise. Now her schedule would be free for her trip to Utah in a few weeks. She couldn't believe it had already been a year. Where had the time gone?

She checked her watch. Six-thirty. Michael was coming over at eight. She had just enough time to get home and make some pasta for them for dinner. They could watch TV for a while and catch up on their day. He usually left around ten since they both left for work in the morning at seven.

It was routine, but they were comfortable with it. So comfortable that she expected a wedding ring any day. They were ready for the next step, especially after a year of dating.

A short chime from her computer indicated that she'd just received a new e-mail. Unable to resist, she sat down at her desk and clicked on the inbox.

She smiled. It was from Jocelyn.

Just wanted to let you know we got the hotel room lined up for the first weekend in June. Can't wait to see you. Emma is coming, but she's a mess. Bring lots of chocolate. Have you heard from Chloe? She thinks she can make it, but I get the feeling something's going on with her. She never complains, but sometimes I wish she'd just open up. Hope you're doing well. I'm going to Seattle this weekend to interview for a teaching position there. Wish me luck!

Lauryn had also wondered if something was going on with Chloe. She was the eternal optimist, but there was something in her voice, and even in her e-mails, that wasn't convincing Lauryn that things were fine. It was definitely time for a Butterfly Girls reunion.

In the twelve years since they'd graduated from high school, the girls had done a pretty good job of meeting each year. Chloe missed one year when her first baby had come prematurely and had been in the ICU for a month. And Jocelyn missed the year she was on her mission.

Lauryn looked forward to spending time with her friends, even though it was only for three or four days. Still, it was enough to keep them going through the year. Nothing kept her from the Butterfly Girls reunion. Not if she could help it.

Clearing off her desk and locking her designs in her desk drawer, Lauryn looked forward to a relaxing night at home with Michael. Even though he thought the Butterfly Girls reunions were silly, and the name even sillier, he knew how much her friends meant to her, and he supported her one hundred percent. That was one of the reasons she loved him.

Just as she turned off the light, her cell phone rang.

"Hello, this is Lauryn Alexander."

"Hey, babe." Michael's smooth voice came on the line.

"Hi, honey, I was just thinking about you," she said, pushing the call button for the elevator.

"Mmm, me too. You have a good day?" he asked.

"It was all right. It will be better when I can see you."

There was a pause on the phone.

"Michael?" Disappointment immediately filled her. "You can't come?"

"Sorry. I'm under the gun with this project. I want it to be just right for my client when we meet tomorrow." Michael worked at

Bennett, Thompson, and Gage, a prestigious architectural firm in Manhattan—high paying and high stress.

"I understand. What are you going to do for dinner?" The elevator door opened, and Lauryn walked inside.

"I'll have something sent up later. I don't have time to eat right now."

"Okay." She couldn't hide her disappointment. He'd been canceling a lot lately. "I'll miss you."

"Me too. I'll make it up to you this weekend."

She smiled. "All right. I guess I can wait until then. Love you."

"Me too," he said.

They hung up, and Lauryn's shoulders slumped. Another night with a microwave dinner and a book.

She didn't want to complain or add to his stress. He worked hard and was busy climbing the corporate ladder. Michael was hoping to add his last name to the firm's name in the next few years, and it would require a huge sacrifice for it to happen. It would all be worth it down the road.

The streets were busy with taxis and pedestrians, all bustling to reach their destinations. Luckily the rain had stopped, but the lingering, cool scent was sullied as it mixed with the scent of exhaust.

Lauryn needed to walk several blocks to get to the subway entrance. She adjusted the strap on her bag and headed for the intersection to cross.

Once on the other side of the street, she passed an Italian restaurant, the fragrance of garlic and oregano tempting her taste buds. Michael loved Italian food, and his favorite restaurant wasn't too far from there.

Lauryn got an idea, and in no time she was on her phone calling ahead for a take-out order. She would surprise him at work with his favorite linguini with meatballs and thick marinara sauce.

Fortune smiled on her as she stepped out of the restaurant with bags in hand. A taxi had just pulled up to the curb. A man and woman stepped out, and Lauryn took their spot in the backseat. She gave the driver the address, and they were off.

Michael's office building was near Rockefeller Center, over-looking the plaza. She was glad to be inside the car as the rain started up again.

At her request, the driver pulled over and dropped her at the corner. She dashed to the sidewalk and approached the entrance of Michael's building, where she managed to catch the door as a woman ran out holding a newspaper over her head and jumped into the taxi Lauryn had left behind.

Excitement tickled her stomach as the elevator lifted her higher and higher. She wouldn't stay long, so he could finish his work, but he had to eat and so did she, so why not eat together?

The receptionist had obviously left for the day, and the front office was empty. The place was quiet and dark.

Bags in hand, Lauryn followed the pathway through the cubicles until she neared the door to Michael's office.

He was going to be so surprised!

Giving the doorknob a quick turn, Lauryn swung the door open and stepped inside.

"Surpr—" The word caught in her throat; her mouth hung open.

"Lauryn!" Michael said, untangling himself from the blond he'd been kissing on the love seat in his office. He jumped to his feet.

Fire-engine red lipstick was smeared across his mouth and cheek. He tried to smooth his tousled hair with one hand and his rumpled shirt with the other.

"Michael . . . I . . ."

"Lauryn," he said with a note of desperation in his voice.

"What are you doing?" she asked.

"It's not what you think it is."

"Then what is it?" Lauryn glanced over at the woman who had pulled a compact from her purse and was busy reapplying her lipstick and rearranging her hair.

"I don't know what to say." He lifted his hands in a helpless gesture, igniting a flame of anger inside Lauryn's chest.

"Let me help you then. For starters, who is this hussy you're with?"

The blond gasped, taking offense at the insinuation.

Michael shut his eyes and dropped his chin.

"Excuse me," the blond said, unfolding her mile-long legs. "I'm Chantelle Thompson, and no one calls me a hussy."

Lauryn pulled back her shoulders and looked the girl straight in the eye. "I call it like I see it. That's my boyfriend you're kissing." Then she corrected herself. "*Was* my boyfriend."

Michael looked up quickly.

"Humph!" Chantelle Thompson sent a satisfied look in Michael's direction.

"So is this how you plan on getting your promotion, Michael? Making out with the boss's daughter?" She laughed. "How long has this been going on?"

"Not that it's any of your business, but tonight's our one year anniversary," Chantelle said.

The news caused Lauryn to drop the bags of Italian food. Marinara sauce splattered across the floor, covering Michael's expensive wool pants and Chantelle's creamy linen skirt.

Chantelle shrieked, bolting to her feet.

Michael looked at Lauryn, but she stood speechless. He'd been dating this woman behind her back for a year?

"Lauryn, I'm sorry."

"Did she know about us?" Lauryn demanded, pulling her gaze from Michael to glare at Chantelle.

"Of course I knew," Chantelle said coolly. "He's been trying to let you down easy."

"I don't believe this," Lauryn said, taking a step back. She had to leave, to get away from them. She looked at Michael, and suddenly all the late nights at work, the sudden calls to the office, the out-of-town meetings, made sense. How had she not seen it!

"Why didn't you just tell me?" Lauryn asked.

"I didn't want to hurt you," Michael said. "I do care about you."

His words struck her as funny. Her only response was the hysterical laughter that bubbled out of her.

"Chantelle," Michael said. "Would you give us a moment?"

"I'll go call my cleaners and see if this sauce will come out."

"No!" Lauryn exclaimed. "Don't bother. I'm leaving."

"Lauryn, don't leave. We need to talk," Michael said, taking a step toward her and reaching for her hand.

Lauryn pulled her hand away like he had a contagious disease. "No, we don't." She blinked away hot tears. She would never let him see her cry.

She took several more steps back. Then taking one last look at Michael and Chantelle, she fled his office.

Chapter Seven

A weekend of staying in bed with several large bags of peanut butter M&Ms did little to raise Lauryn's spirits. She'd just wasted a year of her life on a man who'd been cheating on her the whole time they'd been together. There weren't enough M&Ms in the world to drown out that fact.

It wasn't like eligible LDS men were in large supply in Manhattan either. Michael had been deemed *the* hottest catch in the tri-stake area, and she'd managed to snag him. Yet, now as Lauryn looked back, she wondered just how strong he was in the Church anyway. He rarely went to his meetings because every Sunday he was either returning from a trip or leaving to go on one. Of course, now that Lauryn knew about Chantelle, he'd probably been with her every weekend.

Had he been pretending to be an active member just to date her? If so, then she was glad it was over. She'd rather be single than be married to someone like him.

The following Monday, Lauryn found herself back at her office, with no clue as to why she was there. She couldn't concentrate on a thing, and at unpredictable moments she broke into tears. She knew she was better off without Michael, but that didn't change how he used to make her laugh, or how incredibly handsome he was, or what a romantic he was—or how lonely she felt.

Out of all the consoling e-mails from her friends, the one from Emma shed a whole different perspective on her breakup. Emma had gone through her own challenges with her divorce.

Dear Lauryn,

I was so sorry to hear about what happened with Michael. What a typical man—always sneaking around and only caring about himself. I want you to know that it's his loss, and he's crazy for letting you go.

You know I understand how you feel. Not since Ava passed away have I been so emotionally distraught as when Doug left me. I didn't know how I'd go on. I felt completely worthless and unwanted. Men are basically scum, and I've decided we don't need them to be happy. You have so much going for you. You are beautiful and talented. Men are all the same, and we don't need any of them. So hang in there. We'll see you soon. But if you need to talk, give me a call. I'll cry with you.

Butterfly Girls Forever,

Emma

Lauryn read the e-mail several times, then shut her eyes and tried to focus on Emma's message.

Michael's rejection hurt, and just like Emma, she did feel worthless and unwanted. But she wasn't sure she bought into Emma's whole anti-men philosophy. There had to be good men out there somewhere. Her whole life she'd dreamed of marrying and having a family. She had to believe that someday she would realize that dream.

A knock on her office door pulled her from her thoughts.

"Come in," she called, directing her attention to her visitor. Her interest nosedived when Cooper D'Angelo stepped into the room. Under the word *outrageous* in the dictionary was a picture of Cooper. He was loud, crazy, fun, and one of her favorite people at Jacqueline Yvonne's Designs. He worked in the accessories department. She just wasn't in the mood for him or anyone right now. She wanted to be alone with her M&Ms.

"Hey, Cooper. What's up?" She snatched a handful of correspondence and acted like she was attending to pressing matters.

Cooper looked out into the hallway in both directions, then came in and shut the door. He quickly took a seat in front of her desk and leaned forward. Speaking in low tones, he said, "We have to talk."

He was acting weird, even for him.

"Oh?" she said, wondering what kind of hair product he used to create the spikes in his hair that looked like they could cut glass.

"I just heard some inside information from the friend of a friend and thought you'd be interested."

Now why would he paint just his thumbnails black? Lauryn wondered. She looked at his red velvet bell-bottom pants and rhinestone belt, signs of his current retro British phase. If he started speaking with an accent, she would put her foot down.

"Oh?" She played along, just to hurry him out of her office.

"Oooh, M&Ms!" he exclaimed when he spied the glass dish half full on her desk. He snatched a few and popped them into his mouth. "I could never keep these on my desk. I'd devour the whole thing, and my trainer would kill me. She's so strict I can't even *smell* carbs."

"Uh, yeah, anyway," Lauryn said, shuffling the papers, "what's the news?"

"Oh yes! You won't believe it." He wiggled his fingers with excitement. Then he leaned in closely again and whispered, "Word's out that Laszlo Molnar is looking for a new designer."

She dropped the papers and looked up. "How do you know? Are you sure?"

Even though Laszlo Molnar was arrogant, eccentric, and egotistical, she couldn't help but admire his brilliant designs. His spring show during New York's Olympus Fashion Week made waves through the entire fashion industry. Copies of his designs spun off in every direction. He had a way of combining cutting-edge fashion with highbrow sophistication. His day wear designs were a staple for most well-off, professional women. But it was his evening wear line that Lauryn, and most of the world—even outside the fashion industry—paid most attention to. Many of

Molnar's gowns graced the red carpet at every Hollywood awards show. He even had his own Oscar for costume design in an Academy Award–winning movie.

Of course, just like most famous people, his celebrity status got his name smeared through the pages of the tabloids right along with models, movie stars, and even rock stars. Scandalous tales surrounded him. There had even been an unflattering write-up about him in *Women's Fashion Review* recently. Lauryn knew that some of the stories probably weren't true, just fabrications to get Mr. Molnar's name in print and generate a buzz with his fashions.

Lauryn's fascination with Mr. Molnar had started the summer she'd interned in Milan. Laszlo Molnar, a Hungarian native, had just previewed his spring line in Milan, and the fashion industry had taken notice. Even then, at the beginning stages, it wasn't hard to tell he was going to be an icon in the fashion industry. His motto was that imperfection was more stylish than being polished and put together. His combination of textures and unrelated looks set his creations apart from mainstream designers. He used leather and silks, sequins, thick zippers, and denim. Women loved the contradiction in style. And so did Lauryn.

Even though she had a more conventional fashion sense, she admired his brazen efforts at breaking molds and crossing barriers. One of her most treasured jackets was a Laszlo Molnar she'd picked up at her favorite store, Century 21. It never failed to turn heads when she wore it, and it made her feel unstoppable.

"This is inside information, so this is just between you and me. I'm not even sure why this person from Molnar's office called to tell me. We're not even friends, but she seemed to think I would want to know."

"Are you going to go for the job?"

"Me? I don't have a chance, but I totally think you should go for it," Cooper said.

"But I love it here with Jacqueline. She's not just my boss; she's a friend," Lauryn told him.

"Come on, girl. You are dying to get out of here and you know it. Didn't you just tell me a few days ago that you thought you'd never get a chance to design the clothes you feel you were meant to design?" This time he just raised one eyebrow in an arch of disbelief.

"Yes." She had forgotten about that conversation until now. "I was just having a bad day. Jacqueline's been so good to me. I can't just walk out on her."

"You're not walking out on anything that can't be replaced," he told her. "Don't take this wrong. You're the best in the industry, but any basic design-school graduate can design outerwear. With Laszlo, you could finally design gowns and dresses. I've seen your sketches, Lauryn. Except for the modesty thing, you are the most talented, versatile designer I know, and that's saying a lot because I *know* my designers."

"Hey! The modesty thing is important to me."

"Yeah, and even with it, your gowns are incredible."

She smiled at her friend. "Thanks."

"Don't tell me you're not tempted to finally have a chance to see some of your work make it to the runway. As far as I know, only a select few know about this opportunity with Molnar. It's a miracle I found out about it."

Lauryn thought about the piles of sketchbooks with her designs in them, designs that might never see the light of day. She knew that Jacqueline recognized her talent, but she already had two valued design assistants, and Jacqueline liked the job Lauryn was doing in outerwear. In all honesty, Lauryn did have her doubts about ever being promoted to assistant. It was possible that unless she took a chance and went for this position at Molnar Designs, she'd never realize her dream.

"I have to think about it," she said.

"Well, don't take too long," Cooper said. "Opportunities like this don't happen very often."

Lauryn nodded. Hadn't she been praying for something good to happen—a change, an opportunity? Could this really be the answer to her prayers? Was this her chance to finally break out and make a mark in the fashion industry?

She always thought it would be with Jacqueline, but lately she'd begun to wonder if it would ever happen. Lauryn knew she had something to offer the everyday woman and girl, not just the ultra-thin, ultra-rich, and ultra-chic. Her designs were not only modest, fun, and comfortable, they were also gorgeous and flattering on any body shape. And she was adamant that they be reasonably priced.

"Let me know what you decide," Cooper said as he snatched a few more M&Ms from her desk and popped them into his mouth on his way out the door.

* * *

Lauryn went to Sbarros to pick up a calzone for dinner. Ever since Michael had broken her heart, she wasn't in the mood to eat healthy.

Lauryn was almost to the register when she spied a luscious piece of three-inch-thick cheesecake. Adding that to her tray, she wondered if it was just a coincidence that most of the food she consumed lately started with *ch:* chocolate, chips, cheesecake.

A vibration in her pocket indicated she had a call. The line was moving slowly, so she answered.

"Darling, the dress arrived today." It was Caroline Nottingham.

"Already?" Lauryn nearly dropped her tray. Suddenly she felt nervous. What if Caroline didn't like her gown?

"It is simply exquisite, completely surpassing my expectations. I just adore it!"

"Really?" Lauryn said with relief. "It fits well? It's what you wanted? Did I make the bodice too tight?"

"It fits like a dream. It might have been a little tight, but I've lost a few pounds, and it's perfection! I can't wait to wear it."

"I'm so glad," Lauryn said, distracted for a moment as she placed her money on the counter to pay for her food. "I was worried since we couldn't have a final fitting."

"Like I said, it's perfect. You've really outdone yourself."

"Thank you. I wanted it to be perfect for you." The dress was black jersey knit with a cowl neck front and deeper cut back. With slim-fitting long sleeves and a shirred waist, it would flatter any figure.

"Darling, really, I want to have you come and stay sometime when you can get away. I can't wait to introduce you to all my friends."

"That would be nice," Lauryn said. Having Caroline Nottingham recommend her to others was a very high compliment.

"We need to discuss payment."

"I won't accept any money, Caroline. I've told you, this is my gift to you."

"But I don't expect you to give it to me. Really, I would like to pay you for your time."

"Your payment is telling your friends about me, and especially having you wear my design. That's worth more than you could pay me."

"Well, all right. I don't really like this arrangement, but if you insist, then please promise me you'll let me know if I can ever help you."

"I will," Lauryn said, appreciating the offer. "I'd love a picture of you in the dress for my portfolio.

"Absolutely. Consider it done. I'll be in touch then."

The two women said good-bye, and Lauryn took her bag of food and went home with a lighter heart. Something good had finally happened. Maybe her bad-luck streak had ended.

* * *

Lauryn sat outside Laszlo Molnar's office. Her palms were sweaty as she tightly grasped her portfolio and fought the urge to walk out while she still had the chance. She couldn't believe she was actually there, but Cooper had a point. A chance like this didn't come along very often. Even though she doubted she would get the position, she decided to try. Her loyalty to Jacqueline was deep, but her growth as a designer was limited there. If she wanted to grow, she had to take a risk. So she was taking it.

"Ms. Alexander, Mr. Molnar will see you now." The well-groomed young man, obviously Molnar's assistant, stepped to the office door and opened it for her.

Lauryn stood, suddenly feeling dizzy. She'd only seen Laszlo Molnar from a distance. And even then she'd been tongue-tied. How in the world could she meet him face-to-face?

"You may go in," the assistant said, holding open the office door.

"Yes, of course," Lauryn said, reminding herself to breathe.

Decorated in contemporary style, the lavish office was larger than her whole apartment. Rich, mocha-colored leather furniture; aqua-colored accents; and large picture windows across two walls made Lauryn think of her own small office with one window. Of course, she realized, one window was better than none, but the open airiness of Molnar's office was still enviable.

"Ms. Alexander." A voice came from the back corner.

Lauryn jumped and turned to see Mr. Molnar approach. He'd appeared from a doorway off the main office.

"Oh, hi. I mean, hello, Mr. Molnar," she said, reaching out her hand to shake his, forgetting that she had her clutch purse underneath her arm. It clattered to the floor, and she quickly bent to pick it up as a flush of embarrassment crawled up her face.

Red-faced, she straightened. "Sorry," she said, attempting to shake his hand again.

"Why don't you put your things on the coffee table, and we can talk where it's more comfortable," he suggested. His Hungarian accent was still strong even though he'd been in the states nearly ten years.

Setting her portfolio on the table and her purse next to it, Lauryn took a spot on the couch adjacent to Mr. Molnar.

Up close, he looked much older and more wrinkled, but his dark, shadowy eyes and square chin made his good looks timeless. Wearing snakeskin boots, jeans, and a black-and-white graphic print shirt with a sleek, black suede jacket, he was the epitome of style.

"So, Ms. Alexander, I read the résumé you faxed over and was very impressed."

"You were?" she asked, wondering how. She hadn't accomplished much in the fashion world. Her designs had always made Jacqueline Yvonne money, and she'd received a few meaningless awards for her styles, but nothing that would impress a designer of his caliber.

"Actually, yes. I was delighted to learn that you had an internship in Milan."

She nodded, wondering if he wanted her to speak or just acknowledge that his information was correct.

"I'm aware of your work here in New York and would like to see what you've brought to show me today."

"All right," she said, feeling her heartbeat finally return to normal. "I don't know exactly what you're looking for, but I brought a sample of all my work."

She opened her portfolio to the first sketch. "Of course you are familiar with my designs for Jacqueline Yvonne, but I have some designs of my own which are geared toward the average woman: average size, average income, average lifestyle. I've also created several styles that are more high fashion, for special occasions. Most of my evening wear is appropriate for black-tie affairs. I also have a few designs I've created for the office. Business attire can be so boring and uncomfortable. I've tried to keep that in mind . . ." She stopped when she realized she was babbling. He thumbed through each sketch, examining them closely, nodding occasionally.

Lauryn decided to talk only when he asked a question. She concentrated on holding her tongue still to keep herself from telling him about the inspiration behind every design he picked up.

Laszlo's expression gave nothing away. Lauryn had no idea what he thought of her ideas. Her heart sank—he probably hated her conservative look, even though she knew her styles were fresh and creative. She realized that Cooper was right and this was the opportunity of a lifetime—one she wanted.

"Ms. Alexander." Laszlo's voice cut through the thoughts tumbling in her head.

"Yes. Sorry," she apologized again, realizing this was the second time he'd had to say her name to get her attention.

"I'm very intrigued with your work, but before I make my decision, I would like you to submit a sketch of a gown. Something that is personal to your creative style, but also could be a fit for the Laszlo Molnar House of Design. Something fresh, something innovative. Are you interested?"

She was speechless for a moment. She was at the door of opportunity; this was her chance to open it. "Absolutely. When do you need it?"

"Tomorrow."

She swallowed. It would be difficult; she probably wouldn't sleep all night. She had a Young Women activity that night that she couldn't get out of, but she wasn't going to pass up this opportunity. "Okay," she said. "I can do that."

"Great," he said without emotion. "Fax it to my office by three. I am leaving town tomorrow and want to take the designs with me. If I like what you present, I will have my assistant call you the following day."

She nodded.

"That's all then." He stood to leave, offering a not-so-subtle cue that it was her time to go.

"Thank you for your time," she said. "It was a pleasure meeting you."

She could almost hear him saying, "I know." She couldn't imagine ever getting so famous she treated people like an inconvenience.

"I trust you can find your way out," he said, turning and heading for the door that took him from the room.

Lauryn nodded, closed the cover of her portfolio, and gathered her things. Taking one last look around the room, she left with a strange mix of confidence and disbelief. The thought of telling Jacqueline Yvonne good-bye gave her a sickening feeling of dread, but she reminded herself this wasn't an opportunity she could pass up. Her whole future was riding on this moment.

* * *

"Where are Melinda and Hannah?" Lauryn asked as the group of Laurels gathered in front of the Manhattan Temple. "Aren't they coming?"

"Their dad lost his job today. Things got a little ugly at their house," LaShondra said.

"Oh dear," Lauryn said. "Does the bishop know?"

"They said their mom called him," LaShondra told her.

"Let's keep them in our prayers, girls." Lauryn looked over the five girls who'd shown up to do baptisms for the dead. She'd come close to canceling the activity because of her assignment from Mr. Molnar, but something had stopped her. She just couldn't do it.

Her thoughts turned to Melinda and Hannah, two of her Laurels. Their dad was an alcoholic and in and out of jobs on a weekly, sometimes daily basis. Tonight wouldn't be the first time she put their family's name on the prayer roll. She was also going to add Chloe's name. For some reason, Chloe had been on her mind lately. Something wasn't right, but she didn't know what.

As they waited for the other girls to arrive, Lauryn found herself thinking of ideas for the sketch she would put together later that night. She consciously pushed the design to the back of her mind, along with the anxiety she felt building in her stomach. She had to focus on her girls and help them have a positive experience at the temple. She knew that what they were doing was important, even more important than her sketches, but she had a long night ahead of her.

Still, if there was one thing she'd learned, it was that blessings came from doing what was right. This was something she constantly tried to teach her girls, and she firmly believed it would be the case for her tonight.

Lauryn could relate to the girls and the issues they faced in their lives. The only way Lauryn had survived her own family struggles was to stay close to the Lord. She hoped she could help each of her girls understand that this was the key to their happiness and to overcoming the challenges and difficulties they faced.

She reflected on how close she had come to not accepting the call. Her job kept her plenty busy, but the bishop had told her that a lot of fasting and prayer had gone into calling her as the Young Women president. When she'd been set apart, he'd said in the blessing that the girls she served would be strengthened by her testimony and example, and that she too would receive unmeasured blessings through her association with them.

She'd thought about that blessing many times since then. Spiritually she had felt the blessings of working with these choice Young Women, but she got the impression that, somehow, blessings would occur in other areas of her life too.

Once all the girls arrived, they received a warm welcome from the temple workers. Leaving her cares behind, Lauryn embraced the opportunity to feel the presence of the Spirit and the peace that came from being inside the temple.

It was after they were finished with the ordinances and were riding the subway home that Lauryn got an idea for a dress.

The Laurels had been talking about an upcoming dance and had expressed their frustration in not being able to find dresses that were modest. Lauryn shared her story about the pageant and how she hadn't compromised her standards and still had been able to win. Her Laurels were fascinated by the story and all vowed to dress modestly, which wasn't easy since fashion did everything to promote just the opposite.

It came to her as she noticed LaShondra standing and holding onto one of the straps that ran along the ceiling of the subway car. LaShondra was a beautiful girl, with ebony skin and black, sparkling eyes. She had a fuller build but carried herself well and exuded confidence. Lauryn noticed that LaShondra had tied her sweater about her hips. Her waist looked smaller and her upper and lower body seemed more proportionate.

Without much effort, Lauryn visualized the style of dress she wanted to sketch, a dress that would look stunning on a full-figured girl as well as someone less curvy.

She could barely wait to get home and start drawing.

"Thanks for taking us to the temple tonight, Sister Alexander," her youngest Laurel, Jazmyn, said. "I was having such a hard day today; I almost didn't come. But now I feel so much better."

"You know what, Jazmyn? I almost didn't come either. But something inside told me I needed to," Lauryn told her.

"Me too!" Jazmyn said. "We got so much homework, plus my mom called and had to work late at the salon, so I didn't have anyone at home to watch my little brother and sisters."

"How did you get away?"

"My neighbor invited us over for pizza. She works in a pizza parlor so she brings home pizza all the time. She said she'd keep the kids while I went to the temple," Jazmyn explained.

"What a nice lady."

"She is nice. She's Baptist, but she thinks our church is pretty cool. Her family in New Orleans got a lot of help from the Church after the hurricane, so she is really grateful for the Mormons."

"I'm glad to hear that. And I'm glad we both came. I really needed it too." Lauryn slipped her arm around the girl's shoulders and gave her a hug. The faith of these Young Women, even amidst such difficult circumstances, was impressive. Lauryn remembered the suffering, heartache, and trials of faith she and her friends had gone through as Laurels, and she knew how hard it was.

A warmth filled her soul. Yes, she was so grateful she'd come that night, and she was amazed at how quickly Heavenly Father had blessed her for making the right decision in going to the temple with her Laurels. She felt blessed and honored to work with these girls, and she was grateful for the strength she drew from their faithful examples.

Chapter Eight

After Lauryn got home from her Laurel activity, she went straight to work without stopping to eat. The ideas flowed as effortlessly as if she were drawing something she'd drawn before. Excitement filled her as she looked at the simplicity of the design and how stunning and flattering it would be on any shape or size. The simple, round neckline and capsleeve, blousy bodice; and tight-fitted hip and flared skirt gave the dress almost a flapper, twenties feel. The shirring at the hips was the perfect accent for the dress, and it also provided camouflage to any body flaws. In a soft, satin fabric it would look sophisticated and be reasonably priced for prom and the younger market; the silk charmeuse with crystal stones sewn around the neckline and through the soft folds of fabric at the hip would be stunning and elegant for a special formal occasion for an older market.

If Mr. Molnar didn't love it she would be surprised—and extremely disappointed. The thought of finally seeing her designs come to life was more than Lauryn dared to dream. Working for Molnar, having his encouragement and guidance, would allow her to finally do what she'd always wanted to do.

But how would she tell Jacqueline?

She chided herself for being silly. Molnar hadn't even offered her the job. It was a remote chance at best that he would.

Her gaze slipped to the design on her desk, and a half smile played across her lips. No, she had to be honest; this dress had the potential to be her breakthrough creation. With Molnar's name recognition, she was sure it would happen.

* * *

First thing the next morning Lauryn went straight to her drawing table. She wanted to check her sketch to see if it was still as good as she'd felt it was the night before. Making a few minor adjustments, she gave it her final approval and turned on her fax machine. She had just enough time to fax the design and catch a taxi to work. She usually rode the train, but she didn't have time to walk to the station, wait for her train, and travel the distance to her office.

She held her breath as her design slowly disappeared through the fax machine and emerged on the other side. She took a breath. It was gone. She couldn't turn back now. She'd prayed with all her might to know if it was the Lord's will that she pursue this opportunity. Her answer would come when Molnar made his decision.

* * *

The door to Lauryn's office was slightly ajar when she arrived. Her concern that someone had been inside was quickly erased as she opened the door to see an enormous floral arrangement consuming half her desk.

Intoxicated by the fragrance, she searched through red roses, pink stargazer lilies, and purple irises to finally find a card.

Special thanks for the lovely gown.

Be ready to answer the door when opportunity comes knocking.

I know that all your dreams will come true!

Love,

Caroline Nottingham

Lauryn tucked the card away in her desk drawer, feeling as though she'd opened a fortune cookie. Caroline had no way of knowing the future, but her words held so much power and conviction they were hard to doubt.

No answer came from Molnar on Thursday or Friday. Lauryn convinced herself that Molnar hadn't chosen her and that she needed to accept God's will and be thankful for the job she had. Jacqueline treated her well and wasn't stifling her intentionally.

But it wasn't easy to sit at her desk facing another season of outerwear designs and trying to pull inspiration out of the same old drawstrings, ties, and pockets when she had thousands of designs for evening gowns and formal wear crowding her brain, just begging to be put down on paper.

As always, after finishing a season's designs, she immediately began to work on the next season. Lauryn always began her design phase by researching the market and scavenging for inspiration. She never knew where it would come from, but somehow it always came, either from a different era, a different culture, some random picture she saw on the Internet, or a person on the street.

Lauryn learned that Jacqueline had just been hired to design the wardrobe for an upcoming movie starring Nicole Kidman. It was a period piece set during the fifties, an era that was Lauryn's greatest inspiration. Since finding out about the project, Lauryn had found herself dreamily sketching out designs for gowns that would work perfectly in such a film. But she knew she was wasting her time, because as much as Jacqueline cared about Lauryn, she was also loyal to her current assistants, Monique and Diondra. Until one of them left, there would be no promotion for Lauryn.

Monique had been with Jacqueline several years longer than Lauryn, but Diondra had been hired about the same time. They'd gone to Parsons together and had been friends at the beginning. But Diondra's competitive side had changed all of that. She was a talented designer, but she was also the type who would do anything to get ahead in the industry, even if it meant stepping on others on her way to the top.

Lauryn tried hard not to hold ill feelings toward Diondra, but she couldn't help wondering what Jacqueline saw in Diondra that she didn't see in Lauryn.

By Saturday, Lauryn had resigned herself to the fact that Molnar hadn't given her the job. She kept herself busy running errands and working on her Laurel lesson for Sunday so she wouldn't dwell on it. Now that she hadn't gotten the job, she realized how much she had wanted it. Losing the job brought up the hurt of losing Michael, which was extra painful because Saturday afternoons were usually their time together. If they weren't picnicking at Central Park, they were shopping or taking in one of the shows on or off Broadway. But it was over. She needed to get him out of her head and out of her heart.

Lauryn clutched her purse between her teeth and balanced a gallon of milk under her arm while she fished in her pocket for her keys. Just as she turned the key in the lock, she heard her cell phone ring. Was it Michael calling to say he missed her and wanted to get together? Or could it be Molnar calling on a Saturday? The door to her apartment swung open, and both bags of groceries went tumbling across the floor. Lauryn didn't even notice as she grabbed frantically for the phone.

"Hello, this is Lauryn Alexander."

"Lauryn, this is Sister Watson. I wanted to talk to you about the combined activity we scheduled for this month."

"Oh, hi Sister Watson." Feeling defeated and foolish, Lauryn stooped to reach a can of soup that had rolled under the kitchen table. "You were wondering about the fashion show?"

"Right. I wondered if you would be opposed to inviting a couple of other wards in our stake to participate. I happened to mention our activity at a leadership meeting the other night, and several of the Young Women presidents thought it sounded like a great activity for their girls."

"That would be great!" Lauryn exclaimed. She'd been working on the modesty fashion show for a few months and was excited about having more Young Women attend. The girls were excited to model the dresses. Who would have thought that all of this had started back when she was a junior in high school, altering her own pageant dress? She actually still had the dress, and Jazmyn was going to wear it in the fashion show. They'd spent several activity nights learning to sew as they'd altered the gowns. They'd even had classes on modeling so they would know what to do out on the stage. Not only had the girls enjoyed the modeling classes, but Lauryn had realized that for some of the girls, learning how to carry themselves with confidence, no matter what their size or shape, had greatly improved their self-esteem.

"I'm so glad you feel that way. By the time word spreads, we may have the entire stake at our activity," Sister Watson told her.

"The more the merrier. Girls need to know that there are ways to dress modestly and look great too."

"I'm so thrilled we have your expertise to draw from. I have a feeling this activity will become an annual event. Don't worry about refreshments or setting up; we'll take care of that. Is your boyfriend still going to be our emcee, like we discussed?"

Lauryn had completely forgotten that Michael had volunteered to emcee the show. "I don't think that's going to work out now. But don't worry," she said. "I'll find someone."

"All right, dear. Let me know if you need any more help. We appreciate all your hard work."

Lauryn hung up, making a mental note to find a new emcee and someone to help with set decorations, something Michael had also volunteered to do.

Just the thought of him acting like such a devoted boyfriend when he was busy two-timing her with another woman made Lauryn's blood boil. She grabbed a bag of rice cakes off the floor and shoved them into the cupboard. She doubted he was still planning to help, but she knew she needed to make sure. She didn't want him showing up unexpectedly.

His number was still programmed on her cell phone. She would delete it after this final call.

"Hello?" he answered.

"Michael, this is Lauryn."

"Hey, Lauryn. How are you? It's great to hear your voice."

She rolled her eyes. "Yeah, well, anyway, I just called to tell you that you don't need to emcee that fashion show."

"Fashion show . . . oh yeah, of course. Are you sure? If you need me I can be there."

"We've got it covered." Lauryn heard a woman's voice in the background.

Michael didn't respond. Apparently he was listening to the other woman.

"Okay, then. Guess that's all." Lauryn wanted to end the conversation as quickly as possible.

"What? Oh, sorry. The waiter was just asking me how I wanted my steak. Well, thanks for calling."

"No problem," she said and hung up, tossing the phone onto the couch cushion. Her heart clenched, and she fought the hot tears that threatened to spill over. She'd cried enough over him. It was time to move on. But to what?

Picking up the phone again, she pressed speed dial. Moments later, Jocelyn's voice came on.

"Lauryn, how are you?"

"I'm good," she lied.

"You don't sound good."

"I'm fine. I just talked to Michael, and it tore open a few wounds, you know?"

"I'm sorry," Jocelyn commiserated. "He's a bum. You know you're better off without him."

"I know. I think I just miss having someone to hang out with more than anything."

"I know what you're saying. I wish I lived close by. We could go out for cheesecake and then come home and watch *The Princess Bride* to make ourselves feel better. But since we can't, we can talk. So tell me, what's new?"

Lauryn began telling Jocelyn about her meeting with Laszlo Molnar and the sketch she'd sent off. It felt good to talk to someone who cared and was understanding.

"Have you talked to Chloe lately?" Jocelyn asked. "I called her last night to see if she could fit me in this weekend. I usually go up every other month for a cut and color. Anyway, we set up an appointment, but there's a tone in her voice that doesn't sound right. I can't even describe it."

"Like she's trying to sound happy, but it's really forced."

"Exactly!" Jocelyn said. "I tried to pry just a little, but she was very closemouthed about it. I don't know what to think."

"I talked to her last Sunday and got the same response, especially when I asked about Roger."

"I hope everything's going okay. I know he's out of work right now, except for his job at the video store."

"That can't pay much. She's probably just under a lot of stress right now," Lauryn said, not wanting to overreact, but feeling deep concern.

"I'm going to see her in a couple of days. I'll try and find out what's going on," Jocelyn said.

"Call me and let me know how it goes, okay?"

"I will."

The two friends hung up, but Lauryn remained seated, staring absently ahead and tapping the phone on the tabletop. What could be going on with Chloe? And why wouldn't she talk to them if there were problems? It was a good thing they were having their Butterfly Girls reunion soon.

* * *

"So?" Cooper said, popping his head inside her office.

Lauryn looked up from her desk, not at all shocked to see Cooper's hair cemented in super-shiny spikes with neon green tips. She was looking through fabric swatches for next year's spring coats. She loved the banana yellow and the lime green and could easily picture a lightweight, thigh-length trench coat out of either color, belted, with big buttons down the front and a big collar.

"Aren't you going to tell me what happened?" Cooper barged in without being invited—so like him.

Resigned to the fact that he wouldn't leave until she filled him in on the details, Lauryn decided to get it over with.

"I met with Mr. Molnar," she said quietly. "He looked over my portfolio, asked me to fax him a sketch, and said he'd get back to me if he liked what I sent him."

"I knew it! This is so amazing! I know designers, top of their class, who haven't been able to even get an interview with him. You walk in and bam, he wants a sketch. Are you still floating on air?"

"Actually, I crash landed on Saturday."

"Why?"

"He said he'd get in touch with me the next day. It's been five days."

"Oh, pooh!" He pushed her words away with his hand. "He's a busy man, that's all. You are the right one. I know it!"

Lauryn held her finger to her lips to tell him to quiet down.

"Cooper, let me ask you something," she said. "Don't get me wrong; it may be possible that you are just a nice guy and like to see others succeed, but I can't help but wonder why you are so happy for me. Like you have some ulterior motive behind this."

Cooper's hand flew to his heart as he gasped with horror at her suggestion. "Ms. Alexander, I'm appalled that you would think that of me."

"I'm sorry," she said. "But people are rarely so kind to others for no reason, especially in this business. I can't help being suspicious. I guess I've lived in the city too long."

"Well, I guess I forgive you then, because . . ."

She knew it; his confession was coming.

"I do have an ulterior motive."

"Ha!" she said.

"But it's not some evil plan or anything like that. I'm just hoping that if you get in with Laszlo, and someday he wants to hire a new accessories designer . . . you'd suggest my name to him." Cooper quickly looked away and, in a flair of drama which he did so well, held his hands up to shield himself.

Lauryn smiled and shook her head. "Is that all?"

Cooper looked up with puppy-dog eyes.

"Enough with the look," she said. "Of course I'd recommend you."

With a sudden burst of excitement, he jumped to his feet. "Yes! I knew it! I've always wanted to design for Laszlo Molnar. He's the one who inspired me to go into fashion design in the first place."

"Kind of like Jacqueline did for me." Lauryn suddenly felt guilty, like she was pulling a "Michael" and courting someone else behind Jacqueline's back.

"Yes. And if I know Jacqueline, she will not want to hold you back from a chance to further your career."

That was exactly the kind of woman Jacqueline Yvonne was. That was one of the reasons it would have been so hard to leave. But since she obviously hadn't gotten the job with Molnar, she didn't have to worry about it.

"Well, it doesn't matter. Molnar chose someone else, so we're both stuck for now." She checked her watch. "And I'm leaving early because I have a fashion show to pull together."

"A fashion show? Ooh, that sounds fun. What kind of fashion show?" Cooper questioned.

"Oh, it's nothing big. Well, actually, it is big, but it's not what you think it is."

Cooper shook his head, totally confused by what she wasn't saying.

"You see, I'm in charge of a group of teenage girls at my church, and each week we have an activity together. We decided to do a modesty fashion show."

"A *what* fashion show?" Cooper said with an expression that looked like he'd just sucked on a lemon.

"A *modesty* fashion show. Our church encourages girls to dress modestly. You know what that is? No bare shoulders, no plunging necklines, no stomachs showing, no short skirts."

"No fun," he added.

"Not true. I'm all about having fun with fashion but not showing off everything a girl has."

"And that's what this show is about?"

"Yeah. We've altered gowns and dresses to show that girls can look fashionable and still be modest."

"I don't believe it's possible by the standards you just listed," Cooper countered.

"Then you should come watch it. I'm on my way to rehearsal." She couldn't believe she'd just invited him, but she wanted to prove her point. "In fact, you can see the Jacqueline Yvonne dress I altered to win a pageant back in high school. You could say it was the dress that started it all."

"I'd love to go," Cooper said, surprising Lauryn more than a little.

If she had to change people's thinking one person at a time, then so be it. People like Cooper needed to open their minds and allow women to restructure the media's image of what women should look and dress like. Stick-thin models wearing barely any clothes were not attractive, nor were they a fair representation of women, at least none of the women she knew.

Cooper was in for an eye-opener.

* * *

"What is this place?" Cooper asked when they arrived.

"It's the cultural hall. This is where we're having the fashion show." She looked around at the basketball hoops, stacks of chairs and tables, scattered chalkboards, and piano.

"*Cultural* hall?" he mocked. "Sorry, I don't see the culture part happening."

"I know. It's used for everything, but it's the only place we've got."

"Then, honey, we have our work cut out for us," Cooper said.

Her brow narrowed. "What do you mean?"

"We want to transform this place into a fashion feast—dresses, decorations, lights, music." Cooper waved his arms around, and Lauryn laughed to think of what he might be picturing in place of the scene before them.

"Wait a minute! First of all, are you saying you want to help? And second, I do have a budget," she told him.

"I love a challenge!" he exclaimed. "Besides, you forget my theater background. My parents have access to scenery, props, costumes—you name it. We can transform this place into anything you want."

"Don't forget, it's a church activity, not a rave party," she said.

He gave her an impatient scowl. "Give me some credit, Lauryn. I understand that. But why not have some fun?"

"Are you sure you have time to help?" she asked.

"Are you kidding? I live for things like this. And I can help the girls with their hair and makeup. I can do it all!"

Lauryn smiled. His enthusiasm was completely contagious. "Wow! I don't know what to say. I wasn't sure I could pull this off, especially since they've invited practically every ward in the tri-state area. You're like a ray of sunshine."

"That's me, spreading sunshine wherever I go. Now stop talking and let's get to work."

As the girls trickled in one by one, Cooper and Lauryn called them over to help clear the cultural hall.

Cooper had no trouble relating to the girls, and they immediately developed a rapport with him. His joking and teasing got the girls laughing, and in no time they had enough space for a makeshift runway and were ready to start rehearsal.

As self-appointed set director and creative consultant, Cooper took over the job of staging the show.

Cooper clapped his hands to get everyone's attention. "Okay, girls, let me share my vision with you." He spread his hands wide to demonstrate the magnitude of what he was about to present to them. "I am going to bring in a platform the exact height of the stage and create a runway. You will come out to the center of the stage and strike a pose, like this." He walked out and demonstrated exactly how he wanted them to come onto the stage, then he stopped, propped one hand on his hip, lifted his chin, and slightly turned his head.

Lauryn had to cover her mouth so he wouldn't see her laugh. Cooper loved to put on a theatrical performance.

"After the pose, you will proceed onto the runway. And when you walk, loosen up your hips and shoulders. Strut your stuff."

Lauryn cleared her throat. "Uh, Cooper, we're not at Bryant Park for fashion week; we're in a church."

"Right, sorry. You girls are gorgeous. I forgot for a moment that you weren't real models."

All the girls giggled. Cooper had his first official fan club.

"Still, I don't want to see any of this." He walked stiffly, his shoulders immobile and his arms straight down to the side. "You need to glide with confidence and joy. I want happy models, not serious, depressed models. My models love what they're wearing so much that anyone who sees them wants to wear it too. You're happy because you love your clothes; they make you feel good."

The girls clapped for him as he finished his walk with one final turn and posed with a dramatic look at the imaginary audience.

"Thank you, thank you. All those years of ballroom dance lessons really paid off, don't you think? Oh . . ." he drifted off for a moment, a sudden memory taking him away. "Those were amazing times. The dancing, the costumes, the applause!" He shut his eyes, clutching at his heart. Everyone watched, unsure of what was going happen next. Suddenly, he snapped out of his trance. "Now, where were we? Oh, yes. I remember. I want each of you to try walking. Line up. Doesn't matter which order right now. And Lauryn?"

She snapped to attention. "Yes?"

"Would it be possible to get more girls?"

"More?" She calculated how many dresses she'd have to pull together if they had more girls.

"Yes, I want at least forty girls. This is a production. If we're going to do this, we might as well do it right!"

Since all the other Young Women leaders had committed to help her, she knew she could handle more girls.

"I'll see what I can do," she told him.

"Fantastic! Now then, let's get started. You first." He escorted the first girl in line to the center of the stage.

Lauryn smiled as she watched him interact with each young woman. A few of the girls giggled more than they walked. Others came out of their shell and showed a whole new side of themselves that Lauryn had never seen—especially Jazmyn, who had a tendency to be shy.

"Wonderful, Jazmyn," Cooper praised her. "I'd say you are a natural."

Jazmyn lifted her chin higher with each compliment. As Lauryn watched the enthusiasm build in each girl, she saw that something else was going on. Most of these girls came from broken homes and poor circumstances, some even worse than she dared imagine. Each day was a struggle for them. But they were trying to do what was right. And they were trying to improve their lives by strengthening their testimonies and in turn, strengthening their families. Yes, the girls were learning the importance of modesty, but they were also learning self-confidence and poise, and they were having fun. The smiles on their faces made all the work Lauryn had ahead of her worth it.

Lauryn heard footsteps behind her and turned to see Jazmyn's mom approaching. The woman couldn't take her eyes off her daughter up on the stage.

"Hi Sister da Silva," Lauryn said. "What do you think?"

"That looks like Jazmyn, but she sure doesn't act like her."

"She's a natural up there," Lauryn told her. "Just watch."

It wasn't hard to see where Jazmyn got her exotically beautiful looks. Her mother was part Latino, and Jazmyn's father was Brazilian. Sister da Silva had gotten married and had Jazmyn before she turned eighteen. A few years later, she'd joined the Church without her husband. Her family—very wealthy, staunch Catholics—had disowned her.

After the birth of their third child, her husband had abandoned the family and gone back to Brazil, leaving her alone to care for their three children.

Sister da Silva worked hard at a hair salon to keep her family fed and clothed. Lauryn was amazed by the woman's strength. And, even at thirty-four, she was still young and beautiful.

"Okay, girls, one more thing!" Cooper shouted. "I will have music going—upbeat, fun, runway music. I want you to walk to the beat of the music, hold your poses for eight counts, then start walking again. Line up and let's try it again. And watch me. I will cue you when it's your turn to enter the stage. In a way, we're choreographing a dance—a wonderful, exciting dance of fashion." He exaggerated the last words by lifting both arms in the air and stomping his feet like a Spanish dancer.

The girls took their places in line, then Cooper began clapping his hands. "Five, six, seven, GO!" At the top of his lungs he began singing "Copacabana."

He was like animation on steroids.

He went from one song to the next, singing his heart out. From the Beach Boys to the Backstreet Boys, Cooper kept them going until every girl had completed her turn on the runway.

In a dramatic climax, Cooper held the last note of the final song, then collapsed in a heap on a nearby chair.

The crowd of girls, several janitors, a handful of boys waiting to play basketball, Lauryn and Sister da Silva, all broke out in applause.

Cooper's fatigue quickly vanished, and he stood for another bow.

When the applause ended, the girls surrounded Cooper, boosting his ego to celebrity status. He thrived on the attention and told the girls that the show was going to be fabulous because they were all so amazing. It was pandemonium.

"My goodness," Sister da Silva said. "Where did you find this guy?"

"He volunteered. We work together."

"What a character. He certainly radiates enthusiasm, doesn't he?"

"He radiates something, that's for sure," Lauryn said with a laugh. Cooper was always a little over-the-top, but right now he was somewhere in the stratosphere. "Here comes the radiator himself."

"Well?" Cooper strutted over. "How do you think that went?"

Lauryn lifted her hands and shook her head. "Words escape me."

"I think you were wonderful," Sister da Silva said.

Cooper stopped to look at the woman, then reached for her hand and bent down to kiss it. "Thank you, beautiful lady. And who do I have the pleasure of meeting?"

His attention reduced Sister da Silva to a stuttering school girl. "I'm a . . . a . . . I'm Rita. Rita da Silva."

"Wonderful to meet you, Rita da Silva. Rita da Silva." He said her name again with an accent Lauryn couldn't quite define as Spanish or Portuguese. "A beautiful name for a beautiful lady."

Sister da Silva giggled.

"So," Cooper said. "You are here to be in our fashion show?"

"Oh, heavens no. I'm too old for that."

"You are here to pick up your sister?" he asked.

Sister da Silva giggled again, along with the girls who'd gathered around them. Some of the girls had gone over to talk to the boys who were waiting to play basketball.

"No," she answered. "My daughter, Jazmyn."

"What?! Jazmyn is your daughter?" His dramatic presence was enough to make Lauryn's eyes roll. Still, she loved how much the girls, along with Sister da Silva, were entranced with him.

"Your daughter carries herself like a dancer."

"She's had a little bit of dance. My mother used to own a studio."

"Really? Ballet, jazz?"

"No. Ballroom."

Once again Cooper gasped dramatically. Just watching him was exhausting.

"Does that mean you dance ballroom?"

"Good heavens, not for years."

"Ah, but you never lose the dance. Come." He grabbed her hand and swung her around, then suddenly stopped. "Oh, wait. Will your husband mind?"

"I'm divorced," she said.

"Yes! The heavens have smiled upon me!" he exclaimed and began dancing with her again. "What style did you dance?" he asked as they danced together.

"All the Latin dances, but I also enjoyed the East Coast Swing and Jive."

"This is fate!" He spun her out, then back into his arms. Then he stopped again.

"You must allow us to dance at the fashion show," he said to Lauryn.

"But I haven't danced for years," Sister da Silva objected.

Lauryn immediately liked the idea of some entertainment. A ballroom dance would be a wonderful addition to the show, but only if Sister da Silva felt comfortable. And if Cooper could possibly rein in his enthusiasm for five minutes.

"Lovely lady, with a little practice, I know you would steal the show!" Cooper encouraged.

"I have to say that was fun," Sister da Silva added breathlessly. "What do you think, Jazmyn?"

"Do it, Mama! It would be fun to see you dance again," Jazmyn said. The other girls begged her to dance with Cooper.

"I guess I could try," Sister da Silva said.

"We will set up a rehearsal schedule. We have to be ready in four weeks, correct?" Cooper asked Lauryn.

She nodded.

"We can do it!" he exclaimed.

"Are you sure?" Sister da Silva asked him.

"Of course," he answered her. Then he turned to Lauryn. "I will have time to rehearse since I already have the set in my mind. My parents will help with that. The girls are naturals at modeling. A few more practices, and they'll be ready for Paris."

That brought another round of giggles from the girls. Lauryn was amazed to see how Cooper had turned them all into putty in his hands. He did have a certain charisma about him, but she'd never seen him turn on the charm like this.

With the Laurels showing newfound confidence, Sister da Silva breaking out of her shell, and Cooper demonstrating interest in a Church activity, Lauryn had a feeling this fashion show was going to do a whole lot more good than she had originally hoped.

Chapter Nine

"Jerome, I've found the perfect pawn," Laszlo said.

"So the game begins. Are you certain you want to go through with this?"

"Without question. This woman has talent, I'll grant her that, but her designs desperately need my help. I'll be able to mold and reshape her. Everyone will think I'm wonderful for helping her and giving her this chance. But that's not even the best part!"

"I'm almost afraid to ask," JL said.

"She's a valuable employee to Jacqueline Yvonne. Right now she's the head of outerwear. But word has it that she is next in line for a promotion, one of Jacqueline's prodigies. She graduated top of her class at Parsons. Barney's bought her senior project, and I understand it was a great success."

"Have you offered her the position?"

"No, I wanted to make her worry for a few days, so that when I did extend the position, she would be certain to take it."

"You're very smooth, Laszlo. But tell me, in the process of trying to take down Jacqueline, you could very well ruin this girl's reputation in the industry. Is it worth destroying her career, too?"

"Once you see her designs, you'll realize she has no chance in the fashion world on her own. If anything, this will give her the only shot she would ever have to make it big. Without my help, she'd hang herself by her own designs I'm afraid."

"And you think she can design an entire collection?"

"She has dozens of sketches ready to go. This is perfect, I tell you. She's so frustrated in outerwear she'll do anything for a chance with me."

"You come out on top once again I guess, " JL said.

"I always do," Laszlo responded. "Now, I must go. I'm a busy man. I have several calls to make and several careers to destroy."

"All in a day's work," JL said.

* * *

By the time Lauryn got home from work the next day, she was exhausted. She'd stayed late to finish some sketches, then stopped to get her dry cleaning and grab some Chinese take-out for dinner.

She put away her clothes and poured herself a glass of cold apple juice to go with dinner, then she punched Play on her answering machine before sinking into the couch with a carton of sweet-and-sour pork.

"Hi, Lauryn, sweetie, this is . . . well, you know who this is," Chloe giggled. "I'm so excited you're coming to our reunion. I've missed you so much, and I promise as soon as my poor Rogee-poo finds a job, we're going to come and visit you in New York. Anyway, that's all. I'm so excited for all of us to get together. Love you."

Lauryn opened a carton of ham-fried rice and took a deep breath before diving in. She hadn't eaten lunch that day and was famished.

"Lauryn, this is Cooper. I've been thinking about our theme. Why don't we do something with a Calypso flair. You know, island music, tropical decorations, fresh fruit for refreshments? My parents are onboard and excited to help out. And get this, when they were newlyweds they had some friends who were members of your church, so they like the Mormons. Which is funny, because I do too!" He laughed. "Anyway, call me!"

Lauryn smiled and shook her head. She couldn't believe Cooper's seemingly unquenchable thirst for this project. All day he'd been dancing around Lauryn's office, even pulling her out of her chair to test different choreography moves for the dance he would be teaching Rita da Silva.

Lauryn finally had to tell Cooper to go to his office and get to work and not come back. He seemed more excited about the fashion show than she did, and she appreciated his enthusiasm, but she needed to get some work done before she took off for Utah.

The next message came on.

"Ms. Alexander, this is Beckham Sherwood, Mr. Molnar's administrative assistant." Lauryn's mouth was suddenly dry, and she nearly choked on a chunk of pork. "Mr. Molnar has authorized me to notify you of the decision he's made regarding the new assistant designer. You have a two-thirty appointment with Mr. Molnar tomorrow. He would like you to arrive twenty minutes early. Bring a copy of the sketch you sent him and any revisions. We will be painting your office tomorrow and offer the choice of Grandeur Gold, Passionate Plum, or Parakeet Green. My suggestion would be the plum, but it's certainly your choice. Please leave a message with your preference this evening so I'll have it first thing in the morning. That way, the painters can have your office ready before you arrive. Welcome aboard!"

The answering machine beeped, signaling the end of the message. Lauryn sat paralyzed for a few moments with her mouth hanging open and her fork dangling from her hand. Then she jumped to her feet and pushed the replay button on the machine.

She got the position. Holy moly!

She clapped her hands over her face, covering a huge smile. Then, taking a deep breath, Lauryn began pacing the room. "What have I done?"

Now that it was a reality, she questioned the wisdom of pursuing the job. How did she tell Jacqueline she was leaving? Jacqueline had been her mentor, her friend. Now she was leaving. How could she leave?

Then she thought more about Laszlo Molnar's offer. She would finally get to design evening wear. This was the whole reason she'd studied fashion design. Her goal was to finally address the issue of modesty in the fashion world. She was convinced that the majority of women weren't built to wear the skimpy gowns most designers offered. Average women weren't built like runway models, nor were they comfortable showing off their bodies like models did.

Laszlo Molnar was giving her a chance to make her dream come true.

She had to take that chance. And she knew Jacqueline would support her in this opportunity, because that was the kind of woman Jacqueline was.

Her heartbeat quickened. Was she really going to do it?

She paced from the living room to the kitchen, ignoring her food and turning back to the living room again.

She'd been so disappointed when she'd thought the position had fallen through. Part of her had believed that it was finally her time to make a difference to women, young and old, to give them clothes that represented who they were and allowed them to have both style and choice.

Cooper's gonna flip when I tell him, she thought. With all the hyper-enthusiasm he was experiencing with the fashion show, she wasn't sure his heart could take this news. But he'd kill her if she didn't tell him.

She dialed his number and waited for him to pick up. Instead, his answering machine came on. "Hello, everyone! I'm sorry I missed your call, but you know that you are important to me. I would love to call you back; just leave your name and number! Thanks for calling and have a fantastic day!"

Lauryn smiled. He really did spread sunshine wherever he went, even with his answering machine message.

"Cooper, this is Lauryn. Call me as soon as you can. I have some amazing news!"

That would get him. She just hoped he got the message before morning. She couldn't tell him at work; he'd blow the roof off the building when he heard about Molnar's offer.

Once the excitement in her stomach settled down, Lauryn finished her dinner, then put the remainder of the Chinese food in the fridge to keep for tomorrow.

Changing out of her work clothes, she put on her comfy yoga pants and a knit top and went to her computer to check her e-mail.

A confirmation for her flight to Salt Lake had come through. There were also several unwanted ads and other spam that had somehow made it through her filter, and there was a message from Andrea, who was now living in southern California.

> *Hey you. Did you get a chance to see me on QVC? I was worried I would mess up, but it went pretty well. They've asked me to come back for the next promotion, so I guess it wasn't too bad.*
>
> *What time do you get to St. George? I thought we could share a rental car. Let me know. I'm excited to see you. I might be coming to New York for a convention in September. If so, we can get together and go to some shows. I haven't seen* Wicked *yet.*

Lauryn had seen Andrea on TV doing a demo for a new fitness product. And she'd been a little alarmed. She didn't want to say anything, but Andrea was even thinner than last year when she'd seen her. The girl had amazing muscle definition, but she was so tiny she looked like she could shop for her clothes at Gap Kids.

Forwarding her flight itinerary to Andrea, Lauryn hoped their schedules did coincide so they could have some private time to talk. She wanted to make sure her friend was taking care of herself. Andrea had struggled with an eating disorder after college. She'd become a certified aerobic instructor and personal trainer, but her obsession with working out had caused problems with relationships. She couldn't understand why her boyfriends never wanted to take their relationship to a serious level. No one had the heart to tell her it was because she was so fanatic about working out and staying thin that she never put a guy first or talked of anything else. Her interests were so narrow, her conversations so single-topic oriented, her whole existence so focused on working out and extreme diets that it was impossible to interact with her on any other level. Besides, she was just too sensitive about her eating and exercising to have a civil conversation about it. Apparently being in shape and being thin were more important than having a husband and a family.

This made Lauryn reflect upon her own life. Was she doing something that was a turnoff to guys? Before Michael, she'd dated several guys on a regular basis. But no one like Michael. She'd honestly thought he was the one.

Now, all she had left from Michael was a nice big hole in her self-confidence. If anything, this job offer from Molnar had helped boost her fragile self-esteem. But none of what she was doing was more important to her than getting married and having a family. She would give up everything for the right guy. As much as she admired Jacqueline, she also saw how lonely Jacqueline was. She was surrounded by employees and people who were fans of her designs, but all she had waiting for her when she got home from work was a housekeeper named Juanita and two shih tzu dogs, Milo and Muffy—not exactly the future Lauryn looked forward to for herself.

The phone rang, and Lauryn recognized Cooper's number on the caller ID. Bracing herself for the volume on the other end of the line, she answered.

"What's this about amazing news?" Cooper asked, cutting right to the chase.

"Well, you're not going to believe this. I'm still not sure if I believe it myself, but I heard back from—"

"Molnar! Shut the front door!" Cooper shouted. "You got the job! I knew it! I knew you'd get it."

"Whoa, how did you know that?"

"Oh, come on, girl. You weren't just a shoo-in, you were a black leather Gucci with a four-inch heel in. Congratulations! If you drank, I'd take you out for champagne! We'll just have to find something else bubbly to celebrate with."

"Okay, that sounds great," she said, appreciating his enthusiasm. "Since you're so excited, do you want to tell Jacqueline for me?"

"Honey, I know you think you are a mutinous scoundrel for taking this job with Molnar, but there is no future for you with Jacqueline. It would be different if you were next in line to design evening wear for her, but you'd have to get Monique and Diondra out of the way, and honey, I don't think even a seven-point earth-quake could move them."

"You're right," Lauryn said with a sigh. "Who knows if I'd ever get to design for her, even though she did promise me years ago that I would."

"Well, there you go. She'll just have to understand. In a way it's her fault you're leaving."

His logic made sense.

"I'm a little nervous about working for Mr. Molnar. At least with Jacqueline, I know what's expected of me," Lauryn confessed. "I feel a lot of pressure. What if I don't live up to his expectations?"

"Well, there's no doubt you are going to have to be on top of your game. From the things I've heard about Molnar, he doesn't settle for anything less than perfection, but if anyone can do it, I know you can."

Lauryn's heart melted. "Thank you, Cooper. You are such a good friend. You are doing so much for me. How can I ever thank you?"

"Are you kidding me, girl? You're letting me dance again; that's a great place to start," he told her. "Rita and I had our first practice today. A friend of mine has a dance studio in her neighborhood, so we got together and went through some of the basics. She's quite a good dancer—a little rusty, but I can polish her in a hurry."

"This might be just the thing she needs. She's had such a hard life."

"Well, that loser ex-husband of hers obviously didn't understand what an incredible lady she is. Did you know that her family disowned her when she joined your church?"

"I did."

"She's got quite a story."

"She does."

"A very classy lady."

"She is."

He didn't say anything else.

"You don't have a thing for her, do you, Cooper?"

"Of course not. She's two years older than I am, and I don't go for older women. Besides, I don't belong to your church, and she already told me that she wouldn't even date anyone who isn't a member of your church."

"I see."

"She did invite me over for dinner on Sunday."

"She did?" Lauryn couldn't hide her surprise.

"She also invited me to church."

"She did?" Lauryn repeated.

"And I'm going."

"You're what!" Lauryn exclaimed.

Now it was Cooper's turn to laugh. "Don't get all freaky on me, girl. We're just friends. I have no intention of joining your church, or any church for that matter, but she has some pictures of her ballroom days that I want to see, and I have some pictures to show her."

"I see," Lauryn said skeptically.

"That's all!" he said.

"Okay. I believe you."

"Good. Now quit worrying about Jacqueline. It will all work out. I'll see you tomorrow at work. In fact, I'll take you to Belly Delly Deli for lunch. If you can't drink, you can at least eat!"

Belly Delly Deli was her favorite place for lunch. Their cheesecake was to die for. "That would be great!"

"And remember, Rita and I are just friends!" he said one last time.

"I'll remember. Good night, Cooper."

* * *

It was time. She'd set up an appointment with Jacqueline for first thing this morning so she could just get it over with.

She left her office with her mind in a whirl. What would she say? How would she tell the woman who'd taken a risk and hired her, believed in her, and tutored her, that she was leaving? She felt like a traitor, but Cooper's comment kept playing over and over in her mind. The chance of her ever moving up to designing evening wear was remote at best.

"Good morning, Ms. Alexander," Jacqueline's personal assistant said as Lauryn approached her desk. "Ms. Yvonne is expecting you.

And by the way, your spring designs were a hit! I loved the kiwi-colored raincoat."

"Thanks, Natasha. I'm glad you liked it. It's one of my favorites, too."

The telephone on Natasha's desk rang. "Hello, Jacqueline Yvonne's office." Natasha waved Lauryn toward Jacqueline's office doors and mouthed the words "go ahead."

With a nod, Lauryn walked to the door and hesitated before going in, taking a moment to pull in a few deep breaths. As much as she hated doing this, she felt good about her decision. She felt like her breakup with Michael had to be for a reason, and whatever that reason was, her life certainly had become more interesting lately than it had been in the past few years.

Jacqueline waved to her when she stepped inside. She was standing by the window talking on her cell phone. Monique and Diondra were at a desk looking at design sketches and fabric swatches.

"The cheetah print is perfect for that wrap dress," Monique stated, holding the swatch next to the sketch.

"Oh no, no, no," Diondra countered in her lovely Italian accent. "We must have solids: black, red, and bronze."

Monique cocked her head and said with attitude, "What is it with you and bronze lately, girl? All our models will look like statues if we have any more bronze. I want bold, colorful, vibrant!"

"Accessories can be vibrant, but the main dress should be basic in color," Diondra argued.

Lauryn watched the interchange, realizing that the two women weren't even aware she was in the room. She remembered how she'd felt the day Diondra had gotten the job as assistant, the day she realized her chance of going anywhere in Jacqueline's design house was limited.

Finally, Jacqueline wrapped up her conversation.

"I'll talk to you on Friday, then," she said into the phone, then made some kissing noises. "Give my love to Dad."

The argument between Diondra and Monique escalated. Jacqueline looked over at them and shook her head. "Creative differences," she said to Lauryn, then laughed. "How are you, dear?"

"I'm well, thanks," Lauryn said as Jacqueline grasped Lauryn's hands, then gave her a kiss on each cheek.

"Wonderful to see you. Love the spring line you've come up with. Fabulous colors and fabrics. The big belts on the trench coats are marvelous."

"Glad you liked them," Lauryn answered, feeling her nerve weaken.

Diondra and Monique continued to argue until Jacqueline suggested, "Ladies, why don't you take a break and get some fresh air, then come back and we'll discuss it."

"I need more than fresh air," Diondra said with a huff.

"You need some fresh ideas is what you need," Monique told her.

Diondra gasped, then said, "Like cheetah prints! Oh, wait, didn't we just do that three years ago?"

"Not three years," Monique shot back. "Oh, hello, Lauryn. I didn't see you come in."

"Come to my office, I'll show you," Diondra said, ignoring Lauryn.

The two women barged out the office doors, leaving silence in their wake.

It was no secret that both Monique and Diondra were passionate about their work and shared a very volatile relationship. Yet, when they joined their creative forces, they were dynamite. Even Lauryn had to admit it.

Jacqueline shook her head. "I've learned that people with great talent and passion usually have strong emotions. I have learned to stay out of their way when they get like that and pray that they work it out."

"Must be exhausting to have that much passion," Lauryn said.

"It's exhausting just being around them," Jacqueline replied with a laugh. "So, enough about them. What is it you wanted to talk about?"

Lauryn didn't know where to begin. Or even *if* she wanted to begin. Part of her was ready to back out. In all honesty, she liked the security of her job. But after watching Monique and Diondra getting so emotional about their work, their feelings and ideas supercharged by their passion, she realized she used to be like them. She used to have that passion, that emotionally driven desire to design and push herself and her creativity to the limits. That was gone.

And . . . she missed it.

"I've been offered another job," she said matter-of-factly.

Jacqueline's face registered surprise. "Another job? I didn't realize you were looking for something else."

"I didn't go out looking for it; it just kind of fell in my lap," Lauryn told her.

"May I ask who the job is with?"

"Yes, of course. It's with Laszlo Molnar."

Jacqueline's eyebrows shot up. "Really?" Then her brows narrowed, her expression pensive. "Which line will you be working on?"

"His premiere evening-wear line."

"Really?" she asked again, as if she still couldn't believe it.

Lauryn didn't know what to think of this. "You seem surprised."

"I am, darling. You see," Jacqueline got to her feet and paced to the window, "I've known Laszlo for many years. He is by far one of the most talented designers in the industry. He's also ruthless and egotistical. I really can't stand the man, but I do respect him for his creations. It's just that I have never heard of him ever hiring an outside designer, especially for his premiere line. I wonder what he's up to."

"Up to?"

Jacqueline opened her mouth to say something, then closed it.

"What is it?" Lauryn asked.

"Honestly, any differences I have with Laszlo are personal; I don't want to impose them on you." Jacqueline walked back across the room. "I know your heart has always been in evening wear, and I haven't been able to give you the chance to design like you've wanted to." She sat down, was thoughtful a few minutes longer, then said, "This is a marvelous opportunity for you, Lauryn. I am thrilled for you and proud of you for taking a chance so you can fulfill your dream. I was daring and brave like you, once. It's quite exciting when you think about it."

Lauryn smiled with relief.

"Don't get me wrong—I'm not one bit happy to have you leave. In fact . . ." She paused and looked away briefly. When she looked at Lauryn again, her eyes were filled with tears. "I regret that I didn't follow up on my promise to you. This is all my fault."

Lauryn was moved by Jacqueline's emotion. "It's not your fault. You have a great team, and I understand. This is my chance to finally do what I've always wanted to do."

With a nod, Jacqueline dabbed at her eyes with a hankie. "You've been a wonderful employee. Laszlo had better be good to you."

A knot formed in Lauryn's throat.

"When do you start?" Jacqueline asked.

"I'm not sure. I wanted to talk to you first."

"Well then, I guess it isn't good-bye quite yet," Jacqueline said. She looked at Lauryn through tear-filled eyes. "You've been like a daughter to me, Lauryn. Please know I am always here for you if you ever need me."

Now it was Lauryn's turn to go misty-eyed. "You've been like the mother I never had. I don't know how to thank you."

"I do," Jacqueline said. "You go out there and make me proud. Be successful. You have amazing talent and great potential. Make your dream come true."

Lauryn couldn't speak for a moment as emotion clogged her throat.

"Goodness," Jacqueline said, fanning her eyes, "I feel like an overprotective mother sending her only child off to college."

They both laughed.

"Best of luck to you, darling," Jacqueline said.

"Thank you for being so good to me," Lauryn replied.

The two women hugged and cried some more.

Suddenly, the doors burst open and Monique and Diondra entered the room laughing hysterically, carrying a tray of Starbucks coffee and a bag from the bagel shop around the corner.

"You won't believe what we just saw," Monique sputtered as she doubled over with laughter.

"This man," Diondra explained, "he was standing on the curb, waiting for a taxi. A woman was standing next to him. It began to rain, so she opened her umbrella."

Monique quickly piped up. "The umbrella got caught in his hair and pulled it right off his head just as he stepped off the curb to get into his cab."

"It was a toupee!" they said together, then howled with laughter.

"He didn't . . . even realize . . . it was gone!" Monique held her sides.

"The woman, she just stood there, with the hair hanging off her umbrella. She didn't know what to do." Diondra wiped her eyes. "I wonder what the man thought when he found out his hair was missing."

They lost it again and had to sit down because they were so weak from laughing.

Jacqueline and Lauryn were also laughing by this time and spent the next few minutes laughing together as they ate bagels. The others drank coffee while Lauryn indulged in her milky favorite, cinnamon dolce cream.

* * *

The final two weeks at Jacqueline Yvonne flew by. The farewell party became another cry session. Lauryn was close to the others in her department and many of the employees at the company. They had all pitched in and bought her a beautiful, black leather Tumi briefcase.

Of course, she stayed close to Cooper through it all as they worked together on the fashion show. His parents, both retired, were young at heart and very excited about designing the set for the show. Lauryn realized that without their help, she would have had a major meltdown with all the preparations for the show and making the transition into a new job. But Cooper and his connections took all the stress away. They were turning a simple Young Women activity into the event of the season!

Even though Cooper didn't say much about his rehearsals with Rita, Lauryn picked up on the fact that the two were developing a close friendship. She cared about both of them and didn't want their situation to become awkward because he was not a member of the Church. But every time she expressed her concern to either of them, they assured her they were "just friends." So Lauryn kept her feelings to herself. She did feel encouraged about the fact that Cooper had been attending their ward quite often and had already endeared himself to many of the members. She'd finally gotten over the shock of walking into church and seeing him sitting next to Rita and her family in his white leather tailored suit coat over bronze, metallic suit pants. She had no idea where it was all leading, but Cooper had never seemed happier; nor had Rita.

Leaving her comfort zone was hard; the unknown that lay before Lauryn pulled insecurities and fears from the depths of her soul. Still, her inner determination and confidence battled any negative thoughts or doubts. A door of opportunity had swung wide open, and she was stepping through it into a new world of possibilities.

* * *

"Good morning," Lauryn said to the receptionist. "My name is Lauryn Alexander. I think Mr. Laszlo is expecting me."

The young gum-chomping girl heaved an annoyed sigh, finished a text message on her cell phone, and said, "Just a minute." She then picked up the phone and, in a surprisingly sweet voice, said, "Beckham, is Mr. Molnar expecting a Ms. . . ." She looked at Lauryn.

"Alexander."

"Oh, yeah, Alexander," she said into the receiver. The girl listened to the person on the other end of the line. "Okay. Thanks Beck. Maybe we'll see you at lunch."

The honey-voiced receptionist hung up the phone and quickly morphed into the annoyed front-desk girl again. "Sasha's waiting for you on the twenty-ninth floor."

Lauryn smiled and said extra sweetly, "Thanks so much for your help."

The girl rolled her eyes, chomped her gum, and began texting on her cell phone.

Lauryn didn't remember this girl from the other day. Maybe this bubble gum–chewing, eyebrow-pierced, Jekyll and Hyde impersonator was just a temp. She hoped so. She couldn't imagine having to face this chick every morning.

As the elevator went up, her stomach went down, right to her feet. She felt light-headed and weak. Clutching her briefcase, she watched as the elevator slowed and approached the twenty-ninth floor. She smiled as she thought about the two-dozen white gerbera daisies with the one deep-red rose in the middle sitting on the coffee table in her living room. The card said, "We know you're going to stand out in the crowd! We love you! Emma, Chloe, Jocelyn, and Andrea."

Knowing she had so many people behind her, supporting her and praying for her, gave her the confidence she needed to rise to the challenge and do exactly that—stand out!

On floor twenty-nine, Lauryn shut her eyes and said one more prayer before the doors opened. She knew that with God's help, she could do this.

Several other passengers in the elevator got off on the same floor. Lauryn wondered if they were coworkers or visitors. The thought of learning the names of a whole office full of strangers didn't appeal to her, but she was determined to make a good first impression. Jacqueline had taught her that you can catch more flies with honey than vinegar, so she vowed to be positive, upbeat, and happy.

A honeycomb of cubicles greeted her. Within the walls, voices buzzed like a swarming beehive.

How in the world was she supposed to find Sasha inside that maze?

"Ms. Alexander?"

Startled, Lauryn jumped, then she turned to see a woman, close to six feet tall, with platinum-blond hair, kohl-lined eyes, blood-red lipstick, and a scowl on her face.

Lauryn laughed. "I'm sorry. I didn't see you."

Sasha's eyes traveled over Lauryn, and Lauryn was keenly aware that everything about her was being scrutinized. Sasha frowned. "Yes, well, follow me."

Not the warm and fuzzy reception she'd hoped for, but she supposed it could be worse . . . couldn't it?

The woman led her to an office overlooking Seventh Avenue, the heart of the fashion district. The walls were a rich, golden brown, and the office was decorated with a black desk and credenza and black chairs, with bright splashes of lime green and turquoise in pillows, pictures, and flower arrangements. The office was much larger than Lauryn had expected, and much nicer than her old one.

"So . . ." The woman turned. "I am Sasha, Mr. Molnar's executive vice president. He asked me to welcome you and give you his regrets that he can't be here himself. He was called out of town on business. But we can get you settled and started. He would like to have your collection ready for the Bryant Park Fashion Week in September."

Lauryn swallowed. "September?"

The woman's gaze narrowed. "I was under the impression you have a lot of sketches already."

"I do, but how does Mr. Molnar know that he even likes—"

"Apparently he loves your work and seems to be confident that he'll like whatever you are working on," Sasha said, the sweetness in her voice more like saccharin than honey.

"Oh?"

"Yes, and he's anxious to see the sketches in your collection when he returns on Friday."

"Well, then, I guess I'd better get busy," Lauryn said, hoping her fake, optimistic smile covered the fact that she was on the verge of a total freak-out. This was the first she'd heard of a collection for Fashion Week. How could she possibly be ready for a debut like that?

"If you'd like to have a seat, I have some forms for you to fill out. We'll need your tax information and your signature on our confidentiality agreement. Here you go," Sasha said, shoving a file folder of forms at her. "Excuse me while I make a call."

Lauryn opened the folder and stared down at the pile of forms. Was she one hundred percent sure she was going through with this? Maybe she should just walk out and go back to Jacqueline's. Designing outerwear wasn't all that bad. And it was possible in a few years she could eventually work into evening wear.

But she didn't want to wait another few years. She remembered Caroline Nottingham's words of advice and knew this was her chance; she had to take it!

Pushing aside her doubts, she wrote her name in the box of the tax form and kept going.

The paperwork went quickly, and she sat for quite a while waiting for Sasha to come back. The cinnamon dolce cream from Starbucks that she'd had for breakfast had gone straight through her, and she couldn't wait any longer. She had to find a restroom. Hopefully she could get back before Sasha did.

Following the hallway, she remembered seeing a ladies' room on the way from the elevators earlier.

She went inside and found a long row of cubicles. Someone at the other end was busy talking on their cell phone.

"Yes!" the woman exclaimed. "I know exactly how you feel. I agree completely!"

Lauryn recognized Sasha's voice.

"I wish I knew what he was thinking when he did this. It's outrageous. Unheard of. A joke!"

Lauryn couldn't say how she knew, but she was positive Sasha was complaining about her to the person on the other end of the line.

"Mark my words. I will get to the bottom of this!" Sasha declared, slamming the door of her cubicle.

Without warning, Lauryn's survival instincts kicked in and she pulled up her feet so Sasha wouldn't see them. The woman washed her hands, then stomped out of the ladies' room.

Lauryn's hands shook, and her mind raced as she hurried so she could get back to the office. She'd have to come up with an excuse as to why she wasn't waiting where Sasha had left her, but the last thing she'd tell Sasha was that she'd been in the bathroom with her!

Maybe it was just her insecurities getting the best of her, but something wasn't right. All Lauryn could think was that maybe someone in Molnar's company had wanted the job and hadn't gotten it—someone Sasha obviously believed deserved it more than Lauryn. And Lauryn worried that Sasha was going to make life at Laszlo Molnar's a living nightmare, which actually wouldn't be hard since it already seemed like a bad dream.

Chapter Ten

By the time Lauryn got to her apartment that night, she was fighting a major headache. A couple of employees at Molnar Designs had poked their head in her office and welcomed her, but the majority of employees had acted as though she had a severe and highly contagious case of leprosy. It didn't make sense to her. How would she ever be creative in an environment where she felt almost smothered with negativity and disapproval?

* * *

In the middle of the night, Lauryn woke with a start. She had it—an idea for a dress she was convinced would steal the show.

Pulling on her robe, she hurried to her desk and pulled out a sheet of paper. Taking one more glance into her living room, she began to draw.

First she sketched the basic body of the dress. Then, taking inspiration from the new drapes in her living room, she added swoops of fabric at the hipline, across the abdomen, then around the other hip. At the back it bunched together, then hung down in a long train. At the top of the sweetheart neckline she added the same swooping fabric, creating a nice, wide-open neck with dainty sleeves that amply covered the shoulders.

In silk charmeuse, the dress would be stunning, with accents in all the right places to slenderize and create curves. It would hide flaws in the bustline, in the stomach, and through the hips—areas any woman would be happy to camouflage.

As one last addition, she sketched clusters of crystals at the center front of the neckline and in the center front at the hipline.

"Brilliant!" she said out loud, then laughed as she added, "If I do say so myself."

It really was lovely and very timeless in style. As usual, her inspiration came from the elegance and glamour of the styles in the fifties. She longed to wear gowns like Audrey Hepburn, Grace Kelly, and Doris Day. The sophistication of style in the past seemed to be lost to the current trend of sexiness, and she hoped to change that.

"Go to bed," she told herself after she put the final touches on the sketch. She knew she had to get plenty of sleep so she would have the mental capacity to deal with her new job. But as she climbed back in bed, she felt a new level of confidence bolster her determination to succeed. She was convinced that when Laszlo Molnar saw this dress, he would love it!

* * *

"Magnificent," Mr. Molnar exclaimed when he saw her most recent design inspired, of all things, by the drapes in her living room. "I am impressed."

Even though the flat, uninterested tone of his voice didn't reflect his words, Lauryn still felt a glow of relief and pride wash over her. He liked her designs, especially the last one.

She smiled at Sasha, hoping for a positive reaction. Sasha responded with a placating smile, then turned her attention back to Laszlo. Laszlo's administrative assistant, Beckham, smiled and gave her a nod of approval. Out of everyone she'd met at Molnar Designs, Beckham was by far the nicest. It would take a while, but she was determined to prove herself to them. She remembered Jacqueline's words about Laszlo never hiring anyone outside his company, so she understood there might be some employees mad at her for taking a spot they wanted. But it wasn't her fault!

"May I ask you a question?" Laszlo asked.

"Yes, of course." She sat up, leaning forward, ready to answer anything he asked.

"I notice that your dresses are, um . . . how do I put this . . ."

"Conservative?" Sasha offered.

"Yes!" Laszlo exclaimed. "Exactly. Very conservative. Beautiful, of course. But not quite what we're used to seeing on the runway."

"I thought that's why you hired me," Lauryn said. "You told me you liked my uniqueness."

"And so I do," Laszlo said. "Yes. Please. I just wondered if there was a reason for this."

Lauryn fought the urge to sidestep his question, even though she knew the answer would set her even further apart from him and his employees. "Let me ask *you* something. When you design, how do you decide where to put a cluster of rhinestones or some type of embellishment?"

"I put it where I want the focus," Laszlo answered.

"Exactly. That is why I design the way I do. I don't think you need to show skin to be beautiful. In fact, in my opinion, a woman who shows off her body distracts from the dress itself. For example, I don't want people looking at a woman's chest; I want them looking at how beautiful she looks in the dress."

Laszlo's eyebrows lifted as he nodded his head in agreement. "I see."

"I personally am not comfortable in skimpy, low-cut gowns, and I'm banking on the fact that most women feel the same way. Still, I refuse to sacrifice style. My goal is to create dresses that fit well, are modest, and on the cutting-edge of fashion."

Laszlo and Sasha exchanged a brief glance, and Lauryn wondered what exactly they were thinking. Did they or didn't they agree? It was hard to tell, yet she knew she was right. Nothing was worse than going to an event and having to stare at the middle of a woman's forehead because it was so frightening to look below her face for fear of what you'd see.

"I guess we're done, then," Laszlo said. "We've discussed the revisions on your other designs. Once you have settled on your fabric choices, we can meet again. I would like to have samples made. I want to see each and every individual gown before we send them to the factory in China. You can work with our sewing department on the twenty-eighth floor. I'll be out of the office the rest of the afternoon," he reminded Beckham. "Will you call JL and let him know I'm on my way?"

"Of course, Mr. Molnar."

Both men exited the room, leaving Sasha and Lauryn alone.

Sasha was busy writing down some notes, so Lauryn broke the awkward silence by saying, "I will have the fabric choices to you by the middle of next week. I'd like to have everything done before I leave."

Sasha's head snapped up so fast Lauryn wondered that she didn't break her neck.

"Leaving?" she repeated. "What do you mean you're leaving? No one told me about this."

"I told Mr. Molnar I had one conflict when I came to work. I have a short trip planned for the last weekend in May. I'm sorry if it's an inconvenience."

Opening her mouth to speak, Sasha changed her mind and closed it again. Then, with a curt nod, she said, "I see. Well, I'll postpone the collection preview until the following week. You will be back then, won't you?"

"Actually, I'll be gone that week." Lauryn felt Sasha's disapproval. "I've had this scheduled for months."

"Yes, well. We'll just have to work around it then, won't we?" Sasha said. "I'll schedule it for the week after that then."

"Thank you, Sasha," Lauryn said. "I don't mean to be difficult."

Sasha didn't answer for a moment as she gathered her files. "I'll let you know when I get things set up."

After Sasha left, Lauryn sat in the conference room alone for a moment. Reflecting back on her decision to change jobs, she tried to recall the feelings and thoughts she'd had as she'd prayed for guidance and for a confirmation that it was right. She had felt right about it. This was an opportunity she was supposed to take advantage of. There was some reason, some purpose to it. But what? Because right now, it all felt like one big, fat mistake.

* * *

At the Young Women fashion show rehearsal, Lauryn found herself so distracted she could barely concentrate on what they were doing. Cooper couldn't make it that night, so she was trying to fill in for him. She found herself sorely lacking in filling his designer shoes. There was nothing of the usual enthusiasm he brought, and everyone's patience was running thin.

"I think we're supposed to walk down the ramp, turn, pose, then walk back and pose again before we walk off," Jazmyn said.

"No, girl, you have it all wrong," LaShondra argued. "He changed it last time. We're supposed to come out and pose first, then walk down the ramp."

"I don't think so," Jazmyn countered. "We tried it, and he didn't like it."

"Whatever! He changed his mind," LaShondra shot back.

"Girls, girls!" Lauryn said, feeling a tightening of stress across her scalp. "I'm sure we can figure this out."

Melinda raised her hand. "Sister Alexander, I remember what he said because I asked him just before we went home."

"Okay, could you show us?" Lauryn said, grateful that Melinda could defuse the argument.

Jazmyn and LaShondra turned their backs to each other, crossed their arms, and watched with the rest of the girls as Melinda walked the pattern for them.

"See! That's what I said," LaShondra boasted.

"It's nothing like you said," Jazmyn challenged.

"All right, I can see we're getting nowhere. Let's find out for sure." Lauryn pulled out her cell phone and dialed Cooper's number as she walked away from the group to speak privately.

"Hi-dee-ho, Lauryn, what's up? How's practice going? Sorry I couldn't make it, but my parents' anniversary is tonight, and I'm taking them to dinner and a play."

"Wish I were with you," she said.

"Problems? What's going on? Are my little divas acting up?"

"I think you've created a few monsters."

Cooper laughed. "Let me guess—Jazmyn and LaShondra?"

"Are they always this bad?"

"You tell me; they're your girls," Cooper said.

"They are both very strong willed and highly driven."

"Sounds like someone else I know," he teased.

Lauryn ignored his comment. "Listen, I just need you to tell me what kind of pattern the girls are supposed to make when they model."

"Let me talk to the girls. I can straighten this out in a jiffy."

Lauryn handed the phone to LaShondra. "He wants to talk to you."

LaShondra listened, making a few agreeable remarks, then handed the phone to Jazmyn. "He wants to talk to you now."

Jazmyn listened for a moment, then smiled. "Okay, I got it."

She handed the phone to Lauryn.

Both girls walked off happily, ready to begin rehearsal again.

"I don't know what you said to them, but it worked."

"I just told each of them that they are a very important part of the show and that I'm counting on them. You've just got to make them feel needed and tell them what you expect of them, and they'll do it."

"I'll try to remember that," Lauryn said.

She hung up and said a quick prayer of thanks in her heart for Cooper. Without him, the show would be a disaster; with him, it was going to be a spectacular success. There was no way she could have ever pulled off this crazy fashion show without him.

* * *

Friday morning, Lauryn checked her packing list one last time to make sure she didn't forget anything. Her plants had been watered, and she'd contacted the post office about holding her mail. She was ready to go.

Her head throbbed with the stress of and concerns about leaving her new job and being gone for the final week of rehearsals for the Young Women "Modest is Hottest" fashion show. In many ways it had turned into the biggest fashion show Lauryn had ever been a part of, let alone in charge of. Not only were Young Women from the entire stake coming, but several girls from wards in surrounding areas were also planning on attending. Luckily, the cultural hall could hold about five hundred chairs. If they had more girls than that, she didn't know what they'd do.

Having that many people attend the fashion show also presented another challenge . . . providing refreshments and accommodations for that many people. The stake Young Women presidency had graciously volunteered to take care of food. The stake Young Men leaders had promised to help set up the chairs and tables for the event.

As for a wardrobe for the girls, each ward was asked to provide formal wear for the girls to model. With the help of the Young Women leaders in each ward, Lauryn managed to address the issues with each dress and found ways to alter most of them to make them modest and more up-to-date and stylish.

Everything was taken care of for the fashion show, which was a great load off her mind. But she still had plenty to worry about. Clearly, the position with Mr. Molnar wasn't working out as well as she had hoped it would. Not only did she feel like an alien in the office, she also felt like she had to defend her designs. She'd asked several of her coworkers for their opinions on elements of her sketches, more in an effort to make friends than anything else. Each time, she had seen obvious objection in their expressions as they'd searched for the right words, some coming out nicer than others. It just proved her theory that the fashion industry was restricted in its current trends. She just wasn't sure how to prove to others that modesty gave her even more creative opportunity.

The phone rang just as she was turning out the lights and wheeling her suitcase to the front door.

It was her father.

"Hi, Dad. What's up?"

"Just checking to see if you're still coming this weekend." His voice sounded tired and strained.

"I'm just leaving for the airport. Are you okay?"

"I'm fine. Just having a bit of a challenge with Logan." Logan was Lauryn's stepsister. She was sixteen going on twenty-six. "I guess you spoiled me, because you were a perfect teenager. I'm not used to rebellion."

Lauryn laughed. "Either you've forgotten about the problems I caused, or somehow you didn't find out about them."

"I guess I have forgotten, sweetie. I actually enjoyed you when you were a teenager. I can't say the same about Logan right now."

"Pretty bad, huh?"

"They don't make a chain strong enough to keep her in line. She's constantly sneaking out and running away. I don't think she's into bad stuff . . . yet, but she's got this boyfriend who's bad news. Ever since she hooked up with him, she's like a different person."

"Yeah, that happens."

"Well, I don't mean to burden you. We'll get through it. But you are coming to stay for a few days, right? You won't be with your friends the whole time, will you?"

"We're just together Friday and Saturday night. I'll be home for church on Sunday."

"That's great news, honey. I'm anxious to see you and hear all about your new job. Logan will be glad, too. She thinks you're close to the coolest person in the world, being a fashion designer and living in New York."

"She does?"

"Are you kidding? Your promise to design a prom gown just for her if she would wait to date until she was sixteen was pure genius. She felt like Cinderella that night. Too bad she met the Big Bad Wolf. I wish he'd go away for the summer."

"Maybe I'll get a chance to talk to her. Although as far as men go, I'm far from being an expert."

"I recall you had a nice boyfriend in high school," her dad said.

"Jace? He wasn't my boyfriend. We were friends. That's all," she clarified. She hadn't thought about Jace in awhile. She had heard a rumor that he'd gotten married and moved to California, or was it Arizona? "But you're right, he was a nice guy."

"Well, we're looking forward to seeing you. Have a safe trip."

"I will, Dad. Love you."

"Love you, too."

She hung up the phone and smiled. They hadn't been close during her growing-up years, but they were now, and she was grateful for that. He'd spent much of her childhood traveling because of his work. He'd missed her dance recitals and school activities. Back then she didn't understand, and she'd resented his absence. But now she knew that her mother had driven him away from home. Over time, she'd been able to forgive him and work through her resentment. He'd done everything he could to make it up to her, and she'd put it in the past. They were very close now. She knew her father and his wife, Cassie, cared about her, and it was nice to have them in her life.

Lauryn wished she could also somehow resolve her relationship with her mother, but she couldn't do it if her mother didn't also make an effort. Her mother showed absolutely no interest in working things out between them. That's just the way it was. Her mother drank too much, had four failed marriages, and was basically living on welfare. It was sad, but she had brought a lot of it on herself and refused any help from Lauryn or Lauryn's father.

It was hard to make sense of it, but Lauryn had come to terms with the situation and realized there was nothing she could do to change it. The Lord had blessed her with the capacity to accept her mother's choices and even love her in spite of them. It wasn't always easy, but she found that hanging onto grudges and other issues was too draining. She knew many people who couldn't let things go, who just wouldn't move on, and she was astounded by the amount of energy they wasted each day being bitter and upset. Her dear friend Emma was the perfect case in point. She seemed to grow more and more negative and pessimistic with each passing year. Lauryn had tried to talk to Emma, to tell her how liberating forgiveness was, but Emma just wouldn't listen.

But hopefully one day Emma would figure it out for herself and unload the burdens she carried around with her.

Taking one last look around the apartment to make sure the lights were off and everything was in order, Lauryn grabbed her bags and headed for the elevator. This trip couldn't have come at a better time. She needed the Butterfly Girls now more than she'd ever needed them before.

Chapter Eleven

After changing planes in Salt Lake City, Lauryn continued the last leg of her trip to St. George.

Out of her window, she watched as the mountains and valleys turned brilliant shades of red and orange. Flat plateaus covered in cactus and housing developments spread out below. St. George and the surrounding area had experienced an explosion in growth since she'd left her hometown. She wasn't happy to see the lava rock mountains and red sandstone hills she'd grown to love covered in sprawling homes, but she understood why so many people had wanted to move to this picturesque part of the West. St. George had a wonderful mixture of small-town charm and big-city convenience.

Weary from her long trip, Lauryn emerged from the plane. The warm evening breeze brushed across her face and lifted her hair. She'd barely set one foot on the tarmac when she heard someone scream her name.

"Lauryn!"

She looked up and saw Andrea bouncing up and down with excitement. With a wave she acknowledged her friend. How much more tan and buff could Andrea get? The woman was so bronzed and thin she almost disappeared in the shadows. Her long, naturally brown hair was now eight shades of blond woven together and pulled back in a high ponytail.

The two friends laughed and hugged. As Lauryn wrapped her arms around Andrea, she felt her spine and the bony points of her shoulder blades through her shirt. Suddenly, Lauryn's concern for her friend escalated.

"You look amazing!" Andrea said to Lauryn. "Wow, living in New York must agree with you. You're so trendy and gorgeous. I love your hair."

"Thanks, Andie." She searched for the right words. "And, wow, look at you! How are you?" Lauryn asked.

"Super great!" Andrea replied. "I'm so glad our flights were close. I just got here fifteen minutes ago. I had some time, so I took care of the car rental."

"That's great, thanks," Lauryn said. Andrea wasn't just a type-A personality, she was type A-plus. She made type A's look like slackers!

They waited at the luggage carousel for Lauryn's bag, then, once they had her suitcase, they loaded it into the car and got inside as well.

Before turning on the engine, Andrea pulled a small bottle of hand sanitizer out of her purse, squeezed some into her hand, then rubbed her hands together vigorously. Then she got something else and sprayed it into her mouth, swished, then swallowed.

"What are you doing?"

"Any time I go to an area that's really crowded and filled with germs, I just take a second to sanitize, to kill anything I might have picked up. I haven't been sick in years, because I'm so careful," she said proudly. "Here," she thrust the supplies toward Lauryn, "want some?"

"That's okay," Lauryn said. "I'll take my chances." Then, changing the subject, she asked, "So when does everyone else arrive?"

"They're already at the Marriott. I guess Jocelyn and Emma made it there earlier today; of course, since they still live here it's easy for them. And Chloe just got here a few minutes before I did. She almost didn't get to come."

"Didn't *get* to come?"

"Yeah, I don't know exactly what's going on with Roger, but I don't think things are good with them at all. He wasn't happy about staying home with the kids. I don't know why. It's not like he's got anything else to do."

"You mean he's still not working?"

"No. He lost his job at Walmart and tried to get on at the gas mart, but even they wouldn't hire him," Andrea explained.

"Poor Chloe. It's a good thing she has her hair salon. She's got to provide for the whole family."

"She's amazing. She never complains, and she's always positive. I don't get it. I would leave the bum if I were her."

"But she loves him, and she believes in him," Lauryn reminded her. "We have to support her."

"I guess. I wouldn't put up with it, though. I don't think any woman needs to put up with a man like that."

Lauryn didn't respond. It wasn't a secret that Andrea was in and out of relationships like a revolving door. She liked a guy at first, but then, when she decided he didn't fit into her life like she expected, she got out if the guy didn't get out first. Lauryn chided herself. Who was she to talk? It wasn't like she'd had any luck with men either.

Then there was Jocelyn. She couldn't be more sweet, more beautiful, and more talented. She was an art teacher at a junior high school and loved her students. It didn't make sense that she didn't date, but that was partly due to the fact that she didn't want to. She openly admitted she hadn't met any guys she was interested in, and moreover, she didn't trust men at all, which was due to the fact that she'd never known her father. Her mother had dozens of boyfriends, but none of them had stayed around to fill the role of father in her life.

It was sad, because Jocelyn would be such a wonderful wife and mother. Lauryn just didn't understand it.

Then there was Emma, the complete opposite. Emma fell too easily and too quickly for men. All of her friends had worried when she'd married Doug, but Emma had assured them he was her soul mate, her sweetheart forever. A month after their marriage she'd found out he was still seeing his old girlfriend. Emma stuck it out for as long as she could, but he informed her that their marriage was a mistake and that she was free to leave. She'd stayed, hoping to work it out, so he left.

Lauryn prayed that Emma would slow down and get her head together before she got involved with another guy. She also wished

Emma would start going to church and making some changes in her lifestyle. Of course, it didn't guarantee that she would find true love and her marriage would be perfect, but Lauryn believed it greatly increased the odds.

"So, tell me everything," Andrea said, breaking into Lauryn's thoughts. "You said something about some big news. What is it? Did Michael come back?"

"Hardly!" Lauryn said with a laugh. "I wouldn't take him back now even if he crawled on his knees. It's just something to do with work."

"Did you get a promotion? Are you doing some designs for the first lady?"

Lauryn chuckled. "Stop guessing already. I'm going to wait until we're all together, then I'll tell you."

"All right," Andrea said with disappointment. "You know how impatient I am."

Lauryn knew too well.

"What about you, Andie? How are you? How's your home gym doing on QVC?"

"Sales are through the roof. My Absolute Abs and Glorious Glutes machines are top sellers. I'm shooting an infomercial next week that'll go on the air this fall. We're just trying to line up a few celebrity endorsements."

"That's exciting."

"It's crazy. But you know," Andrea's tone turned serious, "I have to be honest. All this success is great and everything, but I wish I had someone to share it with, you know?"

"Yeah, I know. It's like going to Disneyland alone. How fun is that?"

"Exactly! I'm so glad I have you girls to talk to. That helps a ton. But it's not quite enough."

"I understand," Lauryn said. "You want someone to go home to at night, to share your ups and downs with. Someone to call during the day, just to see how they're doing. Someone to eat dinner with and snuggle on the couch and watch TV with."

Andrea sighed. "Yeah, that's what I want."

"Me too." Lauryn's tone matched her friend's.

"I didn't think turning thirty would bother me so much," Andrea confessed. "I mean, look at me. I'm in the best shape of my life. I've never felt better or looked better. I'm successful, and I have great friends. But when I turned thirty, it hit me really hard. I'm alone, and that doesn't look like it's going to change anytime soon. Besides that, where in the world would I find a man? I'm never home long enough to go to my own ward, so I won't meet him at church. The guys I meet at the gym and in my profession are so self-absorbed they can't even hear the word commitment, let alone consider marriage. Besides, none of them are members. Where in the world are all the eligible LDS guys? Where?"

"Not in Manhattan," Lauryn assured her. "Michael's LDS, but the only reason he goes to church is to meet girls."

"Pathetic."

"I know."

Andrea pulled into the parking lot of the hotel and parked in a stall. She turned to Lauryn. "I so needed this weekend. You guys always help me feel like everything is going to be okay."

"Same for me," Lauryn told her. "And it *is* going to be okay. We're doing everything we can, right? The Lord will bless us. We have to have faith."

"You're right," Andrea said. "We can't give up." She gave Lauryn a smile. "Come on, let's go have some fun. I'm starving. Have you eaten yet?"

"Are you kidding? All I've had were three bags of pretzels and a bagel I happened to shove in my bag at the last minute. I'm starving."

* * *

"We stayed up way too late last night," Chloe said, rubbing her mascara-smeared eyes. She'd shared one of the queen beds in their room with Lauryn and gave her a push with her foot.

"Hey!" Lauryn protested. "I'm asleep here."

"I forgot what a bed hog you were," Chloe told her. "I call dibs on the rollaway tonight."

"No way am I giving up the rollaway," Emma told her. "This bed is uncomfortable, but at least it's all mine. What time did we finally go to bed?"

"It was after three. And the only reason I'm ever up at three in the morning is to nurse a baby or clean up vomit." Chloe covered a yawn then stretched her arms overhead.

"Ew! Thanks for starting our day off with that mental picture," Emma said.

"When you're a mother, you'll get used to it," Chloe said.

"We'll let you take a nap later," Lauryn said, covering a yawn. "Besides, I'm on eastern standard time, so I'm even more tired than you."

"You two stop whining. It was worth it, especially watching Andrea eat something other than that disgusting tofu crud and all that whole wheat gunk." Emma never was one to hold back her feelings. "Where is she anyway?"

"I think she went for an early-morning jog," Lauryn said. "She said she'd be back in time for breakfast."

"I'm starving," Emma said. "Hey, I know, let's go have breakfast and get chocolate chip pancakes and chocolate-dipped strawberries. In fact, let's have chocolate every meal we eat!" Emma suggested.

"Stop saying that word!" Jocelyn's muffled voice came from under the pillow. "I think I have a chocolate hangover. My head is killing me. I'm not as health-conscious as Andrea, but I totally OD'd on chocolate last night. You guys are a bad influence on me."

"Sorry, but that dessert last night was worth every fat gram and calorie, as far as I'm concerned," Chloe said.

"Yeah, but did we have to come back to the hotel and eat an XXL bag of peanut M&Ms?" Jocelyn asked.

"Yes!" the others chorused in.

Just then Andrea burst through the door. "Good morning, girls! Time to get up. You're wasting the best part of the day."

Emma threw her pillow and hit Andrea in the face.

"Hey!"

"Will you just put a lid on that perkiness?" Emma said. "We're all hung over from chocolate."

"You wouldn't feel that way if you went jogging. The fresh air would invigorate you and help burn some of the fat grams from all those sweets."

"Honestly, Andrea, you could use a few fat grams. I swear, you have the body of a thirteen-year-old, except you're more flat-chested," Emma told her.

"Emma!" Andrea exclaimed indignantly. "I can't help it. I have a genetic defect. I've never been busty, even when I was fifty-five pounds heavier in high school. I always wanted Lauryn's body," Andrea said.

Lauryn burst out laughing. "Are you kidding me? Why would you want my body?"

"You look great in jeans, and you have a nice chest," Andrea told her.

"It's true," Chloe said. "We've never told you this, but we were the ones who nominated you for Best Bod our senior year."

"What? You traitors! That was humiliating!" Lauryn exclaimed. "I hated getting that award. Like the boys needed any more reasons to say crude things to me!"

"Kids were cruel in high school," Andrea agreed. "You should've heard the fat comments I used to get. Maybe I'll go to our fifteen-year reunion just to make a few people eat their words. Maybe by then I'll be married, too. And as for your comment, Emma, I'll have you know I'm scheduled for a little surgery at the end of the summer after I finish my promotional tour."

"Andrea, really?" Lauryn asked. Maybe Andrea was a little flat-chested, but because she was so ultra-thin, she looked fine as far as Lauryn was concerned.

"Oh, don't worry. I'm not going to do something drastic, but let's be honest, I'm in the business of looking good, and that's one area of my body I can't fix with any amount of diet and exercise," Andrea defended. "I think it will help me feel better about myself, too. With all the time I've spent in therapy, I'm finally working through some of my issues."

"Wow, Andie," Emma said, "I didn't know you had to go to therapy."

"Yeah, well, it wasn't easy being the fat girl in the group all through high school."

Lauryn opened her mouth to object, but Andrea stopped her.

"I know you girls never said anything about my weight. I never felt like it was a big deal to you, but it was hard to go shopping and never be able to buy anything but earrings and shoes because none of the clothes ever fit me. And I hated going out to dinner and watching all of you pig out and still stay so skinny."

"Oh, Andrea, sweetie," Chloe scooted next to Andrea and put her arm around her, "we love you because of who you are inside, not what you look like on the outside."

"Besides that," Lauryn told her, "I was always jealous of your hair."

"You had really great hair in high school," Emma agreed. "And I was always jealous because you were just so nice to people. You still are."

"See, honey," Chloe said. "We all think you are beautiful."

"Thanks, you guys." Andrea wiped the corner of one eye. "It's hard for me to believe, because I don't have a man in my life, you know?"

"Men are useless," Emma said. "Sorry, Chloe, no offense."

"That's okay," Chloe said.

"You don't need a man to complete you," Jocelyn told Andrea. "I actually don't mind being single. I'm very content with my life."

Lauryn exchanged glances with Andrea. Both of them knew that Jocelyn and Emma were just rationalizing. There were bigger issues here that they just weren't talking about.

"What about you, Lauryn?" Emma asked. "Now that Michael is out of the picture, don't you feel more free, able to do whatever you want?"

Lauryn knew that Emma was hoping she would validate her feelings by saying that she thought men were useless. The problem was, she didn't think that.

"Can I be honest?" Lauryn asked.

"Of course," Emma said, the springs creaking as she sat up in her rollaway bed. All the girls were propped up on pillows and listening.

"You guys remember how weird it was for me growing up. My mom was a nut case and my dad was never around. But my dad and I have really gotten close these last few years, and I see how happily married he is and what a good father he is to Cassie's kids and to me, too. Then I look at my mom, all alone, in and out of bad relationships, and I have to say, it's not hard to decide which life is more appealing. I don't like being alone. I would give up everything I'm doing right now to get married and have a family."

Emma's brow furrowed. She was obviously unhappy with Lauryn's declaration.

"Good for you!" Chloe erupted.

"How can you comment?" Emma asked. "Would you say you have an ideal marriage?"

Chloe lifted her chin and said, "No, I don't have an ideal marriage, but my Roger is a good man; he's a loving father and husband. We've gone through some rough times together, but all that is changing."

"What's going on, Chloe?" Andrea asked.

"Roger is going back to finish college and earn his accounting degree. He thought he could make it on his own, but he realized that he's really good at accounting. He starts in the fall. I'm so proud of him!" Chloe beamed with pride, and it was hard not to be thrilled for her.

"That's awesome news, Chloe," Lauryn said. "He's lucky to have such a supportive wife." Jocelyn and Andrea echoed Lauryn's comment.

Emma was hesitant at first, then she said, "That really is great. I'm happy for you."

"Thanks, Emma. I know you guys are just looking out for me, but I'm committed to my husband and family. Our temple covenants are very important to us, and we are working hard to make our marriage a success." She looked at each of them and spoke with an unfamiliar tone of seriousness. "I know there's something really wonderful inside of Roger. I can see it waiting to get out. And that's finally going to happen now. In the meantime, I've been able to establish my business and build my clientele, so it's worked out really well." She returned to her perky, bubbly self. "Things are going great for me. But how about you, Lauryn. Didn't you have some news you wanted to share?"

"Actually, yes. I did." Lauryn paused for dramatic effect, "I just changed jobs and am now designing for Laszlo Molnar!"

Emma and Andrea shrieked with delight.

Chloe and Jocelyn looked at each other, then realized it was obviously a good thing and got excited for her.

Emma noticed their confusion and helped them out. "Laszlo Molnar is like *the* hottest designer in New York. Whenever you watch the Academy Awards, half the dresses the celebrities are wearing are Laszlo Molnar's designs. Oprah loves him. The guy is huge!"

"Wow," Chloe enthused. "I had no idea."

"That's so incredible, Lauryn," Jocelyn said. "Congratulations!"

"Thanks, you guys. I will show my first line this fall in New York during Fashion Week in September," she told them. "I hope you can all come. I need your support more than you know."

"Are you serious?!" Emma exclaimed.

"Of course. I can get tickets for all of you," she answered.

"That might be hard with school," Jocelyn said.

"Yeah, Roger will be in school then," Chloe said.

"Are you kidding me?" Emma erupted. "Do you know how big this is? If you start now, you can figure out a way to be there. This is the chance of a lifetime. And we need to be there for Lauryn."

"You're right," Chloe said. "Roger's mother can come and stay with the kids while I go."

"And I can get a substitute for my class," Jocelyn said. "I've always wanted to come to New York. I'll be there."

"Me too," Andrea said.

Lauryn smiled at her friends. They were a crazy bunch, but she loved them. Somewhere between her breakup with Michael and the icy reception she'd received at Molnar's, she'd forgotten how good it felt to have unconditional support from the people she loved.

"Thanks, you guys. It helps knowing you will be there," she told them.

"I thought you and that Jacqueline Yvonne were close friends," Jocelyn said. "Was it hard to leave?"

"Totally. She's been so good to me. But she was very supportive and said it was a great opportunity."

"It will be fun to come back and see where you live and go to some shows," Jocelyn said.

"As soon as I know the date, I'll let you know so you can start planning," Lauryn told them.

"We are totally going to our next class reunion," Andrea said. "Maybe Lauryn can design dresses for all of us to wear."

"I'd love to," Lauryn agreed. She glanced around at all the excited expressions on their faces, except for one. "Emma, are you okay?"

Emma swallowed and nodded. "It's just that you are all so successful. Look at me—I have a failed marriage, I work in retail, and I live in an apartment."

"You manage a whole department," Chloe said. "That's something to be proud of."

"And I'll help you look for a home you can afford," Jocelyn offered. "I love home shopping. I'll even help you if it needs fixing up. It's amazing how inexpensively you can decorate if you try."

Emma gave a weak smile. "I don't mean to be a wet blanket. I just thought by the time I reached thirty I'd be doing something different than I am."

"Life doesn't always turn out the way we plan," Jocelyn told her. "But you have nothing to be ashamed of. You've done well."

Emma smiled. "Thanks, girls. I can always count on you to give me a boost. In fact, I was just telling Sandra Stephens the other day about how we get together every year."

"How is Sandra?"

"Great. She's married and has three kids."

"That's crazy," Andrea said. "Three kids."

"I always liked Sandra," Lauryn said. "We had math together. She helped me out a lot."

"She's planning the next reunion and asked if I would be on the committee since I still live in town," Emma explained.

"Are you going to do it?" Chloe asked.

"I don't want to, but I couldn't turn her down. She was desperate. She needs help tracking down classmates. It got me thinking about some of the kids we went to school with. Whatever happened to your old boyfriend, Lauryn?"

"My old boyfriend? I never had a boyfriend." Then she realized who Emma meant. "You're talking about Jace?"

"Yeah, Jace. Whatever happened to him?" Emma asked.

"I hear from him occasionally, but it's been a while."

"I thought he got married to that girl he met at BYU," Chloe said.

"Thta's what I had heard too. I wonder how things worked out for them. I know he used to travel out of the country a lot, because every once in a while he'd send me a postcard just to brag that he was in Switzerland or Thailand or Italy." Lauryn smiled. "He always sends me an e-mail on my birthday, but I haven't actually *talked* to him in like five years. I'm sure he's married by now."

"I don't think he's married," Emma said. "Sandra said something about him. That's why I got to thinking about him."

The news came as a surprise to Lauryn. "He's not married?"

"According to Sandra he's not," Emma answered.

"Whoa . . . wait a minute!" Andrea exclaimed. "Didn't you and Jace make a promise to each other?"

"What promise?" Lauryn asked.

"You did!" Andrea exclaimed. "I remember. You guys promised each other that if you weren't married by thirty, you would get married to each other. Don't you guys remember?" Andrea asked the others.

"I remember," Jocelyn said. "You told us the night after Ava's funeral, at our first Butterfly Girls meeting."

"That's right!" Chloe said, her eyes growing wide. "Lauryn, you're thirty, you're not married . . . aren't you supposed to meet him?"

Long ago Lauryn had stopped thinking about the promise she'd made to Jace. It was a silly joke. He hadn't meant it . . . had he?

"Lauryn?" Jocelyn asked with interest. "When *did* you two decide to meet each other?"

"At noon, on . . ." she hesitantly told them, not wanting to finish for the ridiculousness that would follow.

"On . . ." Emma coaxed.

"June first," she said.

Just as she expected, her friends reacted like a bunch of teenagers.

"That's this Monday!" Emma declared. "Oh, my gosh! This is so cool! What are the chances that you'd be here!"

"I don't believe this," Chloe swooned. "It's so romantic."

"Just like a movie," Andrea said.

Jocelyn looked closely at Lauryn's expression. "Are you okay?"

"I'm fine." Lauryn tried to speak with conviction, but inside she was suddenly nervous. "I'm not meeting him, if that's what you think. It's been forever since we've talked, but he would've said something, wouldn't he?"

"Who cares!" Emma threw her hands in the air. "You have to go. What if he's there?"

"He is not going to be there!" Lauryn told her.

"But what if?" Chloe said, dreamy-eyed. "This is the stuff romance novels are made of."

"Give me a break, you guys. Even if he's single, why would he want me?"

"You promised you'd be there," Andrea reminded her. "You have to go; it's a matter of integrity."

Lauryn rolled her eyes.

"I agree," Emma said. "Even if he's not there, you have to hold up your side of the promise. Do it for us. For the sanctity of marriage. Do it to help me see there is still hope for love in the world."

"How did you not go out for drama in high school?" Lauryn asked her.

Chloe clapped her hands excitedly. "Jace was always such a cutie-pie with his dimples and that gorgeous smile. I agree; you have to go."

"No, I don't. I'll look like a fool." Lauryn wasn't about to let them talk her into it.

"If we have to carry you there ourselves, you are going!" Emma threatened.

Lauryn looked at Jocelyn for help, but Jocelyn shrugged her shoulders. "Sorry. I want you to go too."

"You guys aren't serious! I tell you, he's not going to be there." She clapped her hand onto her head. "Why did I ever even tell you about this?"

"Because it's fate," Emma replied. "We have to help you live up to your end of the bargain."

Lauryn looked at each of her friends, who were ready to haul her off to the temple on their backs. They were serious. But she'd find a way out of it. There was no way Jace would be there waiting for her.

Was there?

Chapter Twelve

"I'm not going to meet him!" Lauryn protested for the thousandth time. It was late Saturday night, and they were sitting in the living room of their hotel suite after a long day of shopping, eating, and laughing. Lauryn had hoped the subject had been dropped since they hadn't discussed it all that day. But the topic came up when Chloe announced that she'd arranged to stay an extra day so she could see what happened.

"It's four to one," Emma told her. "You're outnumbered."

"Um, hello? This is my life. The decisions I make are not up for vote," Lauryn informed her.

"Well, we feel like you need a little help with this decision," Andrea said. "That's why we've decided to give you this."

From her suitcase, Andrea presented the rosewood Butterfly Girls box. "You've got a lot going on right now, and we decided you need it the most."

"When did you decide that?" Lauryn asked, annoyed that they were talking about her behind her back.

"While you were taking your shower this morning," Chloe answered, her gaze slipping to her cohorts.

"All four of you honestly think I should do this?"

They all nodded.

"We love you and hate to see you pass up someone as wonderful as Jace," Jocelyn said.

"But how do you know he's still wonderful?" Lauryn questioned.

"We don't know for sure, honey," Chloe said. "But there's only one way to find out."

"All right; I can see none of you are going to give this a rest. I'll go, but I can predict exactly what's going to happen. He's not going to be there. And I'm going to look pathetic standing there by the steps of the temple waiting for him."

"We're the only ones who will know why you're there," Andrea assured her.

"And that's another thing," Lauryn added. "None of you are going to watch."

"What!" Emma exclaimed. "You have to let us watch."

"No, I don't. I'll meet him on one condition. That none of you are there watching. I'll feel stupid enough as it is."

"It's such a coincidence that you are here at exactly the right time, don't you think?" Chloe remarked.

"That's because it's meant to be," Jocelyn said.

"I agree," Andrea added.

"It really is kind of amazing," Emma admitted. "What have you got to lose?"

"Other than my pride, nothing, I guess." Lauryn didn't want to agree with them, but it was uncanny that she was in town at exactly the right time. Or wrong time, depending on how it turned out.

"Anyway," Andrea said, pushing the box toward her. "This box will hopefully bring you good luck, because we'll be praying for you."

Lauryn looked at the box, its gold plating still as flawless as the day she'd first laid eyes on it. She'd had the box once before and kept it where she could see it every day to remind her of her friends' faith and prayers in her behalf. It was reassuring knowing they were behind her then, and she felt that same reassurance now.

"Okay, I accept the box and all that goes with it," Lauryn said. "I need all the help I can get for the next little while."

Lauryn bent down and gently lifted the box onto her lap. "Well, I guess this means it's time for the ceremony." Every year when the box was opened, it was as if all the memories they shared from the past, both happy and sad, spilled out of the box, bringing with them emotions just as potent as the day they were first felt.

Lauryn inserted the small key and heard the lock open with a tiny click. She slowly opened the lid and removed the movie, *Sabrina,* from the box. Several years ago, she'd finally changed it from video to DVD. "Are we still up for watching this tonight?"

"Of course!" Chloe said, clapping her hands. "It wouldn't be the same without *Sabrina.*"

The rest of them agreed it was a tradition they didn't want to break.

Next she pulled her crown from the box. "I really need to replace this with something else," she said, putting the crown on her head.

"Are you kidding?" Andrea exclaimed, snatching the crown from Lauryn's head. "This is the icon of our group."

"Just think how much that pageant changed your life," Jocelyn observed. "Who knows where you would've ended up if you hadn't won that pageant and met Jacqueline Yvonne? Without that crown, you might not be designing dresses today."

Lauryn couldn't deny it.

"Every girl is a princess," Andrea said, the crown on her head.

"Hey." Jocelyn thought for a moment before continuing. "Do you get to have a name for your clothing line, or do you just use Laszlo Molnar's name?" she asked Lauryn.

"I don't really know. Why?"

"You really should call it the Butterfly Girls Collection," Jocelyn suggested.

"And you could put a little crown on the label," Andrea added.

"That is so cute!" Chloe joined in.

Even Emma had to admit it was a good idea.

"I like it. If I get to name my collection, I'll use it." She wasn't sure how Mr. Molnar planned on marketing her designs, but she hoped she could use the Butterfly Girls name on her label.

Lauryn passed the box to Emma, who pulled out the bungee-jumping T-shirt. "This T-shirt represents each of us taking a chance, getting outside our comfort zones, and making our dreams come true."

"That totally describes our little Lauryn," Chloe said like a proud parent.

Lauryn smiled. If they only knew how far out of her comfort zone she'd gone.

"And of course," Emma said, removing the photograph from the box, "the picture." Emma's eyes began to glisten as she looked at the group in the photograph, twelve years earlier, at their graduation. "The pain never really goes away, does it?" She passed the picture around.

"No, but thank goodness hair styles do," Jocelyn exclaimed. "Why would you guys ever let me wear my hair like that? It was hideous."

Andrea took the next look. "At least yours doesn't look like you had shock treatment. Could my hair be any bigger?"

With a laugh, Chloe glanced at the picture and passed it along. "I'm just glad mine grew back in time for graduation. I hope my clients never see pictures of me when my hair fell out from over-processing. They'd never trust me with their hair again."

Lauryn took the next look and felt a wave of nostalgia wash over her. They had changed in many ways, and yet they all seemed the same. A person's spirit didn't seem to age at the same rate their body did. She didn't feel thirty inside.

Emma passed the box to Andrea, who held up the bottle of hand sanitizer. "This, of course, represents a hope for protection, which we've received in a physical sense, thank goodness. I wish there was some way to protect us emotionally, but I haven't found anything yet. Luckily we have the strength we give each other to help us through our challenges and heartaches. And, I have to say, I've gotten much better at not being so paranoid about germs."

Emma scoffed.

"I have. It takes time, but I'm doing better." She reached into a grocery bag next to her and lifted up a bag of Tootsie Rolls. "Next, there is the ceremonial changing of the Tootsie Rolls, which means we get to eat these," she said, taking the old bag and ripping it open with her teeth. "I have to admit I really look forward to this."

She passed around the candy bag. Lauryn noticed that Andrea didn't take any.

"Well, Chloe, it looks like it's your turn," Emma said.

"Oh, me already?" she said. "Um, okay." She popped a Tootsie Roll in her mouth, took the box from Andrea, and reached in. First, she pulled out the plastic baggie containing the lock of Ava's hair. "I know this sounds crazy, but sometimes I have conversations with Ava in my head. Oh, don't worry," she said with a laugh, "she never answers back." Her usually perky voice became serious. "But I feel close to her when I talk with her. She always was a good listener, and sometimes, when I'm feeling down, she's the easiest one to talk to." Chloe stared down at the lock of hair in her hand.

Lauryn and Emma exchanged looks with each other, then with Andrea and Jocelyn. When was Chloe ever feeling down? Was she just missing Ava or was there something else?

"Sorry," Chloe finally said, shaking her head to clear her emotions. She then reached for the rhinestone clippie, holding it in her outstretched hand for several moments. "Oh my," she said, staring at the clippie, then blinking her eyes several times.

She didn't speak, but continued looking down.

"Chloe?" Emma said. "What's going on?"

Chloe wiped at her cheek. Something was definitely wrong. It wasn't that they weren't used to seeing Chloe cry. She cried in movies. She cried when little kids sang in church. Even commercials made her cry. But when it came to real-life stuff, especially her marriage, she was a rock.

Lauryn became concerned when she didn't speak.

Andrea scooted over and put an arm around Chloe's shoulders.

Suddenly, Chloe burst into tears and buried her head in Andrea's neck.

Andrea looked at the others in alarm.

Emma shrugged her shoulders. Jocelyn and Lauryn looked at each other for answers, but no one knew what was going on.

"Hey," Andrea said in a soothing voice, smoothing Chloe's hair. "It's okay. You can tell us."

"I know," Chloe said between sobs. "I haven't wanted to say anything, because I've been hoping things would improve. But . . ."

They hung on her words, waiting for her to continue.

"Roger and I are getting . . . separated." The last word came out in a heavy sob.

"Oh dear." Andrea hugged Chloe while she cried.

"Chloe, we are so sorry," Jocelyn told her as she put an arm around her from the other side.

Tears filled Emma's and Lauryn's eyes. It was painful to watch Chloe's heart break right in front of them. It was especially distressing to realize how difficult it must have been for her to go on pretending everything was fine when she hurt so much inside.

For several minutes they continued to cry with Chloe, saying nothing, just sharing her sorrow and pain. All of them wished there was something they could do for her.

Finally, when her well of tears had run dry, Chloe placed the hair clippie back in the box and began her story. "I haven't wanted to say anything, because I feel like I need to set an example as the only married one in the group. I have tried so hard to save my marriage, but Roger is struggling, and I can't seem to do anything to help him if he's not willing to help himself."

"Can you tell us what it is?" Andrea asked.

Chloe shut her eyes, as if praying for strength, then she said one word. "Pornography."

Lauryn quickly put her hand over her mouth, which hung wide open in shock. Emma shook her head with disgust. Jocelyn stroked Chloe's hair and tried to soothe her. Andrea got a sick look on her face.

Chloe then opened her eyes and laughed sardonically. "You want to know how it happened?" She laughed again. "It was that video place he worked for." She took a deep breath. "Editing out all the bad stuff eventually got to him. It just goes to show that even the strongest person can break down after constant exposure to something bad. I don't care what anyone says; pornography is evil. It's one of the adversary's greatest tools."

"I'm so sorry, Chloe," Jocelyn said.

"If only he hadn't taken that job," she said, now anxious to talk. She seemed to feel a sense of freedom at finally being able to bring it out in the open. "I watched him change from an adorable, loving husband and father—my hero, the love of my life—to this negative, dark, moody, secretive person. Oh, to everyone else he hid it well. No one knew. A lot of people close to us still don't know. But that evil influence was like a sickness taking over. He's going to lose me and the girls, and he doesn't even care. It's still not enough. I can't stay with him any longer. He doesn't even want to change. He won't even try. He wants us to—" A sob caught in her throat. "He wants us to leave," she choked out.

"Have you talked to your bishop?" Lauryn asked.

"Yes. He told me this problem is more common than we could ever imagine." Chloe found her inner strength again and sat up tall, her head held high. "I don't want to leave Roger. I love the Roger I married, but this man isn't Roger. I know he's in there somewhere. But I have to think of the girls. The environment isn't good for them. And I'm worried about what he's capable of right now."

"I can't believe this has happened," Andrea said. "I knew Roger wasn't perfect, but criminy, you two had the perfect marriage."

"Marriage is hard enough without something destructive like this to deal with," Emma said. "In my case, Doug didn't need pornography; he had a girlfriend. You'll be better off without Roger," she advised Chloe. "I doubt I'll ever get married again. It's just too risky."

"I don't think so," Chloe told Emma. "I love being married. I love having a husband who's my best friend, my sweetheart. When things were good, before all of this happened, it was heaven. It really was. I still want that. I still want Roger. I still want to believe he can change and this can get better. I need your prayers, girls, more than ever before."

"You need to take the Butterfly Box with you," Lauryn said. "You need it way more than I do."

"No," Chloe said. "Right now all I need is faith and prayers to fix my problem. I know the Lord is aware of what's going on and that He cares. That's one thing I know without a doubt. And as hard as this is, I'm not alone. Please pray for my Roger, that he'll start fighting back."

"We will," Lauryn told her. "You know we will."

Chloe gave them her classic, optimistic smile. "Thanks girls. I sure love you."

Hugs went around the circle.

"Hey, Jocelyn," Chloe said. "You've been awfully quiet. Are you okay? I'm sure Emma and I have scared the rest of you out of getting married, but really, it can be so wonderful and fulfilling. You have to believe that."

Emma pulled a face.

Chloe gave Jocelyn a hug. "Someday you'll find a man who you can laugh with. He'll take care of you and be your best friend. And you'll be very happy. I know it."

"I hope so," Jocelyn said with a weak smile. "I hope we all find companions we can be happy with."

"I'm not giving up on my marriage. I'm making a very hard choice to leave. For now, it's what I believe is best. I know that Satan is doing everything in his power to destroy marriage. But we can't let him win."

Emma rolled her eyes while the other three nodded their heads.

"It's your turn, Jocelyn," Andrea said gently.

Jocelyn reached for the box and pulled out the strand of colored beads on boondoggle string. "Of all my memories growing up, girls camp is at the top of the list," she said.

"That year we made the necklaces was so much fun," Andrea exclaimed. "I loved Sister Berrett. She was the best camp director we ever had. I can't believe she actually dressed up as Wonder Woman for that skit."

"She really should have been given some kind of award for that." Emma laughed.

That was also the year Ava and I tipped over in the canoe in the middle of the lake," Lauryn said.

"That's right!" Chloe exclaimed. "We thought you guys were goners for sure. I still don't know how you made it back to shore."

"I really don't know either. Ava and I always felt like angels helped us, because neither of us were great swimmers, and the water was as cold as melted snow. Actually, it *was* melted snow. My arms and legs were completely numb by the time help reached us."

"How about when the eighth ward toilet-papered our camp?" Andrea remembered. "They used like fifty rolls of toilet paper."

"Remember we started cleaning it up, and the eighth-ward girls showed up and had to do it." Lauryn began to laugh. "It was their own fault, but they were mad at us for such a long time."

"Yeah, like the time we asked them to toilet-paper us!" Chloe remarked.

"I hated the hikes back then," Andrea said. "They nearly killed me. But the s'mores, mmm, they were the best at camp."

"S'mores and tinfoil dinners," Lauryn reminded them.

"Remember that year it rained, and we tried to put a picnic table over the fire so it would keep going long enough to cook our dinners?" Jocelyn said. "That was insane! We could have burned down the entire camp."

"I forgot you guys did that," Emma said. "But I was jealous, because all the girls in my ward had to eat soggy cereal for dinner."

"We had so much fun together when we were kids." Lauryn was grateful for the memories.

"And now we're all grown up," Emma replied.

"And we're still having fun," Chloe added.

"I guess we're done then?" Andrea grabbed the movie. "Do you guys want popcorn?"

"Wait!" Emma stopped her. "I don't think Jocelyn was done."

"I'm done," Jocelyn said, closing the lid on the box.

Every year the other four wondered if she would say something about the other item she put in the box. And every year the small box remained sealed and untouched in the bottom of the Butterfly Box. They knew better than to pressure Jocelyn. One year they'd tried to goad it out of her and only succeeded in reducing her to tears. It wasn't worth it. She'd tell them when she was ready.

"Okay, then. I guess we are done," Emma said. She slid the box toward Lauryn. "This is yours for safekeeping until next year."

"Thanks, girls," Lauryn said. "I'll take good care of it."

"All right, then," Andrea said, unable to sit still much longer than a first grader. "Can we watch the movie now?"

They popped popcorn in the microwave and grabbed Andrea's bag of Tootsie Rolls, then they all crowded onto the beds to watch their favorite movie.

Lauryn settled back on the pillows between Andrea and Jocelyn and tried to enjoy the beginning of the movie, but now that the talking had stopped she couldn't get thoughts of meeting Jace out of her mind. What would happen if he actually showed up? When they'd had the conversation twelve years ago, they'd never really discussed that part of the scenario. Lauryn knew it was ridiculous to think he would want to just waltz on in to the temple and seal the deal. And if he did, she would turn around and run! But yet, as she thought about it, she was surprised to realize that she really hoped Jace would be there. A wave of excitement rippled through her. Even if nothing did happen between them, she would love to see his smile again.

Chapter Thirteen

"Are you nervous?" Chloe asked Lauryn over the phone.

Lauryn lied and told them she wasn't, because her friends didn't need any more emotion to feed on. They were already in emotional overdrive.

"Call if you need anything. You sure you don't want me to come and do your hair?"

"No!" Lauryn said a little too quickly. "I mean, thanks, but I've got it." Lauryn fingered one of the soft, blond curls that hung below her chin. "I'm actually having a pretty good hair day, so I'll be okay."

"You'll call one of us as soon as you're done at the temple?"

"I promise," she told her.

"Okay then. We'll say a little prayer for you, sweetie." Chloe had always had a motherly quality about her.

Lauryn had barely turned off her phone when a knock came at her door. She was staying at her dad's house and appreciated the fact that they had a spare room just for her that actually had her old bedroom furniture and some of her other things in it. In fact, she still had boxes of her stuff in their storage, which she needed to go through someday. She'd always planned to take the rest of her belongings when she got married and moved into a house.

"Come in," she said.

The door cracked open and Logan, her sixteen-year-old stepsister, poked her head inside. "Are you busy?"

"Hi, Logan. No, I'm not busy. Come in and talk to me while I finish putting on my makeup." Even though there was a huge gap between their ages, Lauryn tried hard to be a friend to Logan and her brother, Sutton, instead of a third parent. She'd always hated being an only child and had wanted brothers and sisters.

Logan sat on the edge of the bed and watched in silence while Lauryn curled her eyelashes, then applied mascara.

"So," Lauryn finally spoke. "How are you? What's new, other than the fact that you have your driver's license?"

"Yeah, a lot of good that does me," Logan scoffed. "Mom and Dad won't let me drive anywhere without one of them in the car. It's embarrassing."

Lauryn paused and looked at her reflection in the mirror. "Gee, do you think it has anything to do with the fact that you got in an accident on the first day you got your license?"

Logan rolled her eyes. "It wasn't my fault. The light turned green and I started to go. I couldn't help it if the lady in front of me was slow."

"You just have to work harder to gain back their trust, that's all." Lauryn twisted the lid back onto her mascara and picked up her lip liner.

"Dad said you were perfect when you were my age," Logan said.

"He's getting old. He's forgotten. I wasn't as perfect as he remembers, believe me."

"I try to be good, but I sometimes don't think before I do something, you know?"

"Yeah. I think it comes with the age. When a cute boy walks into the room, our brain seems to walk out." She finished lining her lips and filled them in with light-colored gloss.

"That's exactly what happens. I lose track of time, then I get into trouble for coming home late. And now that school's out, they still want me to have a curfew of ten-thirty on weekdays. It's so stupid!"

"You know they are doing it because they love you, right?" Lauryn turned and looked at Logan to see if she was getting through.

"I know," Logan said. "I just feel so confined sometimes. I can't wait until I graduate and can move out on my own."

"I remember feeling that way," Lauryn said. "But I soon realized that being at home is a lot easier. You don't have to worry about anything. Don't be in too big of a hurry to get out on your own."

"They just don't understand. I'm not a kid anymore." Logan reached over, picked up a compact of eye shadow, and examined it.

"I hear you have a boyfriend. Tell me about him."

Logan got a big grin on her face. "Well, his name is Brody. He's out of high school and just got a job as a mechanic at Syd's Garage." She spoke with pride, as if he'd just been accepted to Yale or Harvard.

"Is he going to college in the fall?"

"Probably not. He wants to own his own garage someday, so he feels like he'll get more out of working than going to school."

Lauryn knew this wasn't the time to launch into the whole "does he realize how hard it is to make it in this world without a college degree" speech, so she just said, "But you plan on going to college, don't you?"

"I'm not sure. I'm thinking about going to beauty school. Some of my friends have sisters who went to college and don't even have jobs that require a college degree. But one of my friend's older sister works at a salon and does nails, and she makes a ton of money."

It wasn't that Lauryn didn't want Logan to pursue her own interests, but she wondered if Logan really understood how vast her choices could be if she pursued her education. And, the more Lauryn thought about it, she had to wonder why Logan was allowed to have a boyfriend at such a young age.

"How serious are you with Brody?" Lauryn asked, also reining in her speech about steady dating.

"Well, of course I still have two years of stupid high school to finish, but we're already talking about getting married." Logan's face lit up like she'd just shared the most wonderful secret with Lauryn.

Lauryn realized that Logan felt very safe sharing her personal information. The girl didn't realize that Lauryn was having to restrain herself from grabbing Logan by the shoulders and shaking some sense into her head.

"We're pretty serious," Logan said. "All my friends are jealous of me because Brody is so hot. He was the football captain his senior year and was voted Hottest Guy at school.

"Didn't he want to play college ball?"

"He had a couple of schools look at him, but he doesn't really like studying, so he wanted to take a break from school. Then this job at the garage happened." Logan shrugged and tilted her head. "Yeah, he's feeling pretty good about everything. He'll have enough money saved by the time I'm through with high school so we can buy a house."

"I remember when you were younger and you wanted to be a dancer," Lauryn reminded her.

"Yeah, well, I still love to dance, but I don't dream about dancing professionally anymore. To do that I'd have to leave St. George and Brody."

Which would probably be the best thing for you, Lauryn wanted to say. "Well, you still have a couple of years to figure it all out. Don't give up on your dreams quite yet." Lauryn glanced at her watch. It was a quarter to twelve. She needed to leave if she wanted to get to the temple on time. She almost laughed at herself. She didn't even need to worry about being on time. Jace wasn't going to be there.

"Sorry I can't talk longer," Lauryn told Logan, "but I've got an appointment at twelve. We can talk later, though, okay?"

"Okay. I'd love to hear all about the clothes you're designing," Logan said.

Lauryn took another look at Logan's outfit—a tight shirt that was about three inches too short and showed her stomach, and shorts that barely covered her rear end—and she didn't like it. There was no question that Logan was making choices Lauryn was certain would bring her heartache and could have disastrous consequences.

It wasn't her place, but Lauryn decided to have a talk with her father about Logan to see what his thoughts were about the girl. She didn't want to interfere, but she didn't want to sit by and watch Logan ruin her life, either.

* * *

The ringing of Lauryn's cell phone made her laugh. She pictured Emma, Chloe, Andrea, and Jocelyn all huddled together around the phone, anxious to get the latest update on their real-life romance novel. *More like a romantic comedy,* Lauryn thought.

"Hello," Lauryn said.

Emma's voice came on the line. "So? Are you there yet?"

Lauryn didn't tell them she'd been sitting in her car across the street, watching the temple steps. She'd seen a couple of small groups of people visiting the temple and enjoying the beautiful grounds. But so far, no single men were lingering on the steps.

"Yeah, but I haven't seen any sign of him," she said.

"Oh," Emma said with disappointment. "Have you looked around a bit? Maybe he forgot you were supposed to meet at the steps."

"I haven't yet," Lauryn said, "but I will. And I promise I'll let you guys know."

"You can just text us if you want. Hey, you could send us a picture of him when he shows up," Emma suggested.

"I'll try," Lauryn said, trying to appease them.

"We'll be here at the hotel, waiting. You sure you don't want some backup?"

"I'm sure!" Lauryn assured them.

"Lauryn," Chloe came on the line, "did you say a prayer?"

"I did first thing this morning," Lauryn told her.

"Good girl. This is all in the Lord's hands, so don't despair."

"I won't, Chloe. Thanks. I'll call you guys in a little while."

"Don't wait too long," Chloe replied. "Maybe you should update us every ten minutes."

"I'll call soon," she said, not agreeing to anything.

"Good luck," they all chorused.

Lauryn hung up the phone and groaned. She still couldn't believe she was doing this. Jace was probably at work right now, wherever he lived, sitting at his desk, looking at a picture of his gorgeous wife and perfect child and their dog. He'd definitely have a dog.

Against her better judgment, she got out of her car. Forcing herself to move, she began the walk toward the temple. It was nearly a quarter after twelve, and as far as she could tell, Jace was nowhere to be seen. She'd been right all along; he wasn't going to show up.

Not that she wouldn't be thrilled for Jace if he were happily married, but if he weren't, she really wanted to meet up with him again. Since neither she nor her friends had gone to their class reunions thus far, they were out of the loop with their classmates. They'd sworn an oath that they wouldn't go to the reunions. There weren't that many kids they ever wanted to see again. The ones they did want to see, they'd made a point to stay in touch with.

Except for Jace. Lauryn still cared enough to want to know how he was doing, but they'd lost contact.

Smoothing her aqua-colored sweater and white capris, Lauryn walked through the gate to the temple grounds. Glancing back and forth as she walked, the only men she saw were the ones with their families.

Trying not to look conspicuous and completely ridiculous, Lauryn strolled up the main sidewalk and casually walked to one corner of the temple, then back across to the other corner of the temple. Nothing. Not a single man in sight.

The day was warm and sunny. It was beautiful. She had missed the wide-open spaces of her hometown—the vivid red-rock mountains; the black, lava-colored hills; and the startling blue sky. In Manhattan she had to look straight up to see the sky, and even then it was just a small, gray square.

By twelve thirty, Lauryn had hit the limit of her humiliation. She wasn't going to sit there a minute longer. He wasn't coming.

She pushed the redial button on her phone as she walked back to her car.

"Hi guys," she said.

"So? How did it go?" Emma asked.

"Great. He didn't show up though."

"I don't believe it!" Emma said. In the background Lauryn heard the others expressing their disbelief also. "I guess he is married," Emma added.

"Either that, or he's single and forgot, or he isn't interested. It doesn't really matter, because I'm leaving and . . ."

She stopped. There on the windshield of her car was a red rose.

"Lauryn?" Emma asked. "Are you there?"

"I'll call you right back," she said into the phone, then flipped it shut.

Quickly, she looked around but saw no one. A few cars were parked farther to the south across from the medical center, but nothing close to her.

Where had the rose come from? Was it random? Just a coincidence?

She turned, squinting against the blinding sun, and saw a figure standing on the steps of the temple.

Her breath caught in her throat. Was it Jace?

Even though her breathing had stopped, her heartbeat raced. Was it him?

Get a grip, she told herself. *Walk back casually, just in case it's not.*

Her thoughts raced and collided. If it was Jace standing there on the steps, what would she say? How would she act? What was she to think?

Keep going. She coaxed herself to cross the street, not daring to look toward the steps any longer.

If it wasn't him, she'd just keep walking to the north side of the temple and leave the grounds, then walk back to her car and hightail it out of there.

If it was him, then how rude of him to make her walk all that way with him watching. She felt completely conscious of how she walked, how she moved her arms, and she wondered if her hair looked okay. Suddenly her lips felt like a dried-up creek bed. She needed lipstick.

Finally forcing herself to look up, she saw the figure take one step down, then another, slowly working his way down the steps.

Then, from behind, she heard a man's voice.

"What do you think, Ned? Is it just a surface crack?"

"It looks that way to me," the man on the stairs replied. "We can repair that in no time."

Lauryn followed the sidewalk to the right, her face burning with embarrassment. The maintenance men didn't notice, but she felt foolish for getting so flustered, foolish for being there, and foolish for thinking Jace would actually come.

She exited the temple grounds by way of the east entrance and walked as quickly as she could back to her car. With a yank, she removed the rose from her windshield, now noticing that several other cars in the parking lot also had roses on them with little tags that said: *Grand opening, The Rose Shoppe, located next to Jensen's Jewelers, for all your floral needs.*

"I'm such an idiot," she exclaimed, throwing the rose onto the passenger seat as she got inside her oven-like car.

Turning on the car, she threw it into reverse and backed out of her parking stall.

"Just like high school," she mumbled as she pulled onto the road. "I let those guys talk me into doing the dumbest things."

She stopped at the light and waited her turn, still shaking her head about how ridiculous the last half hour had been.

Before the light turned green, she quickly dialed Emma's cell phone.

"Lauryn! What happened?" Emma practically shouted.

"You guys owe me lunch," she said sardonically.

"Uh-oh."

"Uh-oh is right! You guys seriously thought he would be there. I can't believe I actually fell for that. I just spent the last half hour walking around looking like a pathetic loser."

"I'm sure you didn't look that way," Emma assured her.

"I sure felt that way."

"Why don't you meet us at that Mexican grill, Durango's, by the outlet malls? They have great salads."

"Fine. I'll be there, but it's going to take more than salad to make me feel better."

"I know where a chocolate place is. They sell mint truffles that are out of this world," Emma said.

Lauryn hung up the phone and felt badly for being so abrupt with Emma. It wasn't their fault he hadn't shown up. But it was their fault *she* had. Still, she didn't need to be mean to them.

She knew she wasn't being completely honest about why she

was so upset. She would never admit it to her friends, but she had been looking forward to seeing Jace after all these years. He had been one of her dearest friends in high school; she possibly wouldn't have survived those years without him. There were even a few times when she thought he might have wanted something more, but that must have been her imagination.

* * *

After lunch and a few mint truffles, which actually did take her mind off the whole Jace fiasco, Lauryn made her way back home. Her dad was coming home early from work so the family could spend some time together before Lauryn went home on Wednesday.

She'd hugged each of her friends good-bye and found parting difficult. Sending Chloe back to her situation made it hard on all of them. Chloe kept a smile pasted on as she assured them she would be fine, but she couldn't hide behind her smile anymore. What she was about to face wasn't going to be easy, but Chloe was determined to make her marriage succeed. And if anyone could, Chloe could.

Andrea promised all of them that she'd take care of herself and they had nothing to worry about. She was eating healthy and being careful. They knew when not to push. Andrea would get very defensive if they got too passionate about their concern. But it was hard not to; she barely weighed a hundred pounds.

As always, Jocelyn never drew attention to herself or expected anyone to fuss over her. She was content to stay in the background and play a supporting role rather than be the star. Lauryn worried about her, since she never dated and seemed to be okay with that. It was one thing not to date; it was another thing not to care. Knowing that Jocelyn had a difficult upbringing helped Lauryn understand Jocelyn's disdain for marriage and men. Her mother had been as horrible a role model for Jocelyn as Lauryn's mother had been for her. But Lauryn had her father and stepmom as an example of a successful marriage, and Jocelyn didn't.

Then there was Emma. Even though she'd encouraged Lauryn's meeting with Jace, Emma was also down on men. Lauryn wished there were a way for her to show Emma that if she'd chosen men who had higher values, she wouldn't be experiencing all her present heartache. Emma suffered the consequences of her choices, and it was a hard thing to watch.

There wasn't quite as much sadness as usual when they said goodbye, since they knew that when Lauryn had her first fashion show they would all be there. This thought kept their spirits light and positive.

Lauryn's cell phone rang, and she noticed her father's home number come up.

"Hi, Dad. I'm on my way. Don't start the fun without me."

"I've been trying to reach you." Her father's voice sounded urgent.

"I ate a late lunch with my friends. I had my phone on silent. Sorry."

"A couple of things have come up."

"Oh?"

"We can talk when you get home," he said.

"I'll be right there."

Her mind raced faster than the car's engine as she hurried to get home. What could possibly have happened in the few hours since she left that morning?

She pulled the car into the driveway and ran inside. Tossing her purse onto a table in the entry, Lauryn called for the family.

"In here," her father's voice answered.

Lauryn found her father and Cassie in the kitchen. Cassie's eyes were red rimmed and puffy.

"Oh dear," Lauryn said, sinking into a chair.

"Hi honey, we've had quite an afternoon. Sorry to drag you into it."

"What's going on?"

"It's Logan," her father said. "She's run away from home."

"What? I just talked to her this morning. She seemed like she was doing great."

"She was, but then she said she was going out with that boyfriend of hers tonight. We told her she couldn't because we were going to spend some family time together. Emotions ignited, tempers escalated, and the whole thing just got out of control. She snuck out and took off with the guy."

"She's with Brody?"

Cassie sniffed into a tissue. "This is all my fault. I lost my patience and said some things I shouldn't have. I pushed her right into his arms. She said she's never coming back."

Lauryn looked at her dad, wishing there was some way she could help.

"We've called all her friends and all the places she usually hangs out, but no one has seen her. Brody was supposed to work this afternoon, but he called in sick. Who knows where they are."

"Or what they're up to," Cassie added, wiping her eyes.

"Logan doesn't strike me as the type of girl to do something stupid," Lauryn said. "I think she's probably just upset and being dramatic; a lot of teens are that way, believe me."

"You never were," her father said.

"I was more than you remember, Dad. And I've been around the Young Women enough lately to know they have a tendency to overexaggerate. She'll come to her senses when she cools down."

"I just hope she doesn't do something she'll regret in the meantime," Cassie said.

"This boy has been nothing but trouble since she met him. It's like she's a different person. He has so much control over what she does, how she thinks, even what she wears."

"I can't remember the last time she spent time with friends," Cassie explained. "She wants to spend every spare moment with him. It doesn't matter how much we threaten or plead—we can't control her."

"I'm sorry," Lauryn said. "I can't imagine how hard this is for you."

"It's horrible when you can see exactly what is at the end of the path your child is on and they won't listen to you," Cassie said.

Lauryn's dad shook his head wearily. "Speaking of roads, I think we're at a dead end."

Cassie nodded and reached for more tissues.

"What can I do to help?" Lauryn asked.

"Just pray for her and for us. I'm sure we'll all get through it somehow. I just wish she didn't hate both of us so much," her dad said.

"Honey, she just says that, but she doesn't mean it," Cassie explained. Then she turned to Lauryn. "She's acting out because of her father's and my divorce. She thinks all her problems are because of that. Yet I know she loves your father as much as if he were her real father. She's just trying to manipulate us to get what she wants."

Lauryn didn't know what to say. The agony on their faces tore at her heart. She certainly knew what it was like coming from a less than ideal family situation, but for some reason she'd never gone through the throes of rebellion like Logan. Her Young Women leaders had surrounded her with love and support, and her friends had always been there for her. Of course, the only boy in her life had been Jace, but he was nothing like Brody, and their relationship had never been more than just friends.

"I need a Tylenol," her father said, getting up and going to the cupboard. "Oh, you got a couple of calls while you were gone."

"I did?" Lauryn said. "Why didn't they call my cell?"

"The first call was from your mother. She called collect and just asked if you'd call her back. I don't think she can afford to talk."

Lauryn nodded. Her mother was basically broke and living a very lonely, unhappy life. Lauryn felt bad for her but wasn't surprised at how her mother had ended up. Lauryn sent money occasionally and tried to help, but her mother was stubborn, and that made it difficult to change her situation.

"I'll give her a call. Any idea what she wants?"

"She didn't say. Probably money," he said. "I can tell she's drinking again. Be careful if you send her money. I'm afraid that's all she'll spend it on."

"I will," Lauryn answered. The one good thing about her mother's choices was that Lauryn saw firsthand how unhappy a life without the gospel and belief in God could be.

"Who was the other call from?" Lauryn asked.

"It was actually kind of a surprise," her father answered. "Do you remember a kid from high school named Jace?"

Chapter Fourteen

"Did you say Jace?" Lauryn managed to croak out.

"Yeah, isn't that the name of the guy you used to hang out with?"

"He called here?"

"He said it took a little work to track us down, but he was trying to find you. I gave him your cell. I thought he'd call."

"What time was this?"

"Around noon."

Her heart dropped; her breath stopped.

She whipped out her phone and checked her messages and missed calls. There, at eleven fifty-eight, was a call from an 801 area code, somewhere in northern Utah.

How had she missed his call?

She hadn't thought to look for a missed call. She hadn't expected to hear from him.

"I think I'll go call them back and see what they both wanted," she said, trying to act nonchalant, even though the thought of calling Jace made her whole scalp and neck tingle.

"All right, sweetie," her dad said. "We'll be right here."

Lauryn felt guilty for leaving them in their hour of need, but she had to make a call. For now, her mother could wait, but Jace . . . he'd actually called her!

Walking into her bedroom, Lauryn closed the door and dialed his number. Her heart pounded so hard her ribs vibrated as she waited for him to answer.

She shut her eyes and said a quick, quiet prayer for help. She didn't even know what kind of help she wanted. Help that it would go well. Help that she wouldn't sound stupid. Help that he'd still be single? Help that her call wouldn't get dropped or that he wouldn't be out of the office or . . .

"Hello?" a male voice said.

"Oh! Um . . . I'm trying to reach Jace—"

"Lauryn, is that you?!" he exclaimed.

"Yeah, it's me. How are you?"

"I'm going out of my mind. I meant to get there. I tried so hard, but on my way down from Salt Lake I had car trouble in Beaver, and they didn't have a part, so I've been waiting to get my car repaired. Your dad said you're in town. Were you there? Did you go?"

He was so upset she couldn't even try to play it cool. And she couldn't believe they were actually talking.

"Yeah, I went."

"You must have thought I was such a jerk!" he exclaimed.

"No, I didn't ever think that," she told him. "I just thought you were probably busy being married and having kids. Your wife, I mean." She stopped blabbering before he hung up and changed his phone number.

Jace laughed. "My wife? No, I was busy trying to track you down. Did you know there are three other people with your dad's name in the St. George area? I called all of them before I finally got to him. And one, get this, has a kid named Lauryn. I nearly died when I asked to speak to Lauryn and this little girl came on the phone."

Lauryn laughed. "I bet. I'm sorry I was so hard to find."

"Your dad didn't answer the first few times I called. I knew he probably had an answering machine, at least. I mean, everyone has an answering machine, don't they? So I kept calling until he finally picked up. He sounded like he wasn't feeling well. I hope he's not sick."

"No, he's not sick," she told him, sparing him the story about Logan.

She heard Jace audibly sigh. "It's been a long time. I can't believe we're finally talking. And that you came," he said. "I'm so sorry I wasn't there. I was willing to hitchhike to get to the temple," he said.

"That's okay. It's enough knowing you wanted to be there," she answered.

"How are you?" he asked.

"I'm good. How are you?"

"I'm good. I want to see you."

She was taken aback by his directness but also appreciated it. She wanted to see him, too.

"When will your car be fixed?" she asked.

"It is fixed. I'm pulling into town right now. When I knew you were in St. George I decided to take a chance and just keep coming. I can be at the temple in ten minutes. Will you meet me there and we can try it again?"

"I'll be there."

They both hung up, and Lauryn hugged the phone to her chest. She was on her way to see Jace!

* * *

"Are you there?" he asked, calling her just as she pulled into the temple parking lot.

"I just got here."

"Let's meet on the steps like we agreed."

"Okay, I'll go there and wait for you," she said. "Just be careful. If I remember right, you have a tendency to speed when you get anxious." She got out of the car, talking as she crossed the road to the temple grounds.

"Now what would make you say something like that?"

"The fact that I was with you three different times when you got speeding tickets. Let's see, one was for the homecoming game we were late for, one was for seminary graduation—that was fun to explain to everyone, especially my bishop—and the third one, let's see . . ." She paused for a moment. "Oh yeah, you got that ticket because you were anxious to go to the Frostop and get your can kicked in pinball."

Jace burst out laughing. "Is that how you remember it?"

She walked along the side of the temple, nearing the steps. "That's exactly how I remember it, because that's how it was."

"I believe I beat you," he said. "And set a new record high that is probably still there to this day."

Now it was her turn to laugh.

She rounded the corner and spied the stairs. "First of all, I had the high score, and second of all, they probably don't even have that machine any—"

She stopped in her tracks. There, on the stairs, was Jace, talking to her on the phone.

"—more," she finished, then shut the phone.

His face broke into a smile. He'd changed in some ways. He was taller—probably about six foot two—broader across his shoulders, and his hair was darker than she remembered. But that smile . . . it was exactly the same.

How is he not married? she had to wonder.

They didn't speak, but his clear, blue eyes connected with hers.

All the worries and fears Lauryn had felt completely disappeared. This was her dear friend Jace.

All the awkwardness she'd felt earlier was gone, and they walked right into each other's arms.

It was so good to see him!

He kept his arms tightly around her. She wasn't in a hurry to pull away.

"I'm sorry I was late," he whispered.

"That's okay," she replied.

"I'm so glad you came."

"I'm so glad you came too," she replied softly.

She shut her eyes for a moment and took a deep breath. He smelled like a mix of fresh laundry detergent and her favorite cologne, Ralph Lauren Romance for Men.

"I wasn't sure you'd remember," he said.

"I thought you'd be married," she replied.

Finally, they ended their embrace, only to step apart and look at each other close up for the first time.

"You're even prettier than I remembered," he said.

Lauryn smiled and felt her cheeks grow hot.

"I thought the same thing about you," she said.

"Really? You think I'm pretty?"

She laughed. "You know what I mean."

"What did you think earlier, when I didn't show up?"

"I thought you were at work, sitting at your desk, looking at a picture of your wife and child, thinking of a million things other than me."

"Let's go sit down," he said, taking her by the hand and leading her to a bench where they could sit in the shade.

"I still can't believe this," she said.

"I know; me neither."

"I couldn't believe it when my dad said you called."

"I couldn't believe it when he said you were in town," Jace said. He kept hold of her hand. "So how is it that we are both still single?"

"Unlucky in love," she said. "How about you? I don't remember . . . what happened to your girlfriend, Miss BYU?"

"She waited a whole six lousy months, then she and her new boyfriend sent me a wedding announcement."

"You've got to be kidding. How hard was that?"

"I won't lie to you; it nearly killed me. Boys who go on missions and leave a girlfriend behind are crazy. There were more guys who got dumped while I was on my mission than guys who didn't. We started keeping a list in the office just for fun."

"I'm sorry that was so hard for you."

"In a way it turned out to be a blessing, because I put all my energy into the work. I decided to tune out everything worldly and just focus on being a missionary. I barely took time to write weekly letters."

"I noticed," Lauryn said. "When you didn't write back, I gave up on you. Of course, I went to Italy and didn't have a lot of time to write either."

"And now look at you," Jace said. "A fashion designer in New York. Your dad is really proud of you."

"How do you know that?"

"He told me when I called and asked about you."

She smiled. Her dad did like to brag about her. "I've worked really hard, but I love it."

"I'm proud of you too," he said.

"Thanks, Jace." She was amazed at how easy it was to talk, how comfortable she felt with him. "What about you? Do you still travel like you used to?"

"I do, but I moved to a new company about five years ago. I work for Rocky Mountain Entrepreneur Mastermind Groups, which is basically a group of small businesses that meet to collaborate, brainstorm, and provide support for each other. I guess you could say our goal is to help our dreams and others' dreams come true."

"I love that. I bet you enjoy your work."

"It's exciting to help someone start their own business, especially when the business takes off and becomes profitable for them. That's what it's all about."

She looked into his face and saw the same boyish charm and a glint of youthfulness in him, but he was definitely no longer the boy she'd known in high school and college.

"What?" he asked when she didn't say anything.

She hadn't realized she was staring. "Sorry." She didn't want to tell him that she was thinking about how attractive he was.

"Have you eaten already? I haven't had a chance to eat yet."

"I had a late lunch, but I'll go somewhere with you while you eat."

"Are you sure?"

She nodded.

He grinned. "Come on, then." He got up and reached for her other hand. "I have an idea."

He helped her to her feet, then together they walked to the same parking lot where her car was parked. "I know the perfect place for lunch."

A gleaming black BMW was parked under a shade tree. Jace pointed the key fob toward the car, and several beeps sounded.

"Nice car," she said.

"I guess when you're as old as I am and you're not married, you can buy cars like this."

"I'm as old as you are and I'm not married, and I don't drive a car like this."

"What do you drive?" he asked, opening the door for her.

She waited to answer until he went around to his side and got in.

"Right now, I'm just borrowing my dad's extra car, but back home I don't have a car," she said. "I either walk, take a taxi, or ride the subway. Parking in Manhattan is outrageous."

"How do you like living there?"

"I love it. It's a lot different than here, that's for sure." She liked how clean his car was, and she noticed that it still smelled new. "I don't think about it until I come home and realize how much more laid back and relaxing life is here. But I have to be honest; I love the energy of the city."

"Tell me about your job. What's it like?"

As they drove to wherever Jace was taking them, she told him about her job with Jacqueline Yvonne and her decision to go to work for Laszlo Molnar. She referred several times to Cooper and how much help he'd been through it all and how much he was doing for the fashion show that would take place in three days.

"So this Cooper guy," Jace said, turning onto the main boulevard, "is he someone special?"

"Cooper!" she exclaimed, then started to laugh. "No way! I mean, don't get me wrong, I love the guy—he's like a brother in a way, but I could never like him romantically."

"He's not . . . you know."

"Absolutely not. In fact, he's hitting on one of the moms of my Young Women. I'm a little worried because he's not LDS, although lately, you'd think he was the ward greeter the way he's practically best friends with everyone at church. I wouldn't be surprised if I come back and they've given him a calling."

"He sounds like quite a guy."

"He is. I would have been lost without all his help with this fashion show. He just sent me at text this morning with a picture of the decorations. I'm telling you, I would have put a few silk plants on the stage and maybe some balloons or something and called it good. Cooper has backdrops, scenery, and even a runway. These girls are having a great time. They all feel like fashion models. It's been great for their self-esteem. With Cooper's coaching, I think they're ready for the famous New York Fashion Week in September!"

"That's great. They'll never forget it."

"I don't think so either."

Jace put on his blinker and pulled into the parking lot of the . . . Frostop. They'd eaten more fries and fry sauce; caramel marshmallow shakes; and double-meat, double-cheeseburgers there than anyone in town. Even the owner said so. This was also where they'd had the famous pinball showdown.

Lauryn burst out laughing. "It still looks the same!"

"Since there seems to be some confusion as to exactly who the Frostop pinball champion is, I thought we could settle the score once and for all."

Lauryn laughed. "Fine by me. But you know my name is in the book. Remember, I even signed it to make it official."

Jace opened his mouth in shock. "Obviously you have a selective memory. You did beat me, but I came back and beat you again. If Wilbur is still there, I'm sure he'll remember. He gave me a free milkshake when I won."

"I won, and I gave you the milkshake because I was getting ready for that pageant and didn't want to get fat."

Instead of using the stalls for drive-up service, Jace found a place to park so they could go inside. "We'll let Wilbur decide. But just in case he doesn't remember, I challenge you to a game."

She hadn't played pinball since . . . since she'd beaten Jace the last time!

"I accept your challenge. Loser pays for the meal," she replied.

"Sounds fair."

"Good. Since you'll be paying, I'm getting extra onion rings."

"You do that. I'm getting triple meat, triple cheese then."

"I'm getting a monster-sized milk shake," she stated.

"I'm getting a jumbo order of cheese fries with extra fry sauce."

"Mmm, that sounds good," she said.

"It does, doesn't it," he agreed. "I just hope we can eat it all."

He held the door for her as they went inside. The same red vinyl and chrome stools and black-and-white checkered floor greeted them. The counter had been updated, and there were now Frostop hats and T-shirts to buy. And in the corner was . . . the famous pinball machine.

"Hi," a young girl with braces and long, curly blond hair said. "Can I help you?"

"Hi," Jace replied. "Is Wilbur still the owner?"

"Wilbur? I don't know any Wilbur." Her face reflected the confusion in her voice.

"Oh. Okay." Jace stated his disappointment. "It has been twelve years since we were here last."

"Wait a sec," the girl said. "I think that's the name of the owner's dad. Hang on."

The girl left the counter and walked through some swinging tavern doors, then came back in a flash with a younger version of Wilbur behind her.

"Can I help you folks?" he said.

"Hi, we haven't been here for about twelve years, but we used to come here all the time. We knew Wilbur really well."

The man smiled, his eyes crinkling just like Wilbur's had. "I'm his son, Ernie. Glad to have you back."

"We've missed your double-meat, double-cheeseburgers," Jace said.

"And your fries. Do you still make them fresh?" Lauryn asked.

"My dad would send a lightning bolt down from heaven if I didn't," Ernie told them.

"I'm sorry to hear he's passed away. He was a great guy. We loved coming here after ball games just to hang out," Lauryn told him.

"Yeah, we still get a good crowd of kids, but it's getting harder and harder to compete with the trendier hangouts."

"We were glad to see you're still here," Jace said.

"You both grew up here?" Ernie asked.

"Pretty much," Jace answered.

"Can I get you folks something to eat?"

"Absolutely," Jace answered. "I'd like a double-meat, double-cheeseburger; a large cookies-and-cream shake; and a large order of french fries."

Lauryn nudged him.

"Oh, and a small order of onion rings and small chocolate milkshake."

Lauryn smiled with satisfaction. She wasn't hungry, but she wasn't about to pass up two of her favorite childhood treats, either.

"I'll be right back with your order," Ernie said.

Lauryn and Jace scooted into a booth and grinned at each other.

"This seems so surreal," she said.

"Like we're in the twilight zone," he answered.

"Exactly. It's so familiar. Everything's about the same, but twelve years is a long time."

Jace reached across the table for her hand. "So, tell me more about your life in Manhattan. Tell me about this new job."

She liked the feel of his hand over hers and the way he followed the bumps of her knuckles with his thumb.

"So you've heard of Laszlo Molnar?" Lauryn asked, trying to concentrate on the question instead of the butterflies in her stomach. She felt as giddy as a sixteen-year-old on a first date.

"Of course. I'm a fan of his menswear. I have several Molnar suits. I don't even know how many ties of his I own."

"Well, he's branched out into women's wear and even has an evening-wear line that I'm working on. I will present my collection at New York Fashion Week in September. Although he's thinking of setting up a collection preview sooner than that to get some media buzz going and some anticipation for the complete line."

"What a great opportunity for you. Congratulations."

"Thanks." She said the word, but her heart wasn't in it.

"You don't sound very enthusiastic about your new job," he observed.

"I know. And I know that every employer can't be as wonderful as Jacqueline. She's managed to stay in the business without becoming vicious."

"Is Laszlo the vicious type?"

"I'm not sure yet. He has a reputation, that's for sure, but he's been fine with me so far. Still, there's an undercurrent I pick up, like something just isn't right. I'm not sure if it's just me feeling like I'm having to prove myself or what, but I don't feel like anyone else wants me there. It's so hard to go to work everyday feeling like an outsider. That sounds silly. I wish I could explain it better."

"Hopefully that will go away with time."

"Yeah, I hope so too."

"So you live right there in Manhattan."

She nodded, eyeing Ernie, who was putting their food on a tray. "I'm in Soho, on West 4th Street. I have a great apartment. I sublet from a member of our ward who is an actress. She moved to Hollywood because she got a role on a television sitcom, so I'm living in her apartment. She could be gone for several years. She's even let me do a little redecorating."

"Here we go," Ernie announced as he approached their table and placed the tray between them. He helped divvy out the food and even had plenty of ketchup and fry sauce for them. "You folks let me know if you need anything else."

"We sure will, Ernie," Jace said. "Thanks. It looks just like I remember it."

Ernie gave a nod of thanks and left them to eat. Because it was the middle of the afternoon, business was slow and they had the restaurant all to themselves.

"So," Lauryn said, stealing one of Jace's fries, "what about you?"

"Well, I told you about my job. I have a home in the Sugarhouse area of Salt Lake. It's close to work, and I love the neighborhood—a lot of kids and nice neighbors who look out for my place when I'm gone on business trips."

"Think you'll ever come to Manhattan?" she said.

"I will now," he said, meeting her gaze.

Lauryn's breath caught in her throat, and she felt a tingling from the back of her neck to the top of her head. She couldn't control the reaction. Looking into his deep blue eyes did something to her. Had his eyes been that blue in high school? She hadn't even remembered they were blue until now.

"You have any trips coming up?" she asked, dipping another fry in fry sauce.

"I think I could arrange something." He also took a fry and dipped it. They ate at the same time.

Lauryn could barely swallow. *What is wrong with me,* she wondered. *I feel like I'm back in high school, yet Jace never had this kind of effect on me then.*

She unconsciously kept chewing and trying to get her throat to work. Finally, she managed to swallow after taking a sip of water.

They talked about friends from high school. She caught him up on Emma, Jocelyn, Andrea, and Chloe. He hadn't made it to any of the reunions either.

Eating and chatting, Lauryn was continually amazed at how easy it felt to be with Jace again. She liked how he looked directly at her when she spoke, like he thought every word she said was important. Michael had never done that. He was always paying attention to something or someone else when she talked, and it made her feel like she never had anything to say that was worth listening to.

"I'm stuffed," she said, pushing away her half-eaten order of onion rings. Of course, she'd helped herself to his fries also. It was all as good as she remembered, maybe even a little better.

He finished his last bite by dunking his cheeseburger in a pool of ketchup and then popping it into his mouth. That was one thing about Jace that hadn't changed; he still loved ketchup. "I really do have better manners than this," he said with his mouth full.

She laughed. He'd always been able to stuff his face with food. She'd learned to eat fast around him or he'd start on her food when his was gone.

"I'll believe it when I see it," she said.

"When I come to Manhattan, I'll take you to the restaurant at the top of the Marriott Marquis and prove it. My business colleagues rave about the place."

"Is that the one that spins around?"

"That's what they tell me."

"Maybe we can go to some plays when you're in town, too," she offered.

"I'd like that," he said, holding his gaze on her.

"Me too," she said, feeling as if she'd fallen under his spell again.

"What are you doing the rest of the day?"

"Nothing," she managed to say.

"Do you have time to spend it with me?"

She nodded, feeling excitement tingle her toes. He wanted to spend the rest of the day with her!

"Let's go," he said.

Together they cleared the remains of their meal, put it in the garbage, and told Ernie good-bye.

"Oh wait," Jace said as they got to the door. "Did you still want to play pinball?"

"No," she said. "I think I remember; you did have the high score."

Chapter Fifteen

Lauryn didn't want the day to end. They went for a drive to see how big the town had grown since Lauryn had last been there. They drove to Snow Canyon and walked around, hiking up some of the easier trails into the red rock. Back in the city, they went to the outlet mall and browsed through stores, more for fun than to buy. They found a store with sunglasses and laughed at each other as they tried on some of the different styles.

At a chocolate shop they shared some truffles, then held hands as they strolled down the sidewalk, enjoying the warm evening and just being together.

As stars appeared, they decided to get some dinner. They found a new-looking Chinese restaurant and were seated in a private corner. As they approached the booth, Jace motioned for Lauryn to sit. She gave him a big smile when he slid in next to her instead of sitting on the other side of the table.

She and Jace had been together nearly eight hours, and they still hadn't run out of things to talk and laugh about. Lauryn couldn't help but remember the stress of her dinner dates with Michael. It had always seemed like his thoughts were somewhere else (she now knew where). She was constantly trying to think of interesting things to say in an effort to impress Michael. But with Jace, she felt like she could say anything and he would want to hear more.

At the end of the meal the waiter brought out their check and some fortune cookies.

Jace took care of the bill, then handed one of the cookies to Lauryn.

"You want to go first?" he asked.

"No, you go," she said.

"Okay." He snapped the cookie open and read the paper inside. "Success will come from an unexpected source."

"Wow, that's an interesting fortune. I wonder what it means."

"It means don't count on it because these things never come true," he joked.

"True. I've gotten some really bizarre fortunes before. In fact, I still remember one that said, 'Worse things are yet to come.' Now what kind of a fortune is that?"

"A bad one."

They both laughed.

"Yeah, well, I like to eat them, but it's silly to even care about the fortune inside." She cracked hers open and popped half in her mouth, leaving the fortune paper hanging out of the other half.

"You don't want to read it?"

"Nope. They're dumb. I don't want to read, 'The end is near,' or 'You will be diagnosed with a horrible disease,' or something like that."

He reached over and pulled the paper from the cookie. He read the paper, then put it down.

"So?" she asked.

"I thought you didn't care what it said," he teased.

"I don't. I'm just curious."

"Okay, well . . ." He picked it back up. "It says, 'You will find your future in your past.'"

"Ha! Give me that." She reached over and snatched the paper from him. With a quick scan she read the paper. "Hmm, it really does say that."

"I like that fortune," he said, dipping his chin and looking intently at her.

"Yeah, as fortunes go, that isn't bad." She looked into his eyes. He held her gaze, and once again she found herself mesmerized, like she was falling into a sea of blue and didn't want to catch herself.

Something was going on. Something unexpected. Something wonderful.

The waiter returned with Jace's receipt, then bowed to them and thanked them for coming.

The spell was broken, but Lauryn found her mind racing. This was all so unexpected and so completely impossible, yet it felt so comfortable and so right. Were the heavens smiling down on her? Was all of this part of a much bigger and better plan than she could comprehend?

If it wasn't, there was no way to explain what was happening here.

"It's nearly nine," Jace said, glancing at his watch. "Do you need to get home or can I keep you a little longer."

She couldn't help smiling as he took her hand and helped her from the table.

"I'm all yours," she answered, sliding her purse over her shoulder.

They walked out into the warm summer evening, and for the first time there was silence between them. It didn't feel awkward, but there just weren't any words to describe the crazy, unbelievable, amazing thing that was going on between them.

"Let's go for a ride," Jace said.

They drove to a spot on the black hill, near the capital *D* that stood for Dixie and found a place to park. From their vantage point, they looked out over the city, the temple shining brightly in the center of it all.

"It feels good to be here," she paused, "with you." She turned in her seat and faced him.

"That's what I was just thinking." He looked over at her and reached for her hand.

"Thanks for your postcards and e-mails through the years," she said. "I always liked hearing from you when you were in different parts of the world."

"I always thought of you wherever I went."

"Why has it taken so long for us to get together?" she asked.

"I don't know, but it doesn't really matter now."

"I wish I didn't have to go home Wednesday," she said.

"I'll have to leave tomorrow night," he said. "I've got a meeting I absolutely can't miss Wednesday morning. I wish I'd arranged to stay longer."

"Me too," she replied.

"So . . ." he started.

She leaned in. "Yes?"

He also leaned in. "I don't mean to sound sappy."

"Go ahead. I like sappy."

"It's just that I don't want it to end."

Her heart beat so hard it hurt. "Me either."

They magnetically leaned closer together.

"So, what do we do?" she asked.

"I don't know. I could come visit you," he said, inching closer, his voice barely above a whisper.

"And I could come visit you," she said, keeping her voice quiet and matching his movement.

"Lauryn?" His face was inches from hers, and his eyes fell to her lips.

"Yes," she whispered.

"I've waited so long."

"Too long—"

He didn't let her finish.

Lauryn's bones went weak, her head swirled dizzily. His kiss was warm, tender, and sweet. In that moment she forgot every kiss she'd ever had, and she knew her lips would never again touch any but his.

"Whoa," she said when he pulled back.

"I agree," he said.

"It's a good thing we never did that in high school," she said, thinking of her stepsister Logan. "You could have really distracted me."

"Same with you," he said.

"I didn't even think you'd show up today," she said with a laugh.

"I was positive I was wasting my time," he said.

"What made you want to see me after all these years?" she asked.

"I never stopped caring about you."

His words touched her heart, and a wave of emotion caught her off guard. She blinked quickly to clear the tears that filled her eyes.

"Hey," Jace said, cupping the side of her face with his hand. "Don't cry."

"I'm not, I mean, I don't know why I am," she confessed. "How silly is that?"

"It's not silly," he said. "I think it's sweet, just like you."

"I'm really not that sweet. I have a very stubborn side."

"I've seen it."

"I have a temper too."

"I know."

"I'm not very patient."

"That's okay."

"I don't cook."

"I do."

"I think I just realized why I'm still single," she said.

"You don't know how glad I am that you are," he replied.

"We live so far apart. Does this even make sense?"

"We'll make sense out of it," he said, drawing her close again.

"This seems like a dream," she whispered.

"No," he said. "It's better than a dream . . . it's a dream come true."

"Mmm," she said. "I feel like the luckiest girl in the world."

Their lips were almost touching.

"Then we make the perfect match, because I am the luckiest guy."

They kissed again, and Lauryn knew this was the start of something wonderful.

* * *

"This is horrible! You can't do this to me!" Logan shouted as Lauryn walked through the front door into her father's house.

She stopped and tried to back away, but it was too late; she'd already interrupted the heated argument.

"Come on in, Lauryn," her father said wearily.

"Sorry, I'll just go up to my room."

Logan had her face buried in her hands and was sobbing like her world had ended.

Lauryn scurried up the stairs to her room, where she closed the door and paused to listen. She was glad to see Logan had returned, but obviously her homecoming was not a joyful reunion.

The shouting didn't resume, but a low mumble of voices and Logan's crying were still audible.

Lauryn didn't like contention and wished Logan could see how much her parents loved her and how shortsighted she was being about Brody. If Logan could look even five years down the road and see what it would be like to be married to him, she might change the course her life was on. Brody didn't go to church, he wasn't ambitious, and he didn't seem to be very caring if he was causing so much trouble between Logan and her parents. But Logan couldn't seem to see past his handsome exterior and the fact that out of all the other girls, she had gotten him.

Wishing there were some way she could help, Lauryn began to change into her pajamas, and thoughts of Jace soon filled her head.

If someone had told her twenty-four hours ago that she would have spent most of the day with Jace and ended it with a kiss, she would have laughed them out of town. It would have been a ludicrous, impossible idea.

But it wasn't ludicrous, and it wasn't impossible. Nothing had felt more right in her entire life. Being with him was as natural as being with her best friends. No amount of time had weakened their bond. But there was a difference now—a big difference. *Friends* wasn't the right term to describe what they were feeling. They weren't quite a couple, but they most certainly were more than friends.

Telling him good-bye that night had been like removing part of her heart. There was something about being with him that made her feel complete.

Was it possible to fall in love that quickly—especially for a grown woman who'd been scorned by love enough to know that heartache was always around the corner?

She knew there was great risk involved, but it just didn't seem to matter, because his feelings seemed completely in sync with hers.

Falling back on her bed, she stretched her arms overhead and closed her eyes. As Lauryn lay still, she once again felt Jace's lips on hers, and her stomach did a backflip. She felt like someone who finally sits still after riding a roller coaster all day, whose body continues to feel the rise and fall, the twists and turns. She really had been on quite the ride today.

Her phone buzzed, and she saw that Jace had sent her a text message. *I miss you. Seven hours and twenty-nine minutes until I see you again.* She smiled. They were going to breakfast together. She texted him back and told him she missed him too.

Her analytical, skeptical side told her to be wary, not to put herself in a position to get burned again. Her romantic side told her to jump in with both feet and never look back.

Footsteps pounded up the stairs, and a door slammed. Lauryn figured it was Logan heading to her room, convinced her life was over. Lauryn wished she could convince the girl that all of this was for her own good.

Another text. *Seven hours, twenty-five minutes.*

Lauryn laughed. She hoped he didn't plan on counting down the whole night. She had wanted to spend more time with him, but it was so late, and she was exhausted from her weekend with her friends. They'd barely gotten five hours of sleep a night.

Keeping the phone with her, she went to the bathroom to wash her face and brush her teeth.

Beach-themed towels and a shower curtain covered in colorful fish greeted her as she turned on the bathroom light. She quickly washed her face, then brushed her teeth.

Her phone buzzed. *Seven hours, twenty minutes. How can we make the time go faster?*

She texted him back, *There's a magic thing called sleep.* She pushed send just as she opened the door. There, in the hallway, was Logan, waiting to get in.

"Oh, sorry. I didn't know you were out here waiting," Lauryn said.

Logan didn't say anything, just sniffed and nodded.

Lauryn felt terrible for her. It didn't matter how wrong the situation was between her and Brody. Logan's feelings were still real, and her heart was breaking. If she could only understand.

"You okay?" Lauryn asked, feeling awkward. She didn't want to pry, but she didn't want to appear like she didn't care, either.

"No," Logan said. "They've forbidden me to see Brody. I knew I shouldn't have come home. They're making this so difficult."

"They're doing what they think is best," Lauryn offered, knowing it wasn't going to help Logan feel better.

"They're just interfering with my life. I can't wait until I'm eighteen and can get out of here. Brody said he'll wait for me."

Lauryn nodded, but inside she thought, *I'll bet.*

"I wish they understood my feelings and how much in love Brody and I are. They don't even care!"

Feeling very much out of her league, Lauryn decided it was probably best if she stayed out of their business. She didn't possess the wisdom to know what to say, and she certainly didn't want to misrepresent her dad or Cassie.

"Well, try to get some sleep. Maybe things will seem better in the morning." Lauryn turned toward her bedroom door to go to bed.

"How did you do it, Lauryn?" Logan asked.

Lauryn stopped and turned. "Do what?"

"Get through high school so easily. Why does it have to be so hard for me?"

Against her better judgment, Lauryn motioned for Logan to come into her room where they could sit and talk. She wasn't going to try and parent the girl, but maybe she could help her broaden her vision a little to see the bigger picture and understand how her choices would affect her future.

"Just a sec," Lauryn said, checking the text that had just come up on her phone. *Good night, dream girl. I'll see you in seven hours and ten minutes.*

Lauryn smiled and texted him back.

Logan noticed what she was doing. "Is that the guy you were out with tonight?"

Lauryn smiled and nodded.

"I guess things went well then?"

"Better than I ever could have dreamed."

"This is a guy you knew in high school? Like twelve years ago?"

"It's him, and he was well worth the wait," Lauryn told her.

"Cool," Logan said. "I hope things work out for you."

"Thanks," Lauryn answered, noticing that Logan seemed ready to start crying again. Before that happened, she spoke up quickly. "Listen, Logan, I'm not a parent or anything, but I have to be honest. When I look at you I see how much potential you have, and I have to wonder if you really understand what a sacrifice you're making for Brody."

"Oh, it's no sacrifice. I'm the luckiest girl in town to have Brody. I would do anything for him."

That raised Lauryn's eyebrows. "I hope not."

Logan chuckled. "Well, you know, within reason."

"Tell me, Logan. What does Brody do for you?"

"Well, he . . ." She was thoughtful for a moment. "Sometimes he'll . . ." She swallowed. "I mean, he's the kind of guy who . . ."

Lauryn wasn't surprised she was having such a hard time coming up with an answer.

"He does a lot of things. Little things. Like he knows exactly what I like to order when we go out to eat. And he sometimes lets me choose the movies we go and see. And he'll let me hang out with him and his friends sometimes."

The words, "Are you nuts!" came to mind, but Lauryn refrained.

"So, does he ever write you little notes or bring you flowers or offer to help you with your homework? Does he support you in your school activities? Does he support you in your Church activities? Does he go to church?"

"Not exactly. I mean, he's Mormon and everything, but his parents don't go, so he's not really used to going. But he says he'll go for me once he doesn't have to work on Sundays."

"So, what is your dream in life? You know, after high school?"

"Well, next year I can start taking cosmetology classes at the tech center. By the time I graduate, I'll pretty much have my license to do hair. Once I get my license, I'll get a job at a salon. Brody and I will probably get married in the fall after I graduate. I've always wanted a September wedding."

"You have no desire to go away to college or travel or see the world?"

"Not really. Brody's enough for me."

"What are you going to do all summer?"

"I'm looking for a job. My friend thinks she can get me a job at a kiosk in the mall. There are a couple of other places I can apply too. I'll go job hunting while Brody's gone."

"Oh, where's he going?"

"For a late senior trip he's going to Southern California with a couple of friends for two weeks. I'm dying that he's going to be gone so long. But one of his buddies has friends who live in Long Beach, where they're going to stay. They're going to car shows and Tijuana and stuff like that."

"Two weeks, huh?" Lauryn had an idea.

"Yeah, that's the longest we've been apart since we started dating."

"You've only been sixteen for six months haven't you?"

"Brody was my first date. My friend lined us up."

"So you haven't dated any other boys?" Lauryn asked.

"Are you kidding? Have you seen the other boys? There's no one as hot as Brody that I would even consider going out with. People say Brody looks a lot like Brad Pitt, but I think he's even hotter."

Lauryn decided she needed to see this kid. Was it possible he was as "hot" as Logan said he was?

"Logan, I have an idea." Lauryn felt strongly about what she was about to say; she just hoped it was the Spirit and not desperation prompting her.

"You do?"

"Yeah, and I haven't asked your parents yet, but, well, since Brody's leaving for two weeks and you don't have a job yet, how would you like to come back to New York with me for a few days?" Lauryn knew it was the worst time to have a guest come stay with her, but this window of opportunity would close soon. It was now or never. Somehow she'd make it work . . . on top of the fashion show and her new job.

"Really? Go to New York with you? That would be awesome! I would love that. Can we go see *Wicked?* Can we go to the Empire State Building? And the Statue of Liberty? And Ground Zero?"

Lauryn laughed, not expecting quite this enthusiastic of a response.

"Do you think my parents will let me go?"

"I hope so."

"Lauryn, you are the best!" Logan exclaimed, lunging for her and giving her a crushing hug. "When I was in junior high I kind of got into drama, and I always wanted to go to New York to a show on Broadway. Since you lived there, my mom said we'd go visit you sometime, but it just never happened, so I gave up dreaming about it."

"Then let's make that dream come true," Lauryn said.

"I can't wait to tell Brody! He's gonna freak."

Lauryn wished he'd *freak* right out of the picture.

"I want to see *Phantom,* too. And *Lion King,* and *Beauty and the Beast.* I love Disney stuff."

"Okay, okay. Don't forget, the shows are a bit pricey, and we do have to talk to your parents."

"I wish we could wake them up now."

"I think they need their sleep," Lauryn assured her. "I'll talk to them in the morning. I'm leaving Wednesday."

"That's perfect. Brody leaves tomorrow, so I can tell him good-bye. And I'll be back before he gets home, right?"

"Right."

"This is super awesome. I'm going to New York!" She danced around the bed and hugged Lauryn again.

"Let's get some sleep then," Lauryn suggested. "We'll work it all out tomorrow."

"You are the best big sister ever," Logan said, giving her one last hug.

"Hey, what are sisters for?" Lauryn said, hoping she wouldn't regret what she'd just done.

Chapter Sixteen

At six o'clock the next morning, Lauryn's cell phone rang and woke her up.

"Come on, Jace. Don't you need any sleep?" she mumbled as she searched for her phone.

"Hello," she said groggily.

"I don't have a picture of you!" her mother said frantically.

"What?" Her mind was still foggy.

"Lauryn, where are all the pictures? Your second-grade picture with your two front teeth missing. I can't find it. And your first dance. Where are they?"

"Mom, you didn't take any of that with you to Florida. It's all here in storage."

"But it's mine, and I want it! I need it. I need it."

"Okay, okay. I can get the pictures and send them to you, okay?"

"Will you, Lauryn? Will you do it today?"

"Yes, if you want me to. But why is this so important all of a sudden?" Lauryn was confused, since her mother had never even carried pictures of her in her wallet when Lauryn was younger.

"I need to see you, Lauryn. I've been a terrible mother and I need to see you. I'm sorry, honey. I'm so sorry." Her mother broke down, sobbing loudly on the phone.

Lauryn sat up and yawned. Obviously her mother needed her medication adjusted. "Mom, it's okay. You don't need to apologize."

Her mother cried for a moment longer, then seemed to calm down a little.

"I do need to apologize. You must hate me. Do you hate me?" she asked as her crying grew louder again.

"No, Mom, I don't hate you." Had her mother been drinking? "I wonder if you should call Dr. Reeves. What do you think?" Lauryn had spoken to Dr. Reeves on the phone several times when her mother had taken too much of the wrong medication or had a bad reaction from combining drugs and alcohol. Sometimes she felt like the parent taking care of a delinquent child.

"I went to Dr. Reeves, and you know what he told me? You know what that good-for-nothing, horrible excuse for a doctor told me?"

"What?"

"He told me I have cirrhosis and that I'm going to die."

* * *

"I'm so sorry," Jace said, pulling Lauryn into his arms and holding her close. "This must be such a blow."

They sat in a corner booth at Village Inn, neither of them eating much.

"It came as a surprise, but I knew my mother's health was bad. She hasn't taken care of herself at all, and she's had a horrible drinking problem for years. It was bound to happen. Her father died of the same thing in his late forties. She knew, and she still wouldn't stop."

"It's so sad, because it didn't have to happen."

It was sad for Lauryn to find out about her mother's disease, but she couldn't seem to make herself feel any emotion beyond pity. "She's consumed by guilt and regret. She apologized for being a horrible mother."

"She did? What did you say?"

"I didn't know what to say. The truth is, she hasn't exactly been the most supportive person in my life, but she is still my mother. I've tried to understand her and love her for who she is. It's funny, but I don't really have any resentment. I just wish it would have been different. I always wanted a mom who was my best friend, you know?"

He nodded.

"How bad is she? Do they know how long she has to live?"

"I called Dr. Reeves, and he said the damage is irreversible. She'll slowly deteriorate. It could take months."

"How awful."

"I need to go see her. I don't know when, though. I just started this job, and they weren't happy I was taking a week off to come here. I'll just have to go spend a weekend with her."

"Have you told your dad?"

"Yeah, he knows. We talked this morning before you picked me up. I need to talk to him about something else, too. I want to take Logan back with me to New York for a few weeks."

"You do? Wow, that's nice of you."

"I know, it really is," she said, then laughed because she knew how that sounded. "I just mean because it's not the most convenient time to have a houseguest. But this is the only time we can get her away from her boyfriend."

"Oh, I get it. You're doing an intervention."

"Exactly. I want to get her out of the whole environment and see if I can get her to open her eyes a little wider."

"I think it's great you're willing to do that."

"Thanks. It may not make a difference, but I feel like I need to do something."

He laced his fingers through hers. "I hope you can still find time to see me when I come to town."

She smiled and placed her other hand on top of his. "You can count on it. Knowing you're coming will help me keep going."

"So, what have you got planned today?"

"I need to talk to my dad about Logan. If she's coming home with me, she needs to know so she can get packed and we can get her booked on my flight. After that, I'm free. What about you?"

"I have an idea, but it's kind of a surprise. You wouldn't happen to know anyone who might like to go on a date with me, would you?"

"I'll ask around, but good luck finding any eligible girls at your age," Lauryn teased.

"My age!" Jace laughed. "Look who's talking." He wrapped his arm around her side and tickled her under her arm.

"All right, I give up!" Lauryn squirmed away from him. "I do know one girl who's free this afternoon. She's *around* your age, and she happens to love surprises."

"Well then, how about if I take you home and let you take care of your family business, and I call the office and take care of some work, then I'll pick you up in a couple of hours. Does that give you enough time?"

"That's perfect." She looked at the sparkle in his eyes and the kindness in his expression and felt a flood of gratitude fill her heart. Jace had come into her life at the perfect time. It was a beautiful feeling to be staring into the eyes of the greatest blessing she'd ever received.

* * *

"So, it went well?" Jace asked as they drove through town.

Lauryn was so busy talking she didn't pay attention to where he was taking her. "Dad and Cassie jumped at the idea. In fact, they gave me a budget to use so I could take her to some of her favorite Broadway shows and show her around town. I just need to figure out when I'm going to do all this. But I think some of the Young Women in my ward would be great to take her shopping and to a few of the sights."

"Is Logan excited?"

"The minute they gave their permission she ran upstairs to start packing. She was so excited she forgot she was supposed to meet Brody at his house so she could tell him good-bye. He called and was a little upset because she wasn't there. It was awesome!"

Jace laughed.

"I feel good about it, though. And if it helps her, great; if not, at least we'll grow a little closer as sisters."

"She's lucky to have you."

"I always wanted brothers and sisters, so I feel lucky."

"Where is her brother, anyway?"

"Sutton left for Scout camp early Monday morning, so I haven't seen him yet. He gets home just as we leave, so I get to say a quick hi and that's about it. He's a great kid, though. Has some really good friends."

"Glad to hear it. Friends make all the difference."

"Don't I know it." She looked out the window and noticed where they were. "Hey, why are we going to the airport?"

"This is the surprise. You know how you've never been to the Grand Canyon?"

"Yes."

"Well, that's where we're going. I have a friend who flies a Twin Otter airplane and takes people on aerial tours. He's always wanted to take me when I came to town. So I gave him a call, and he happens to be free this afternoon."

"I can't believe it! I've always wanted to see the Grand Canyon." She looked at him, her heart spilling over again with gratitude. "This is already the best date I've ever had, and it hasn't even happened yet. This is the nicest thing anyone has ever done for me. Thank you."

"You are welcome. And really, it's not like I planned this for months; it was just a quick phone call."

"Still, you thought to do it. That's the best part. Tell me again, how is it that no girl has snatched you up already?"

"Guess none of them were the right girl," he answered, pulling into a parking stall in front of the terminal.

"I'm glad they weren't," she said.

Before opening the door, he leaned over and kissed her.

"Sorry," he said. "But I didn't get dessert at breakfast."

"If you're a good boy, you can have seconds," she teased.

"I'll hold you to it." He got out of the car and came around to open the door for her. Hand in hand, they walked toward the airport where they were greeted at the doors by a refrigerator-sized man with a bald head and big smile.

"Jace, buddy, long time no see." The man pulled Jace into a hug that nearly lifted him off the ground. "How are you?" He looked over Jace's shoulder. "Nice wheels."

"Thanks, you'll have to take it for a spin," Jace offered.

"I'd love to. And who's your pretty lady friend?" he asked, turning to Lauryn.

"This is Lauryn Alexander. We went to high school together. Lauryn, this is Caleb McCollough, my dad's best friend. Caleb's like an uncle to me."

Caleb smiled. "Jace has been my buddy since he was a little tyke playing in the cockpit while his dad and I worked on engines. Sure miss your ol' dad."

"Yeah, me too," Jace said.

"I feel close to him when I'm in the air. I call him my heavenly copilot."

Jace laughed.

"So you two want to go see the Grand Canyon, do ya?"

"I've never seen it," Lauryn said.

"Girlie, this is the best way to see the Grand Canyon, from the air, just like God sees it every day. One of the seven natural wonders of the world, you know."

"I did know that," she said.

"Well, come on then. Let's take you up. I'm not sure how long you've got, but there's plenty to see on the way there and on the way back."

"We're all yours," Jace said, taking Lauryn's hand and giving it a squeeze.

"Well, that's a scary thought, but I'll do my best to bring you two back alive."

"That'd be nice, Caleb," Jace said.

They followed the man through several doors that finally took them outside onto the tarmac. Near the hangars sat the Twin Otter, Caleb's pride and joy. Another man stood nearby, with a clipboard and cell phone.

"Hey, Wink, we all set to go?" Caleb asked.

"Sure thing, Caleb. Perfect day to fly."

"You remember Jace, don't ya, Wink?"

"Sure do. Hey, Jace. Good to see ya."

"And this is Jace's friend, Lauryn. She's never been to the Grand Canyon. Lauryn, this is Wink. His real name is Winthorpe, but he was getting teased too much with a pansy name like that, so now he's known as Wink."

"Hi, Wink," Lauryn said, thinking the nickname suited him much better than his given name.

With no other passengers in the nineteen-seat plane, Jace and Lauryn found seats together next to a large, oversized window. Caleb explained to them that the Twin Otter was specially designed with the wings set high on the plane so as not to obstruct the view from the oversized windows.

"Caleb's done this for years. You don't need to worry."

"I'm not worried. He seems like a great guy."

"After my dad died, Caleb took good care of my mom and our family. He brought his son over every Saturday morning and helped with yard work. He fixed things around the house when they broke. He was the one who taught me how to drive. He's been a great friend to our family."

"I can tell."

"Okay, folks, buckle up and we'll be on our way shortly. We'll take you above the Virgin River, then on to Zion National Park and Kolob; then you'll see Cedar Breaks, Bryce Canyon, and Lake Powell. Don't worry, we'll get you to the Grand Canyon, too. We're just taking the scenic route. Make yourselves comfortable. There's no stewardess on board, so if you need anything, just holler, and Wink will put on an apron."

Jace and Lauryn laughed as the engines roared to life. Soon they were off the runway and in the air.

Lauryn turned at an angle to look out the window and leaned back against Jace's chest, who wrapped his arms around her and rested his chin on top of her head. For a moment, she shut her eyes, trying to absorb not only the fact that she was in Jace's arms, but that she wasn't freaked out by the fact that she was in Jace's arms. He'd never been more than a friend in high school, their relationship never having turned romantic, yet nothing seemed more natural than to sit close to Jace and feel his presence near her. She felt strengthened next to him—capable and brave. She'd never felt that kind of assurance and confidence with Michael. Never.

"Hey, you'd better open your eyes and see what you're missing.

Look at that," Jace said as the majestic red cliffs and multicolored sandstone folds of Cedar Breaks appeared before them. The beauty heightened as they flew on to Bryce Canyon and drank in the vivid colors and breathtaking shapes and forms of the giant natural amphitheater. But nothing prepared Lauryn for the grandeur of the Grand Canyon.

Caleb took them deep into the sandstone slot canyons carved by wind and rain over the course of thousands of years. The sheer magnitude brought Lauryn's emotions to the surface.

"What do you think?"

"I don't know the right words to explain it," she said. "It's more than beautiful; it's more than breathtaking."

He pulled her close and held her tight.

"I can never get enough of the big hole in the ground," Caleb joked over the intercom. "That's probably one of God's best masterpieces, in my opinion. Unless there's something else you'd like to see, we'll head back now."

Lauryn and Jace fell silent, knowing that when they returned, their time together would come to an end.

The thought of saying good-bye to Jace was difficult to accept. Had she known it would be this wonderful with him, she would have tracked him down long before now. But perhaps there was a reason it worked out this way. Perhaps she wouldn't have been ready for these strong emotions. Perhaps this was how Heavenly Father intended it to be.

But that didn't make the thought of being separated any easier.

"We're almost there," Jace said. She could feel his lips near her ear.

"I know," she said. "I don't ever want to land. I want to just fly off into the sunset."

He chuckled and gave her a squeeze.

She didn't want to let him leave without a plan, without some kind of understanding for what happened now and when they would be together again. But she didn't want to be demanding or overwhelm him, so she kept her questions to herself.

When the plane's wheels touched the ground, Lauryn felt her heart drop. Why did it have to end?

Jace and Lauryn thanked Caleb and Wink for a wonderful flight. Caleb gave her a hug, nearly crushing her spine, and told her that Jace was a lucky fellow. She kissed Caleb on the cheek, making him blush.

"Next time you're in town, girlie, we'll take you back up. You name the place," he offered.

"It's a deal," Lauryn answered.

"You're awfully quiet," Jace said as they walked back to his car.

"Am I?" she asked. "Sorry, I'm just thinking."

"About what?"

"About how perfect this day has been. Actually, these last two days."

"Well, not quite perfect," he said.

"Oh?" She didn't like hearing that.

"We never got to play pinball. You owe me a game."

"Aha! You're right."

"We don't have time today, but I was thinking, how about a week from Saturday?"

She stopped and looked at him with confusion. "I won't be here then."

"But I'll be in Manhattan. They do have pinball machines in Manhattan, don't they?"

Lauryn jumped toward him and threw her arms around his neck. "Yes, they have the best pinball machines in Manhattan."

He wrapped his arms around her and spun around once.

"I'm so glad you're coming. I wanted to ask you to come, but I didn't want to appear pathetic," she said.

"I figured you'd need some help taking care of Logan. Maybe I could treat both of you girls to a little arcade fun, then we could go to dinner and a show."

Lauryn shut her eyes for a moment so she could absorb the absolute wonderfulness of this man. How in the world did she get so lucky? It would have been worth going through fifty guys like Michael to finally get one guy like Jace.

She opened her eyes and smiled. "I think that could be arranged," she said.

"Good. Because that's about as long as I think I'll be able to stand being away from you," he told her.

"Are you going to text me the countdown until we're together again?"

"Of course. I'll count down the days, and then as it gets closer, I'll count down the hours. But remember, I'll be thinking of you every minute."

"You are such a romantic," Lauryn said as she slid into the passenger seat. Jace walked around to the driver's side and started the ignition. "You weren't like this in high school, were you?"

"I never had a girlfriend to find out."

"Why not?" she asked, seriously. "You didn't really date much at all that I remember."

"The only girlfriend I wanted, I couldn't have."

"Oh really? Who did you like back then? Was it Ava? You kind of had a crush on her in junior high, didn't you?"

"It wasn't Ava."

"Don't tell me it was Kinley Maxfield. Every other boy in school was in love with her." Kinley had been head cheerleader their senior year.

"No, definitely not Kinley. She drove me insane in biology. I'd never heard more stupid questions come out of one person's mouth."

"Then who did you like?"

"You."

Lauryn's mouth dropped open.

Jace's eyebrows arched. "You really didn't know I had a crush on you all that time?"

She shook her head slowly. All that time they'd spent together, Jace had secretly liked her.

"Sometimes I thought . . . maybe, but . . . why didn't you say anything?"

"I tried to hide it because I knew you didn't like me the same way. Sometimes it was hard."

"I guess I was too busy dealing with my parents' relationship issues to handle one of my own," she told him. "I'm sorry if I ever hurt you."

"Oh no, you never did. I was glad to at least have you as a friend. But I always dreamed of being together with you like this. Of course, as we got older and went our separate ways, I moved on. But when that date finally arrived to meet you at the temple, I was surprised at how much I was hoping you would be there."

"Me too," she said. "But I didn't dare let myself get too excited, because I was positive you'd gotten married since the last time we talked."

"I'm really glad I hadn't."

"So am I."

He pulled over in front of her dad's house.

"What do you think would have happened if I'd liked you back in high school?" she asked.

"I don't know, but obviously it wasn't supposed to happen then, or it would have. And it seems pretty clear that we were supposed to meet again now."

"I'd have to agree with you. I don't think I was ready before now."

"Ready for what?" Jace asked with a smile.

"Ready for . . . everything," she answered.

"Everything," he echoed, locking her gaze into his own. "Maybe our friendship in the past somehow helped prepare us for the—"

She gasped when he stopped, because they both realized what he was saying.

"That is so bizarre," he said. "Really."

"I know; I can't believe that fortune cookie was right."

They both laughed.

She hated the thought of him leaving, but she knew he had to go. "I'd better go in. You have a long drive."

"Yeah, I'd better get going. So I'll see you in nine days and four hours."

"The longest nine days and four hours of my life," she said.

"Mine too."

They parted with a final kiss.

"Thanks for everything," she said. "The plane ride was unforgettable."

"You're welcome."

She opened the door and mentally forced her legs to move out of the car.

"Bye, Jace."

"Bye, Lauryn. I'll see you in nine days, three hours, and fifty-eight minutes."

She laughed and closed the door.

As Jace drove away, Lauryn felt as if she'd left part of her heart sitting in his passenger seat. She knew she wouldn't feel that wonderful wholeness until they were together again.

Chapter Seventeen

"Lauryn, do you think I'll need a swimsuit?" Logan stood in Lauryn's doorway with a bathing suit dangling from her hand.

"I kind of doubt it, but you might as well take one." Lauryn tucked her blow-dryer and round brush into her carry-on bag.

"Okay. I just have to throw this in my suitcase and I'll be ready to go."

"I'll meet you downstairs," Lauryn told her. Her phone beeped, indicating an incoming text. It was Jace with the hourly update. The messages had started at six A.M. and had been regular, on the hour. Sometimes there was a short note, but usually just the countdown. It always made her smile and gave her a warm feeling inside.

She was nearly packed when her phone rang. It was Andrea.

"Are you still in St. George?"

"I'm just getting ready to fly home. I'm taking my stepsister, Logan, with me."

"That sounds fun. Has she ever been to New York?"

"Nope, this is her first time. What's up?"

"Oh, I'm at the airport. I'm on my way to San Diego for a fitness convention. I was just thinking about you. Are you doing okay?" There was concern in her voice.

"I'm great, why?"

"Well, you know, after the whole Jace thing, so soon after breaking up with your boyfriend. I just wondered how you're holding up."

Lauryn realized that she'd been so busy with Jace and so preoccupied with her mom and Logan that she hadn't called any of her friends to update them. They were going to freak!

"Actually, Andie, I'm holding up really well. Hang on," she said while she lifted her suitcase off the bed and plopped it onto the floor. "I haven't told anyone yet, but Jace showed up."

"What?!" Andrea shrieked. "You saw Jace?"

"Not only did I see Jace, but we've spent every possible moment together the last day and a half, and he's coming to Manhattan next week to visit."

Andrea screamed into the phone. She was indeed "freaking out."

"Andie, calm down! The people in the airport are going to think you're nuts."

"This is so cool! Oh, my gosh. How come you didn't call us? I can't wait to tell Emma, Jocelyn, and Chloe. They won't believe it."

Lauryn laughed and pulled up the handle of her rolling suitcase so she could wheel it down the hallway to the stairs. "I know. I've been meaning to call, but Jace left last night, and I've been busy with family stuff."

"How is he?"

"Well," she paused, "he is absolutely incredible."

"No way!"

"I'm not kidding."

"What does he look like? He was kinda cute in high school."

"He's very good-looking, very classy, businesslike, but still kind of outdoorsy too."

"And?"

"And we had a wonderful, amazing time together."

"And?"

"And what?"

"And . . . did he kiss you?"

"Andrea!"

"I knew it. You and Jace kissed. That just seems so weird, yet so cool!

Lauryn rolled her eyes at how juvenile this all seemed; yet inside, she felt the same way.

"I don't even believe this," Andrea continued. "Here we've all thought he didn't show up and you're at your dad's house being sad and lonely. Instead you've been having the time of your life with Jace Reynolds. This is crazy!"

"It is. But it's the best kind of crazy there is." She glanced at her watch. "Andrea, I gotta go so we can get to the airport on time. Can I call you back?"

"You'd better! In the meantime I'm going to make a few phone calls of my own. We may have to have a conference call tonight so you can fill us all in on the details."

"We'll do it."

"Okay, I'll let you go. Call me!"

Lauryn hung up the phone and shook her head. She anticipated a call from each of her friends before the night was over.

At the bottom of the stairs, Logan stood by her suitcase and carry-on with an excited look on her face. "I'm ready!"

With hope that the next two weeks wouldn't be overwhelming and praying for extra help from above so she could handle all of it, Lauryn smiled at Logan and said, "Great, then let's go. Where's the family?"

"Sutton's eating breakfast, and Mom and Dad are here somewhere," she said, then she yelled, "Mom! Dad! We gotta go."

The chair legs at the kitchen table scraped across the floor as Sutton left his bowl of cereal to come and tell them good-bye. He'd already voiced his opinion about how unfair it was that his sister got to go to Manhattan with Lauryn, but he was promised a trip by himself sometime, too.

"Don't have too much fun without me," Logan told her brother as he gave her a halfhearted hug.

"Yeah, well, don't hurry home," he said.

"Are you guys leaving?" Cassie said as she joined them. She'd gotten showered and dressed after her morning workout. Lauryn liked how she took care of herself and stayed in good condition.

"Honey, it's time to go," Cassie called out to her husband.

"Already?" he exclaimed as he came in from his office. He looked at his watch, "I didn't realize it was so late. Let's get your bags loaded."

"Now, Logan, don't stay on the phone all day with Brody, and try to be good for Lauryn and pick up after yourself, and make sure you—"

"Okay, Mom, I got it. You already told me all this."

"You two have fun," Cassie said, giving her daughter one last hug. Then she turned to Lauryn. "Thank you," she said as she hugged her.

Lauryn knew there was much more to those two words than she was saying. They were depending on her to give Logan an experience that would make a difference in her life and hopefully show her that there was so much more she could do with her future than settle for marrying Brody at eighteen.

Moments later they were on their way to the airport. Much of the morning traffic was gone by then, so they didn't have to worry about getting there on time.

"I've e-mailed some pictures to your mother so she'll settle down for now, and I will mail her the prints later today," Lauryn's dad said as he drove.

Lauryn appreciated her dad's help with her mother's request. Since she had no childhood photo albums at her apartment, she couldn't really help her mom.

"She's probably already forgotten about the phone call, but I'll send them just in case," he said.

"Thanks, Dad. She probably doesn't remember, but she was so upset when she called."

"I'm sure she's doing a lot of soul-searching right now," her father said. "She may not be so happy with the discoveries she's making."

Lauryn and her father had talked at length about the choices her mother had made and about her priorities. They both knew they hadn't been at the top of her list.

"Oh, look," Logan said. "There's the garage where Brody works." She pointed to a grungy building surrounded by parked cars, stacks of old tires, and rusted car parts.

"So how was it telling Brody good-bye?" Lauryn asked Logan.

Logan rolled her eyes. "He made me kind of mad. He was trying to be cool in front of his friends, so he wouldn't even give me a hug. It was stupid. He said he would try and call if they weren't too busy."

"You don't sound happy about it."

"It's just that he wants me to be there for him whenever he snaps his fingers, but if it's not convenient for him, he won't even bother being there for me."

Lauryn held her tongue and caught a knowing glance from her father. Logan was finding out what her boyfriend was really like on her own. That was the best way—for her to see it for herself.

"What did he say about you going to New York?"

"That was the best part. I could tell it totally bothered him. He was like, 'What do you need to go there for? Don't you need to be looking for a job?' I couldn't believe it. He can go have fun with his friends, but I can't go to New York with my sister? Whatever!"

"I'm glad it worked out so you can come. I'm going to be crazy busy for the next few weeks, but I promise to make your trip memorable."

"It's okay if you're busy," Logan answered. "Just being in New York is going to be so way cool."

They arrived at the airport with a few minutes to spare. Lauryn's father got their luggage out of the trunk of the car and walked them to the ticket counter. After they checked their bags and got their boarding passes, they took a minute to say good-bye.

Lauryn got the first hug from her dad. "It's been so great to see you, Dad. You need to come to New York soon to visit me."

"You're right. We do. I'll talk to Cassie and see when we can plan a trip."

"Thanks for letting me borrow your car while I was in town."

"No problem, sweetie. Come as often as you can. We love having you."

Lauryn gave her dad a kiss on the cheek.

Logan was next to hug her father. "Thanks for letting me go with Lauryn," she said. "I promise I'll look for a job when I get back."

"We'll keep an eye out for you," he told her.

"But nothing in fast food or a grocery store. Maybe a job at the mall or something," Logan suggested.

Logan's phone buzzed. She grabbed her phone from her back pocket and checked her message. "Brody!" she announced. "I should just ignore it."

To no one's surprise, she read the message immediately.

"Oh, that's so sweet," she gushed. "He feels badly about how we said good-bye. He misses me."

She immediately punched in a reply, and Lauryn and her dad exchanged glances. They didn't need to talk; both had the same thought: somehow they needed to get Brody out of Logan's life.

* * *

Logan slept most of the flight. Lauryn missed Jace's hourly countdown. He knew exactly how to appeal to the romantic in her. But there was something inside her that prompted her to be cautious. She'd been in enough bad relationships to know that some men could get her so caught up in romance that she forgot to be sensible and notice the warning signs that were screaming at her to slow down. Jace seemed so amazing and wonderful. But could anyone be that perfect? Something had to be wrong. She just didn't know about it, yet. Just like Chloe's husband, Roger. He'd seemed perfect. Now look at what they were going through.

Was she just feeling these doubts because she was away from Jace? Or was being away from him helping her to think more clearly?

Lauryn pushed the thoughts out of her head. She gave herself permission to enjoy it for now. She'd deal with reality later. It felt so good to be valued and to feel special. That's how Jace made her feel, and it was too hard not to enjoy, even if only for a moment, especially after what Michael had done to her.

With Logan snoozing on one side of her and the woman on the other side of her also asleep, Lauryn pulled out her notebook and began to sketch some ideas she had for dresses and fabric, inspired by her weekend. People would laugh if they knew where some of her inspiration came from. For example, while her friends had chatted away during their lunch at Durango's a few days ago, Lauryn had focused in on the ruffled edge of a cabbage leaf mixed in to her grilled chicken salad. Now, she used her pencil to transform that cabbage leaf into a crinkly, gauzy-weight fabric with a ruffled edge—a flared skirt cinched at the waist with a wide, shirred band, then a simple bodice using the same cabbage-leaf edge for a sleeve gave the tea-length dress a lightweight airiness to it. She wanted color, bright and bold. Last season the pallet was neutrals: tan, beige, cream, butter yellow. Those colors were fine for day wear and career separates, but for evening wear, prom night, or other formal occasions, she wanted rich, jewel tones or vivid colors.

Recently, the trend in evening wear had taken on the look of lingerie, something that didn't belong on the street or at a dance or party. The gowns were sleek and flowing, but they did little to cover the full-figured woman, and they looked dull and shapeless on younger or thinner girls.

Always influenced by the style and pizzazz of fifties glamour gowns, Lauryn used images of Grace Kelly elegance and Doris Day charm in her designs. These women managed to look sophisticated and beautiful without resorting to showing too much skin or dressing like a trollop. If a woman had to use double-sided tape to keep a body part covered up, it wasn't appropriate. Lauryn wanted women to feel comfortable and confident in their clothes. She didn't want them to have to be afraid to bend over or take a deep breath for fear of the dress shifting or sliding.

"Wow, that's beautiful. I love it," Logan said as she stretched her arms overhead.

"Thanks. I had some ideas pop into my head so I thought I'd sketch them before I forgot."

"You've always done that, haven't you?"

"Sketched ideas? Yeah, I guess. You never know when inspiration is going to strike. The smallest thing can give me an idea. I've learned to act on it when I get it, because I usually can't get it back," Lauryn explained.

"I know just the hairstyle for that dress," Logan said, pointing to the tea-length gown.

"Here. Show me your idea." Lauryn handed her the pencil and notebook.

Logan sketched an updated version of a French twist. It was rough, but Lauryn got the idea.

"I love that," she told Logan. "Very elegant."

"That might be too much if a girl wore this to a high school dance, so she could do this." She drew the hair hanging straight and full, with teasing at the crown to add lift and height. "Then a strip of the same fabric, tied around her head, like a headband."

"Cute!" Lauryn exclaimed. "I love that."

"If that isn't Audrey Hepburn, I don't know what is," Logan said.

"You like Audrey Hepburn?" Lauryn asked.

"Are you kidding? Have you seen her in *Funny Face*?"

"I love her in that show. When she's walking down the steps in that red dress—"

Logan cut in. "And she's saying 'take the picture, take the picture.' I love that. I want to be her. Oh, and the black dress when she's holding the balloons in front of the Louvre. Those are the clothes I want to wear," Logan told her. "Feminine and fashionable."

"How would Brody like you in a dress like this?" Lauryn asked, showing her the sketch of another design, this one a long, flowing evening gown with an amazing bodice more structured than most of her designs, but one that would slenderize and shape any woman's figure. Shirred bands of fabric wrapped and crisscrossed from the cap sleeves at the shoulder to the hip. Then the skirt, made of yards of silk, hung in a narrow column that would lift and flutter when the person walked.

It was a masterpiece, if she did say so herself.

"Wow, Lauryn. That is the most gorgeous dress I've ever seen. Of course, Brody always says I look like a grandma when I wear clothes that cover me like that. But I think that dress would look fantastic. What do you think about making the neckline a sweetheart instead of just rounded?" Logan suggested.

"Like this?" Lauryn erased the round line and added a sweetheart line.

"That's it. Oh, my gosh, Lauryn, that dress is incredible!" Logan exclaimed.

"I can see this in a bronze, shimmery fabric, or deep purple."

"The purple would be so awesome!"

Lauryn added a few finishing touches and looked at the sketch with approval. This dress would take her into the big leagues.

"You put a sleeve on every dress, don't you," Logan observed.

"I have some dresses with just a little cap sleeve, like this one. That's about as close to sleeveless as I get. I just don't want to go there. It's my signature, you know? I want to build a reputation for designing clothes any woman would be comfortable in. I'm not about to sacrifice style or fashion, but I don't really have to. I've never felt like sleeves held me back from my designs. Just like pants have two legs in them, or a shirt has a neck hole, you know?"

"Do people say anything about all your clothes having sleeves?"

"Are you kidding? I get comments all the time, most of them negative. I've had some designers be outright rude to me about it. They tell me that because I'm not willing to bend my standards, I'll never have broad enough appeal to make it big. In fact, I think that's one reason my old boss, Jacqueline Yvonne, never promoted me to assistant designer. She knew I would design to my standards, not hers. That's why she stuck me in outerwear. You rarely see a sleeveless coat, right?"

Logan laughed.

"But I can't go against who I am and what I believe. If I want Heavenly Father to bless me, then I'd better be doing what I'm supposed to, don't you think?"

"Yeah, I guess so. I don't really understand why it's that big of a deal though. The women wearing your clothes don't have the same standards as you do," Logan countered.

"True, but I also have a theory that not all women in the United States are built like runway models, and so they can't wear a lot of the popular styles anyway. I'm not designing for the too-thin, too-rich crowd. I'm designing for the everyday woman who wants to look fabulous for that special occasion, and for young girls who shouldn't be dressing like runway models in the first place!"

"Excuse me." The woman next to Lauryn sat up and rotated in her seat so she could see the drawing. "May I look at that?"

"Uh, sure," Lauryn said, handing the notebook to the woman.

The woman slid her sunglasses down her nose and peered closely at the drawing. She'd worn the glasses the entire flight, even sleeping in them. She also had on a Mets baseball cap and was wearing a sweat jacket and jeans.

"How would that dress look in emerald green?"

Lauryn noticed the woman had thick red hair pulled back in a long ponytail. "I love jewel tones. Emerald would be fantastic."

"You designed this dress?"

"Yes."

"Is this a hobby, or is it your profession?"

"It's always been a hobby; I just happen to get paid for it now. I work for Laszlo Molnar."

The woman's expression turned to one of distaste. "His ego far outweighs his talent, in my opinion."

Lauryn didn't know what to say. She was well aware of his ego, that was for sure.

"I asked him to design a dress for me for a red-carpet event, and the gown was the most hideous thing I'd ever seen. First of all, it wasn't right for my body, and second, there was nothing to it. I might as well have worn my slip."

Lauryn took a closer look at the woman after hearing the words "red carpet" and realized this was a woman she'd seen in a recent movie. She just couldn't remember the woman's name.

"Now, something like this, with structure and style; that would work for me. I mean, let's face it, girls," she said to them, removing her glasses completely, "like you were just saying, I'm one of those women who wasn't born with the body of a runway model. That doesn't mean I don't like to look good, though."

"Weren't you in a movie called *The Broken Soul?*" Lauryn asked.

"I was," she said with a smile.

"You were amazing! Except, I'm sorry, I can't remember your name." Lauryn hated to admit this fact.

"Vanessa Cates," the woman said, extending her hand, which Lauryn shook.

"It's so wonderful to meet you, Ms. Cates," Lauryn said. "I'm Lauryn Alexander, and this is my stepsister, Logan."

"I thought you looked familiar," Logan said to Ms. Cates.

"Oh, sweetie, I try not to when I travel. It's so nice to be able to just sit and relax and not be bothered." Then she held up the sketch. "Now back to this dress. Where can I look at it? I've got a premiere coming up and I need something fantastic to wear. I love this dress. It would totally hide my rear end and make my top look smaller. Ever since junior high, I've dressed to minimize my chest. I got so tired of the comments from boys. I'm still a little testy about it."

"I know what you're talking about. I had that same problem. That's why I decided to go to design school. My clothes are for the everyday woman."

Vanessa smiled. "Finally."

"If you're serious about this dress, I could come up with a sample for you to try," Lauryn said.

"I'm very serious, enough that I'll overlook the fact that you work for Laszlo. But I want this dress to have your design name on it. Not his. I won't wear it if he gets credit for it."

"Of course not. This will be a Lauryn Alexander original."

Vanessa borrowed Lauryn's pencil and wrote down several phone numbers. She pointed to one. "This is my personal cell phone, which I only give out to certain people. You can always reach me at this number. Call me when you want me to come for a fitting. I'll be in town for the next few weeks."

"How about this weekend?" Lauryn said, hoping she could pull it off that quickly.

"You name the time and I'll be there. *Stones of Blood* is an important movie for me. I want to make a lasting impression at this premiere."

"What's the movie about?" Logan asked.

"I play a photojournalist in Sierra Leone doing a documentary on the blood diamond conflict. I get captured by rebel soldiers. It's very gritty and was probably my most difficult movie to make yet—very physical."

"Wait a minute. I read something about this movie in a magazine. The critics are saying you will definitely be nominated for an Oscar."

"That's what they're saying, but you never know," Vanessa said.

"I have to tell you, Ms. Cates—"

"Please, call me Vanessa."

Lauryn swallowed, a little overwhelmed at who she was talking to. "I just want you to know that I admire your work. That magazine article I was reading recently really impressed me. You seem to play by your own rules, not by Hollywood rules."

"I won't lie to you. My line of work is filled with all sorts of filth and scum. I recognized it right off the bat and made a goal to not sink into that sort of thing. My parents taught me values that aren't appreciated by Hollywood: I don't smoke, I rarely drink, and I don't sleep around. But one thing Hollywood does understand is talent and box office draw. I've made some good choices in my first few films that have put me in a position where I don't get offered the garbage that other actresses get. I'll never be cast as the femme fatale, because I don't have the body or the look, which was difficult for me growing up, but now it's something I view as a blessing. I'm recognized for my talent and my acting abilities, not my body or my love life. I don't give the paparazzi much to write about."

"That's awesome," Logan said.

Vanessa held up the dress sketch and said, "Just like your dress, Lauryn. I would never have guessed you design for Laszlo Molnar. Your designs have class, distinction, and sophistication. I would much rather be seen in your dress than one of his pathetic frocks any day."

"I get a lot of criticism for the type of dresses I design, but it's just like I was telling Logan. I would rather have a man look at me because of what I'm wearing, than because of what I'm *not* wearing."

"Exactly!" Vanessa exclaimed. "Well put, Lauryn. Listen to her," she said to Logan. "This woman knows what she's talking about."

Logan nodded her agreement. Then she said, "In our high school, we have a bench in the main hall where guys sit and rate girls as they walk by. They actually make number cards and hold them up."

"No, they don't!" Vanessa was appalled.

"They do. They even have negative numbers."

"That's exactly what I'm talking about! I know how those girls feel, because I had to put up with that garbage growing up. Why doesn't the administration stop them?"

Logan shrugged. "They probably don't know about it, or care. I don't know. I avoided that hall all year. I walked halfway around the building to get to some of my classes."

"I'd love to give those boys a piece of my mind," Vanessa said. "Don't you let them get to you. You are a beautiful, talented girl. You don't need some boy to validate who you are. No girl does."

Lauryn wanted to high-five Vanessa.

"My success came from being true to myself. Oh dear, excuse me." Vanessa reached into the pocket of her sweat jacket and pulled out a Blackberry.

Lauryn and Logan leaned in toward each other. "Can you believe we're sitting here talking to Vanessa Cates?" Lauryn whispered.

"And she wants you to design a dress for her!" Logan added.

"I know. This is amazing." Lauryn wasn't normally a fan of flying, but she'd met two outstanding women on planes. She definitely needed to fly more.

"Whoa!" Logan exclaimed as something out the window caught her eye. "Is that the city? It's so huge!"

Lauryn remembered how excited she'd been the first time she'd come to Manhattan. Nothing could have prepared her for the experience. The shows, the food, the people, the shopping—it was all so overwhelming. Living here was certainly a lot different than visiting here, and it had taken a lot of getting used to, especially for someone who had grown up in a small, southern Utah town. She had felt claustrophobic at first, but now she found herself entranced by the constant beat of the city.

"First time here?" Vanessa asked. She tucked her Blackberry into her pocket again.

"Yes, I'm so excited," Logan answered. "We're going to some shows, and we're going shopping and sightseeing."

"You know my favorite place to shop?" Vanessa said.

Lauryn was certain they couldn't afford to shop where Vanessa Cates shopped.

"My favorite store is Century 21, across from the World Trade Center Memorial."

"I've been there," Lauryn said. "Brand names, great prices."

"It's a madhouse most of the time, but I've never been disappointed," Vanessa said. "When I first started in this business, I needed to dress the part even if I couldn't afford the dresses. But now, even though I can afford to shop at nicer stores, I'm still a bargain lover, and I like to choose my own clothes."

The flight attendant's voice came on the loudspeaker and reminded the passengers to stay seated and keep their seat belts fastened. Within moments the wheels touched down on the runway.

Vanessa slid her glasses on and pulled her baseball cap down low on her forehead. No one would know it was her, especially dressed as casually as she was.

"Is there any way we can do the measurements on Saturday?" Vanessa asked.

"Sure," Lauryn answered. "Whatever works best for you."

"Great, I'll see you two on Saturday around ten."

"Here's my number in case you need to call." Lauryn gave her business card to Vanessa. "This is my old business card, but it has my new information on it."

"You used to work for Jacqueline Yvonne?" Vanessa asked.

"Until about two weeks ago."

"She's a wonderful woman—a great designer and a good person, too. I've actually worn a couple of her designs to some events—of course, none of her originals, just off-the-rack gowns. At the time, I couldn't afford anything else."

"It was hard to leave her company. She gave me my first chance in the business, but I was stuck designing outerwear. My real love is evening wear."

"I can see that," Vanessa said.

It was their turn to file into the aisle and leave the plane. The three women walked together until Logan requested a pit stop at the ladies' room.

"I guess this is where we say good-bye then," Vanessa said.

Lauryn reached out to shake her hand, but to her surprise, Vanessa gave her a hug instead. "I'm so glad we met."

"So am I. I'll do my best to make the dress work for you."

"I know you will," Vanessa said. "And you, Logan, have a wonderful time in New York." She gave Logan a hug before she disappeared into a crowd of passengers headed for baggage claim.

Chapter Eighteen

Getting through the airport to baggage claim was like trying to go the wrong way on a crowded escalator. They'd take a few steps forward, then be pushed back even farther. The airport was packed with outgoing and incoming flights. Lauryn held on to Logan's hand as they forged their way to get their luggage then finally get outside where they could wait on the curb for a taxi.

Lauryn laughed when she saw Logan's wide-eyed, mouth-hanging-open expression.

"Hey, are you okay?"

"That was crazy!" Logan said.

"It can be. We arrived at a busy time." Lauryn held up her hand and hailed a taxi. The driver pulled up in front of them, then he got out and threw their suitcases into the trunk while they climbed into the back. Lauryn gave him the address, and he swerved into traffic and sped off, trailed by several honks and a few shouts from other drivers.

The driver steered the car in and out of traffic, generously using his horn and hand gestures to negotiate the roads.

Logan barely spoke as she watched the view of high-rise apartment buildings, iron-gated homes, and high-fenced school grounds. "Do you ever feel claustrophobic?" she asked.

"Actually, I did at first. It took some getting used to, not seeing the sky or anything but buildings. I went to the top of the Empire State Building a lot when I first moved to the city so I could have a clear view instead of just looking at the high-rise across the street."

By the time they got into Manhattan, the sky was dark, but it was hard to tell, because the city lights lit up the sky like noonday. Logan's face was glued to the window. She said "wow" about every five minutes at billboards for Broadway shows and ads for stores she'd only dreamed of shopping at.

The driver honked and changed lanes and attacked the traffic with all the aggressiveness of a bargain shopper at Walmart the day after Christmas.

Both Lauryn and Logan heaved a sigh of relief when they finally stopped in front of Lauryn's apartment building.

"I can see why you don't own a car," Logan said.

"It's amazing they don't have more accidents, isn't it?" Lauryn asked her as they gathered their purses and carry-on bags.

They joined the man with their luggage on the sidewalk. Lauryn handed him some cash, and the man was off with a blast of his horn to get back into the flow of traffic.

Logan just shook her head and followed Lauryn up the front stairs to the entrance of the apartment building.

"We're on the sixth floor," Lauryn told her. "Just pray the elevator works. Last week Mrs. Pederson got stuck inside for about ten minutes. She was crying and screaming for help. A few of us stayed by the elevator door, trying to talk to her and calm her down. As soon as they fixed the elevator, she got out, and boy was she mad because she'd gotten stuck in the first place. Didn't even say thanks or anything."

Just as Lauryn had predicted, the elevator didn't work.

"You'd think for as much as these apartments cost each month, the elevator would work more than once a week. I don't use it unless I have a lot to carry up the stairs."

"Like now?"

"Yeah," Lauryn said with a laugh and a grunt as she picked up her suitcase. "Like now."

They struggled and dragged the bags until they finally arrived at the landing on the sixth floor.

"Living here is just too much work," Logan said. "I'm spoiled back home. I like being able to drive my car up to the front door and unload my stuff right there."

"You get used to it," Lauryn said as she pulled out her keys again. She undid three different locks before the door finally swung open.

She flipped on a light, and they both stepped inside.

Logan turned around to get a full view of the living room/ kitchen/dining room. "This is great!"

"Thanks. I just did a little redecorating. The girl I'm subletting from let me deduct it from my rent because she's wanted to redecorate but never has time, nor does she really know what to do, so she just let me do it for her." Lauryn closed the door. "You can put your suitcase in the bedroom. I have a love seat in there that folds out to a bed. That's where you'll sleep."

While Logan got settled, Lauryn checked her messages. Most of her close friends called her cell phone, but there was still a backlog on her machine.

The first message was from Sister Watson, just making sure everything was set for the fashion show and offering to help in any way she could, which reminded Lauryn she needed to call Cooper. He'd left a couple of messages on her phone to call him. One sounded urgent.

The next few calls were sales calls. She deleted the messages before they were even finished.

The final call caught her off guard.

"Lauryn, this is Sasha. You have a seven-thirty meeting Thursday morning with Mr. Molnar. He expects a full report on your progress. I wouldn't disappoint him."

The call ended with a click of the phone.

"Don't worry. I won't," Lauryn answered to herself. Other than an Arctic cold front in January, nothing was as icy as the tone of Sasha's voice. Lauryn couldn't figure out why Sasha held her in such contempt.

"Who was that?" Logan asked as she joined Lauryn in the kitchen. She'd changed into pajama pants and a T-shirt.

"A woman from work. She's Laszlo Molnar's assistant."

"She sounds like a real witch."

"And I'm her Dorothy. She's out to get me, and I don't know exactly why."

"Are you ready for the meeting she was talking about?"

Lauryn shrugged. "I don't know what Mr. Molnar is expecting me to report. He knows where I'm at with my clothing line. He's seen all the sketches."

"Not the ones you did on the plane," Logan reminded her.

"Oh, you're right. I want to add the cocktail dress to my collection, but not the dress I'm doing for Vanessa." Vanessa's dress was certainly one of her most brilliant ideas. She could do a version of the dress with a few minor changes, so it wasn't exactly like Vanessa's. "Logan, do you mind if I take some time and sketch these out? I would like to have them to take in the morning. Which reminds me, what are you going to do all morning?"

"Are you kidding? I plan on sleeping until noon. Then I'll get some lunch, watch TV, and hang out until you get home."

"Don't forget, we have the fashion show tomorrow night."

"I know. I'm excited."

"Which reminds me, I've got to call Cooper. Last I talked to him everything was under control, but he left an urgent message. If you're hungry, help yourself. I'm not sure what I've got to eat. There's cereal, but I don't think I have milk. And there's some frozen stuff."

"I am a little hungry," Logan replied. Just then a faint beep came from her cell phone in the bedroom. She bolted from the room, nearly knocking over the end table and lamp in the process, but Lauryn was quick to rescue them.

Brody!

It was possible that Brody was a decent guy. Lauryn certainly didn't want to judge him, but she agreed with her father and Cassie that the situation wasn't right for Logan, especially with her being only sixteen, and especially if Brody wasn't active in the Church.

Lauryn sat at her desk and rubbed her temples. A headache was beginning to form. How was she going to help Logan wake up and take a good look at Brody and her life and set her goals a little higher—actually, a lot higher. She had big plans for Logan while she was here, but at the moment it seemed like everyone was counting on her to work miracles . . . with Logan, with the fashion show, and at Molnar's. She couldn't work miracles, but she could take things one step at a time. And before she did anything, she needed to call Cooper.

Speed-dialing his number, she stood up and paced anxiously while the phone rang.

"It's about time you called!" he scolded right off the bat.

"I'm sorry. I noticed you called, and I meant to call back. I just kind of forgot."

"Oh, thanks. That makes me feel good."

"I'm sorry," she apologized again. "It's been so hectic, bringing my stepsister home with me and everything. Anyway, your message sounded urgent. What's up?"

"Oh, my message sounded urgent? That's because it *was* urgent! You are never going to believe what happened."

"Is it the fashion show? Do we have a crisis? I can't handle a crisis right now, Cooper."

"It's not the fashion show, honey. Don't worry about that. In fact, this fashion show is going to put both of our names on the map. And our dance, girl, you should see our little Rita. She's like a new woman."

Lauryn was relieved to hear that everything was going well. Cooper's creative juices had become a tsunami of ideas. He loved being needed and having a chance to show off his talents. This fashion show was perfect for him.

"So, what's all the urgency about?"

"I hope you're sitting, because if you aren't you'll be flat on the floor when I tell you this."

"What?"

"First, have you heard from Jacqueline Yvonne?"

"You mean has she called me? No, why?"

"Because she fired Diondra on Monday."

"Whoa!" A whoosh of air escaped her lungs. "I can't believe it. Why?"

"Diondra was caught leaking some top-secret information to another designer, and Jacqueline gave her the boot, just like that. Jacqueline still hasn't found out who was receiving the information, but she's got someone working on it for her. And get this: she wants you back!"

"She does? Yes! This is great. No, wait. This is terrible. What about Molnar? I just started there."

"Molnar? Tell the dude to step off. You don't like it there anyway."

"There's no way I can quit now. Molnar would drag my name through the mud if I did. He's too powerful. He'd find a way to ruin my chances of success."

"True. He's vicious and vindictive."

"I'm learning that firsthand. But I'm up for the challenge. Besides, I have a secret weapon."

"Ooh, you little devil. Do tell!"

"Does the name Vanessa Cates mean anything to you?"

"I love Vanessa Cates! She's done some great independent films, but she's got a big film coming out soon that is supposed to be considered for best picture at the Oscars. Not to mention a best actress nomination for her."

"Well," Lauryn paused for dramatic effect, "we met her on the plane from Salt Lake City."

"Shut the front door!"

"That's not even the best part. She noticed a dress I was sketching, and . . ."

"And what? My goodness, Lauryn, will you spit it out already! You are killing me!"

"She wants to wear my design to the premiere of her new movie."

"Are you for real?" Cooper exclaimed. "Oh, my goodness, I think I'm going to faint."

"Don't faint. I need your help. She's coming over Saturday so I can measure her and show her some fabric swatches. I'll need your help with the sample."

"You're going to let me help? I get to meet Vanessa Cates? I'm getting light-headed. Oh my goodness, this is too much."

"Stop talking then and breathe, Cooper. Keep your head together. This could be the big break I've been waiting for."

He didn't reply.

"Cooper, are you there?"

"I'm breathing."

"Okay, you breathe. I'm going to bed. I'm exhausted."

"How can you sleep? I'm never going to get to sleep tonight. This is better than Christmas! Laszlo Molnar is going to crawl on his knees and beg you to stay after Vanessa debuts your dress on the red carpet."

"Yes, well, the way things are with Molnar, I don't see me staying there. But I have to stick it out until after the show. It wouldn't make sense to pull out now. I need to talk to Jacqueline to find out how to handle this. And by the way, Cooper, Vanessa could use a really great pair of shoes and a clutch bag to go with the dress." Lauryn waited for the explosion of excitement.

She didn't have to wait long.

"You are killing me! I'm going to die, right now. Forget fainting—my heart is stopping. I can't handle all of this amazing news. I will design the most fabulous shoes she's ever worn, with a clutch to match. Oh my." He breathed heavily for a moment. "This is unbearable. I'm staying up tonight to work on some designs."

"No you're not, Cooper. Go to bed. I need you to be at your best tomorrow. You've got a big day. You can do the design tomorrow night, after the fashion show is over."

"You're right. The show's going to be dynamite. It really is. And as far as Molnar is concerned, he won't know what hit him."

"That's possible. And if my collection is as brilliant as I want it to be, I'll have even more bargaining power. If Jacqueline wants me, she'll have to be patient. I know this sounds crazy, but I know I made the right decision to work for Molnar."

"All right then. I'm behind you all the way."

"Thanks, Coop, that's what I wanted to hear."

"So I guess I'll see you at the church tomorrow. The girls are coming around five to dress and do hair and makeup. There's no way you can get there at five is there?"

"I'll try, but I won't be later than six. My sister could come and help with hair and makeup, though, if you need it."

"Absolutely! Tell her I'll pick her up on my way. We need all the willing hands we can get tomorrow."

"And you're sure you can emcee, along with everything else?"

"Honey, are you kidding? I thrive on chaos. And with all this good news, I feel like I could conquer the world! Bring it on, baby!"

Lauryn laughed. "Maybe you should do the staging when I show my collection."

"Can I?!"

"I don't see why not, unless Mr. Molnar has his own *people* he wants me to use. I'd rather have you do it. You know me. You know what I like and what would represent me the best."

"After I get some killer shoes and a bag designed for the fab Ms. Cates, I'll draw up some ideas and we'll talk."

Lauryn hung up the phone, completely exhausted. Cooper had the capacity to do the work of ten people. He astounded her, especially that he was so willing to help her. And her payment to him . . . the opportunity to do it! It made absolutely no sense at all.

Lauryn's headache faded as she felt a calming peace come over her—a quiet assurance that everything was going to work out. If she had to explain how the next few weeks would come together, she would be at a loss. But the peace remained, and she felt like a child being guided by an all-knowing parent.

* * *

"What's that?" Logan asked as she munched on a handful of dry Cinnamon Toast Crunch cereal as Lauryn unpacked her suitcase.

Lauryn held up the object and let it glisten in the light. "That, Logan, is the famous Butterfly Box."

Logan's response was a confused expression.

"After my friend Ava died on graduation day, my friends and I got together and created the Butterfly Box. Lauryn explained how they had each contributed to the contents of the box and how they passed it around, taking turns as keeper of the box. "Of course, we know there's no real magical power, just the power that comes from all our faith and prayers, but having the box in my possession reminds me that others are praying for me. That's a very powerful feeling. Just like you should feel knowing how much your parents are praying for you every day."

Logan nodded. "Yeah, I guess so. That box is pretty cool. Can I see what's inside?"

"No!" Lauryn said. "We only open the box when we get together each year. The things inside are very private and special to us."

"What kind of secrets are you guys hiding in that box?"

"It's not like that. You've seen too many movies. It's just stuff that means something only to us, as a group. That's all."

Lauryn pushed her jewelry box aside to make room for the Butterfly Box on top of her dresser. "I'm almost unpacked, then I'll let you get to bed. I'm just going to finish those sketches for my meeting. Are you sure you don't mind helping Cooper tomorrow?"

"Not at all. I can't wait to meet this guy. He sounds completely insane."

"He can be. But his heart is pure gold. I don't know what I'd do without him."

"Why haven't you two ever hooked up?" Logan asked.

"It's not like that between us. He's more like a brother to me. I think you'll like him."

"The show sounds like it's going to be huge."

"With Cooper in charge, it's bound to be." Lauryn closed her suitcase and stored it inside her closet. "There, I'm done. You can go to bed now. Or are you and Brody still texting each other?"

"He responds every once in a while when they aren't doing anything."

"Is he having fun?"

"He says he is. They went to the beach today, and they're going to get something to eat now. I guess his friends met some girls at the beach, so they're hooking up with them."

"That doesn't bother you?"

"No," Logan said with assurance. "I trust him completely."

Lauryn nodded, wondering how honest Brody was being with Logan. She didn't want to suggest he was lying, but how many eighteen-year-old boys sat by and let their friends have all the fun?

"I'm going to go finish those sketches. Holler if you need anything."

Pulling the bedroom door shut behind her, Lauryn went to her desk and pulled out her sketch pad. It bothered her that Logan was so naive, but then again, the girl was only sixteen and hadn't been dating long enough to know how complicated relationships could be. She just hoped Brody wasn't taking advantage of her stepsister.

It took several minutes for her to get her focus. Too many things were whirling through her mind. Mr. Molnar, Vanessa, Logan, and of course, Jace.

Finally, as she managed to shut out the noise in her head and tap into the essence of her ideas, her drawings began to take shape. Unsure of where they came from, she felt new angles and thoughts pop into her head, giving her creations even more elegance and sophistication. Details, draping, lines, and shape all came together.

Sitting back, she took a final look at her work.

"Wow," she said. "That's good."

The dress for Vanessa, in emerald green, with a trim of green and aurora-borealis rhinestones, turned out beautifully. With the waist placed just a fraction of an inch higher, the dress would accent Vanessa's small waistline and create a longer silhouette, giving Vanessa a slimmer appearance and even more height.

The other dresses she would show Mr. Molnar were equally as stunning and some of her best creations. But she was keeping Vanessa's her secret.

Slipping the sketches into her attaché case, she turned out the light and made her way to the bedroom. The faint buzz from her cell phone caught her ear. It continued until she retrieved her phone. Her heartbeat sped up. It was Jace.

"Hey you."

"Oh, hey," he said. "I'm sorry, I didn't expect you to answer. I just wanted to leave a message."

"Should I hang up?" she teased.

"Nah, I'd rather talk to you in person, but I know how late it is there."

"I'm still up. I was working."

"Making up for all that play time?"

"Yeah, 'you play, you pay,'" she said. "I have an early meeting I needed to get ready for."

"I won't keep you then," he said. "I was thinking about you, and I just wanted to tell you that."

"I'm glad I answered then."

"Would it be cheesy to tell you that I already miss you?" he asked.

Lauryn smiled. "You know how much I love cheese," she reminded him.

He laughed.

"I miss you too," she said. "The good thing is, I'm going to be very busy this weekend and all next week, so the time is going to fly."

"I've been looking online for tickets to some of the shows. I'll e-mail you and Logan all the options, and you can let me know which show you want me to take you to."

"Sounds good. That sure is nice of you."

"I want our time together to be unforgettable," he said.

"If it's anything like our last date, it will be."

"All right, beautiful girl, I'd better let you get some sleep."

Lauryn loved the way his voice sounded when he called her that. Her knees felt weak.

"Good night, Jace."

"Good night."

Lauryn hung up the phone and held it in her hand for a moment. Was all of this too good to be true? Was she putting her heart on the line just to get burned again?

Jace's words, *All right, beautiful girl,* echoed in her mind, and she smiled. Whatever lay ahead for her and Jace, any future heartache was worth the complete joy she felt now.

She let herself fall to her knees and say her prayers. She wasn't sure how long she'd been on her knees before she woke up and crawled into bed.

Chapter Nineteen

Well before seven-thirty, Lauryn was in her office organizing her thoughts and her sketches. If Laszlo wanted something fantastic, she was going to give it to him.

She was busy thumbing through fabric swatches when she heard the elevator doors open and a familiar, icy voice break the silence.

Her skin prickled. Sasha.

"I just got here. The place is dark," Sasha said.

Since no one replied, Lauryn figured she was on her cell phone.

"Exactly. I agree with you. Yes, I talked with JL's assistant last night. He'll call you at nine this morning, just before his meeting with Camilla. I guess Prince Charles won't be there, which disappointed JL, but he's thrilled to be meeting with Camilla."

Again, she was quiet.

"I'm not sure what the proper term for her is. I'll give you a call after I meet with Ms. Alexander. That is, if she's here like I told her to be."

Lauryn gritted her teeth. This comment epitomized the cold reception she'd received at Molnar's. Whatever Sasha's problem was, Lauryn was going to figure it out and break through it. She was determined not to let this woman intimidate her.

A moment later, Sasha appeared at her door.

"So, you made it," Sasha said crisply.

"I did," Lauryn said. "I guess I misunderstood the time, I thought you said be here at seven-thirty."

Sasha's eyes narrowed. "Yes, well, Mr. Molnar had more important issues come up. He asked me to meet with you and give him a report."

"Great." Lauryn welcomed the challenge. "Why don't you have a seat and we can get started."

Sasha took a seat across from Lauryn, crossed her legs and her arms, and said, "I'm ready," as if daring Lauryn to impress her.

Lauryn steadied her nerves with a calming breath and deflected Sasha's negative vibes. The woman wasn't going to get to her.

Armed with confidence and preparation, Lauryn began her presentation. She explained the origin of inspiration for several of her gowns, explaining her desire to provide playful and flirty styles, along with glamorous, sophisticated styles. Several of her designs were cocktail dresses that Lauryn knew would be a hit. After seven years in the business at Jacqueline's heels, she'd learned how to anticipate trends in the fashion world. She felt strongly that her designs were the direction styles were heading. She was willing to take risks with her creations, to give her collection a unique quality that would inspire women to want her dresses. She'd had this experience once before during her last year at Parsons, when Barneys of New York bought her entire senior collection.

She felt it inside of her, the creativity, the foresight, the talent. And not even Sasha's disapproving glare and curt comments could take that away from her.

After showing the final sketch, Lauryn finished by saying, "I'm still working out the details on the fabrics for those recent sketches, but I'll have those by the end of the day. We can get to work on the samples as early as this afternoon."

Sasha hadn't moved from her position. She gave Lauryn a level look and said, "That's it?"

"Excuse me?" Lauryn said, unsure if Sasha wondered if she was finished or if that was the best she could do. Lauryn supposed the latter.

"I'll warn you right now, Mr. Molnar was hoping for something a little more spectacular. He's putting a lot of money into this collection. Your styles have a certain amount of elegance in their simplicity, but they lack . . ." she searched for the right word, "pizzazz."

Lauryn paused before responding. She needed to choose her words carefully.

"Mr. Molnar approved most of these drawings last time we met. He never expressed that feeling then."

"Well, you have to understand, he doesn't want to discourage you, but he's quite concerned that perhaps he made the wrong choice."

Lauryn felt her face flush but reminded herself to stay strong.

"These designs seem to lend themselves to something between prom night and a formal event for a matronly woman. I can see why Jacqueline had you in outerwear. Your designs there were actually quite brilliant."

Balling her fists, Lauryn kept her composure. Laszlo had never given her the impression that her designs weren't what he was looking for.

"I'm not sure what you're saying." Lauryn spoke through gritted teeth but fought to maintain a pleasant expression. The only way Sasha won was if she knew she'd gotten to her. She would never give the woman that satisfaction.

"I'll tell you what." Sasha finally uncrossed her arms and legs and walked around the desk to the stack of sketches. She shuffled through them, pulling out a cocktail dress and two evening gowns, neither of them the most stellar of the collection. "Why don't we go ahead and have samples made of these three designs; then we can see if Mr. Molnar even wants to continue."

Lauryn knew what Sasha was doing, and Lauryn wasn't going to let her sabotage everything she'd worked for. It was obvious Sasha was out to bring Lauryn down before she even presented her collection to the public. Lauryn had no idea why Sasha was after her, but she wasn't going to let her win.

With her head held high, Lauryn put her faith in her designs and in Mr. Molnar's prior approval, and then she did one last thing. She pulled one of the drawings that Mr. Molnar had shown great interest in and switched it for one Sasha had in her hands. It was a spectacular dress that would work on nearly any body type, and it was Lauryn's favorite dress in the collection. "I think he would like to see this one first."

Sasha glanced at the sketch. "Fine. I'll get these to the dress-making department right away. They'll have something ready by tomorrow."

Lauryn dipped her chin in agreement, still stunned by Sasha's blatant show of animosity toward her. But she wasn't going to shrink down into a corner. "Great. I'll go down later and check to see how it's coming. I'm sure they'll have plenty of questions. I'm very hands-on with my designs," she informed Sasha. "I plan on being involved in every step of the process."

Sasha avoided eye contact as she took the drawings and left the room.

Lauryn fought hard to keep back the angry tears that threatened. She looked with blurred eyes at the rest of her drawings sprawled upon her desk.

Most designers struggled for years before they made it big, and Lauryn had paid her dues. Counting all her years in school until now, she'd spent ten years learning about the fashion industry. She'd worked in every area of design and knew the process forward and backward. And she knew her designs were good.

Could it be that Sasha had wanted Lauryn's position? It seemed unlikely since she already held an even higher position at Molnar's. Lauryn just couldn't understand why this woman seemed to be waging a personal vendetta against her. Even with all the negative emotion surrounding her, Lauryn still felt the peace of the night before. For all her haughtiness and disapproval, there was some-thing Sasha didn't know. There was a guiding force in Lauryn's life, a source of strength and inspiration that reassured Lauryn all was well. She had put her life in Heavenly Father's hands, and she knew He was capable of making more out of it than she was. If things were supposed to happen with her designs, they would. If things were supposed to happen with Jace, they would.

So she dried her eyes, pushed Sasha's face from her mind, extinguished the feelings of inadequacy Sasha had ignited inside of her, and went back to work. The dress for Vanessa was going to be spectacular. When Laszlo and Sasha saw it, they wouldn't doubt her talent again. She would show them.

* * *

"I'm coming," Lauryn shouted into her cell phone. The noise of the subway made it difficult to hear Cooper's reply. "I just got off the train."

"Well get that booty over here. We need your help."

"I'm hurrying. How's Logan?"

"You didn't tell me what a great makeup artist she is. You should see her in action. She's a pro at getting these girls glammed up. And her ideas for hair . . . you'll just have to see it when you get here. The girls love her."

"How are you?"

"Honey, I am in my element, but I could use your help, so haul those buns to the church. You won't believe it when you see it."

Lauryn's stomach churned with nerves and excitement. She had barely managed to get through the stressful day at work. She'd spent the afternoon helping with the dress samples. For once she had been received with kindness. The three Asian women who worked in that department complimented her on her designs and appreciated her hands-on help. They were used to working with designers who had large egos. For them, Lauryn was a welcome change. And bless their hearts, they were staying late so they could finish cutting out the dresses and start sewing in the morning. By tomorrow afternoon, the samples would be ready.

Half jogging, half speed-walking, Lauryn hustled to the church and arrived breathless and sweating but on time.

"Our fearless leader has arrived," Cooper announced when she walked into the multipurpose-room-turned-dressing-room. The Primary room was designated for hair and makeup.

"Did you take a look yet?" Cooper asked as he paced the hall.

"At the stage? Not yet." She unloaded her purse and bags onto the floor in the corner and greeted the girls who were still in the room changing. "Tiffany," Lauryn said to the young, thin fourteen-year-old. "Wait just a minute. I want to make an adjustment." Tiffany's mother had been a dancer on Broadway, and Tiffany studied ballet, spending summers at workshops with the New York City Ballet.

Grabbing a handful of straight pins, Lauryn made a tuck in the back of the dress that pulled the dress in to better fit Tiffany's tiny frame.

"There," Lauryn said. "It looks great, but if you sit or move too much, you might get poked."

"I'll be careful. Thanks, Sister Alexander."

Cooper smiled. "I'm still not quite used to the brother and sister thing," he said. "A few of the girls called me Brother D'Angelo, and it made me feel geriatric."

"Brother D'Angelo. That has a nice ring to it."

"I sound like a monk. Come on, we've still got a lot to do. Some of the girls haven't even shown up yet. But you've got to see this ramp."

They walked down the hall and paused at the doorway to the cultural hall.

"Shut your eyes," Cooper told her.

Lauryn indulged him and shut her eyes. He then opened the doors and led her inside.

"Okay," he said. "They're just putting on the final touches, but you'll get a good idea of how it's going to look. Open your eyes."

Lauryn slowly opened one eye. Then both eyelids flew open.

"Whoa!" she cried. "I love it!" She turned to Cooper, giving him a giant hug, then rushing to the stage. "This is fantastic!"

A long ramp extended from the stage nearly twenty-five feet, nice and wide so the girls would have room to walk and turn. She'd expected something completely over-the-top, but this was absolutely stunning.

Cooper had incorporated her love for vintage styles in his decorating. Taking his inspiration from the late fifties and early sixties, he'd used aquas and browns with splashes of orange and pink. Clean lines, geometric shapes, and era-inspired furniture decorated the stage. It looked like something out of the Doris Day movie *Pillow Talk*.

The backdrop for the stage had large, blown-up pictures of Audrey Hepburn in *Breakfast at Tiffany's*, Grace Kelly in *Rear Window*, and Doris Day in the appropriate movie *Pillow Talk*, all dressed in clothes that portrayed an era of glamour and elegance.

"Lauryn, darling, there you are!"

Lauryn turned to see Cooper's mother, Doreen, hurrying toward her.

Bending over so she could embrace the tiny, five-foot-one bundle of energy, Lauryn attempted to thank her for all the work she'd done.

"Don't be silly, darling. We haven't had this much excitement around our house since *Cats* opened on Broadway. And these girls— where did you find so many beautiful Young Women? My goodness, I've never seen anything like it."

"Is that Lauryn?" a gruff voice said from behind a panel of electronic switches and cords.

"Hi, Mr. D'Angelo," Lauryn called.

The man came from behind the panel, limping toward her.

"Are you injured?" Lauryn flashed a worried look at Cooper.

"No, no, just a bit of arthritis. My joints aren't like they used to be."

"She doesn't want to hear about your joints, Harry," Mrs. D'Angelo scolded.

"She asked. What am I supposed to do, lie?"

Lauryn gave him a hug. "Thank you for your help. This is so much better than anything I ever could have put together. I don't know how to thank you."

"Are you kidding me?" Harry replied. "We're happy to have something to do with ourselves. Retirement is for old people."

Lauryn laughed.

"Well," Doreen said, "forty-five minutes until showtime. We've got to do a sound check. Are you ready, Cooper?"

"Sure thing, Mama," he said, taking the microphone from his mother.

"I guess I'll go check on the girls. You need any more help in here?" Lauryn asked Harry and Doreen.

"We've got more hands than a clockmaker," Harry replied. "You go do what you need to do. We'll be ready before the doors open."

Lauryn left the cultural hall and found the Primary room, where most of the excitement was. All of the Young Women greeted her with enthusiasm. The level of excitement was enough to launch a space shuttle, and Lauryn immediately felt herself caught up in it. After weeks of planning, preparing, and rehearsing, it was finally time for the show.

She spied Logan in a corner, making barrel rolls in Jazmyn's updo.

"Jazmyn, you look beautiful with your hair up like that," Lauryn said.

The young girl really was stunning. Her olive skin, jet-black hair, and exotic looks were perfect for the leopard-print dress she was wearing.

Leopard-print dress?

"Jazmyn, I thought you were wearing my Jacqueline Yvonne dress."

"Oh, sorry, Sister Alexander, but it's way too big in places, and it's too long."

Lauryn glanced at the clock. Even with duct tape and pins, she didn't know if they had time to alter the dress, and if they did, she was afraid the dress wouldn't look very good.

Disappointed, Lauryn smiled at her. "That's okay; I guess we didn't really need it in the show then. We'd better make sure Cooper knows."

"He knows. He was the one who helped me decide. A few other girls tried it on, but no one is really built right for it."

"Is that your pageant dress you're talking about?" Logan asked Lauryn as she set Jazmyn's hair with a heavy layer of hairspray.

"Yes, it seemed fitting to end the show with the dress that started it all, but I'm sure the show will be fine without it."

"I bet it would fit you, Logan," Jazmyn said, looking at Logan's reflection in the mirror.

"Me? I'm no model. I wouldn't even know what to do if the dress did fit."

"Wait a minute!" Lauryn exclaimed. Jazmyn had a great idea. Logan was taller than Jazmyn, and even though Logan was thin, she was much more developed on top. "Logan, it would mean so much to me if you'd wear it."

"Lauryn, I can't even walk in high heels. And all I brought are my flip-flops."

"That's fine. We have tons of shoes to choose from. We can find something. Logan, would you please try it on, just to see?"

"I'll go get it," Jazmyn said, rushing off to find the dress.

Logan looked at Lauryn with concern. "I don't know how to model. I'm a klutz. I'll probably fall off the stage."

"We have time to show you how to walk. It's not difficult." She reached for Logan's hand, but Logan was reluctant.

"Just give it a try," Lauryn coaxed. "If you don't want to do it, you don't have to. But just try, for me."

"Okay. But if I fall off that stage, you're in big trouble."

"Spoken like a true sister," Lauryn said.

They hurried to the stage, where Cooper was finishing up his sound check.

"Cooper, we need to show Logan the walking pattern. She's going to model the Jacqueline Yvonne dress at the end."

"Ooh, lucky you!" he exclaimed. "There's nothing to it. The pattern is simple; it's the attitude that sells the dress. You have to love wearing it and send that love to the audience, like this." He strolled from stage right and struck a pose in the center of the stage, then he began to walk forward. At the end of the runway he did several turns, cocking his head this way and that, tossing his pretend hair and rolling his shoulders. It was all Lauryn and Logan could do not to laugh. He looked ridiculous, but modeled amazingly well just the same.

"Oh, that I was five inches taller and ten years younger," he exclaimed as he came back to the center of the stage. "Now, Logan, you try it."

Logan rolled her eyes. "I'm not sure about this."

"You're going to be wonderful. Now go!"

Timidly, Logan followed the pattern like Cooper had shown her. She looked stiff and scared.

"Honey, you did great," Cooper encouraged, "but you didn't put any 'tude in it, sweetie. Now, once more, with feeling. Wait! I have an idea." He waved to the control booth. "Yo, Daddy-o, we need some music. Something with attitude."

A moment later the song "Dancing in the Streets" by Martha and The Vandellas started playing.

"That's it!" Cooper exclaimed. "Now, show me your stuff, Logan!"

Logan began walking.

"Loosen up, girl; roll the shoulders. Have fun! Dig that beat." He started singing with the music.

Logan laughed, and immediately her body language reflected the difference. When she wasn't quite so nervous, she let the music dictate her pace and her poses. Playfully, she turned, looked over her shoulder, then flipped her head and walked back.

"Yes! Now you're getting it," Cooper cried, then started singing and dancing across the stage. "There'll be singing, swaying, and record playing, dancin' in the streets!"

Logan returned to center stage and held her pose. Cooper grabbed her and gave her a hug. "That was perfect. Now go get that dress on!"

Excitement replaced fear, and Logan darted off the stage.

"I'll be right there," Lauryn called after her. Then she turned to Cooper. "I don't know how you do it, but you can work miracles!"

"Most people call it being overbearing, but I like what you said better. Now," he said, giving her a playful push off the stage, "You go get the girls ready. Rita and I are going to run through our dance."

"You are amazing, you know that?"

"My parents tell me that every day. I could take out the trash and they'd say it was the most phenomenal thing ever."

"You're lucky to have that kind of support."

"That's true. I never take them for granted." Lauryn was surprised at Cooper's unusually serious tone. "I want to help all of these girls who are having struggles at home. I want them to believe in themselves and who they are. I heard them reciting that pledge at the beginning of a meeting, and I thought, you go girls! If they'd just believe it, they could really rock this world."

"Oh, you mean the Young Women theme?"

"Is that it? Your church teaches some pretty cool stuff."

Just then, Sister da Silva walked up the stairs in costume and literally took Lauryn's breath away.

"But we can talk about that later," Cooper said, with his eyes on Sister da Silva. "I think my partner is ready."

Her costume was a black top with long sleeves and a high neck. Her full, black skirt fell to the middle of her calves. Rows of lime green, hot-pink, and vibrant-orange ruffles were sewn around the bottom of the skirt, the sleeves, and the entire bodice of the shirt. On the colored fabric, rows of sequins in matching colors caught the light and shimmered when she moved.

Her hair was slicked back in a low bun at the back of her head, with a swoop of bangs heavy across her forehead. A glittery clip that matched her costume was fastened near the bun. Her makeup was dramatic and colorful. She looked like a completely different person.

"I'm so glad you changed your mind," Lauryn told her.

Sister da Silva smiled. "Me too. And you should see Cooper's shirt. It matches perfectly."

"Where did you get these costumes?" Lauryn asked.

"You forget, my parents have connections in the theater," Cooper told her. "Just a few phone calls and we were set."

Sister Watson came rushing in. "We have a line at the door. When should we let people in?"

"Five minutes," Cooper said. "We just need to run through our dance." Glancing at his watch with the wide, black leather band and large, square face surrounded in faux diamonds, he said, "Whoa, and I've got to get changed."

"You look magnificent," Sister Watson exclaimed as she took Sister da Silva by the hands. "This is so exciting! I'll go tell the others."

"Good grief, I'd better get to the dressing room," Lauryn said.

She raced from the stage as Latin music blasted from the speakers.

First she checked the multipurpose room, which was littered with clothes. All the girls were gone, which was a good sign. Poking her head into the Primary room, which was a swarm of satin and taffeta, Lauryn nearly choked from hairspray inhalation. She grabbed a handful of pins and made a few little adjustments here and there, but overall, the dresses seemed to fit beautifully.

The other Young Women leaders helped get the girls lined up, and Lauryn began at the front of the line, giving a final inspection. Some girls needed more jewelry; some needed less. Some needed a bit more makeup; others were given a few more adjustments to their hair. Lauryn found herself wanting to make minor changes to some of the dresses but knew that overall the dresses were fine. Besides, most of them weren't even her creations, so she couldn't begin making changes to those dresses just minutes before the show started.

"Girls, girls." Sister Watson got their attention. "The audience is getting seated, and the show will begin shortly. Why don't we take a moment and start with an opening prayer. Sister Alexander, would you mind saying it?"

"Not at all," Lauryn said, grateful for the opportunity. She knew this was the perfect way to calm her nerves.

In her prayer, she expressed thanks for the abundant blessings they had received and especially for the opportunity they had to perform the fashion show. She asked that their purpose would be fulfilled, that the Young Women in the audience would be committed to wearing modest clothing, and that this fashion show would convince them that it was possible to look stunning and modest at the same time.

In unison they closed the prayer with "amen," and the hugs began.

Lauryn stepped back and looked at the Young Women, most of them from her ward, some from neighboring wards, all of them a beautiful reflection of who they were inside and what they believed.

From the other side of the circle, Lauryn watched as Jazmyn whispered something in Logan's ear. Logan smiled back, and Lauryn could tell she said, "Thank you."

Warmth filled Lauryn's chest. No matter which Broadway shows they saw or which famous landmarks they visited, she hoped this Young Women fashion show would be the best memory for Logan.

After the prayer, Sister Watson had slipped out to see if Cooper was ready for the show to start. She came back in the room all aflutter.

"Girls, girls, it's time. We have a packed house. In fact, the Young Men are setting out more chairs so people don't have to stand."

"What are the Young Men doing here?" one of the girls exclaimed. The others chimed in their concern.

"Apparently the Young Men leaders thought it would be helpful for the Young Men to learn about the importance of modesty so they could be more respectful of the Young Women. I'm thrilled they've decided to join us. I think we have close to three hundred people out there."

"Three hundred!" Lauryn exclaimed. Originally the activity had been planned for the Young Women in her ward and their mothers. "We're never going to have enough refreshments."

"Each ward brought something to share. The kitchen is bursting with goodies. We'll be fine. I put Sister Bronson from the stake in charge of getting the refreshments out after the show. She'll make sure we have enough."

From the cultural hall, music began to play, which meant the opening prayer had been given and the show was ready to start.

The girls lined up in the order they'd practiced, the level of excitement hovering near the ceiling.

Lauryn stood at the front of the line and said, "I know some of you didn't want to participate in the fashion show for one reason or another, but look at all of you. I'm so proud of you. Have fun tonight. Don't worry if you turn the wrong way or do something different than you rehearsed. You're perfect just the way you are."

"We're ready," Sister Watson said.

The first girl turned and gave the other girls a smile, then lifted the front of her full skirt and sashayed from the room.

"Sister Alexander," Sister Watson said, "why don't you slip out and go watch the show? I've got things under control back here."

Sister Watson had read her mind. She desperately wanted to go watch the girls on the runway. "Are you sure?"

"My husband is videotaping the whole thing. I can watch it later. Go on!"

Lauryn thanked her and hurried down the hallway to the back doors of the cultural hall and slipped inside.

The cultural hall was dark, the only lights on the stage and runway. The song "My Girl" by the Temptations was playing.

Dressed in a sleek, black tuxedo with a vibrant lime-green vest and tie, Cooper stepped onto the stage. The audience cheered, already in a good mood from the upbeat music and anticipation of the night's events.

Cooper welcomed them and announced the first model as she walked out and struck a pose in the center of the stage.

"Nicole Abrams is wearing a trumpet-cut evening gown with black lace overlay."

Nicole strutted forward, followed by the spotlight controlled by Cooper's father.

Lauryn got chills as Nicole reached the end of the runway, lifted her chin, and made a perfect turn. She flipped her head, looked over her shoulder, flashed a giant smile, then started back up the runway. The crowd cheered.

From that point on, the audience, and Lauryn, were completely captivated.

Girl after girl came onto the stage, some in prom gowns, others in formal tea-length gowns. The ones that had been altered and modified to fit the standards set in the "For the Strength of Youth" pamphlet were described by Cooper so the audience would know that dresses that started out strapless or sleeveless could be modified without taking away from the look of the dress.

Songs from Sonny and Cher, Diana Ross and the Supremes, the Beach Boys, the Beatles, and Smoky Robinson played in the background. The timeless tunes caused even the youth in the audience to clap along.

It was nothing like the runway shows Lauryn had seen during Fashion Week or any other place. It was so much better! She loved the color, the fun, and the upbeat feel.

Finally, Cooper announced the last model. Lauryn held her breath as Logan stepped onto the stage. At first, Logan looked timid and shy, but as she walked down the runway with the crowd clapping and cheering, her body visibly relaxed, and her face showed her delight.

Lauryn wasn't sure why, but seeing Logan in her old pageant dress brought tears to her eyes. To Lauryn the dress symbolized so much: staying true to her standards against opposition, taking a chance and getting out of her comfort zone, and even making her dreams come true. These were the things she wanted for Logan. Maybe the dress would be as lucky for Logan as it had been for her. Lauryn blinked tears away quickly so she could finish watching Logan's turn on the stage.

Thunderous applause followed her exit, and Lauryn joined in.

With twenty-five girls taking turns to model, the show took close to forty-five minutes. And when Logan finished her walk, the crowd cheered for more. Lauryn was relieved that Cooper had planned his performance for the end so the audience could have one last exciting moment.

The lights went dark, and there was shuffling and sliding on stage. Then, without warning, the spotlight switched on, and standing center stage was Rita in a deep lunge, her colorful dress spread out around her with Cooper holding her steady with one hand, his other arm lifted high into the air.

The audience was already so energized and excited they nearly raised the roof with their applause.

Suddenly, the song "Let's Get Loud" by Jennifer Lopez started, and the level of applause died quickly as Cooper and Rita started dancing. Their synchronized footwork and bigger-than-life movements brought the stage to life. Cooper spun Rita in every direction, then at one point, she leapt into his arms and he twirled her around then put her on the floor and she kept twirling. In the next moment she was down in the splits with Cooper kicking his leg over her head, then grabbing her and pulling her back up.

Lauryn's mouth dropped open with amazement. They were astounding!

Using every inch of available space, Cooper and Rita continued the dance, making it difficult not to get up and dance right along with them.

Lauryn didn't know a lot about ballroom technique, but as far as she could tell, they had all the moves and couldn't have been more entertaining had they been professionals.

When the dance ended, the audience jumped to their feet and cheered until Cooper finally put his hand up to get them to calm down.

Cooper went to the microphone. "You are all too kind. I've never seen such an audience. Whoo hoo!" he screamed, and was echoed by the entire crowd. "I love it! I just want to take you all home with me. Now, before we pray, I'd like to ask someone to join me up here."

Lauryn's stomach dropped to her ankles. She tried to step back into the shadows, but someone from her ward spied her and gave her a friendly push toward the stage. Cooper didn't miss the movement and pointed her out so his father could beam the spotlight on her.

Practically blinded, Lauryn stumbled up to the stage, trying to figure out a nice way to wring Cooper's neck, but knowing she owed him the moon for all he'd done to make the night a huge success.

When she got to him he whispered, "Be a good girl and say something nice to the audience," then stepped aside to give her the microphone.

"Well," she said, still not sure what to say, "I want to thank all of you for coming tonight, and for your enthusiasm." There were a few whoops and hollers from the audience. "I also want to thank the Young Women, who were terrific models." That brought a full-on cheer from the crowd. "Also, all the wonderful leaders who pitched in to make this night happen." She joined in the applause. "But none of this could have happened tonight without Cooper D'Angelo and his family." She stepped to the side and pointed at Cooper while the crowd applauded and cheered. "He's worked tire-lessly on the fashion show and on his performance with Sister da Silva. Weren't they incredible?"

The crowd showed their agreement with loud applause.

"Anyway . . ." She wrapped it up. "Thank you for making this night memorable. And I hope you've all learned that modest really is hottest!"

The audience clapped wildly, then quickly stopped when the person giving the prayer approached the microphone.

All heads bowed, and the prayer was said. Then, after a resounding "Amen!" the house lights came on, and there was a mad rush to the refreshments.

"I guess that's all she wrote," Cooper said with disappointment. "It's like the day after Christmas, you know, a letdown."

Lauryn looked at him like he was nuts. "Cooper, this fashion show has consumed you for weeks. How can you say that?"

"I live for the spotlight, I guess."

"Your dance was fabulous! You and Rita were like professionals," she exclaimed.

"Really, you're not just saying that?" He clasped his hands together excitedly.

"You should keep dancing together. You two were amazing."

Sister Watson pushed her way through the crowd and grabbed both of their hands, her face beaming. "Oh, Sister Alexander, Brother D'Angelo, that was just . . . Well, what can I say . . . And that dance . . . Oh, my goodness!" Her words tumbled out, one on top of the other. Moments later, other leaders joined them, along with parents and even youth with requests to make this an annual event. There were also requests for Rita and Cooper to go to the various wards and teach ballroom to the youth.

Lauryn had noticed that Rita was engaged in a conversation with one of the Young Men leaders from another ward, a man Lauryn happened to know was also single. A smile tugged at her lips. Sister da Silva was a quiet woman, never one to draw attention to herself. But suddenly, people were seeing her in a different light.

Cooper had gone to find his parents, and Lauryn anxiously went to find the girls to tell them what a great job they'd done.

As she stepped into the foyer, a woman with a notepad stopped her. The woman looked familiar, but Lauryn couldn't place her. Was she the mom of one of her Young Women? Someone from the stake?

"Ms. Alexander, do you have a moment?"

Lauryn felt her phone vibrate, indicating an incoming message. She was positive it was Jace, wondering how the fashion show went and giving her the countdown, but she'd have to wait to check.

"Uh, yeah, sure."

"I'm Bernice Thomas, from *Women's Fashion Review*."

"That's right! I thought I knew you from somewhere."

Bernice was a powerhouse at the weekly newspaper and had done a feature article for the newspaper last fall when Jacqueline Yvonne had presented her spring line during fashion week. Several of Lauryn's pieces were presented at the show. Bernice had the power to make or break a designer, especially one starting out. For the life of her, Lauryn couldn't figure out what she was doing here.

"I got a call from your friend Cooper telling me about your show. He thought it might make an interesting piece for the paper. And since his parents and my parents are longtime friends and I've known Cooper my whole life, I couldn't turn him down."

"I didn't realize you and Cooper were so close."

"He was like my brother when we were growing up," she said. "And I'm so glad he called. This was quite an event tonight. Do you have a minute to tell me what brought on this whole concept? I'm not exactly sure what you hoped to accomplish tonight, but I can say the crowd was pleased."

Lauryn began telling Bernice about the dress that started it all and how her whole career path began with that dress and the coincidental meeting with Jacqueline Yvonne. She explained her goals with her designs and how she wanted to make dresses that women and young girls looked at, had to have, and were dying to wear— dresses that were exquisitely beautiful but comfortable, and above all, modest.

"Most women," Lauryn explained, "aren't comfortable showing their bodies. Let's face it, what percentage of the female population is built like a supermodel?"

"Certainly not me," Bernice remarked. "But that doesn't mean I can't dress fashionably."

"Exactly!" Lauryn said.

"I noticed that your models were beautiful, but they were also normal, average girls. Does this have anything to do with the trend to get a healthier body image on the runway, like what recently happened during Spain's Fashion Week?"

"I'm definitely in favor of presenting a healthier image for women," Lauryn told her. "The girls I used are a perfect representation of the Young Women I design dresses for. Now, not all of these dresses were mine. Some of them are dresses we altered to make them more modest."

"Lauryn, I'll be honest. This is certainly against everything the media, the celebrities, and the other designers are doing. How are you going to break through?"

"I've recently left Jacqueline Yvonne Designs and am working for Laszlo Molnar. I'm hoping to show my first collection soon."

"Laszlo Molnar? Why haven't I heard this? Your designs are nothing like his. He's never hired outside of his company like this before." Bernice quickly wrote something down in her notebook.

"To tell you the truth, I'm about as baffled by all this as you are."

Bernice's brows narrowed, the reporter in her wanting more facts. "I may have to look into this. This is a bold move, even for him."

"Well, if you find anything out, please let me know."

"Interesting." She twirled her pencil in her fingers. "Why would he hire you when he has several designers in his company he has been grooming for this position?"

"Like I said, I don't know. I may never know."

Bernice was thoughtful a moment longer, then she brightly said, "But what a great opportunity for you!"

"Yes, it is. And even though it was difficult to leave Jacqueline, I knew this was the opportunity of a lifetime."

Bernice nodded and chewed her bottom lip for a moment, lost in thought, then she jotted something else down. A moment later she looked up. "Would you let me know when you're having your show? I want to cover it myself. I hope you don't mind, but I'd like to stay close to this story. I'm fascinated with the dynamics of what's going on here."

"You've always seemed fair to me, Bernice. I'd love to have you around. And I will let you know about my show as soon as I have a date. But you'll be able to see a debut of my work before then. This needs to be off the record for now. No one knows yet, but I promise, you can have the scoop to write about it when it happens."

Bernice looked at her with interest. "Do tell."

"Vanessa Cates will be wearing one of my designs at the debut of her new movie, *Stones of Blood.*"

Bernice's eyes grew wide. "There's Oscar buzz for Best Actress and Best Picture for that movie."

"I know!" Lauryn exclaimed. "She wants me to design her dress for the Academy Awards too."

"You know you'll be hit with an explosion of demand if she wins that award. Are you ready for that?"

"I'm ready. I just hope Mr. Molnar is."

Bernice jotted down the information in her notepad, then said, "When I first met you and saw your designs, I was impressed and knew you were someone to watch."

"Thank you," Lauryn said. "A good friend taught me that after you set your goals, you need to work hard and be prepared so that when opportunity knocks, you can answer."

"So true," Bernice said. "You have certainly proven that." She made a few more notes. "Well, I think that's it. Boy, to think I almost sent my assistant to cover this. I predict great things are about to happen for you, Lauryn. But a word of warning." She lowered her voice. "I'm not at liberty to give you any details, but I'd watch your back if I were you."

Chapter Twenty

A light rain was beginning to fall when Lauryn and Logan finally left the church, so Lauryn hailed a cab, and they jumped inside just as the rain began falling heavily.

"Thanks for helping out tonight. I know I told you this earlier, but you looked spectacular in my dress," Lauryn told her.

"You're welcome. But in the future, just remember, I'm happier on the other side of the curtain. Being out there in front of everyone scares me to death! I'd rather be doing hair and makeup."

"You don't need to worry. I'll never make you do that again."

"I had fun getting to know Jazmyn and a couple of the girls. They were wondering what I'm doing while you're at work tomorrow. They said they'd take me sightseeing and around town."

Lauryn wasn't sure at first, but the more she thought about it, the better she felt. Her Young Women were responsible and sensible. They would probably be the best ones to take Logan around the city.

"I think that would be fine. You'll keep your phone with you and stay in touch through the day, right?"

"Of course," Logan said, holding up the phone just as it vibrated with an incoming text.

But to Lauryn's surprise, Logan didn't practically rip the phone apart like she usually did. Instead, Logan looked out the cab window as they rode to Lauryn's apartment.

"Is everything okay?" she asked Logan.

"Yeah, it's great," Logan replied.

"Are you sure? Did you just get a message from Brody?"

"Probably," Logan said without enthusiasm.

"Aren't you going to read it?"

"No."

Logan wasn't offering information, so Lauryn didn't know whether or not to pry.

They sat in silence, the cab winding through the busy streets, when suddenly, Logan turned and said, "I called him after the show because I wanted to tell him how much fun it was, and that, even though I hadn't really even rehearsed, I did a pretty good job. You know?"

Lauryn nodded. "You did a great job, are you kidding? I was so proud of you."

"Thanks. So I call Brody, and this girl answers. And she's giggling and saying that Brody can't talk because he's busy, and I can hear music in the background and other people talking and laughing."

"What did you say to her?"

"I didn't know what to say. I was so shocked I just hung up. He tried to call a few minutes later, but I don't want to talk to him."

"What are his text messages saying?"

"That it's not what I think it is, and he doesn't even know that girl," Logan said skeptically.

"And you don't believe him?"

"No."

"But Logan, if you two are as serious as you say you are, shouldn't you have more trust than that?"

"Probably," Logan replied. "But it's hard because he's always been such a flirt, and I've caught him flirting with other girls before."

"What does he say?"

"He says that the girls don't mean anything to him and that he's just having fun, but it bothers me."

Lauryn remembered the shock, disappointment, and embarrassment she felt when she found out that Michael had cheated on her. She hoped the same thing didn't happen to Logan.

"Have you told him it bothers you?"

"I tried to, but he thinks I'm being immature when I say that. He tells me that I should be able to handle it."

"How would he like it if you were flirting with other guys?" Lauryn asked.

"Are you kidding? He'd freak out!"

The driver pulled the cab over to the curb. Lauryn paid him, and they got out.

Lauryn slipped her arm around Logan. "Sorry you're having a hard time. I'd like to tell you that it gets easier when you get older, but I'd be lying."

"Really? You have a hard time dating?"

Lauryn nodded.

"Guys should be falling at your feet!" Logan exclaimed. "I mean look at you. You're gorgeous, you're successful, you're nice, you're funny, you're . . ."

"Stop!"

"It's true. Anyone would be lucky to get you," Logan said.

"Thanks, kiddo. I think the same about you."

The stepsisters hugged.

"I'm starving. Should we go around the corner and grab some Chinese?" Lauryn offered.

"And could we get some cheesecake with chocolate, too?"

"I know just the place," Lauryn said.

* * *

"I'm going to take a shower and get ready for bed," Logan said. "The girls want to take me for bagels and hot chocolate in the morning, then I'm not sure what we're going to do. What if they want to do the Statue of Liberty or Empire State Building? Should I save that to do with you?"

"Nah, you go ahead. I've been to those places so many times I don't mind skipping."

Logan went to shower, and Lauryn sat down on the couch and put her feet up to relax.

Shutting her eyes, she thought about the evening and the positive comments from the girls who'd participated, the leaders, and the audience members. Overall, the show was a great success. Moms were grateful for the help in proving to their daughters that fashion could be fun and didn't have to be boring just because it was modest. The leaders wanted to make the fashion show an annual event, with more entertainment thrown in. Of course, Cooper was happy to oblige and promised two dance numbers next year and even bigger and better stage props.

Cooper's parents not only enjoyed being part of the event but were also impressed with the quality of the youth and how well-behaved they were. They'd been around youth groups and worked with inner-city kids through drama camps and community plays. They were used to the foul language and rough demeanor that accompanied some youth groups. They were impressed to see a group this big that was so respectful and clean-cut.

Even Sister da Silva had caught the attention of one of the single men in the ward who was a Young Men leader. She was very excited after they talked and hoped he called like he said he would.

Lauryn's thoughts drifted to Jace. She missed him. She felt closer to him after spending two days together than she'd felt with any guy she'd dated after two months.

It wasn't like her to be thinking so far down the road this early in the relationship, but Lauryn couldn't help acknowledging to herself that Jace had every quality she wanted in a husband. She knew he wasn't perfect—no one was, but he was darn close.

The ringing of her phone startled her. It was about time he called; she was dying to talk to him.

"Hey there," she said.

"Lauryn, sweetie, I got the pictures. You're father sent them Federal Express so they'd make it overnight."

"Hi Mom," Lauryn said, glad her mother was happy, but a little disappointed it wasn't Jace.

"I just looked at the pictures of you as a little girl and," her voice cracked, "I just can't believe how much has changed since then. Oh, Lauryn, I just feel terrible about things. I really do."

"Mom, it's okay. It's in the past. There's nothing we can do to change it. Really."

"You don't know what it's like to know your days are numbered and more than anything to want to make peace with the important people in your life."

"Mom, I understand. But there's nothing to make peace about. We're fine. We've worked through all of this."

Lauryn's mother sniffed and stayed quiet.

"Mom?"

"I just don't feel like we're quite there yet."

"Mom, I love you. I forgive you. Really, everything is good with me. You've got to forgive yourself."

"How can I? I wasn't there for you. I was selfish and stupid. I lost you and your father, the only good things in my life."

Lauryn wasn't sure what to say. "Mom, don't worry. Why don't you get a good night's sleep. I need to get to bed too; I have a busy day tomorrow. Could we talk this weekend?"

"You'll call me?"

"Of course I will."

"And you'll tell me when you show your clothing line?"

"As soon as I know the date."

"I want to come," her mother said with urgency.

"Really? I'd love to have you there." Lauryn had heard promises like this her entire life, but she never quit hoping. "You just take care of yourself. I'll come and spend a weekend with you soon."

More sniffling on the phone was her mother's reply.

"Thanks for calling, Mom. I'll call you Sunday afternoon."

"You're a good daughter."

Lauryn hung up the phone and took a long, deep breath. She always felt physically and emotionally drained after talking to her mother. She didn't know what else to do to help her let go and move on. Certainly she wished that her childhood could have been different, but she also knew that she couldn't change anything about it. She'd learned to let go and realize she was who she was today because of what she'd been through. Dragging a bunch of baggage around with her only held her back from achieving her goals and making her own dreams come true. As soon as she'd let go and forgiven her mother, her whole attitude toward her mother had changed. Instead of resentment and anger, she felt compassion and love. And now that her mother was terminally ill, she was grateful that Heavenly Father had blessed her with the capacity to forgive. And she prayed her mother could do the same before it was too late.

Pulling an afghan over her, she remained on the couch waiting for Jace's phone call. The stress of the long day caught up with her, and she quickly fell asleep with the phone resting on her chest so it would wake her up when he did call. But he never did.

* * *

Lauryn arrived at her office early the next morning. She wanted a jump on the day before Sasha, Laszlo, or anyone else showed up to ruin it.

Taking the elevator down one floor, she let herself into the sample room to check on the progress of her designs, hoping to get an idea of how they were shaping up.

One of the dresses was completely cut out, the other one, lying on the cutting table, was waiting to be cut. The dress she'd designed with swags of fabric hung on a dress form, pinned together, waiting for final adjustments before sewing.

Lauryn loved the creative process of taking a sketch and turning it into the real thing. It always seemed like a miracle when she could actually hold and touch—and wear—a piece that days before was merely a thought in her head. She'd had her share of disasters, that was for sure, but she'd learned from every mistake she'd made, so she valued even her failures.

Pulling up a stool to the dress form, she began moving pins and fabric pieces to get the fabric to drape and hang so it would create a more flattering look.

The crimson silk shimmered in the morning light that poured through the horizontal band of windows in the room.

As the dress took shape, she pictured where she wanted to place the stones and beading. A ripple of excitement coursed through her veins. If they could get this dress sewn together before noon, Sasha would be eating her words for lunch today. Lauryn's dresses were going to be stunningly beautiful, and she was certain Laszlo would agree.

After an hour of tucking and pinning, stepping back and viewing the dress from a distance, then tucking and pinning some more, Lauryn finally achieved the exact look she wanted. The private time gave her a chance to reflect on Jace. It was hard not to speculate over reasons why he hadn't called last night, but remembering her resolve to enjoy the relationship while it lasted and not psych herself out by being overly cautious, she chose to be sensible and hope he had a good excuse. Besides, she didn't have time for distractions. She had to make sure these three dresses were perfect, since her future career as a designer depended on them.

Voices outside the door caught her attention. Praying it wasn't Sasha or Laszlo, she stepped back from the dress form and braced herself for their entrance. Instead, it was one of the young Asian girls who helped with the sewing. These girls could work miracles with a sewing machine, despite their young age, which Lauryn guessed couldn't be over twenty.

Lauryn gave her a smile and said, "Good morning."

The girl shyly returned the smile. She pointed at the dress form. "Very beautiful," she said.

"Thank you," Lauryn answered.

"You need help?" the girl asked.

"I think I've got it ready. Are you the one who's going to sew the dress?"

"Yes, I can sew it for you."

"That's wonderful . . ." She stumbled over her words, not knowing the girl's name.

"I am Toshiro."

"Oh, Toshiro. Thank you. I will cut out the other dresses while you sew."

"You?" Toshiro remarked with surprise.

Lauryn knew it was unusual for designers to spend time in the preparation of the samples, but Lauryn wanted everything just right.

"Yes. If you have any questions I will be right here for you to ask."

"Very good," Toshiro said.

Laying the pattern pieces on the fabric, then pinning them in place, Lauryn carefully cut through the shimmery layers of purple silk. For her preview, she wanted colors that were bold and eye catching.

Lost in concentration, Lauryn worked steadily, taking the cut pieces of fabric and draping and pinning them onto another dress form.

Other workers joined them, and all went straight to work, focusing on getting her three dresses done for Laszlo to see later that day.

They worked quickly and tirelessly, the dresses nearing completion within several hours. In-house models came for a fitting, and alterations were made to get the fit just right.

With all three dresses almost finished, Lauryn sat in a chair and rubbed her temples. A headache was coming on, probably from lack of sleep and too much stress.

"You okay, miss?" Toshiro asked.

"Just a headache," Lauryn replied.

"Oh, let me help you."

Toshiro told Lauryn to shut her eyes and try to relax. She then began to massage the back of her neck and into her shoulders, putting deep pressure on several areas that hurt at first, but then the pain slowly subsided. By the time she was done, Lauryn's headache was gone.

Lauryn turned to the young girl. "Toshiro, thank—"

The door burst open, revealing Sasha's bulging eyes and blood-red lipstick. "There you are," Sasha exclaimed when she saw Lauryn. "Laszlo wants to see you in his office right away."

The workers froze, the look of fear in their eyes. Apparently, Lauryn wasn't the only one Sasha had this effect on.

Sasha left in a huff. "I may need to come back for another massage," Lauryn joked with Toshiro, but Toshiro only looked at her with pity, which Lauryn welcomed. She would rather face a guillotine than a large helping of Laszlo in a bad mood with an order of Sasha á la Freak on the side.

"Wish me luck," Lauryn said as she left the room.

Her phone buzzed as she walked toward Laszlo's office. She'd have to look at it later; right now she was about to face the verbal firing squad.

Beckham looked up like a frightened puppy as she approached his desk.

"Mr. Molnar is expecting you," he said.

No kidding, she wanted to say.

Beckham pushed a button and received a buzz for an answer.

"You can go right in."

Pausing before she opened the door, Lauryn said a quick prayer. She'd already turned her life over to the Lord, but just in case, she wanted to make sure He saw what was happening in hopes that maybe He'd send some very powerful guardian angels her way.

Turning the knob, Lauryn slowly opened the door.

"Come in!" Laszlo barked.

Lauryn jumped, then pushed open the door, steeling herself for what was about to take place.

There to greet her were the grim reaper and the angel of death, Laszlo and Sasha.

"Sit down," Sasha commanded.

Lauryn sat down, a mantra of "be strong" running through her head. She looked at them with her head high.

There wasn't a hint of what to expect until Laszlo tossed a sheet of paper toward her, printed off the Internet.

At first glance all it looked like was fashion advertising and headlines. Then, upon closer inspection, she realized what he wanted to show her.

"Breakout designer holds private fashion show," read the title.

Oh no! The title sounded bad; she was scared to read the article.

"Do you want to explain this?" Laszlo asked.

Lauryn scanned the article, which wasn't too long. Still, it only took one sentence, one word, to be misrepresented.

After reading it, she realized there was nothing wrong with it, except for the mention that she had several surprises up her sleeve and that Bernice Thomas promised to reveal more at a later date.

Lauryn relaxed.

"It's nothing," she said.

Sasha's eyebrows shot up to her hairline. "Oh, really?"

With a smile, Lauryn began her explanation, knowing that they, of all people, were not going to be impressed with her answer. "In my church, I have the responsibility to work with Young Women ages twelve to eighteen. We've been talking a lot about dressing appropriately for dances, formal and informal, and the message a girl sends by the way she dresses."

Sasha turned her head slightly. Lauryn noticed a smirk on her face, which fueled her defenses.

"One thing led to another, and we decided to have a modesty fashion show. Some of the dresses were old designs of mine, others were dresses they had bought for previous school dances that we altered to make more modest. It wasn't as big as Bernice made it sound."

"Still, this is something I would have liked you to clear with me first," Laszlo said.

"I'm sorry," Lauryn replied. "Really, I was shocked Bernice was there. I think this whole modesty thing intrigued her. She didn't realize that there were teenage girls who really cared about dressing modestly."

"And you think there are?" Sasha asked with amusement.

"I know there are," Lauryn responded directly, catching Sasha off guard.

"Maybe a select few," Laszlo said. "But our research shows that girls even as young as twelve want to dress to look older and more mature."

"And dressing sexy is the way to do that?" Lauryn asked.

"That's what sells," Sasha informed her.

"I don't agree. I believe there's a larger market out there for fashionable but modest clothes. You make it sound like modesty is a bad thing."

"It's boring," Sasha said.

"It's classy," Lauryn dared to say. "And if it's done right, it doesn't even have to be an issue. My goal is to prove that a dress can be beautiful, fashionable, and modest."

"Are you saying you won't design anything that isn't?" Laszlo asked. "I'd say that limits your creative abilities, wouldn't you?"

"Not at all. In fact, if anything, it pushes me to be even more creative and cutting-edge. When you have a strapless gown, you lose the ability to design everything from the chest up. That's where I like the focus to be, around the neck and face. Otherwise, a lot of the focus is on the waist and bottom of the dress. I think that after you see my samples, you'll agree."

"And when will they be ready?" he asked with annoyance.

"Tomorrow at the earliest," Sasha said.

"Actually, they're ready now," Lauryn corrected. "I came in early to help."

Sasha dipped her chin and looked Lauryn square in the eyes. "You did what?"

"I came in early. I do know how to cut a pattern and sew."

"But that's highly irregular," Sasha argued.

"I'm sorry. It was important to me to have control over these samples, since they will determine what happens with my line."

Most of her exchange was with Sasha, but Lauryn noticed an interesting expression on Laszlo's face. Almost like he was impressed, but she doubted he would ever admit it.

"Sasha, get dressmaking on the line and have them send the dresses on models to my office right away."

Sasha jumped to make the call.

"So, how did Bernice Thomas end up at your show?"

"My friend Cooper D'Angelo knows her well. He asked her to come as a favor."

"And what are the surprises she referred to?"

"The preview of my collection. She promised to be there to cover the event."

"Which we'll decide on after we see the samples."

Everything depended upon the three dresses he was about to see.

The more Sasha and Laszlo tried to intimidate her, the more determined Lauryn was to stand her ground. She felt secure in her principles and confident with her designs. Plus, she did have one more ace up her sleeve.

It didn't take long before a buzz from Beckham alerted them that the models had arrived.

Lauryn felt her heart stop for a moment, which wasn't good since she was also holding her breath.

Laszlo buzzed back, and the door opened. In walked the first model, a tall, leggy girl with long, black hair. Her dress, the rich, deep-purple silk charmeuse with the curtain swag sleeve and neckline, was draped beautifully on her slender frame. She walked forward, the silk billowing effortlessly with her movement, causing Lauryn to catch her breath. It was everything she'd dreamed it would be.

She didn't want Laszlo and Sasha to know she was watching them, but out of the corner of her eye, she looked to see their reaction. Sasha showed no expression on her face. Laszlo wore a challenging look, as if daring the models to impress him.

The model finished, pausing at the door before exiting. She then stepped out, and the next one came in.

This dress was a deep burgundy with a shimmer of bronze in the fabric. The exquisite color gave the style a regal elegance suitable for the fanciest formal occasion. The sleeve and neckline followed a three-inch band around the shoulders and chest, then dipped in the back. A lower waistline was flattering to any body shape, especially because it camouflaged any lower-body flaws. The skirt hung in three layers, creating a long, statuesque silhouette.

It was all Lauryn could do not to cry out how beautiful the finished product was. So far, each of her designs had surpassed her expectations, in spite of how quickly they'd been made.

The final design was a tea-length dress for a teenager. A modified version would be available for adults. The model was older but wore the teen version, which came with a simple cap sleeve and scoop neck, drop waist, and billowing skirt. This one was in black taffeta. Lauryn's favorite part of the dress was the large white sash tied around the waist with a bow at the back—very Audrey Hepburn.

"Dreadful," Sasha said. "Every bridesmaid's worst nightmare."

Laszlo made some sort of noise that could have been translated either positively or negatively, Lauryn didn't know for sure, but she ignored Sasha's remark. In her opinion, these three dresses epitomized the theme of her collection: elegance and sophistication brought together with the glam factor of the fifties and sixties. She loved it, and she believed that not only would women want to wear these dresses but that most women would look amazing in them.

After the last model left, Sasha, Laszlo, and Lauryn sat in silence. Laszlo said nothing, but held his expression. Sasha wrote something on a notepad in front of her, and Lauryn waited for a verdict.

"Well, Lauryn," Sasha finally said. "Would you say this gives us a pretty good idea of what to expect from your collection?"

"Absolutely," Lauryn said proudly. The dresses were some of her best work. "It's exactly what you can expect." She had a whole list of reasons why she thought the market was ready for this look. And getting in now, with her signature style, would establish her as a serious designer. But she kept these thoughts to herself.

"I think Mr. Molnar and I need to discuss a few things before we decide," Sasha said.

"Okay." Lauryn stood up, keeping her attitude and voice upbeat. She was determined not to let them see her sweat. "I'll be in the sewing room. There are a few little alterations I want to make."

She turned on her heel and left the room, ready to blurt out that she was designing a dress for Vanessa Cates, just to see the look on their faces. But she decided to keep that information quiet just a little while longer.

Keeping her cool until she stepped outside the office, she collapsed onto a chair in the reception area. Beckham was away from his desk, and Lauryn was grateful. She needed a moment to recover.

There was no doubt Sasha was out to destroy Lauryn's chances for success at Molnar's. Lauryn just hoped that Laszlo would tune out all of Sasha's negative comments and make a decision based on his own opinion of the dresses. Laszlo's expression had been impossible to read. She didn't know if he outright hated her designs or if he was surprised at how good they were.

With her head in her hands, she pulled in a long, steadying breath. "What was I thinking?" she said out loud, wondering why she'd voluntarily hopped out of the warmth and security of the frying pan into the Laszlo Molnar fire. Sure, working for Jacqueline hadn't been the most stimulating job, but she did have satisfaction in her work, and she especially loved seeing her creations on the street or, occasionally, on a celebrity. And if she'd just been patient, she would have ended up with the job she wanted. Yet she knew she'd followed the promptings of the Spirit when she'd taken this job. It just didn't make sense.

A rumble of voices in Molnar's office caught her attention. The door wasn't completely shut, so as the voices got louder, they also became clearer.

"You told me she had no talent!" came Laszlo's voice.

"I didn't think she did!" Sasha snapped back.

"This whole news article is going to ruin everything! We're talking *Women's Fashion Review* for crying out loud!"

"I know. I'm the one who found the article!" Sasha cried.

"Then there's the small fact that she is giving all the credit to Jacqueline. The whole point of this was to bring that woman down!"

Lauryn's mouth dropped open.

"I'll get Bernice Thomas on the phone. She would never want to make an enemy out of you," Sasha assured him.

"You'd better do it now," Laszlo threatened. "This whole thing is about to blow up in my face! I want to end this whole fiasco as soon as possible. I've had it! Now make that call!"

Before Lauryn got caught, she took off around the corner and found cover in the ladies' room.

Grateful she had Bernice's number in her contact list and not daring to talk out loud, she texted Bernice and begged her to not accept Sasha's call until she talked to Lauryn first.

Luckily, Bernice sent a text right back and asked why.

Lauryn told her she'd call within the next fifteen minutes and asked her to just please not talk to Sasha.

After several minutes, Lauryn dared to leave the ladies' room. Instead of going back to her office, she got on the elevator and went to the top floor where she found the roof exit. As soon as the warm wind hit her face, her eyes began to sting, and she knew that tears were not far behind. As much as she wanted to cry, she had no time to waste. She had to call Bernice right away

* * *

"Beckham, get in here, now!" Laszlo's voice boomed through the intercom. Beckham leapt from his chair and sprinted into Laszlo's office.

"Sit down," Laszlo commanded. Beckham immediately dropped into one of the brown leather chairs across from Sasha, who fixed him with an icy gaze. Laszlo sat behind his spacious desk, gazing out the large windows with his back turned toward them. "I have a job for you, and perhaps you can try to get this right for a change. Ms. Alexander has become a threat to me and this company." He quickly turned his chair to look directly at Beckham. "She must be destroyed. That's where you come in. Now, do you think you can handle one, simple little task for me?"

Beckham nodded his head obediently. His leg was twitching, making him look like a scared child.

"Good. Now listen closely. Sasha is going to inform Ms. Alexander that we are moving ahead with her show. Tomorrow, I want you to speak with Ms. Alexander and give her the impression that everything is being taken care of—venue, guests, advertising, set design . . . everything. Then, over the next two weeks, I want you to keep an eye on her. Become bosom buddies, or whatever it is you have to do to stay up on what she's doing. I'll expect a full report every day."

"I can't wait to see the look on her pompous little face when she arrives for the show and discovers there is no show!" Sasha chuckled menacingly, and Laszlo joined in.

"Uh . . . excuse me, sir." Beckham's voice squeaked.

"What is it?"

"It's just . . . um, well . . ."

"Spit it out, fool. I haven't got all day."

"Well . . . what if Ms. Alexander invites her own friends and family to the show?"

"You're not following me, are you?" Laszlo sounded tired and annoyed. "I *want* her to invite her friends. You see, when they arrive for a show that doesn't exist, I'll simply accuse her of planning a private showing behind my back, which will give me grounds to fire her and end this whole charade."

Beckham stared first at Laszlo then at Sasha.

"What are you waiting for?" Sasha demanded. "Go!"

Chapter Twenty-one

"What do you think is going on?" Bernice asked after Lauryn explained the precarious situation at Molnar's.

"I wish I knew, Bernice. And I wish I knew what Sasha's going to say when she calls you. For some reason they want to make me look bad, and I know it has something to do with Jacqueline Yvonne."

"It's no secret that Laszlo Molnar is fiercely competitive with Jacqueline. The funny thing is, Jacqueline doesn't get caught up in his ridiculous games. Frankly, I'm glad this is happening. The man needs to be exposed. But not yet. I want to see if we can find out a little more first." Bernice's phone beeped. "Hold on, that might be her. Let me look."

Lauryn waited anxiously.

"It is. I'll call you right back."

"Thanks, Bernice."

"For the record, Lauryn, Laszlo is an egotistical troll who treats people like dirt, and I've been snubbed by that witch Sasha more times than I can count. Don't worry, we'll get to the bottom of this."

Lauryn hung up so Bernice could take the call.

Lauryn's mind raced, and she couldn't get her hands to stop shaking. Now she understood why Laszlo and Sasha acted like they were out to get her. They wanted Jacqueline, and for some reason they thought they could use Lauryn as a pawn to bring her down.

To keep herself from breaking down while she waited for Bernice to return her call, she checked her messages. There were two from Jace and one from Cooper, both asking her to call them.

Jace said it was urgent; Cooper said it was life or death. Knowing Cooper, he was trying to decide where to go to lunch that day. He was the original drama king.

She tried Jace first but got no answer. He was hard to pin down at work, so she left a message telling him to text her when he could talk and she'd call him. Lauryn couldn't allow herself to even consider what might be so urgent; her emotional stability was already teetering on the edge of a cliff.

Next she called Cooper. He would flip when she told him everything that was going on, but until she had all the details, she was going to wait to fill him in.

"It's about time you called. I'm having an aneurysm here!"

"What could possibly be that urgent?" she asked.

"Are you sitting down?" he asked.

"No."

"Then brace yourself. I have some news that will blow your mind."

She felt as though her mind were already blown. She leaned back against the wall, knowing she couldn't take much more.

"Jacqueline called me into her office this morning. She offered me your old job!"

A sudden pang went through Lauryn's heart. She had no right to feel protective of her old job, especially with her good friend Cooper. More than anything, she felt regret. Leaving Jacqueline Yvonne had been the dumbest thing she'd ever done. Look what she'd gotten herself into.

"Coop, that's great. I'm so happy for you, really. You're going to do a superb job."

"She also wants to talk to you. She wants to make sure you're coming back. She regrets not giving Diondra the boot when you were getting ready to leave. I guess she'd been having trouble with her for a while but wanted to give Diondra another chance."

"Tell Jacqueline she's got me, but tell her not to say anything yet. Something big is going on."

"What is it?"

"I'll call you after work and fill you in."

"I hope I survive until then," he said. "I'm super stoked you're coming back. I've missed having you around. No one else will ballroom dance with me in the office."

Lauryn laughed. "Speaking of ballroom dancing, how's Sister da Silva?"

"Actually, not bad. I guess she's got a date with that guy from the fashion show."

"The Young Men leader?"

"That's the one. She's smitten."

Lauryn's phone beeped. It was Jace. "Hey, I'm getting another call. Can we talk after work?"

"You know my number."

They hung up, and she clicked the line to answer Jace's call.

"Hey there," she said. "How have you been?"

"Busy. Sorry," he answered. "We've had some crazy developments here at work, and I've been in meetings nonstop."

"Oh. I've missed your countdown."

"Yeah, uh, I need to talk to you about that."

Lauryn shut her eyes and fought the urge to scream. She didn't know what he was going to say, but she didn't like where the tone of his voice was taking the conversation.

"There's no good way to put this." He paused. "Believe me, if there was anyone else who could do it, they would, but I'm the only single partner. The others are married with families."

She didn't want to ask, but she had to. "What is it?"

"I have to move to London for a few months. We've got something big going on over there, and I need to be there full time for a while."

"Months?" Lauryn felt herself sinking. Were her fears coming true? Had she let her heart get caught up in another one-sided relationship? Maybe their time together in Utah wasn't what she thought it was. Maybe it was just a nice couple of days . . . an incredibly nice couple of days.

"I suppose it could be worse. I'll be able to visit occasionally. Maybe you could come to London sometime. It's not a bad flight."

She tried to brighten her voice. "Sure, that would be fun."

"Lauryn," his voice was serious, "you need to know how hard I tried to get out of this. I know we haven't had much time together, and I'm not sure how you feel, but I was with you enough to know that I want to pursue this relationship we have. You are very important to me."

Tears filled Lauryn's eyes. Jace had thrown her the life preserver she needed at this stormy time in her life.

"I feel the same," she managed to say.

"Then we'll make it through. I'll arrange a night's layover in New York on my way to London."

"That would be nice."

"I'm sorry about our weekend together, but I'll make it up to you and Logan. I promise."

"I know. It's okay. I'm just disappointed."

"Me too. There's something else I need to tell you. I have a friend who's an attorney down here, and he told me that there has been a breakthrough in Ava's case."

"What do you mean?"

"Not many people know this, I guess, but he told me that after the police reenacted the crash, they went back through the old crime scene investigation files containing lists of everything found in Ava's car. He couldn't tell me what they found, but he said the puzzle pieces are all coming together to create more than just a suspicion of foul play. Lauryn, they don't think it was an accident."

Lauryn nearly dropped her phone. "Jace, you mean they think someone meant to kill Ava?"

"That's what he said. He doesn't really want it to get out until after the investigation. You might not want to tell your friends quite yet. I know how they talk."

"I can't believe this. I mean, I'll admit it was such a freak accident it didn't seem possible that it even happened the way it did. But I still can't believe someone actually meant to kill Ava. Who would have done that? Who would've wanted to see Ava dead?"

"I guess that's what they're going to try to find out. I'll let you know if anything develops."

They hung up, and Lauryn remained leaning against the building with her eyes shut. She felt droplets of rain on her hands and face. She opened her eyes and noticed the dark clouds closing in.

Perfect! Even the stormy weather reflected what she was feeling inside.

She reminded herself, though, that at least Jacqueline wanted her back. In fact, she didn't know what was stopping her from charging into Laszlo's office and quitting on the spot. But something was. She wanted to wait to find out more about what was going on. She couldn't quit without letting him know he couldn't treat people like this.

* * *

After stopping at the water fountain to take some Tylenol for her headache, Lauryn went back to her office and received a surprise.

"Sasha, what are you doing here?" she asked as she sat in her chair and pulled herself up to her desk.

"Laszlo's made a decision. He wants to premiere your show in two weeks."

"Two weeks? But why so soon? We can't have the gowns ready by then."

"Of course we can. Laszlo can have anything he wants!" Sasha reminded her.

"But—"

"We've already started making arrangements."

Fury burned in her bones. This woman was ruthless. Lauryn stood up quickly, pushing her chair back.

"I don't want to rush my collection. It can't be done that soon. What if I refuse?"

Sasha leaned close and said, "Then you will never work in this industry again. Now, I suggest you get a good night's sleep tonight, because it will be the last one you'll get for two weeks."

Lauryn teetered between bursting into tears and throwing furniture. Instead, she pulled in several deep, calming breaths, then collapsed into her chair.

Whatever they were up to, she wasn't going to let them win. And when it was over and the dust settled, she would still be standing.

* * *

In a flurry, Lauryn rushed into the apartment, startling Logan.

"Whoa, Lauryn, are you okay?"

"Vanessa's coming over tonight."

"Vanessa Cates is coming over here?" Logan jumped to her feet.

Lauryn walked up to Logan and grabbed her by the shoulders and looked her squarely in the eye. "Listen. Something crazy is going on at work. These next two weeks are going to be hectic and stressful, and I can't promise I will even be able to have a spare minute to spend with you." She walked away, running her fingers through her hair. Then she turned back to Logan. "Why don't we send you back home and have you come out again when things settle down?"

Logan shook her head. "No. I want to stay. I can help you. I don't want to go home. Not yet. I can't."

"You can't?"

"Please, Lauryn. I won't be any trouble. I'll take care of the house and have meals ready for you. I can run your errands. I don't want to go home yet."

Lauryn didn't understand. "What about Brody? Doesn't he come home in a few days?"

Logan's face hardened. "He's a jerk, and I think he's lying to me about being with girls in California. I don't like that he gets to call all the shots in our relationship. I don't want to be there when he gets home. Besides, I haven't seen enough of New York."

"But you can come back. We'll do shows and dinner and sight-seeing then. Besides, your parents wouldn't want you hanging out alone all day while I'm at work."

"I have Jazmyn and the girls to hang out with. We had so much fun today. Please, Lauryn, let me stay a little longer."

Lauryn couldn't deal with this right now. "Okay, fine. I'll talk to your parents. But if it doesn't work out, let's send you home and bring you back when my life is normal again."

"Thank you!" Logan gave Lauryn a big hug. "Now, tell me what is going on at work."

While Lauryn got ready for their guest, she told Logan all about her meeting with Laszlo and Sasha. There was nothing about it that made sense. Free publicity, like Bernice Thomas' article, was always welcomed by designers trying to make their mark in the industry, especially in a prestigious newspaper like *Women's Fashion Review.*

The doorbell rang.

"She's here?" Lauryn said, smoothing her hair and tucking her blouse into her skirt.

"You look great," Logan assured her.

"Thanks." Giving Logan a thumbs up, she opened the door.

Vanessa rushed inside and closed the door.

Startled, Lauryn asked, "Is everything okay?"

"I think someone on the elevator recognized me and tried to follow me," she said, pulling off her hat and sunglasses. "I wanted to get inside before they saw where I went."

Lauryn felt sorry for the woman, having no privacy.

"Could I trouble you for some water? I'm a bit thirsty."

"Oh, sure," Logan said. She went to the fridge for a bottle of water.

"Thank you for agreeing to come tonight," Lauryn said to Vanessa.

"When you told me what was going on, I was happy to do it. Who does that Laszlo Molnar think he is anyway, treating people like this?"

Lauryn smiled, feeling so fortunate to have met Ms. Cates.

"I've got some fabric samples for you, and a final sketch," Lauryn said. "We can tweak it however you want. I just need to take some measurements, then I can get started on the dress."

"Fabulous! *Access Hollywood* contacted me and will be at the premiere. I will be sure to tell them who designed my dress."

Lauryn and Logan exchanged excited glances.

After getting all the measurements she needed, Lauryn showed Vanessa the samples of fabric that would work for that particular style of dress. To her delight, Vanessa chose the emerald-green burnout velvet. The rich, textured fabric would hide any figure flaws and drape in elegant folds to the floor.

"That was my first choice, too," Lauryn told her.

"I've never been able to be quite so involved in the creative process," Vanessa told her. "I appreciate you being willing to address my needs and listen to my ideas."

"Why wouldn't I? I want you to love the dress."

"I already do," Vanessa said.

"I guess we're finished then," Lauryn said as she made one last note to herself about a pattern adjustment. Vanessa wanted a longer train, to give the dress more dramatic effect.

"It's going to be wonderful, Lauryn. I like you, and I want to help you any way I can. I plan on getting many more dresses from you in the future. Now, what are you girls doing for dinner? I'm starving."

"We don't have any plans. I have some frozen dinners we could heat up. Would you like one?"

Vanessa pulled a face. "No thanks. I ate more than my share of frozen dinners when I first moved to New York. I know a wonderful Thai restaurant that delivers. Eating out is just too much effort for me. I am not up to dealing with the paparazzi tonight. Mind if I call in some food?"

"Are you kidding? We'd love it!" Lauryn and Logan exchanged glances again. No one was going to believe they were hanging out with Vanessa Cates.

"Oh, one more thing!" Vanessa exclaimed. "I want you two to attend the premiere next weekend!"

Lauryn and Logan squealed with excitement.

"This is like, totally the coolest thing that has ever happened to me!" Logan exclaimed. "See, Lauryn, I have to stay."

It was true. There was no way Lauryn wanted Logan to miss an event like that.

"Oh, I almost forgot!" Logan said. "I saw the billboard for your new movie in Times Square today."

"Nothing like seeing yourself the size of King Kong on a bill-board," Vanessa said.

"Vanessa, are you sure you want us at the premiere? I mean, we've only just met." Lauryn was stunned by her generosity.

Vanessa smiled at both of them. "Don't be silly. It's my pleasure. It's not often I get to meet people as genuine as you two. I'll even send a car for you that night so you don't have to mess with taxis and such. To be honest, it feels good to hang out with nice people like yourselves. This is the most *normal* I've felt in years. I grew up in a small town, spending time with my family, climbing trees, and weeding the family garden. Nothing fancy about my childhood. Tonight I just feel like one of the girls."

"You are!" Logan said. "Except with you, instead of wondering what it's like to kiss George Clooney like you did in your last movie, we can ask you directly!"

"Logan!" Lauryn exclaimed.

"Sorry, I'm just wondering. He's so hot!"

"Well," Vanessa said with a sly smile, "to give you the honest truth, he kisses every bit as good as you'd think he would."

"I knew it!" Logan erupted. "You are so lucky!"

"He's such a gentleman, but probably the biggest tease I've ever met," Vanessa confided. "I wouldn't mind making another movie with him. I hope our food hurries. I'm supposed to be losing weight for my next movie, but I'm starving. I can't eat another carrot stick!"

While they waited for their food to arrive, Vanessa gave them the scoop on more Hollywood actors and actresses—the perfect distraction for Lauryn after one of the worst days of her life.

* * *

"Did you sleep at all last night?" Logan asked Lauryn when she came into the kitchen the next morning.

"I got a few hours. I wanted to get Vanessa's dress cut out. I ended up pinning it to the dress form also. I'm so excited about this dress."

"She's such a great person. I like her a lot."

"Me too. What a nut. I've never known anyone who could burp the Pledge of Allegiance."

"Wasn't that funny?" Logan said with a laugh. "She's so cool. And she invited us to her premiere!" Logan added with an excited squeal.

"We'll have to find something fancy to wear."

"You should wear your Jacqueline Yvonne dress."

"Me?" Lauryn asked. "It's old and dated."

"It's vintage and beautiful."

"I'll have to think about it. I like the significance of wearing it. I'm just not sure how I'd look in it anymore. It may be too young for me. You could wear it though."

"Really? I'd love to. I've got some ideas for hair, too."

Lauryn rinsed her cereal bowl. "I'm off to work. I need to get there early, before the sharks infest the waters. I'm keeping a close watch on everything. No telling what they plan to do with my designs." Lauryn put her cereal bowl in the dishwasher. "What are you going to do today?"

"Jazmyn is getting some girls together, and we thought we'd check out the Empire State Building and do some shopping at Bloomingdale's and Macy's. We might even try to do baptisms for the dead if we can arrange it."

Lauryn smiled at her stepsister. "That sounds like a great day. I wish I could join you."

"You will soon. You just need to get through these next two weeks."

"Stay in touch, will you?" Lauryn asked.

"Sure thing, sis."

Lauryn stopped and looked at Logan as she poured herself a bowl of cereal.

"What?" Logan said, glancing up at Lauryn.

"Nothing. I'm just really glad you're here."

"So am I." Logan smiled. "Brody asked when I was coming home, and I said I didn't know. He totally freaked. It's interesting." She put down the cereal box. "Now that I'm away from him, I'm starting to see him differently. I'm not so sure how I feel about him anymore."

Lauryn fought the urge to jump for joy. "Funny how that can happen, isn't it," she said instead. "You'll figure it out."

Logan nodded. "I know. I think I was supposed to come here for a couple of reasons."

"Me too. I'll see you later."

* * *

Lauryn opted to walk to work, since the streets were deadlocked with traffic and she could travel the distance faster on foot. While she walked, she called her mother to tell her about the fashion show. She'd have to call her friends later, since they probably wouldn't appreciate her calling them at three-thirty in the morning.

"Lauryn, is that you?" her mother said, sounding like she was already at death's door.

"Mom, are you okay?"

"I'm fine. I'm just so tired."

"Are you following the doctor's orders? You're supposed to get a lot of rest, and you're not supposed to drink anymore."

"I know. It's just so hard."

Lauryn couldn't imagine being a slave to alcohol. When she needed to numb the stress of her life, she used exercise and yoga—and chocolate. After seeing her mother's life deteriorate under the constant need for a drink, she was more sure than ever that she'd never touch a drop of alcohol.

"I'm going to come see you soon, Mom."

"You are?" Her mother's tone brightened.

"Yes. I just have to get these next two weeks out of the way, then I'm going to come spend a weekend with you."

"Oh, my, that's such wonderful news," her mother said. "I know how busy you are."

"You have no idea," Lauryn said as she paused at the street corner to wait for the walk signal to flash. She looked up and saw a giant billboard on top of one of the buildings advertising Vanessa's new movie. Vanessa was driving a Jeep, and behind her was the fire from an explosion. It looked very intense and intriguing.

"What's causing you so much stress?" Her mother's question jarred her from her distracted thoughts. She still couldn't believe Vanessa would be wearing her dress to the premiere of her new movie.

"You don't want to know. I do have some exciting news, though. My collection is going to be presented at a private show two weeks from Saturday."

"A private show?" her mother asked.

"Yes. My first show featuring my designs exclusively."

"I can see why you're stressed."

"Yeah, it's a little intense right now," Lauryn told her as she entered the building through the revolving door. "Hey, Mom, I gotta hang up now. I'll talk to you soon. Take care of yourself."

"I will, honey. I'll say a prayer for you."

Lauryn hung up the phone and stepped into the elevator. Had her mother just said she would pray for her? That was a first. Her mother had never been religious.

She wondered if maybe she should contact the bishop in her mother's area and see about having someone go over and give her mother a blessing. She hated the thought of her mom suffering alone.

When she got to her floor, she went straight to the cutting room to see how her designs were coming. She was stunned when she walked in.

Nothing had been done. No fabric had been cut; no patterns were even in sight.

She dared to hope that maybe there were gowns in the sewing room, but no. To her complete despair, nothing had been sewn.

What was going on?

She took one final look around, then prepared herself for the next step. She was going to confront Laszlo.

Chapter Twenty-two

In her office, Lauryn tried to organize her thoughts so she would be prepared to talk to Laszlo. It was time for him to take off the mask and tell her outright what his plans were for her collection.

Turmoil filled her chest and head until she thought she'd explode. She needed to deal with Laszlo, she had to get Vanessa's dress done, and she was worried about her fashion show coming together—not to mention her mother's illness and Jace's move to London.

It was too much. How was a person supposed to handle all of this at the same time?

Tears filled her eyes. Angry, frustrated, frightened tears.

For a brief moment, everything had seemed wonderful and glorious. Jace was back in her life, her new job seemed exciting and promising. So many good things had happened all at once. And now things couldn't seem worse.

Not wanting anyone to see her like this, Lauryn went to her office door and locked it.

Then, she fell to her knees at her desk. And she prayed. Sharing her burden with the Lord, she poured out her heart, her fears, and her concerns. She prayed for guidance and the ability to clearly see what she should do and how she should handle the situation. She prayed for the capacity to handle the enormous burden she carried. Somehow she had to find time to make Vanessa's dress. So much depended upon the success of the dress. It had to be perfect. She prayed for Jace. If his moving to London was right, then she prayed that everything would go well for him. She cared about him enough to want him to be happy and successful. They'd been apart more than ten years; what was another few months? She prayed for her mother. After all this time, after all they'd been through, her mother's heart was finally softening. Maybe once and for all they would be able to make real peace with each other and heal the wounds of the past.

By the time Lauryn finished praying, she was exhausted. She was already physically tired from staying up most of the night, and now she felt emotionally drained. Yet spiritually, she felt at peace. No action plan had suddenly come into her mind. The answers weren't yet clear. But an undeniable sense of peace filled her. It would all work out. Somehow, it would all work out.

Staying on her knees a moment longer, she cupped her chin in her hands and took a deep breath. The fear of talking to Laszlo was gone. In fact, she wasn't going to talk to him. She was going to take charge of her collection. If he wanted to talk to her, then he could. As far as she knew, she had a fashion show in two weeks. And she would make every effort to pull it off. As far as Vanessa's dress was concerned, the hardest part was done. She could sew it tonight, then have Vanessa come for a fitting. With Vanessa trying to rapidly lose weight for her next movie role, Lauryn would have to do a final fitting right before the premiere. As for the embellishments and stonework needed, she could teach Logan how to do it. Sewing on crystal wasn't hard; it was just time consuming. Logan had the time.

As for Jace, well, she knew she cared about him and wanted to pursue their relationship, but it seemed that now just wasn't the time. He had things he needed to do, and so did she. It would be hard because she missed him desperately. He made her laugh. He helped her feel confident and strong. But she could be patient and wait until the time was right.

And then there was the fashion show. She wasn't even worried about that. The arrangements had been made, the venue secured, the models booked—even the set design was begun. And she could have those dresses done. The women in the sewing department were amazing and quick. She would be there with them, and they could pull it off.

But she would need some moral support, especially during the week of the show. And she knew just who to call.

With her thoughts organized, she got up off her knees and went to work.

* * *

"Ms. Alexander." Beckham, Molnar's assistant, poked his head inside the door of the sewing room. "There's a delivery for you."

Lauryn glanced up from her machine to acknowledge him.

"Thanks, Beckham. Would you mind bringing it in here?"

"Sure thing. By the way, um . . . how's it going?"

Lauryn stopped sewing. Was that sincerity she detected? Did Beckham actually care?

"Um, so far so good. We're starting to make some progress."

He nodded his head. "I'm glad. I, uh . . . I wanted to let you know that everything else is on track for the show. I've got the venue secured, and it looks like we're going to have several big names there for publicity."

"Really? What big names?"

"Oh, um . . . well, there's . . . oh, what's her name? Well, don't worry. I've taken care of everything. Just remember to leave it all up to me." Beckham turned on his heel, knocking over a dress form that was set up behind him.

"Sorry about that. I'll go get your delivery," he apologized as he picked up the dress form and shuffled quickly out of the room.

That was odd. Beckham had never seemed so fidgety before.

Lauryn cut the threads on the piece she was sewing, then began moving scissors, pins, and fabric scraps from a cutting table to make room for the food.

Ever since Toshiro and the other girls had arrived that morning, Lauryn had shifted into overdrive.

Toshiro told her that Sasha had given her strict orders to wait for her okay before they began working on Lauryn's designs.

Lauryn realized it was pure sabotage, for whatever reason, and she wasn't about to let Sasha destroy all her hard work. If Sasha had a problem with them working on her designs, then Sasha could come and talk to her about it.

Even though Toshiro knew she could be putting her job in jeopardy for not obeying Sasha, she also knew that she was invaluable to the company as head seamstress. Molnar couldn't afford to let her go.

"Here we go," Beckham said when he returned. In his arms was a large cardboard box filled with food from Belly Delly Deli—Lauryn's treat to the girls who had so willingly given up their lunch hours to help her.

"Let's take a short break and have some food," Lauryn announced to them. "I know this isn't much, but I promise, I'll make all of this up to you."

The women had committed to helping her, even if it meant staying late, working through lunch, and coming in early. Lauryn wasn't surprised to learn that many of the seamstresses had felt stepped on for years at Molnar's, never receiving anything but criticism for their work. She sensed that they were taking this opportunity with Lauryn's designs to show Molnar who really had the power in his design house.

"I've heard this place is good," Beckham said, pointing at the food.

"It's one of my favorite delis in the city," Lauryn replied as she handed out sandwiches and drinks. "There's plenty here; would you like some?"

"Oh, no, that's okay," he said.

"Really, we'll never eat all this. You should try it. The turkey club is out of this world."

Beckham shrugged. "Okay, yeah. I guess I have a couple of minutes. The answering machine is on for lunch anyway."

Lauryn handed him a sandwich, a bag of chips, and a drink. She'd gotten plenty of food so she could keep the workers happy.

Beckham looked around the room at the half-sewn dresses and sighed. "These gowns are going to be beautiful."

"I think they're coming together pretty well," Lauryn remarked, confused by the hint of sadness in his voice.

"I hope you'll let me know if I can do anything to help."

Was he kidding? Her expression must have reflected her confusion.

"I'm serious," he said, his eyes finally meeting hers.

Was it possible that Beckham was tired of being treated like a lesser form of life and didn't like seeing her get the same treatment? Was it possible he wanted her to succeed?

"Maybe you could warn me when Sasha gets back to the office. Just so we can be prepared."

"You bet. And Mr. Molnar isn't expected until later today, if at all."

"Great," Lauryn exclaimed. The less intrusion she had, the better. "Thank you, Beckham."

"You're welcome. You know," Beckham said between bites, "I'm actually pretty good with a sewing machine."

"You are?"

"My mother was a seamstress, and I used to help her. Of course, none of my friends knew that I could sew. They would have beaten me up for sure if they had known. I discovered that I liked clothing and design, so I went to Parsons and graduated a year ago."

"That's where I got my degree."

"I noticed that when you came in about the job. I've also noticed how nice you are. That quality kind of stands out around here." He smiled.

"Thanks, Beckham."

"I want to get into the design world. I'm just waiting for my break. I was hoping this job would help me get my foot in the door."

"Be careful; it might get stomped on," Lauryn said.

Beckham laughed.

"If you're serious about design, my advice would be to not wait for your break, but to create it. You have to work hard if you want to get into this industry. Just be prepared. It's not as glamorous as it seems."

"Believe me, I know. I've seen the dark side," he joked. "I've seen it all." His eyes said more, but he didn't continue.

"If you want a chance to design, you ought to try Jacqueline Yvonne's. She's the best at hiring beginners and giving them a chance."

"I've heard that. You really think she'd consider me?"

"Absolutely. Tell her I sent you," Lauryn said. "She's an incredible woman."

"So why did you leave her employment?" he asked.

"Don't think I don't ask myself that question every day." Lauryn didn't tell him that as soon as the fashion show was over she was going back to Jacqueline Yvonne's.

"I wasn't sure what kind of people they had working over there. I met one of Jacqueline's assistant designers recently," Beckham said.

"Oh?"

"Deidra, Dandra . . ."

"Diondra?"

"That's the one. The Italian," he said. "Either her stilettos were much too tight that day or she was just in a bad mood, but she was one witchy woman the day she came to meet with Laszlo."

Lauryn remembered when Jacqueline promoted Diondra to assistant designer. Lauryn had hoped for the position, but Diondra's career-wear line had made headlines, and she was considered the hot designer to watch. Diondra knew how much that job meant to Lauryn, but it hadn't mattered to her.

"I'd watch out for Diondra. I don't think I'd trust her," Lauryn said.

"Kind of like Sasha?" Beckham asked.

Lauryn nodded. "Exactly."

"I appreciate the recommendation," Beckham said.

"If you have a portfolio, I'd be happy to take a look at it and tell you what I think," she offered.

Beckham smiled. "Thanks, Lauryn. And I can come in after work tonight and help for a couple of hours."

"You can?"

"Sure. I think your collection is fresh and innovative. I'd love for your show to be a success."

Lauryn heard a hint of sadness in his voice again . . . or was it regret? Lauryn smiled anyway. "I appreciate that. And I can use all the help I can get."

"Then I'll see you later." He wrapped up his sandwich. "I'd better get back to the phones. By the way, this sandwich is incredible. I can hardly fit my mouth over it, it's so loaded."

"You need to go there sometime. Try their cheesecake. It's amazing. And don't forget to let me know if Sasha comes in."

"Will do," Beckham said as he opened the door.

After he left, Lauryn looked around at the busy women bent intently over their sewing machines. A warmth of appreciation wrapped around her heart. God's hand was working in her life. Her problems weren't going to magically fix themselves or disappear, but she knew if she worked hard and did her part, He would make up the difference.

* * *

There was no sign of Sasha or Laszlo all day. It felt good not to have them pestering her or causing her more stress than she already had.

The sewing department buzzed with the constant whir of sewing machines. In-house models came in for fittings and alterations. Several designs needed extensive reworking. Lauryn took those projects on herself. Others came out perfect the first time. Most of them needed tweaking and adjustments here and there, but overall, things were on schedule.

At the beginning of the day, Lauryn had sent out a text to each of her girlfriends to notify them of the date of the fashion show. During the day, she'd received responses from each of them. Andrea was the first to reply, promising to come the Wednesday before her show to help. She had managed to set up a business meeting at the same time so she could write off her trip as a business expense.

Jocelyn wasn't sure she could get away. She'd taken on a summer job teaching art and didn't know if she could cover all of her classes.

For Chloe, getting away was tricky, since she had small children. She promised to try her best to be there. Her message was filled with encouragement. Roger was now meeting with their bishop on a regular basis. It sounded like he was at least trying to overcome his pornography addiction.

The last one to reply was Emma. For the first time in a long time, she sounded happy in her message. She'd finally met someone, a "gorgeous Greek man," whom she was totally smitten with. She said he treated her like a queen, and even though they'd only known each other a few weeks, they were already talking about a future together. She hoped to come to the fashion show and bring Nicholas along so everyone could meet him.

This sudden turn of events in Emma's life worried Lauryn. Emma had been down on men and everything about them. Could she really be ready for a new relationship? Lauryn hoped Emma would slow down and not rush into anything she might regret later.

In hopes that all four of her best friends would be there, Lauryn went back to work. The women in the department were committed to helping Lauryn meet her deadline and promised to stay late and return early the next morning. Somewhere between those two times, Lauryn needed to work on Vanessa's dress.

The pace was crazy and grueling, but she knew she could handle it for two weeks. She had to. And with Heavenly Father's help, she would.

* * *

Lauryn walked into her apartment just after nine o'clock that night, barely able to move her feet. She dropped her purse on the floor just inside the door and kicked off her shoes.

What a day.

Yet even though she was exhausted, she was invigorated. Her visions and sketches had come to life—some exactly what she'd hoped for, others exceeding her expectations. A few needed some serious help. But there wasn't anything she couldn't handle.

She smiled as she thought about Toshiro's suggestion to lock the dresses in her supply closet. She'd had the same thought. There were people she couldn't trust. So with the help of the team of seamstresses, she had moved all the extra dress forms and equipment out of the closet and made room for the racks of clothes. She'd sleep better knowing her gowns were safe. That was, if she managed to get to bed at all that night.

The place was quiet. Logan had mentioned she was going to dinner with some of the girls from the ward, so Lauryn expected her soon. She was actually grateful for a few minutes of peace and quiet so she could recover from her day and launch into her night of sewing Vanessa's dress.

But first she needed to change into something comfortable.

Pulling on pajama pants, a T-shirt, and slippers, she already felt revived. There was something relaxing about comfy clothes.

She was about to go into the kitchen and find a bite to eat when her eyes rested on the Butterfly Box sitting on top of her dresser.

Lauryn reached out and lovingly touched the symbol of support and faith. Knowing that her friends' prayers were being sent up to heaven just for her gave Lauryn an added sense of peace and the feeling she wasn't alone.

Pulling the box from the dresser, she sat on the bed and placed it on her lap. She knew she shouldn't, but slowly she opened the lid. Each item she removed had an emotion attached: sadness, laughter, melancholy . . . confusion.

She held the small box from Jocelyn, wondering what could possibly be inside. It was taped shut, untouched for all these years. It was strange to think she knew Jocelyn so well, yet here was proof that there was something about her friend, something so private, that Jocelyn wasn't willing to talk about it or even hint toward what it might be.

Entranced in thought, Lauryn didn't hear Logan come into the apartment.

"Hi," Logan said from the doorway.

Lauryn jumped. The box lid slammed shut, and the items she'd removed scattered across the bedroom floor.

"Sorry," Logan said with a laugh, reaching for the things that had landed near her feet. "I thought you heard me come in. What are you doing?"

With a sigh, Lauryn helped gather up the items. "Just getting a little help from my friends."

Logan handed her the box. "You're lucky to be so close to them. I've spent so much time with Brody I don't have very many friends anymore."

"It's not too late," Lauryn told her. "You shouldn't have to give up everything for a boy."

"I know. Especially when he hasn't given up anything for me. He still has friends. He even hangs out with girls."

"You're sure about that?"

"Yeah. He blabbed it to one of the guys at work when he got back from California, and that guy told Lynette, a girl I worked with. She's probably the closest thing I have to a friend right now. She texted me and told me what Brody was saying. He's a jerk."

"You should probably hear the story from him before you take someone else's word for it."

"He'll just lie to me like he always does." Logan sat on the bed.

"Are you okay?" Lauryn reached over and grabbed Logan's hand and gave it a squeeze.

"Actually, better than I thought I'd be. If I were still home I'd probably be a wreck, but being here has helped me see that I was settling for him. I've decided I've got a lot more I want to do with my life than marry a loser like him."

Lauryn was so happy she burst out laughing. "Really!"

"I've decided I'm going to college. I still want to attend beauty school, but I think I need to go to college and work on a business degree. I don't want to just work in a salon. I want to own my own salon."

"You'll have to talk to my friend Chloe next week if she comes. She owns her salon."

Logan bounced on the bed excitedly. "That's great. And Vanessa said she could get me in to talk to the makeup people in her next movie so I can see what they do."

"That will be fun."

"It'll be awesome!" Logan exuded. "I'm just really excited about my future. I have so much I want to do. You know how you talked to me about windows of opportunity? Brody was like this big, fat, curtain covering up my window. I had to move him out of the way so I could look out and see how much life had to offer."

Lauryn laughed. "That's a very good analogy. I think we all have our curtains. We just have to figure out how to move them."

"Exactly," Logan exclaimed proudly. She looked at the small box Lauryn still held in her hand. "So what's inside there?"

"I don't know. It's something Jocelyn put in, but she hasn't wanted to tell us yet."

"Really? After all these years? Don't you get tempted to open it?" Logan asked, reaching for the box.

Lauryn quickly snatched it away. "No. I mean . . . yes. I can't help but wonder. But I figure she'll tell us when she's ready."

"You don't think the others have opened it up and just haven't said anything?"

"Of course not." Lauryn looked at the box to see if it appeared as though someone had tampered with it, but it didn't.

"I bet they have. They just replaced the tape with a fresh piece."

Lauryn looked closer.

"I think you should open it."

"I'm not going to open it."

"You don't have to tell anyone you did it. Maybe you should know what's in there. What if it would help your friend if you knew?"

There were a lot of things Jocelyn held inside. Lauryn had often wondered if they really knew exactly who she was.

"She asked us not to. She will tell us when she's ready."

"What if something happened to her and she never got to explain it? What if it's a key to something important?"

Lauryn hadn't thought of that before.

"No one will know if you do open it. I won't say anything."

Should she?

Lauryn looked at the box again, wondering if the others had opened it when the Butterfly Box was in their possession. Chloe had never been able to keep a secret. Emma wouldn't feel like she was doing anything wrong by opening it. Andrea wouldn't, though. Andrea could be trusted.

Still, she wondered if the others had opened it?

"Open it, Lauryn," Logan coaxed.

Peeling up just the corner of the piece of tape, Lauryn agreed with Logan—no one would really know. Then she stopped. She would know. Jocelyn trusted her. Jocelyn's heart would be crushed if she knew Lauryn had opened her private box.

"Nope," Lauryn said, sealing the tape down with her fingernail. "I'm not going to do it."

"Aw," Logan said with disappointment.

"Sorry, but I'll wait for Jocelyn and find out when she's ready. Besides," she said as she put the box inside, shut the lid and locked it, then placed the Butterfly Box back on her dresser, "I've got a dress to make."

"Can I watch?"

"I'd love to have you keep me company so I stay awake. You can tell me about your day."

While Lauryn pinned and measured, Logan told her about the fun she'd had that day. Even though Jazmyn and the other girls didn't have a lot of money, it didn't stop them from going shopping. They'd taken Logan to H&M, Strawberry, and Century 21. Logan's mother had agreed to let her buy a few new things, so Logan had found a cute pair of capri jeans and several tops. She had even found a fun pair of flats to wear for summer.

Lauryn felt bad that she wasn't the one taking Logan shopping and sightseeing, but Logan didn't care. She was having fun, and she knew that what Lauryn was doing was important.

Working into the early-morning hours, Lauryn sewed the dress together, then unpicked seams and tried again in hopes of getting everything perfect for Vanessa's fitting. Logan fell asleep on the couch, and Lauryn didn't have the heart to wake her. She looked at her young stepsister and thought about how close they'd become. She saw a lot of herself in Logan, remembering the struggles she'd faced as a teenager and how confusing and overwhelming life had been at that age. Lauryn's heart swelled with pride for the choices Logan was making. Logan was outgoing, energetic, and thoughtful. She had what it took to make her dreams come true. She was going to be just fine.

It was close to three when Lauryn finally turned off the light on her sewing machine and went to bed. At Parsons, she'd had a definite advantage over many of the other students because she had sewing experience. Lauryn understood how the cut-out pieces from a pattern fit together and how they were constructed to create the right look and fit. When she took pattern-making classes, she grasped the concepts immediately, because she already knew how patterns worked.

Wearily, she fell to her knees beside her bed and fought sleep as she expressed the feelings of her heart in prayer. Handing over her burdens and praying for strength, she prayed with heightened fervency. She knew that without the Lord, she would never make it through these final days of preparation.

With her faith strengthened and her heart comforted, she climbed into bed. As her head hit the pillow, Lauryn's thoughts began to settle so she could fall asleep. There was nothing more she could do until tomorrow.

Chapter Twenty-three

"How are you?" Jace asked over the phone. They talked while Lauryn walked to work the next morning.

"I'm hanging in there. When are you flying to London?"

"Next Monday. Do you have any plans that night?"

"None that I know of, but if I did, they'd be cancelled."

"I'm glad to hear that. I get in around four thirty, so I'll be in the city about six. Can we meet for dinner at the Marquis?"

"I would love that." She stopped and waited for the light to change. The day was overcast, and the air smelled of exhaust and rain. She always kept an umbrella with her just in case, so she pulled it out of her bag and opened it. "I wish you could be here Saturday for the premiere. Vanessa's sending a limo for us to arrive in style."

"I wish I could too. I've never been invited to a premiere before, but if I don't work all weekend I'll never be ready to leave on Monday. You'll have to take a lot of pictures."

"I will," she said, trying to hide her disappointment. "I can't wait to see Vanessa in her dress."

"How are you feeling about the rest of your collection?" he asked.

"I'm excited, Jace. I feel like it's my best work, and I'm proud of it. I'm meeting with Jacqueline today for lunch. I have pictures to show her. She said she would give me her opinion and advice."

"Call me later. I want to hear what she says."

"I will." Droplets of rain began to pelt the top of her umbrella. Lauryn picked up her pace.

"I miss you," he said.

"I miss you too."

"I'll keep you in my prayers so you have a good day."

She smiled. "Thanks, Jace. I need all the prayers I can get. And thanks for waking up to talk."

"You're welcome. It's worth it. I don't like going days without talking to you."

"Me neither." She appreciated his understanding. Because she was so swamped during the day, she could never talk. And because he was busy after work, he could never talk. "I hope you can go back to sleep."

"I will. Don't worry."

A loud siren went off around the corner. Lauryn tried to respond, but Jace couldn't hear her.

Finally, between wails from the fire truck as it tried to get through the mass of yellow taxicabs and pedestrians, she told him good-bye. They'd have to talk later.

The truck managed to maneuver its way through the congested streets, and the hustle and bustle returned to normal.

Lauryn arrived at work just a few minutes before seven-thirty. But, just as she'd done the past few days, instead of going to her office, she stopped on the floor below and went straight to the sewing room. This department was vital to Molnar's operation, because this was where the final fittings and pattern adjustments took place. Once the samples made in this room were approved, they were sent overseas for production.

When Lauryn walked inside, she turned on the light and was startled by the movement of a pile of fabric on one of the tables in the corner.

"Hello?" she said cautiously, ready to run if she had to.

"Hello?" came a garbled reply. The fabric parted, and a figure sat up.

"Beckham?" Lauryn asked, not sure if the rooster-tufted hair and squinty eyes belonged to Molnar's administrative assistant.

"Ms. Alexander. I'm glad it was you. Sasha would have used me for a pin cushion if she'd caught me here."

"What are you doing?"

"I stayed late last night, sewing."

Lauryn's mouth dropped open with the news.

"I wanted to help you finish the collection."

"Thank you, Beckham, but you didn't need to do that."

"Yes, I did." Beckham looked down. "Ms. Alexander, I need to tell you something, and I'm afraid you're going to hate me when you hear it."

"Beckham, you just spent the entire night slaving over a sewing machine. I could never hate you." Lauryn slid out of her raincoat and fluffed her deflated hair.

"You haven't seen my work yet."

"True," she teased.

"Listen," Beckham began. "Yesterday I told you that everything was set to go for your show, and well . . . it isn't."

"I don't understand."

"I'm so sorry. I knew you'd hate me. I'm probably going to lose my job for telling you this, if that's any consolation. You see, Mr. Molnar told me to tell you everything was on track for your show. But it's a lie. He's not planning a show for you, Lauryn."

"What?" She looked at him in disbelief. "Why would he tell me he wanted to move forward with my collection then?"

Beckham looked sheepish. Lauryn didn't have time to read between the lines. Something had told her not to count on anyone but herself to make this show a success. And even though Beckham worked for the enemy, she trusted him.

Lauryn and Beckham stood in silence for several moments. Finally, Lauryn looked up. "Beckham, thank you for being honest with me. I've made a decision. This show is going to happen whether Mr. Molnar likes it or not."

"But Lauryn, I've been around here long enough to know that you're already behind schedule. You don't know anyone who knows how to stage a fashion show, do you?"

Lauryn started to laugh.

"I don't understand what's so funny," Beckham said.

"You'll understand soon enough. I've got a phone call to make."

"And I need to get cleaned up and get to my desk. Mr. Molnar hates it when I'm not at the phones by eight."

"I can't thank you enough for all your help, Beckham."

Beckham smiled." You're the real deal Lauryn. Let me know if there's anything else I can do."

He took off in a rush so he could make it upstairs before most of the employees came in to work.

As soon as he left the room, Lauryn pulled out her phone and dialed a number.

"Well, well," Cooper said when he answered the phone. "I guess you haven't forgotten all the little people you used to work with."

"Cooper, I need your help."

"What's wrong?" he asked with alarm.

"Meet me for lunch. Jacqueline's coming too."

* * *

"Lauryn, darling, it's good to see you again," Jacqueline said when she joined Lauryn at their table. They were in the back corner of the restaurant. Lauryn wanted something out-of-the-way and private. Jacqueline pulled off her oversized, black-rimmed sunglasses and put them in her bag. With long, red, acrylic nails she finger-combed her jet-black, chin-length bob into place. "Horrible weather today."

"It's good to see you too."

Jacqueline's eyes scanned Lauryn's face, taking in the smeared mascara that framed the dark circles under her bloodshot eyes. "Sweetie, I hate to say this, but you look terrible." Jacqueline hung her purse over the back of her chair and sat down.

Lauryn didn't even have enough energy to give a clever come-back. "I know."

"Is it that bad over there?"

"I don't know what's going on, but I'm in the middle of something really weird. I desperately need to talk to you."

"First, may I see your collection? I'm anxious to see your pictures."

"Yes, of course." She pulled the digital camera out of her purse and clicked on the first photo. They leaned in together and scanned through the twenty-five photos.

"Well," Lauryn said, noticing that Jacqueline hadn't said a thing. "What do you think?"

Jacqueline still had her head tilted down to look at the image on the camera. She sniffed, then wiped at her eyes with one hand.

"I can't believe I let you go," she finally said.

"You didn't really have much of a choice," Lauryn replied. "I pretty much told you I was leaving."

"How did I not see this before?" She looked at Lauryn with tear-filled eyes. "Sweetie, this collection is brilliant."

Lauryn's eyes opened wide. "Really, you think so?"

"Absolutely. It's fresh, it's fun, it's glamorous . . . it's you. I underestimated you. If I'd just given you a chance to show me what you really had inside of you . . ." Jacqueline's voice was filled with regret.

"It's okay," Lauryn said. "Maybe I had to leave for both of us to see what we had together."

"I want you back," Jacqueline said. "I'll do anything. You can even continue your own line, but I want you to be part of my design house."

"That's great news, because as soon as this fashion preview is over, I'm quitting. Molnar is too difficult to work with."

"What exactly is going on over there?" Jacqueline asked.

Lauryn explained the situation with Molnar and Sasha, the promises that had enticed her to come work for Molnar, then the quick change in attitude when she'd started.

"It's as if they hired me thinking I had no talent, which doesn't make any sense, and then when they found out I did, they were furious," Lauryn told her. "And Jacqueline," she continued, "it sounds like Mr. Molnar is really out to get *you.* I don't understand the connection, and I can't think of what I possibly could have done to deserve this treatment."

Jacqueline rested her head in her hands for a moment, then looked at Lauryn.

"This is all my fault."

"Your fault? Why do you think that?"

"How in the world did I miss this? You'd think I'd been in this business long enough to know that Laszlo is capable of something like this. He said he'd do it, and he is."

"Do what? What are you talking about?"

"Lauryn, Laszlo Molnar is using you."

"Using me how?"

"He's using you to get to me."

"I don't understand."

"This goes way back, but I know exactly what he's up to." Jacqueline laughed sardonically. "He's only gotten more vicious as time goes on. You see, Lauryn, we both emerged onto the fashion scene about the same time. Both of our collections were the biggest hit at Fall Fashion Week. He had a more eclectic look—edgy, different, with a lot of attitude. Mine was more refined, but strong. My dresses appealed to a classier woman with a strong sense of who she was. Politicians' wives, celebrities, and wealthy socialites all bought my clothes."

"So you two have always been in competition?"

"For as long as I can remember. I'll be honest, though. I wasn't as willing to play the game as he was. Creating my designs and building my business has been much more important to me than schmoozing with the rich and famous. That's just not my style. But Laszlo is a constant face in the social scene, at parties and premieres. It's worked to his advantage a lot of the time, but in some ways I think it's also worked against him."

"Like the bad press he recently got?"

"Exactly. And if anyone knows Laszlo Molnar, I do. I know exactly what he's up to, and we can beat him at his own game."

"What is he up to?"

"Darlings!" Cooper's voice echoed through the entire restaurant.

Jacqueline and Lauryn looked at each other and laughed. No one lit up a room like Cooper.

"Kiss, kiss," he said as he greeted both of them, air kissing them on each cheek. "Great bag, Jacqueline. I designed that when I went through my safari phase."

"It will be a smash this fall," Jacqueline said.

"So," Cooper said, clasping his hands together underneath his chin, "what are we talking about?"

Lauryn brought him up to speed with Laszlo's latest antics and Jacqueline's explanation of why he was being so conniving.

"That dirty dog!" Cooper exclaimed. "You're telling me that he would literally step on you to destroy Jacqueline's career?"

"That's exactly what he's doing. Lauryn is merely a pawn in his game to get to me," Jacqueline said. "He made some horrible threats to me after that whole fiasco with the models."

"When you banned thin models from your show?" Lauryn asked.

"Yes. I was merely trying to make a statement to the media, to push for a better self-image for women, along with a whole contingency of designers who jumped on the bandwagon, and he acts like we're all out to get him. He literally accused me of trying to destroy him. And he said he would destroy me first."

"He did not!" Cooper exclaimed, slapping his hand on his chest for emphasis.

"It's true. Then, when I got Designer of the Year, I thought he was going to strangle me himself."

"Is it that important to him, really?" Lauryn asked, unable to comprehend Laszlo's extreme desire for power, money, and recognition.

"Oh, Lauryn," Jacqueline leaned over and put her hand on Lauryn's cheek, "you've been in this business a while, but there is something you need to learn right now. Actually," she turned to Cooper, "both of you need to learn this. It is a dog-eat-dog industry. You will encounter wonderful, talented people, but you will also encounter those who are so hungry for the top that they will do anything to get there. Laszlo is feeling threatened, especially after his little hijinks at that party where he bad-mouthed the first lady and threw his drink at the waiter. I think it must have pushed him over the edge when I got the bid for the Nicole Kidman movie. They had Laszlo lined up to do it, but after his outburst, they decided they didn't want any of his bad press tied to the film. I should have anticipated that he would retaliate, but I never, ever thought he would hurt innocent people along the way. It shouldn't surprise me, though. This is Laszlo Molnar we're talking about."

"I guess that explains why I can't figure out what I possibly could have done to be treated like this," Lauryn said.

"Well, the article Bernice did about you in *Women's Fashion Review* probably did a lot to expose you to the design world, but it was the worst thing that could happen for Laszlo's plan."

"Why do you think that?" Lauryn asked.

"I think he wanted to redeem his reputation by taking a young designer like yourself and receiving all the credit for launching your career. He's trying to reinvent himself and polish his tarnished image. And by recruiting one of my designers, whom I admit I was stifling, he would run my name through the mud in the process. But look at you, Lauryn. You *are* making it on your own. Without any of Laszlo's help. He can't stand that. And," Jacqueline pointed to the camera, "you have created a collection that will help you break out on your own. This has got to be killing him." Jacqueline laughed.

"What do I do? He's trying to sabotage my preview. I just know it."

"Then we don't let him. How's the show coming along?"

"I found out from his assistant that I'd better get my own plans going for the show."

"That's where I come in," Cooper said. He clapped his hands. "I know just what to do. Oh, my gosh! After our last show—"

"Last show?" Jacqueline asked with confusion, "Oh, you mean the one in the paper?"

"Right," Cooper said. "I've been thinking about what I would have changed and done differently. And now I get to do it!" His voice raised an octave in all the excitement. Lauryn and Jacqueline laughed at his exuberance. "How long do I have?"

"A week and a half," Lauryn told him

"Jacqueline, I may need some time off to work on it," Cooper said.

"Are you kidding? You have my whole staff at your disposal. What about the gowns, Lauryn?"

"We're keeping them locked in the sewing closet at night. I don't trust anyone."

"Keep your guard up, darling. I hate to say it, but Laszlo is capable of anything at this point. I'm certain he will stop at nothing to destroy your show. You have to understand, dear, he doesn't want anyone to see your talent, because then they'll know he did nothing for you, and his plans will be ruined. In fact, I think we should consider finding a safer place to keep your gowns. Now, what about publicity? Do you have any connections with the media?" Jacqueline asked.

"Bernice has been really good to me. She's getting the word out to her colleagues. Representatives from *Vogue, Elle,* and most of the other leading fashion magazines will be there."

Jacqueline nodded her approval. "It would be great if we had a few celebrities there, you know, to really give the media something to feed on. We need to surround the show in a frenzy of excitement."

Lauryn and Cooper looked at each other, then at Jacqueline.

"What?" she asked, sensing their excitement.

"I actually have two powerful friends coming. One is Caroline Nottingham."

"I know Caroline," Jacqueline said. "Great woman. I hear she's writing a book."

Lauryn nodded. "She had me design a dress for her and has told all her friends about me."

"She has very wealthy friends," Jacqueline said, impressed.

"True, but more important is that she's highly respected."

"Who's the other person?"

Lauryn and Cooper exchanged looks.

"Vanessa Cates!" Cooper blurted out. He clapped his hand over his mouth when he realized that all the people in the surrounding booths and tables were looking at him.

When the attention turned away, Jacqueline said in a quiet tone, "Are you kidding me?"

"No," Lauryn answered. "She's wearing one of my designs to her premiere this weekend. She invited me and my sister to join her."

"She's one of the biggest stars in Hollywood right now. How did you get her?" Jacqueline asked.

Lauryn gave her the short version of meeting Vanessa on the plane.

"Good grief, darling, you don't need my help at all," Jacqueline said. "I'm afraid that at this point, Laszlo better just step aside or he's going to get trampled in the crowd that will be trying to get to you."

Lauryn was flattered by her words but not convinced. "I don't want a lot of attention."

"You're going to get it."

"That's not what I'm after," Lauryn said.

"And that's exactly why you're headed for a long, fruitful career. You still need to know how to handle the press and the attention, though."

"I've learned from the best," Lauryn told her.

Jacqueline smiled, and her bottom lip quivered. "You are such a sweetheart."

"The feeling is mutual. As soon as all of this is over, I hope I can come back to work for you."

Jacqueline shook her head. "I'm sorry, darling. I'm not sure that's going to work anymore."

"What?" Lauryn asked with surprise. "You don't want me?"

"Oh, by all means, my dear, I would love to have you. But you don't want to work for me when you can have your own design house."

"My own? Oh, no, I don't think—"

"We'll talk after the show. You know you always have a place with me. But Lauryn, I think there are bigger things in store for you."

Cooper grabbed her hand. "So do I."

Lauryn's eyes began to sting as her tears surfaced. She wished she could have the kind of confidence in herself that her friends were demonstrating. She felt so small and insignificant at times. Did she really have the talent and the drive to create her very own design house? At the moment, she didn't know if she even had the guts to dream about it.

* * *

With only one week to go, Lauryn lived on adrenaline and peanut M&Ms. Every morning when she pulled the dresses out of the sewing closet, her heart swelled with pride. This was her very best work. The gowns were absolutely breathtaking. She felt strongly that they would appeal to the major retailers. She already had a good relationship with Barneys, but if they didn't want her collection, Bloomingdale's or Saks were both great options.

By Saturday, Lauryn was exhausted. She'd survived on barely four hours of sleep each night, some nights even less. There was nothing left to give.

"The premiere's tonight!" Logan sang as she bounded into the bedroom and plopped onto Lauryn's bed. "I could hardly sleep last night."

Lauryn was awake, but she didn't have enough energy to lift her eyelids to prove it.

"Hey," Logan said, poking her, "are you dead?"

"Yes."

"Come on, Lauryn, wake up. I want to plan our day. Are you sure you're okay with me wearing the Jacqueline Yvonne dress? I keep thinking about how perfectly it fits you. And should I wear my hair up or down?" She pulled her long, light brown hair into a ponytail and twisted it onto her head.

"Yes. Up." Lauryn felt like someone had pulled her plug and all her energy had drained out.

"Also, your cell phone has been ringing like crazy," Logan informed her.

"Whoizit?" Her words slurred into each other.

"Just a sec. I'll go check."

Logan left the room and came back in a flash. "Looks like Jace called, Vanessa called, and your mom called."

"Did they leave a message?"

"I'll check." Logan pushed buttons and listened to the messages for her. "Jace said he'll call back." She listened some more. "Vanessa called to see if we want to get our hair done by her stylist. And I am definitely going to call her back with a big *heck yeah!*"

Logan didn't waste a second dialing the number. She calmed herself down and waited for someone to answer.

"I'd like to speak to Ms. Cates please," she said, sounding very professional. "I'm so excited!" she whispered to Lauryn while she waited for Vanessa to come on the line.

"Hello?" Vanessa said.

"Hi, Vanessa, this is Logan."

"Logan. Hi. You got my message."

"Is it too late to go with you?"

"I'm on my way right now. I wanted to swing by and pick up the dress. I can just pick you girls up at the same time. Does that work?"

"Sure does. We'll be ready."

Logan hung up the phone and shrieked, "This is so cool!" then fell onto the bed and rolled over, crushing Lauryn. "You have to get up. She's coming right now."

"Right now?"

"She wants to get her dress, so we can go with her right now."

Lauryn groaned. "Okay. I just need to sleep for five more minutes."

"Now I know how my mom feels when she's trying to wake me up for church," Logan said.

"Okay, okay. I'll get up." Lauryn forced her limbs to move so she could get out of bed. "I don't care about my hair," she said. "I just want sleep."

"You can sleep later." Logan was digging through her side of the closet for something to wear. "There it is," she said as she whisked a shirt off a hanger. "I'm so glad I went shopping this week."

The more Lauryn moved around, the more she woke up. Her head throbbed, and her neck ached too. She'd probably slept on it wrong.

Just as she got dressed, the doorbell rang.

"It's Vanessa!" Logan announced.

* * *

"Can I talk to you girls about something? I could use your advice." Vanessa pulled a pepperoni off her pizza and poked it into her mouth. They all sat with their feet up, toes freshly polished, eating the pizza Vanessa just had to have.

"Our advice?" Lauryn asked with surprise.

"Yes. I trust your opinions. You see, I've always said I would never do a nude scene in a movie, for obvious reasons." She patted her rear end. "But also because I'm not comfortable doing it. Even if they get a body double, people are going to think that's my body up on the screen, not to mention the fact that my family will be watching the movie." She put the semi-eaten slice down on her plate. "I've been offered a movie from a director I have wanted to work with since I started in this business. The script is brilliant, and it's a part I really want to do. I love the character, and I feel like it's the perfect film for me. But it has a very steamy love scene in it." She looked at Logan. "You couldn't even go see my movie and keep your conscience happy."

Logan shook her head.

"Lauryn, what do you think?"

"I've never seen a movie where there's been a romantic scene in it that I've felt even had anything to do with the plot. Scenes like that are just put in there to attract a certain audience, not to improve the plot or the characters," Lauryn answered.

"I usually leave and get popcorn or go to the bathroom," Logan said. "Brody would never leave, and it always bothered me."

Vanessa thought about their objections.

"Let me ask you this," Lauryn said. "Would the story be the same without the love scene?"

Vanessa chewed her bottom lip for a moment as she processed the question. "To be absolutely honest, yes." She sat up. "That scene does nothing to move the plot forward or build the characters." She lifted her chin. "I'm not going to do it. I'll tell the director that I will make the movie on one condition—that we take out that scene."

"Good girl!" Lauryn exclaimed. "Instead of lowering yourself to their level, make them come up to yours."

"You're absolutely right." Vanessa thumped the arm of the chair with her fist. "I mean, look at you and your designs. People have tried to pressure you into designing dresses against your personal standards, but you haven't budged, have you?"

"No," Lauryn said. "I couldn't look myself in the mirror in the morning if I did. It wouldn't make me a better designer if I did, so why would I do it?"

"Exactly. I won't be a better actress for taking off my clothes."

"What if you lose the movie over it?" Logan asked.

"Then I'll find another movie," Vanessa said.

"Wow," Logan said, nodding her head. "That's very cool." She looked at her stepsister. "You guys are both very cool."

Vanessa and Lauryn looked at each other. "We're cool," Vanessa said. "I like that."

They all laughed.

"Speaking of cool, that's a huge understatement for that incredible gown you've designed," Vanessa said to Lauryn. "I've never been so excited to wear something in my life. And the shoes and bag your friend Cooper designed . . . absolutely fantastic. The shoes are every bit as gorgeous as my Manolo Blahniks, but three times more comfortable."

"I'm so glad you like them," Lauryn said. "He's very creative. You'll see when you come to the fashion show. He's designing the set. I think it's going to be quite a show if it all comes together."

"Well, I'm happy to help any way I can," Vanessa said.

"Wearing my dress and coming to my show is more than I can ask of you," Lauryn replied.

"I've invited over a dozen of my closest friends to come. All we need is Sarah Jessica and Renee and a few others and, honey, you're going to be one busy lady!"

At the moment, being busy held no appeal for Lauryn. But the possibility of finally realizing her dream was exciting. Lauryn felt lightheaded and weak at the thought. Things were falling into place. She prayed nothing would go wrong.

Chapter Twenty-four

"How do I look?" Logan said as she walked out of the bedroom.

The Jacqueline Yvonne dress, with its soft, turquoise chiffon and beaded bodice, looked stunning on Logan. Vanessa's stylist, Antoine, had woven three different colors of brown into Logan's hair to create a rich, textured look that complemented her coloring. He also added a row of extensions around the bottom, then styled her hair in long, loose curls that hung below her shoulders and down her back. Her makeup was subdued, with most of the focus on her eyes.

"I feel like a princess going to the ball."

"You look like one," Lauryn told her.

"Let me look at you," Logan said, admiring Lauryn's hair again and her elegant black gown—a column dress with sheer, long, black sleeves. A touch of sparkle at her ears and neck completed her look. "You look amazing. I love the highlights he put in your hair."

So did Lauryn. Caramel hues accentuated her naturally honey-blond hair, giving it shine and texture. Long, loose layers framed her face and balanced the pure elegance of the gown.

"I wonder how much he charges," Lauryn said. "I doubt I could afford him, but he's so good he might be worth it."

"It was awesome of Vanessa to do this for us," Logan said. "She's such a nice person for being as famous and important as she is."

"That's why I like her. Not because she's famous, but because she's nice."

"And funny," Logan added. They both laughed as they recalled the way Vanessa had paraded around the salon with foil in her hair, walking on her heels with her toes lifted in the air so she didn't ruin her pedicure.

After careful consideration, Lauryn had decided that it might be wise to help advertise her gowns by wearing one of the creations from the new collection. Neither she nor Logan dared sit, for fear of crushing their gowns. Lauryn had nearly fallen asleep leaning against the wall. She'd taken some painkillers for the headache she still had and hoped they would help the scratchiness in her throat. She peeked out the window as they waited for Vanessa's limo to arrive.

"Is the car here yet?" Logan asked.

"I don't see it. I'm sure the driver will call to let us know when he's close."

"I'm so excited; my stomach is inside out."

"Mine's a little upset too," Lauryn said.

"Oh, I almost forgot my purse. I have to have my camera and lip gloss and phone. And breath mints. I can't forget breath mints." Logan rushed into the bedroom in a flurry to grab the beaded bag that matched her gown. When she returned, she asked, "Can you see them yet?"

"Not yet," Lauryn said, looking out the window again. Then, her breath caught in her throat. A long, white limousine rounded the corner. "It's here."

The phone rang, and the driver informed them that he was waiting.

"This is it," Lauryn said as she hung up the phone.

Both of them clasped hands and squealed with excitement.

"Okay," Lauryn said, gaining her composure. "We have to be cool."

"I know," Logan agreed. "But it's going to be so hard!"

They left the apartment and took the elevator down to the lobby. Taking a deep breath, they emerged from the building to see the driver waiting for them with the limo door opened. He had his back turned to them, but when they approached, he turned.

Lauryn let the driver help Logan climb in first, then he reached for her hand to help her inside. Looking up to tell the driver thank you, Lauryn's knees buckled.

"Jace!"

"Hey, beautiful girl!"

Tears immediately filled her eyes, and she threw herself into his arms. "What are you doing here? How did you get away?"

Jace held her, then gave her a soulful kiss before he answered. "Let's get inside, and I'll tell you all about it."

The actual limo driver waited for them to get seated before he pulled the car away from the curb and merged into traffic.

Lauryn's cheeks hurt from smiling so much. How was it possible Jace was here?

She looked at Logan, who was beaming like a lighthouse. "Wait a minute, did you have something to do with this?"

Logan burst out laughing and nodded her head. "I told Vanessa how much it would mean to you if Jace could be here. And you know Vanessa . . ."

"So all this time you told me you had meetings just to throw me off?" she scolded him.

"Sorry. I didn't mean to lie, but I didn't want to spoil the surprise. By the way," he said as he took one of her hands in his and lifted it to his lips, "you look incredibly beautiful tonight. So do you, Logan."

Logan blushed. "Thanks, Jace."

"Is this one of your dresses?" he asked Lauryn.

"From my new collection. But wait until you see Vanessa. Her dress turned out extraordinarily beautiful."

"I can't wait to meet her and thank her for inviting me," Jace said.

"You're going to love Vanessa," Logan exuded. "She's the neatest, nicest celebrity I've ever met. I mean, she's the only celebrity I've ever met, but still. When we're together it's just like hanging out with a best friend. She always wants to order food and just sit around and eat and talk. When we were getting our hair done, she ordered in pizza even though she's supposed to be on a diet. She's so us!" Logan continued rambling on about Vanessa, but Lauryn and Jace weren't listening. They were busy gazing into each other's eyes. Lauryn still wasn't quite over the fact that Jace was there, putting James Bond to shame for how dashing he looked in his tux.

"I'm so glad you're here," she said to him.

His dimpled smile nearly melted her bones.

"So am I. I've missed you."

Crazy things were happening in her heart. Could falling in love cause a heart attack?

Sparkling cider had been placed in a bucket of ice for them. Logan spied it first and offered to pour them drinks.

With crystal in hand, they toasted Vanessa, the night, and being together. And much to Logan's delight, Jace and Lauryn finished the toast with a kiss.

* * *

Standing in a section reserved for VIPs, Jace, Lauryn, and Logan watched as stars from the film walked down the red carpet. Lauryn didn't know many of the actors and film crew, but some of the bigger stars were impossible to miss. But no one came close to making the entrance Vanessa Cates made when she stepped out of her limo and onto the red carpet.

Logan screamed right along with the rest of the crowd, but Lauryn stood speechless as she watched Vanessa slowly and regally make her way up the red carpet. She looked absolutely breath-taking.

With her red hair curled in long ringlets all over her head but clipped back on the sides, her neck looked long and elegant. Dangling emerald earrings and an understated emerald necklace gave just the right sparkle to frame her face. But it was the exquisite, flawlessly fitted, emerald-green silk gown that trans-formed Vanessa into the Hollywood royalty she was.

And last of all, Cooper's sequined bag and matching shoes completed the outfit to perfection.

Lauryn heard comments coming from the crowd behind her.

"Who designed that gown?"

"I've never seen anything like it."

"It's absolutely exquisite."

The whole experience was so overwhelming Lauryn could barely stand it. Her breathing became shallow, and she got light-headed and broke out into a cold sweat.

"Lauryn!" Jace said with alarm. "Are you okay? You're as white as a ghost."

Lauryn felt weak at the knees, and luckily, Jace circled his arms around her to steady her.

"I don't . . . feel . . . so good."

"You look terrible. We need to take you home," Jace told her.

"No, no. I can't leave. I want to see Vanessa's movie."

"But you're sick."

"I'm not sick, I'm just overtired. I'll snap out of it. I haven't eaten much today. Maybe if I could get some juice or something."

Jace held on to her but got Logan's attention, which wasn't easy, since Logan had joined the throng of overexuberant fans screaming at the tops of their lungs.

"Logan!" Jace hollered, then tugged at her purse strap.

"Hey!" Logan screamed, turning quickly to see who was trying to pilfer her purse, then realized it was Jace. "Oh. What's going on?" she asked, noticing Lauryn slumped in his arms like a rag doll.

"Lauryn's not feeling well. She needs juice or something to eat. Can you try to find something for her?"

"Of course," Logan said, forgetting about the red-carpet parade of stars. "I'll be right back."

Jace found a spot where they could sit and helped Lauryn into a chair. She felt weak, shaky, and cold. Why hadn't she brought some kind of shawl or wrap?

Not sure how long she had dozed, she stirred when she heard Logan's voice. "Thank goodness Vanessa saw me. She helped me get all of this." Logan held out bottles of juice, cookies, and some little sandwiches on a plate.

"Perfect. Thanks, Logan." Jace popped the bottle lid and helped Lauryn take a sip of the cool, sweet liquid. "How's that?" he asked.

Lauryn knew if she didn't snap out of it, he would take her home, so she answered with all the perkiness she could muster. "Much better. That's exactly what I needed."

"How about a bite of cookie?" he asked.

She didn't tell him that the thought of eating a cookie made her stomach turn inside out. Instead, she said, "That sounds great." She took a small nibble of the white chocolate chip macadamia nut cookie and managed to swallow it. "Mmm, good."

Forcing her eyes open, she gave them both a smile and said, "I feel a lot better. Thanks, you two."

"Are you sure you feel better?" Jace leaned in closely and examined her face.

"Positive. It's just been a long week."

"That's for sure," Logan said. "I don't think she's gotten more than three or four hours of sleep a night."

"You feel well enough to stay?" Jace asked.

"Of course. In fact, give me another bite of that cookie." Lauryn faked it as best she could. She wasn't about to miss the opportunity of a lifetime, nor the chance to support Vanessa.

"I think we need to take our seats," Logan said. "That guy over there is waving all the VIPs into the theater."

"Let's go," Lauryn said, wondering if she really could make it to her seat without collapsing.

"Here," Jace said, helping her to her feet. "I'm going to hang onto you, just in case."

Together with the rest of the crowd, they filed into the theater in anticipation of the night of entertainment and celebrities.

* * *

"So, how did you like the movie?" Jace asked Lauryn.

"It sure was exciting," she answered.

"Are you basing that response off the first five minutes you watched before you fell asleep or the credits at the end when you finally woke up?"

"I was awake for more than the first five minutes," she said.

"Oh? Then how do you explain the wet spot on my shoulder where you slobbered while you were asleep?"

Lauryn pulled a face. "Really?" She looked at his tuxedo closely. Sure enough, there was a wet spot the size of tennis ball, just like he'd said. "That's gross. I'm sorry."

"How are you feeling?"

"Better, actually. That little nap helped. But what do I tell Vanessa when she asks how I liked the movie?" Lauryn felt terrible about missing Vanessa's big part.

"She was superb. If they don't give her an Oscar for her performance, I'll never go see another movie again."

"Really? She was that good?"

"Yeah, she was. Just tell her that you think she deserves an award for her performance."

Lauryn thought about it. "That works. I can't lie to her, but I don't want to tell her I slept through the whole thing. At least, not tonight."

"My question is, though, are you ready to go home? I think you need to get some more sleep. You're still pale, and I can tell by your eyes that you don't feel well."

"I look that bad?"

"You look beautiful," Jace said. "But you just don't look like you feel well."

"I want to see Vanessa first, then I'm ready to go. Where's Logan, by the way?"

"You won't believe this, but she's been talking to that teen idol, Trey Matthews."

"The one from that Disney movie?"

"Yeah, and he seems to be very interested in Logan."

"Where are they?" Lauryn asked, sitting up so she could see. Jace pointed to where they were standing, and Lauryn got the same impression. Logan was resting back against a large, marble column, and Trey had one arm stretched up above her head and was leaning in closely, talking to her. "He's getting a little too cozy, don't you think?"

"Yeah, but look at her face. That's the face that represents every teenage girl in America."

"We need to get a picture," Lauryn said, glad to be feeling a bit better after her nap. "Logan's the one who brought a camera though."

"I can use my cell phone," Jace said. "I think I can get close enough without disturbing them."

Jace strolled over to the hors d'oeuvre cart and casually put a sushi roll on a small plate, then walked away slowly, pausing long enough to snap a picture of Logan and Trey.

He returned to Lauryn triumphant. "I got it. She's going to love showing this off to her friends." He showed Lauryn the picture, which was surprisingly clear for a cell phone.

"There's Vanessa," Lauryn said, spying the starlet over Jace's shoulder. "She looks so beautiful, doesn't she?"

"She really does. I've never thought of her as a beauty," Jace said. "In all her movies, she plays such gritty, down-to-earth characters; it's interesting to see her so glamorous. A lot of that is due to that fantastic dress you made for her."

"Thanks, Jace," Lauryn said, stifling a yawn.

"Let's go talk to her, then I'm taking you back to your apartment, whether you like it or not!"

"I won't fight you. I just want to crawl into bed and pull the covers over my head."

He helped her to her feet.

Arm in arm, they walked over to Vanessa, who was surrounded by reporters and fellow actors. They waited several minutes before Vanessa spotted them and stopped what she was doing to identify them. "Everyone, I want you to meet someone. Her name is Lauryn Alexander, and she's the designer of my gown. You'll be seeing much more from her next week when she gives a preview of her new collection."

Suddenly, all eyes were on Lauryn.

"Stay close to me," she whispered to Jace. He pulled her in close, and they joined Vanessa in front of the cameras.

Vanessa continued praising Lauryn and told all the details about Lauryn's preview and how many fashion magazines and celebrities were going to be there. "I guarantee you'll be seeing more of Ms. Alexander's dresses on the red carpet."

Digging deep, Lauryn found the strength to perk up, put a smile on her face, and have her picture taken with Vanessa. A couple of reporters asked to be invited to the preview, and Jace jotted down their names so Lauryn could leave them a VIP pass at the gate. The photographers admired Lauryn's own gown and took several pictures just of her. Then someone spied another star, and the crowd of reporters and photographers shifted away from Vanessa.

"So, how did you like the movie?" Vanessa asked.

"Incredible," Jace said. "The show blew me away. If I hadn't heard all the good things Lauryn's been telling me about you, I'd be afraid of you. You're a pretty tough gal in that show."

"That's why acting is so much fun," Vanessa said. Then she looked more closely at Lauryn. "Are you okay? You look like death warmed over."

"I think I overdid it this week," Lauryn said. "Nothing a good night's sleep won't cure."

"I hope that's all it takes. You've got a big week ahead of you. I can call my driver if you're ready to go."

Lauryn felt a wave of chills come over her. Her knees went weak.

Jace held her close. "I think that would be a good idea," he said as everything around Lauryn went black.

Chapter Twenty-five

"Hey there, Sleeping Beauty." Jace's voice came through the fog in Lauryn's head. "How are you feeling?"

Lauryn wanted to speak, but her mouth wouldn't move. Instead, she groaned.

A hand rested on her forehead. "Your fever's finally gone," he said. "You really scared me there for a while."

He felt both of her cheeks. "I bet you're thirsty."

She managed to dip her chin, indicating that yes, she was thirsty.

"Here," he said, slipping a straw between her lips. "Take just little sips."

With a little effort she managed to suck a few drops of the cool water, which slid down her parched throat.

"Thanks," she whispered. "Is it morning?"

"Yes," he said.

"I don't think I can go to church today."

"I don't either," he said, "seeing as it's Wednesday."

"What?" Her eyes flew open, the brightness causing her to quickly squint. Panic struck her heart.

"You've been a very sick girl," he told her. "Don't you remember anything?"

The last thing she remembered was Vanessa's premiere, and even that was a blur. The reality crashed down on her.

"The show!" she exclaimed. "It's in three days. There's no way I can be ready for it." Tears filled her eyes as despair filled her heart. "Oh, Jace, I worked so hard."

Jace chuckled. "It's going to be okay." He reached over and stroked her forehead.

"I can't believe it's over," she said, her tears falling faster. "I lost my chance. And the worst part is, Laszlo won."

"Lauryn, you are very talented, and a lot of people believe in you. You'll get another chance."

Trying to be strong, Lauryn nodded, but she knew in her heart that if first chances were nearly impossible in this business, second chances didn't exist. She could go back to work for Jacqueline. That would be okay. She missed working there, and Jacqueline loved her designs. Perhaps this was what was supposed to happen after all. "I'm a has-been even before I was a could-be."

Jace chuckled.

"I wanted to show Laszlo what I could really do, you know? I wanted to prove to him that he was wrong."

"There's something you need to know." He leaned in close to her and looked at her intently. "I hate to have to tell you this, as weak as you are."

"What?" she asked. "Is someone else sick? Has someone been hurt?"

"No, nothing like that."

She waited a moment for him to go on, but he didn't. "Jace, what is it? Just tell me."

"Okay. That guy from Molnar's office called, his name is Brock or Bic or—"

"Was it Beckham? He's Molnar's administrative assistant."

"Yeah, that was the guy. I wrote his name down in the kitchen. Anyway, he seems like a really nice guy. He called to let you know that . . ."

Lauryn waited, wondering what was so hard for him to say.

"Well, you see . . ."

"Jace, please, tell me what happened."

"A fire broke out in the sewing department. All of your samples were ruined by smoke and water damage."

"A fire?" she said. "My samples?"

"I'm so sorry." Jace reached for her but stopped when Lauryn unexpectedly broke out in laughter.

"Lauryn?" He felt her forehead, but it wasn't hot.

She couldn't stop laughing long enough to explain why she found it funny.

Logan appeared at the doorway of her bedroom. "What's going on?"

Jace lifted his shoulders and shook his head. "I just told her about the fire."

Logan's face reflected Jace's same expression of confusion. "And she's laughing?"

"I don't get it either."

"Maybe she's still a little out of it," Logan said. "You know, the high fever and being so sick."

Lauryn held up her hand and took a few deep breaths. "I'm fine." She chuckled again. "It's just that—" She paused to wipe the tears of laughter from her eyes. "Oh, my goodness, I don't believe this."

"Lauryn, please, tell us what's going on!" Jace insisted.

With another deep breath and a quick sip of water to clear her throat, Lauryn told them the news. "Those dresses weren't the final product. All the gowns are hanging in Jacqueline's warehouse."

Logan and Jace both looked dumbfounded, their expressions making Lauryn laugh again.

Finally Jace asked, "How did you know to move them?"

"It was Jacqueline's idea. She was afraid something might happen to them."

"Do you think Molnar is responsible for the fire?"

"I really don't know, but when I asked the seamstresses to help me sneak the dresses out, they didn't blink an eye. Those women have seen plenty around that place, and they completely agreed when I told them I wanted to store the gowns at a private location."

"This could be huge if the press found out about it," Logan said.

"I don't want to create a scandal," Lauryn replied. "But I do know one thing."

"What's that?" Jace asked.

"The show must go on! Give me my phone."

* * *

After making calls to Cooper, Jacqueline, and Vanessa, Lauryn felt a surge of energy take over.

Her next call was overseas, to Zurich.

"Caroline Nottingham, please," she said when she called the number Caroline had given her.

"Lauryn!" Caroline's excited voice came on the line. "I heard you were sick. How are you?"

"Much better."

"Good! I wish you had time to come to Zurich for a little recovery."

"That sounds wonderful, but I'll have to take a rain check. Right now I've got a show to put on."

"Your friend Jace told me about the fire. I was so sorry to hear about your gowns."

"Don't worry, Caroline. The gowns are safe. But I am working against the clock. I've got Laszlo working against me, too, but I'm not going to let him destroy me."

"Good girl!" Caroline exclaimed. "What can I do to help?"

"Just having you come to the show and bring your friends will help. Your presence will give a lot of credibility to my show."

"I'll be there. Can you reserve me ten seats?"

"Of course, Caroline. Anything for you."

"All right. Good luck with all the preparations. Call me if you need anything. I have a whole staff in Manhattan who can pitch in if you need them."

Lauryn thanked her, then offered a quick prayer of thanks in her heart, because she knew exactly where all of the blessings were coming from.

* * *

"I need to go to my office," she said to Jace after she took a long, refreshing shower.

"Why?" He had set up a makeshift office at her kitchen table while she'd been sick.

"To pack up my things. And to give them my notice."

"You want me to come with you?" Jace asked.

She smiled. "I was hoping you'd ask. I seem to remember you playing some very convincing roles in our high school plays. Do you think you could dig up some of that talent and pretend to be my legal counsel, you know, just in case things get a little ugly?"

"It would be my pleasure," he said, clicking a button on his laptop and saving his document. "I can finish this later."

He got to his feet, and Lauryn walked over to him and gave him a hug.

"Mmm, what was that for?"

"For being here. For staying by my side the entire time I was sick. I know you were supposed to be in London on Monday."

"It was more important for me to be here with you," he said, giving her a kiss on her forehead. "I would have been worthless in London. At least here I was able to still get some work done while I was with you."

"I'm so lucky to have you."

"I feel pretty lucky myself," he said.

They hugged again.

"Are you ready?" he asked.

"Ready to get this over with."

* * *

"So, this is the famous Molnar House of Design," Jace observed as they walked down the hallway together.

"Yes, and this," she said as she led him into a room, "is my office."

His eyebrows lifted as he looked around the room. "Not too shabby. You sure you don't want to stay? That's quite a view." He looked out the window.

"No view is worth working here," she said, plopping the empty box on top of the desk. "I just have a few things to gather up."

She began emptying her drawers of her belongings. There wasn't much to pack, since she hadn't been there all that long.

Jace was still looking out the window, and Lauryn was getting the last of her things when Sasha entered the room.

"Well, well," she said.

Lauryn looked up and noticed Sasha's smug expression.

"Hello, Sasha."

"I see you're feeling better."

"Yes, thank you."

"I gather you were informed of the mishap in the sewing room."

"Yes, such a shock," Lauryn said, wanting to add the word, *NOT!*

"Well, these things happen. Too bad your collection was ruined. I'll alert the media today that the show will be cancelled."

"Oh, you don't need to. I've already contacted the media and taken care of everything."

One of Sasha's eyebrows lifted. "You did?"

"Yes, but I told them the show would go on."

Sasha's mouth dropped open. Then she snapped it shut and said, "Why would you do something like that?"

"Because I will be having my show."

"You have no gowns, no facility, no models. It's impossible!"

"Actually, I do have gowns, I've secured a facility, and I'm taking care of the models."

"But how?! Mr. Molnar will never put his name on something like this. He has a standard of excellence to maintain."

"To be honest, Sasha, I don't really want his name associated with mine in any way. So, I guess that brings me to my next item of business." Lauryn squared her shoulders. "I quit."

Sasha lifted her chin, her cheeks sucked in aristocratically. Then she said, "May I remind you that you signed a contract?"

Jace stepped forward, falling into his role as legal counsel right on cue. Sasha had yet to recognize his presence in the room.

"May I inform you that my client has kept a detailed log of her experience here with Mr. Molnar. Every conversation, every e-mail, every action by every employee," he told Sasha. "We're prepared to fight this if we have to. It will get ugly, and it will make headlines. I'm sure Mr. Molnar has a lot at stake. He might want to think of his reputation, as tarnished as it already is."

"Well. I think I'd better report all this to Mr. Molnar!"

"Yes, you probably should," Jace said. "Just have your attorneys contact me if they have anything they want to discuss." He retrieved a business card from his pocket and handed it to her, but she didn't take it.

"I knew this was a bad idea from the start," Sasha said, glaring at Lauryn.

"Funny," Lauryn said, folding the flaps on the box. "So did I."

Jace picked up the box, and together, he and Lauryn walked out of the office, leaving Sasha frozen in her spot, her mouth hanging open.

* * *

"I can't wait to see this," Lauryn said as she and Jace stepped out of the taxicab on Fifth Avenue by the New York Public Library. They were at Bryant Park, where events like the HBO Film Festival and the New York Fashion Week were held.

With Jacqueline's help, Cooper had been able to reserve the spot near the pond, a favorite ice-skating spot in the winter, where a large white tent had been temporarily constructed for the show.

Jace took her hand, and together they walked across the expansive lawn as the white canvas tent came into view.

"There it is!" Lauryn exclaimed. "This doesn't seem real."

Giving her hand a squeeze, Jace pulled her forward. Cooper was expecting them.

They walked quickly until they stood in front of the tent doors. "Are you ready?" he asked.

Lauryn squared up her shoulders and smiled. She felt like a kid at Christmas.

Jace pulled open the door while Lauryn stepped inside.

From the back of the room, Lauryn and Jace got a full view of the layout. Lauryn got goose bumps.

The runway cut the room in half. On either side were rows of chairs and an area on each side for the media. The ramp was covered in some sort of mirror-like material that reflected the overhead lights. A small stage was set with a staircase and decorated in stark black and white, reminiscent of the fifties. Hanging as backdrops were the pictures of Audrey Hepburn, Doris Day, and Grace Kelly from the modesty fashion show.

Breathless, Lauryn followed Jace to the front, where workers were still putting finishing touches on the ramp.

Suddenly, a supercharged Cooper came onto the set like a whirlwind. He stopped when he saw Jace and Lauryn.

Clasping his hands together, his expression lit up like Times Square. "So, what do you think? Isn't it fabulous?"

"It's amazing, Coop, but I didn't expect anything else. You're brilliant!" She walked up the set of stairs and joined him on the runway, where they hugged.

"I'm so glad you like it. Don't you feel like you've stepped back in time?"

"Totally. I love the whole Hollywood glam feel. It's perfect."

"Your gowns are going to pop with this background," he said. "All of that color in front of the black and white will make them stand out even more."

"Did the dresses arrive?" she asked.

"They're in the back. When do you expect the models?"

"They'll be here anytime."

"You were able to get enough?" Cooper asked.

"I think so. Jacqueline said she'd make some calls if I need more. I also might need more help with hair and makeup." She groaned with frustration. "All of this was supposed to be lined up by Molnar."

"Molnar? Who needs him? This show is going to blow anything he's ever done out of the water," Cooper assured her.

"I hope so. I'm encouraged after seeing this." She motioned to the extravagant set and runway.

"You've done a great job, Cooper," Jace said. "Anything I can do to help?"

Cooper's eyes lit up. "Actually, I could use your help in the back. Are you handy with a saw? I'm trying to build a ramp for the girls, because the stairs will be difficult in their dresses."

"I'll give it my best shot."

"I'm going to check on the dresses while you do that," Lauryn said. She was anxious to see how her gowns had survived storage.

Lauryn passed through the curtain and walked backstage. There they were, lined up in the corner next to the dressing tables—five racks filled with colorful silk, chiffon, taffeta, and lace. She stroked the first dress on the rack—a floor-length, silk gown in dark magenta. It was hard to explain why, but Lauryn felt tears welling up in her eyes. The dresses on these racks were more than unique and beautiful gowns that she hoped would launch her career in evening wear; they were her love and her inspiration come to life. Touching them was like touching a dream.

Lauryn carefully checked each garment and pulled the dresses that had loose rhinestones and other things that needed some repair. The big challenge would be fitting the models and making the alterations. She mentally prepared herself to stay up all night.

Setting her sewing box on a small table, she opened the lid to make sure she had plenty of pins for the fitting, then she checked to see how many full-length mirrors Cooper had managed to secure. She found four full-length mirrors and four vanity tables with mirrors where models could sit and get their hair and makeup done. More would be better, but hopefully it would be enough. Threading a needle, Lauryn began to secure loose rhinestones and other trims that had come unstitched. The task before her seemed to stretch out to even bigger proportions when she realized just how long it would take to do each dress. How was she ever going to be ready?

Voices near the curtain separating the dressing room from the stage caught her attention. The models were early.

Even though she wasn't quite ready for them, she was anxious to get started on the fittings. The more time she had to work, the better her chance of being ready for the show.

Lauryn looked up as the curtains parted, and her mouth dropped open.

"Surprise!" Andrea cried, rushing over to Lauryn. Right behind Andrea were Emma, Chloe, and Jocelyn.

"What? How? Oh, my gosh, you guys," she babbled as she hugged each one. "I don't believe this."

"Jace told us what was going on," Andrea explained.

"And we thought maybe you could use some help," Chloe said. "We can do hair and makeup or help with the dresses if you need us to."

"What about Roger and your girls?"

"We're working through it," Chloe told her. "He realizes that he could lose us. He's working really hard to get his life together."

"I'm so happy to hear that," Lauryn said, hugging Chloe again.

Tears filled Lauryn's eyes. "You don't know how badly I need your help."

"That's why we came," Andrea said. "But you'll have to save your tears for later. I think your models are on their way. Jace said something about it when we came in. And by the way, who's that other guy taking charge out there?" she asked with interest.

"My friend Cooper. He's done this whole production."

"He's cute," Andrea said. "Is he available?"

Lauryn smiled at Andrea. "Well, yes, actually, he is."

"Maybe you can introduce us."

"Of course I will." Lauryn gave her friend a hug. "I still can't believe you all came."

"Jace called when you were really sick and said if you got better in time he was going to try to help you pull off the show. Then that fire happened, and we weren't sure the show would go on," Jocelyn said. "We decided we were coming either way. You needed us."

Lauryn shook her head. "I'm so lucky to have you guys."

A commotion at the curtain caught their attention. Then the curtains parted, and in walked Jazmyn, LaShondra, and several other Young Women. Her models had arrived! It was time to get busy.

Lauryn watched the girls fawn over the gowns, and her heart warmed. Who else but these beautiful girls would come to her aid?

No one was going to believe that she would take a risk like this and not use professional models, but Lauryn was determined to make a bold statement with this show. She wanted people to connect with the models so they could see themselves in her dresses. Her designs were for the everyday woman and girl, so who better to model them than average girls of all shapes and sizes? She'd called Jacqueline to bounce the idea off her. Jacqueline had immediately loved it.

"You'll turn the fashion world upside down," she had responded. "You'll also make a bold statement to the media by using these girls. You may have a little to lose, but I think you have more to gain by doing it. And the mere fact that Vanessa and her friends are going to be there will add a level of legitimacy to your fashions. It's risky, but with great risks come great rewards."

"You know, Jacqueline, you taught me something many years ago, and it's something I've never forgotten. In fact, I've tried to live my life by it."

"Really. What was that?" Jacqueline asked.

"You told me that all that glitters isn't gold. I want to be successful, of course—without success I can't use my talents to help other people—but the real success has been seeing how many wonderful friends I have, especially in my time of need."

"Darling, then you have learned the secret to happiness. Molnar has success, but I wonder how happy he really is."

"No success would be enjoyable for me if I had to use others the way he does."

"I'm very proud of you, Lauryn. Very proud."

With that said, Lauryn knew the show would be complete.

And as she looked at the beautiful, eager young faces in front of her, these amazing Young Women, she knew they would be perfect. And after the last fashion show, she had complete confidence in her girls. Many of them had been given a boost to their self-esteem and had been inspired by their participation in the last show to take better care of themselves by exercising and eating healthier. They were taking a little more time to fix their hair, put on a little makeup, and dress nicely, instead of wearing only baggy jeans and oversized T-shirts like some of them had.

With the support of her friends, not to mention the four extra pairs of hands for pinning, sewing, hair, and makeup, Lauryn just knew the show was going to be a huge success.

* * *

Lauryn spent the next several hours answering her cell phone, making alterations, and running around like a crazy woman. Her dad had called to let her know they weren't going to make it. She had a hard time being too disappointed, because he had such an awesome excuse. He'd just been called as the bishop and had to get his counselors called.

Lauryn was so proud of her father and the changes he'd made in his life. She knew he would be there in spirit and that he would be praying for her, just as she would be praying for him.

Caught up in the commotion, Lauryn wasn't aware of how late the hour was or the fact that she hadn't stopped to have anything to eat, even though her friends had brought food in for everyone.

It was Jace who finally cornered her.

"Hey," he said, pulling her into a quiet corner of the dressing room, secluded by dress racks. "How are you holding up? I'm worried about you."

She smiled and hugged him tightly. "I'm fine. My body is used to being pushed like this."

"But you need to take care of yourself or you'll get sick again. We can't have you collapsing tomorrow." He tucked a piece of hair behind her ear and kissed her on the forehead.

She rested her head against his chest and enjoyed the strength of his arms around her.

"Listen," he said. "The set is completely finished. The alterations are almost done, thanks to the *dream team.*"

"Thanks to you for calling them," she said. "They've been life-savers. I don't think I could have pulled this off without them. I think they're almost done, too."

"Don't thank me. I just made the call. They're the ones who dropped everything to come."

"Yeah," Lauryn said, taking in a long, calming breath, "that's the kind of friends they are."

"I know."

"But Jace," she said, pulling back so she could look up into his eyes, "none of this would have happened without you. You've sacrificed your job and your time for me. Are you worried you might lose your job? Why would you do this?"

"Can't you tell by now?" He put his hands on each side of her face. "I'm in love with you."

Tears filled her eyes as he kissed her.

For several moments after, he held her close in his arms, where she felt secure and strengthened.

"As for my job," he said, "I guess I should probably let you know that I gave my notice. I'm not going to move to London."

"You're not?"

"It's too far away from you."

"Does that mean you're moving here?"

"Would that be all right with you?"

"Oh, Jace," she said, wrapping her arms around his neck. "That would be wonderful. You are wonderful. Everything is wonderful."

He laughed as they hugged again.

"Thank you," she said.

"For what?"

"For taking care of me. But most of all," she paused to control her emotions, "thank you for loving me. I love you, too, Jace. I think I always have."

"Me too," he said with his familiar, dimpled smile.

"What took us so long to figure this out?"

"I don't know," he said. "I'm just grateful we did. And I'm never letting go of you, now that I've got you."

"Promise?" she asked.

"Promise."

Chapter Twenty-six

The next morning at eight o'clock, surprisingly refreshed after only four hours of sleep, Lauryn and Jace arrived at the tent, ready for the biggest day of her career.

"You look beautiful, by the way," Jace told her as they walked hand in hand toward the runway.

"I thought I'd better look presentable, just in case the media shows up in droves, like Vanessa said they would. I know Bernice is going to be here. She's the most important one as far as I'm concerned."

"The woman from *Women's Fashion Review*?"

Lauryn nodded. "She's been following this story from the beginning, when I did the show for the Young Women. I think she's curious to know what I'm really capable of. Plus, she's determined to bring Laszlo Molnar down."

Jace gave her a curious look.

"What?"

"Is that how you feel?"

"Actually, it's not. I really can't stand the guy. I don't like how I was treated while I was at Molnar's, but in a way, he's part of my having this chance to show what I can do."

"I don't know if I'd go that far."

"It's true. I feel like he freed me from a cage—no doubt a gilded cage. I loved working for Jacqueline, but I never would have been able to see if I could fly had he not opened the door. And I'm flying, Jace. It's really happening. But I also know that I never, ever could have done it without everyone's help: Cooper, Vanessa, Caroline, Jacqueline, Logan, my *dream team,* and you. To risk sounding cheesy, you guys are the wind beneath my wings."

Jace chuckled. "Yeah, that's pretty cheesy. But it works." He gave her a quick kiss. "Now, what are we doing here so early?"

"I just need to go over everything one last time—the set, the show outline, the dresses—in case there are any last-minute changes."

"All right, then. Let's do it."

* * *

By ten in the morning, the tent was abuzz with excitement. Of course, anytime Cooper was present there was excitement.

He entered the tent, singing, "Start spreading the news. I'm leaving today. I want to be a part of it, New York, New York."

He climbed up on the ramp and did a chorus line kick the rest of the way. "If I can make it there, I'll make it anywhere." Then came his big finish. "It's up to you, New York, New York!"

Jace and Lauryn burst into applause, and Cooper took a bow.

"Thank you, thank you," he said, as if he were receiving an award.

They laughed as he joined them offstage.

"I'm so excited. I didn't sleep a wink all night. I racked my brain trying to think of anything I needed to change or fix on the set, you know, maybe improve it so it would be perfect."

"Oh, no! You can't change anything," Lauryn exclaimed. "It *is* perfect."

"I know. I couldn't think of a thing," he agreed. "It really is. Oh, and look!" He unzipped the garment bag in his hand, "How about this tux? Isn't it to die for?"

He displayed the tuxedo he would wear when he emceed the show. It had a white jacket with black lapels, cuffs, and buttons. Perfectly fitting for the stage design.

"That is great!" Lauryn said. "You didn't have it made especially for this, did you?"

"No, actually, I had it hanging in my closet. I've been waiting for a chance to wear it again."

"Only you would have something like this in your closet."

"So true," Cooper said. "I amaze even myself some days. So, what can I do to help?"

"I can't think of anything," Lauryn said. "We're just waiting for the models to arrive so they can get their hair and makeup done. My friends and Logan will be here any minute."

"Really?" Cooper straightened his collar and smoothed the front of his shirt.

"Any particular reason you want to look so spiffy?" she asked.

"No, not really. Just a big day, you know."

Lauryn had noticed that after she'd introduced Cooper and Andrea, they'd managed to find ways to bump into each other throughout the evening. She wasn't sure what she thought about the two of them hooking up, but then again, they had barely met. Who knew if anything would come of it? The good thing was, Cooper was still attending her ward and had become good friends with the missionaries. In fact, his parents had the missionaries over for dinner once a week.

"Just, uh . . . let me know when your friends arrive," Cooper said as he left to get ready before his parents showed up for the final sound and light check. Lauryn and Jace smiled at each other as they watched Cooper whip a comb from his back pocket and run it through each side of his fauxhawk, *Grease* style.

He had just stepped off the stage when the door opened and in walked Lauryn's four friends and Logan, bringing even more excitement with them.

Hugs were shared, then Andrea, who nonchalantly glanced around the entire tent, finally asked, "So, is anyone else here yet?"

"He's in the back, getting changed."

"He? Who do you mean?" she asked innocently.

"I'm sorry, I meant Cooper is here. He's getting changed."

Andrea's face lit up. "Oh, good. Well," she said. "I think I'll go visit the powder room and freshen up after that taxi ride. I probably smell like stale cigarette smoke."

"I need to go too," Logan said. "This is what happens when I get excited!"

The group watched them walk away, then burst into conversation.

"Cooper is all Andrea talked about last night," Emma said.

"You'd think she'd met Johnny Depp the way she went on and on about him," Jocelyn added.

"I think it's cute," Chloe said. "Andrea hasn't been excited about a man for a long, long time. And Cooper is completely adorable."

Emma frowned. "You make him sound like a puppy."

"He is adorable. And so fashionable. I think he and Andrea would look cute together."

"Let's give them five seconds to get to know each other first," Emma said.

Chloe raised an eyebrow at Emma's comment. "And this is coming from a woman who is ready to get married and move to Greece with a man she's only known for three weeks?"

"I'm not going to get married and move to Greece right away," Emma countered.

Lauryn felt concerned. Emma wasn't convincing. Was it possible she was thinking about it? "Emma, you really aren't going to, are you? I mean, Nicholas sounds wonderful, and I can't wait to meet him, but you should take this really slowly. He's not even a member, right?"

"Well, no. But I'm working on it. He's a good man, and he treats me like a queen. That's got to say something about him."

"I met him once," Jocelyn said. "But only for a minute. He seemed really nice, and he is very handsome."

"Thank you," Emma said.

The doors opened, and in walked Lauryn's Young Women.

Lauryn took a deep breath. *Here goes nothing,* she thought.

"All right, girls. First we're doing hair and makeup, then you can get dressed. Cooper had the shoes delivered, so we'll also need you to come and find a pair to wear for the show. Some of you can work on getting shoes, and the others can be getting ready."

Chloe helped take over and moved the groups of girls into the dressing room to get started.

Several of the Young Women leaders and mothers had offered to help, so they followed along.

Lauryn closed her eyes and offered a quick prayer of thanks, and another one for a blessing that all would go well today. She knew she would need heavenly help to pull this off.

Her phone buzzed, indicating an incoming call. She glanced at it and recognized her mother's number. Lauryn just didn't have time to talk. She'd have to call her later. Right now, she had to focus on getting ready for the show.

"Hey," Jace said, pulling Lauryn aside. "Have you had anything to eat? You need to keep your strength up."

"I'd love a cinnamon raisin bagel with cream cheese if you can find one," she said.

He kissed her forehead. "Consider it done."

Lauryn watched him walk away, her heart pounding in her chest. Her thoughts were carried away with him.

"Sister Alexander!" one of the Young Women called from the curtain, pulling Lauryn from her entranced state. "Chloe needs you."

"I'll be right there," Lauryn answered, hurrying to the dressing room.

* * *

"Girls," Lauryn said as the time drew near for the show to begin. She pulled all the models and backstage help together so she could express her gratitude to them. "Without you, I wouldn't be able to make my dream come true. Thank you." She choked up as they applauded quietly so they wouldn't create a disturbance for the audience already seated and waiting for the show to begin.

"You all look amazing. To be honest, I can't think of anyone I'd rather have wearing my gowns in this show." The excitement in the faces looking back at her reassured Lauryn that she'd made the right decision.

"All I ask is that you don't be nervous. Just have fun. That's the message I want people to get from my creations."

"Sister Alexander," Jazmyn quietly spoke up, "we have something to give you." A large bouquet of flowers and a card signed by all of them was handed forward from the back of the group. The card read, "Thank you for believing in us, so we can believe in ourselves."

Blinking quickly to clear the moisture from her eyes, Lauryn looked up at the lovely Young Women of all shapes, sizes, and colors and felt an overwhelming surge of love for them. No matter what happened out on that runway, this moment would be what she treasured most.

"Girls, girls, you look fabulous, every one of you!" Cooper exclaimed as he charged into the group. "Is everyone ready?"

The girls nodded.

"All of you take a five-minute final check—hair, makeup, and dress—then we'll get this party started!"

The crowd of models dispersed to the mirrors and makeup stations for one last inspection.

"How are you holding up?" Cooper took Lauryn by the hands and looked her directly in the eyes.

"Actually, I'm more calm than I thought I'd be. I'm more excited than nervous."

"Good, because the place is packed. Vanessa and her friends arrived in style, making quite a production of it. Of course, I got it all on video. Vanessa really worked the media and sang your praises, declaring you to be the hottest new designer in the city and letting everyone know that you would be designing all of her dresses in the future. Of course, the media was in a frenzy because of the Oscar buzz surrounding Vanessa. She's brilliant, by the way. If you ask me, we've got more than our share of media covering this event."

"Probably here to see if I'm going to fall on my face."

"Probably. Which you won't," Cooper assured her. "Then again, some are here out of curiosity. Oh, and Bernice is here. She interviewed me and wants to catch you after the show. Of course, I told her she was your top priority."

"Nice job," Lauryn said.

"Your friend Caroline Nottingham and her group of highbrows arrived."

"Caroline made it!" Lauryn was relieved. Caroline's private plane had encountered engine trouble, so she'd had to fly commercial and had had a difficult time getting a flight in time.

"And there's someone else out there you might want to be aware of."

"Oh?"

Cooper hesitated a moment before he spoke. "Well, you're going to find out, so I might as well tell you . . . Laszlo Molnar arrived just a few minutes ago."

"What's he doing here?"

"It doesn't matter what brought him here. What matters is that when he leaves, one foot will be in his mouth and the other one will be kicking himself in the tush. I've got my video camera ready."

Lauryn laughed at the image but couldn't help feeling added anxiety knowing *he* was in the audience.

"We're ready to start whenever you are," Cooper said.

"Are you nervous?" Lauryn asked, knowing how much of the show's success depended upon him.

"Me? Absolutely not. I live for moments like this—bright lights, an audience, performing—I was born for the stage."

Lauryn shook her head in amazement. "I can see that. Broadway's missing her brightest star."

"Don't think I haven't thought about it," Cooper replied. "But I can decide that later. We go on in less than three minutes."

"Oh, my! Okay. Get going; I'll have everyone ready."

Cooper ran off, and Lauryn took the quiet moment to say one last prayer of thanks and a plea for help. Everything had to go as planned. It just had to.

"Hey there." She felt a pair of arms circle around her.

A smile creased her face. "Hey there." She turned and slipped her arms around Jace's neck. "Where have you been? I was getting a little worried."

"Sorry. I got delayed. I got your food, but you probably don't have time to eat it."

"I'm okay. I'm too nervous to eat."

"Did you see the crowd out there?"

"I haven't had a chance," she said.

"Come here; you gotta see this." He guided her by the hand to a crack in the curtains so she could look out.

Her breath caught in her throat as she looked out over the packed tent. Every seat was taken, and many people were standing in the back by the entrance. "Whoa," she said. "This doesn't even seem possible."

"Did you notice who was sitting in the corner on the front row?" he asked.

"Don't tell me Laszlo managed to get a front-row seat," she grumbled, splitting the curtains again. Her gaze followed the row of chairs and stopped on a thin-framed woman, looking very much out of place.

"Mom?" She turned and looked at Jace. "What in the world is she doing here?"

He didn't have to answer. Guilt was written all over his face.

"You?"

He nodded. "I hope you're not mad."

"She said she wanted to come, but I didn't really think much about it. She's never cared about what I'm doing before."

"She cares more than you think. She was thrilled when I invited her."

"She's broke. How in the world did she find the money?" Lauryn asked.

"I helped out a little."

She narrowed her gaze.

"Okay, I helped a lot." He sighed. "Listen, I probably stuck my nose in where it doesn't belong, but this event is a huge accomplishment for you, and I thought it was something she should see."

Lauryn wasn't sure how she felt about having her mother there. Mostly, she was just surprised that her mother would even come. Lauryn prayed that she was sober.

Taking another glance through the curtain, Lauryn looked at her mother again. The woman looked like she'd aged forty years and shrunk to half her normal size. Lauryn's heart went out to her. Maybe it was her own fault that she was like this—sad, lonely, empty, and in bad health—but Lauryn still felt twinges of love and loyalty for her. She still wished things could have been different for them, that they would have had a close relationship and shared in each other's lives. Maybe things could change.

"Showtime!" Cooper announced as he raced through the dressing room making the announcement.

Lauryn let the curtains fall together and shook off the sadness that had come over her. She could deal with all of that after the show. Right now she had to be focused and in charge.

"All right, girls. Line up. And remember, have fun!" Lauryn told them.

The house lights went off, spotlights came on, and the familiar strains of "Luck Be a Lady" from *Guys and Dolls* began pulsing through the huge speakers hanging from each corner of the tent ceiling. Lauryn and Cooper both had the vision that they wanted the audience to not just attend the show, but really experience it, by tapping into a nostalgic thread of old Hollywood glamour and days gone by.

The first girl, Juanita, took her spot and, on cue, strutted onto the stage in a shimmering gold gown with layers of silk and glittering rhinestones. Lauryn couldn't stand it. She had to peek through the curtain and see it firsthand.

Juanita's family was from Puerto Rico, and she had beautiful brown skin and thick, black hair. The gold color was exquisite on her.

Lauryn smiled as Juanita executed the runway walk exactly as Cooper had shown her. Her hair was in an updo, which gave her a very sophisticated, mature look, even though she was only seventeen. Under the runway lights, Juanita glowed, her smile as captivating as the dress she wore.

Applause accompanied her as she turned at the end of the runway, posed, turned, posed again, then turned and walked back.

"How's she doing?" Jace asked as he stood behind Lauryn and slid an arm around her waist.

"Incredible," Lauryn whispered back.

Of course, Cooper was in his element announcing the girls and their dresses.

Lauryn noticed Jocelyn hurrying over to her with a worried look on her face.

"What's wrong?"

"One of the girls is throwing up. She can't go on. She thought it was nerves, but I think she's sick."

"Oh, no!" Lauryn dropped the curtain and hurried over to the group of girls. "Who is it? Who's sick?"

"Jazmyn," one of them said. "She said it's been going around her family."

Lauryn located Jazmyn, who was laying on the floor on top of a pile of clothes. Lauryn knelt beside her. "Honey, how are you feeling?"

Normally dark skinned, Jazmyn looked as pale as milk.

"I feel terrible."

Lauryn felt her forehead; it was burning up.

"I put the dress on that rack over there," Jazmyn said, trying to point. "I didn't want to barf on it."

Lauryn laughed. "I appreciate that. Do you need anything?"

Jazmyn shook her head. "My mom wanted to come today, but she was sick."

"Are you okay for a minute then? I need to find someone to wear that dress, then I'll be right back."

"I just want to sleep," Jazmyn said, shutting her eyes.

"Okay. I'll check on you in a minute." Lauryn grabbed the dress and rushed back over to the group of girls, trying to decide who the dress would fit. Then it dawned on her—Logan could wear it.

Last time this had happened, she'd promised Logan that she never would have to model again. Somehow she had to get Logan to put the dress on. If Lauryn quickly unpicked the hem, it would fit Logan perfectly.

"How's Jazmyn?" Logan asked when Lauryn approached her.

"She's not doing so well. There's no way she can model."

"That's too bad; she was really looking forward to it." Logan was putting makeup back into cases. "It's a good thing she's at the end of the show. Who are you going to have wear her dress?" She stuffed some curling irons and hairspray into a bag.

"There's only one girl who can really fit into the same dress as Jazmyn."

Logan continued cleaning, then she stopped and looked at Lauryn with sudden understanding. "No, Lauryn. I did it once, and you told me you'd never make me do it again. That's scary out there. I can't do it."

"Please, Logan. This is one of the most important dresses of the collection."

"But there are news people and photographers."

"You won't even see them. Just go out and model like you did before. It won't even take five minutes."

Logan shut her eyes and groaned.

"You know I wouldn't ask if I weren't desperate."

Logan didn't answer for several moments. "Oh, all right then. But you so owe me *Wicked* tickets."

"I promise. That's the first thing we'll do."

"Fine." She snatched the dress out of Lauryn's hands. "And to think I always wanted a big sister. Ha!"

Logan went to change, and Lauryn went back to the curtain where Jace had been watching the show.

"How's it going?" she asked.

"The audience is eating them up. You've got to take a look."

Peeking through the curtain, Lauryn scanned the faces in the crowd and was relieved to see everyone smiling and nodding approvingly—everyone, that is, except Laszlo Molnar, who looked over the top of his wire-rimmed Armani sunglasses and followed each model with a disapproving glare.

But Lauryn didn't care. Most of the shows she had been to had been serious, dramatic affairs, where everyone tried to outdo one another. Lauryn had always vowed that her show, if she ever got to have one, would be an enjoyable experience, one that would be memorable, not just because of the clothing.

Lauryn beamed as Martha, one of the heavier-set African-American girls, stepped onto the stage. She looked absolutely stunning in a dandelion-yellow-colored dress that skimmed her curves with flattering drapes of silk. No one could work the runway like Martha. She strutted and engaged the audience with her beautiful smile and gorgeous eyes.

"Would you look at her?" Jace said. "She's stealing the show!"

"I know. I had her in mind when I designed the dress. I don't care what size a woman's body is; she still deserves to have clothes that make her feel wonderful. The average, everyday women are the ones I want wearing my dresses, not just the rich and famous. I mean, don't get me wrong; I love Caroline and Vanessa and definitely want them to wear my dresses too, but you shouldn't have to have an eating disorder to be able to fit into one of my designs."

Jace hugged her. "Have I told you how proud I am of you?"

"Yes. At least a million times."

"Just checking. Because I am, you know. This is incredible."

"Thanks," she said, enjoying the feel of his arms around her and the satisfaction of finally seeing her gowns on the runway. Her dreams had come true.

Chapter Twenty-seven

"Did you see that standing ovation?" Cooper exclaimed as he barreled down the stairs toward Lauryn. He grabbed her and swung her around. "The show was a hit!"

Lauryn made an appearance at the end of the show, walked several steps onto the ramp, then hurried off the stage. Now she knew how Logan felt, walking out in front of all of those people. It was terrifying!

The commotion behind the curtains nearly matched the commotion in front. All the Young Women were celebrating the fact that none of them had tripped or fallen off the ramp or done anything seriously embarrassing. Poor Jazmyn slept through the whole thing, but at least she'd stopped throwing up.

Tingling with excitement and relief that the show had been successful and was over, Lauryn began hanging dresses on the racks for transportation back to the warehouse.

"Hold on there," Jace said, stopping her as she gathered another armful of dresses. "You need to get out there and meet your fans. We can do this."

"I don't want to," Lauryn said. "It's too scary."

"That's part of the deal. You've got to go meet them so they can understand why your collection is so amazing."

Lauryn lifted up on her toes and gave him a kiss. "How have I survived all these years without you?"

"I've been asking myself that question ever since the day we met at the temple."

"I'm so glad this is over," she said, feeling the exhaustion kick in.

"I hate to break this to you, but this is just the beginning."

She laughed. "I guess this is what I've always wanted. But what do I do now? I'm done with Molnar. I can go back to Jacqueline's, but part of me doesn't want to lock into that completely, either."

"How about going at it on your own?"

"You mean starting my own design house?"

"Yes."

"That would be ideal, except there's one thing I don't have," she said.

"What's that."

"Money."

"Hmm." He gave her a kiss on the forehead. "I knew we made a good team. I just happen to know an investor who would be very interested in helping you get your own business started."

She studied his face to make sure he was serious. "Really? Who?"

"Your friend Caroline. She wants to meet for dinner while she's in town and talk about it."

Was this really happening? Lauryn was amazed that everything was finally falling into place. Sure, it had taken nearly ten years and had nearly cost her health and sanity, but it was worth it. She'd learned that dreams didn't come true on their own. A person had to make them come true. Talent was one thing. But hard work and perseverance seemed to be the magic ingredient in making dreams happen.

"You'd better get out there," he told her. "We can talk about all of this later."

"Okay." She gave him a quick kiss and stepped away, then stopped. "Don't go too far," she said.

He held up dresses and hangers. "You know where to find me."

Lauryn paused at the curtain before stepping through. She needed to prepare herself for the attention she was about to get, good or bad. She knew better than to expect rave reviews; she just hoped the critics wouldn't be too harsh, especially with Laszlo in the audience.

She parted the curtains and slipped through unnoticed. Several crew members were taking down chairs. Many audience members clustered in groups, talking, and several news channels were capturing interviews on camera.

Lauryn smiled as Vanessa answered questions about her association with Lauryn and the phenomenal hit her recent movie had been at the box office.

Sidestepping a large speaker, Lauryn caught a glimpse of Bernice Thomas with a cameraman. To Lauryn's horror, Bernice was interviewing . . . her mother!

"Tell me, Mrs. Alexander, when did you first know that Lauryn had the talent to be a designer?"

"Well," Lauryn's mom thought for just a moment, "I suppose it was when she was a little girl and used to cut dresses out of scrap fabric and make clothes for her Barbies. She was always working on some little project and really enjoyed working with her hands. She can crochet a mile a minute!"

"How did you enjoy today's show?" Bernice asked.

"Oh, my! Well, I have to say that it was the most remarkable thing I've ever seen. I can't believe that my little Lauryn designed all those beautiful gowns." Lauryn's mother's voice trembled with emotion as she spoke. "She's always believed in herself, even when I didn't believe in her. I am just so proud of her."

Those were words Lauryn hadn't heard in her entire thirty years of life. And she was amazed at how much power those words had to move her.

"Thank you, Mrs. Alexander," Bernice said, turning back to face the camera. "And there you have it from Lauryn Alexander's mother herself. From Barbies to the Big Apple, Lauryn Alexander is on the brink of becoming a household name. Not only did she wow the audience with her creations and classic designs, but she did something no other designer has dared to do . . . she used models who were average women, just like you and me, and she transformed them into glamorous Hollywood stars. She made me believe that even Bernice Thomas could feel like a celebrity in a Lauryn Alexander dress."

"Oh!" Bernice exclaimed as she glanced sideways and saw Lauryn standing in the shadows, wiping away tears. "There she is now. Let's see if we can have a few words with the designer herself."

Lauryn wanted to run, but she knew that wasn't an option.

Dabbing at her face with the corner of her sleeve, she tried to put on a happy smile before the camera light blinded her.

"Lauryn, could we have a moment?" Bernice asked.

"Of course, Bernice."

"It seems as though the show was a great hit. There was something very fresh and appealing about each style. Some were elegant enough for the red carpet, some for an expensive evening on the town, and some for a school prom—quite a range of styles. Where do you get your inspiration?"

"My inspiration comes from the people I design for. I don't just imagine who those people are, I know who they are. They're my family, my friends, my associates and neighbors, and their families and friends. Right now, I'm going through a Hollywood glamour phase. I love the styles and elegance of the fifties, when clothes made a statement and so did the women wearing them."

"I noticed that not only were the dresses breathtaking, but the shoes were out of this world. I didn't recognize the designer."

"The shoes were designed by Cooper D'Angelo, the man who also produced and emceed the show."

"Those were D'Angelo shoes?" Bernice seemed surprised. "Perhaps we can have a few words with the genius behind the show and the shoes." She switched the focus quickly back to Lauryn. "So, Ms. Alexander, now that you have your first show out of the way—your first prominent show, I should say—where do you go from here? You've worked with Jacqueline Yvonne and Laszlo Molnar; what are your plans?"

"Well." Lauryn paused, catching a glimpse of Jace over Bernice's shoulder. His presence made her feel confident and strong. She smiled at Bernice, "My experience with Mr. Molnar proved to be a great learning opportunity and, I must say, that without my experience there I would never have had the chance to put on my own show, so I want to give him credit for that." Even though there was a lot of mud she could sling at that moment, she chose not to. Bad-mouthing Molnar wouldn't benefit her in any way, and she didn't want to appear vengeful or manipulative. "But I will no longer be working for him. I will, however, continue working with Jacqueline Yvonne, but as an independent designer. I've decided to start my own design house."

Bernice's brows lifted with surprise. "That's an ambitious under-taking."

"It is. I know there are risks involved. But I have a great deal of support. A very good friend taught me to take advantage of opportunities when they come along. That's why it's important to always be ready. You never know when that opportunity is going to present itself."

Bernice gave her a nod of approval. She turned to the camera. "Great advice from new designer Lauryn Alexander." She turned back to Lauryn. "Thank you for your time, and again, congratula-tions. We will watch you with great anticipation. Also, word has it that Vanessa Cates, who most likely will be nominated for best actress, will be wearing one of your designs at the Academy Awards this year."

"That's right. Ms. Cates has graciously asked me to design her gown. It's very exciting."

The interview ended, and Lauryn breathed a sigh of relief. Hopefully she hadn't made a fool of herself.

"Let's find Cooper and get an interview from him," Bernice told the cameraman. The guy nodded and left the camera to find Cooper.

"Great job today," Bernice told her. "You were very gracious about Mr. Molnar. You could have chosen to expose him, you know."

"I know. He did everything he could to sabotage my show. The mere fact that I pulled it off and that it was successful says more than any of my words ever could."

Bernice nodded. "You're a class act, Lauryn."

"Thanks, Bernice. You've been great through all of this."

"What can I say? I like underdogs and risk takers. And you, Lauryn, have just become the poster child for both! The modesty thing worked!"

They laughed together, and Bernice even gave her a hug.

"Good luck with everything. Give me a call when you're ready to launch your next line. You aren't going to try for Fall Fashion Week are you?"

"No," Lauryn said. "I'm sure that would kill me. I'm going to spend the next few months recovering from all of this and getting my design house underway. I'm shooting for spring next year, but even that will be a push."

"Keep me posted. I'm a big fan. In fact, I would love to talk to you about a couple of those cocktail dresses I saw today. I've got a White House gala to attend, and I think one of them would be perfect for the event."

"Call me Monday," Lauryn said. "We'll schedule a fitting."

"I've got Cooper!" the cameraman called to Bernice.

"We'll talk soon," Bernice told her, then hurried off to continue her interview.

Lauryn was about to go back to the dressing room and help load the racks of gowns, when a movement out of the corner of her eye caught her attention.

She turned to see Beckham, Mr. Molnar's assistant, coming her way.

With a smile, she greeted him, and they hugged.

"I'm so glad you came," she said. "You know, without your very timely confession, I would be looking pretty foolish right now."

"I know," he said.

She knew he was teasing, but it was true. He'd sacrificed greatly to help her.

"Why did you do it? You risked your job by helping me."

"I've been around Molnar long enough to recognize talent when I see it. I knew you had something special. And I guess I got sick of the way they were using you."

"Did you know exactly what his motives were?" she asked.

"As closely as I work with Mr. Molnar, this wasn't something he ever talked to me about. A lot of it was his vendetta against Jacqueline. You were just a pawn in his plan. He didn't care if he destroyed you if it helped bring her down."

"Well, it all backfired on him, didn't it."

"It sure did. He left during the standing ovation. I'm not sure, but it looked like he was about to cry."

They both laughed.

"Well, I hope you don't suffer back at work for being involved with me."

"That won't be a problem. I quit. I can't work for him anymore."

Lauryn felt bad that Beckham had quit because of her. Then she got an idea. "You know, Beckham, I'm just in the beginning stages of developing my own design house, but I sure could use someone like you once I get things up and running."

"Are you offering me a job?" he asked excitedly.

"I'm not sure how long it will take until we're in business, but I'm already getting calls for gowns."

"Lauryn, that would be great! I would love to work for you."

"You're sure? I told you I would talk to Jacqueline about you. I'm sure she'd hire you."

"That's tempting, but I think I'll take you up on this offer. We already know that we work well together."

Lauryn laughed. "We sure do. Well, I'll be in touch then. And Beckham, thanks again for everything. This all happened today because of you."

"Thanks, Lauryn."

They hugged again, and he waved good-bye.

He was eager and loyal and hardworking. He would be a great help in starting her new business.

Her phone buzzed in her pocket, and she checked her text messages.

"Have you seen your mom?" Jace had texted.

She hadn't seen her mom since right after her interview. It had been so hectic they hadn't yet spoken with each other.

Where had her mother gone?

One of the workers helping to put away chairs and take down the tent told her he thought he'd seen a woman who fit her mother's description going outside.

Lauryn pushed through the doors and stepped out into the hot afternoon sun. Squinting against the sunlight, she shielded her eyes with her hand and scanned the grounds, hoping to see her mother.

Just as she was about to pull out her cell phone and call her, she spotted her mom sitting on a bench under the shade of a tree.

As she approached the bench, Lauryn noticed again how thin and frail the woman looked. There was a time when her mother had seemed so strong and powerful, so in charge. Now she looked like a shell of that person. The choices her mother had made in life had cost her everything: her health, her career, her family.

Her mother looked so sad and lonely. She didn't even notice Lauryn approaching until Lauryn was just a few feet away, then she looked up, and her expression brightened.

"Hi, Mom."

"Lauryn." She jumped to her feet. "I didn't think I'd see you. You must be very busy."

"I have a lot of help," Lauryn said. "What are you doing out here? Let's sit down."

They sat together on the bench.

"I didn't want to get in the way," she said. "But the show was so wonderful. Just wonderful." Her mother got a tremor of emotion in her voice.

"Thank you. I'm glad you liked it. And . . . I'm glad you could be here for it."

Her mother looked at her, blinking her eyes quickly to clear the moisture in them. "You are?"

"Yes. It means a lot that you were here."

"Oh." Her mother lost the battle as more tears collected in her eyes. "That's so nice of you."

"Mom. I want you to be part of my life. I've always wanted you to be part of my life."

"But after all—"

"None of that matters," Lauryn interrupted. "I don't know how much time we'll have together, Mom, but I want us to spend more time with each other."

"You do?"

"Yes. In fact," Lauryn said quickly, before thinking too much and changing her mind, "I want you to move here, to New York, with me."

Her mother's mouth dropped open.

"That way we can be together, and you can get the best doctors."

"But you're so busy, and I would be in your way."

"No, Mom. In fact, it would be nice to have you. You're right, I am busy. Sometimes too busy to even cook or do laundry. Maybe, if you felt up to it, you could help me out that way a little."

"Of course I could. I could keep your place clean and have meals ready for you. Look at you, you're skin and bones."

"See, I need my mom to come and take care of me."

"Oh, honey, I would love to," her mother said, wiping at her tears.

Lauryn slid her arms around her mother's shrinking frame and gave her a hug. She knew that they wouldn't have much time together, but whatever time they had left, they would spend it together, making up for all the years they had been apart.

* * *

Saturday evening, once everyone had gone back to their hotels, Lauryn and Jace decided to go out to dinner, since they hadn't really spent any time alone since he'd come to New York.

With a view of the city from the top of the Marriott Marquis, they looked out at the sparkling city lights below and enjoyed a moment of peace and contentment together.

"Good day?" Jace asked.

"Fantastic day," she replied.

"You were the fantastic part," he told her.

"Thanks. You were pretty fantastic yourself. I mean, hanging up gowns, gluing on rhinestones. In fact, did I see you putting bobby pins in one of the girls' hair?"

"Hey, don't be so shocked. I have sisters."

"You know what really touched me?" she said, reaching across the table to take his hand.

"What?"

"I watched you check on Jazmyn and roll up someone's sweatshirt to put under her head for a pillow. Then you put a couple of jackets over her to keep her warm. You are always thinking of others, aren't you?"

"You make me sound like Mother Theresa."

She smiled. "It's just that I've never known a man quite as thoughtful as you are. It's one of the reasons I love you."

"Oh, really? That means there are more reasons?"

"Yes," she said, "many more." She scooted her chair close to his and snuggled against his chest in his embrace. "I'm so glad you're moving here. I don't know what I'd do if you were leaving for London."

"I couldn't go," he said. "In fact, I don't ever want to leave you again."

"I feel the same way."

"Well," he held her by the shoulders and looked at her intently with his blue eyes, "I guess that means there's only one thing to do."

"What's that?"

"Get married."

She jumped back, startled at his words. "Jace, are you serious?"

"I have never been so serious in my life."

She couldn't deny she'd been having the same thoughts. Never before had anything felt so right. Every time she thought about marrying him, a warm peace filled her heart.

"Are you saying what I think you're saying?"

"I'm saying . . ." He slid his chair back and took hold of both of her hands. Then, to her surprise, he knelt down on one knee. "Lauryn, will you marry me?"

Lauryn looked at him through tear-filled eyes. "Yes, Jace. I will marry you!"

He stood up and pulled her into a hug that lifted her off her feet. Together, they laughed and cried. It was wonderful and magical and perfect.

Chapter Twenty-eight

The next day, several articles appeared in the fashion newspapers and online, along with Bernice's interview, which aired on *E! News* and *FashionTV.* Unaccustomed to seeing herself on film, Lauryn had a hard time watching. Did her voice always sound so nasally? And why did she keep putting her hair behind her ear? Regardless of what she thought of herself, Lauryn appreciated Bernice's positive review of the fashion show. Several other fashion reporters hadn't been quite so glowing in their reviews, but they hadn't really attacked her, either. For the most part, the exposure was flattering.

Lauryn was in a hurry to get ready for church when her cell phone rang.

"Hello?" she said, expecting one of her friends, or hopefully, Jace. He hadn't gotten back to his hotel until nearly two A.M., after hours of talking and dreaming about their future.

"Hey, Lauryn, congratulations!"

"Michael?" She nearly dropped the phone.

"Wow, you're all over the papers today. I didn't know you were having a show yesterday. I would have loved to come."

"Why?" she asked, zipping up her skirt. She shoved her feet into her shoes. Jace would be there any minute to pick her and Logan up. She didn't have time to talk to Michael. Ever.

"Because this was a big thing for you. I would have loved to have been there to support you."

Holding the phone between her ear and shoulder, she rolled her eyes as she fastened her watch on her wrist.

"It's been a long time since we talked. Do you have time this week to go to dinner so we can catch up?"

"Actually, Michael. I don't. There's not really any point in us getting together, and besides that, I'm engaged. I don't think my fiancé would appreciate it." It was the first time she'd said the word fiancé, and she was surprised at how easily it came out of her mouth.

"Engaged? But we haven't been apart that long. Aren't you rushing into things a bit? Who is this guy?"

"I've known him since I was in high school. What can I say, Michael? When it's right, it's right." The phone beeped, indicating she had an incoming text. "You know what? I have to run, but it was nice talking to you. Good luck and . . . good-bye."

She hung up the phone and shook her head. There was a time that phone call would have meant the world to her, but hearing his voice, having him call, did nothing for her. She felt nothing except the excitement of seeing Jace and spending the rest of eternity with him.

* * *

While at church, Cooper was able to meet Rita's boyfriend, the Young Men leader whom she'd met after the Young Women fashion show. He was now taking ballroom dancing lessons with her.

Cooper was genuinely happy for her, especially now that he had other interests, namely Andrea. Even though it was strange to see them sitting next to each other in sacrament meeting and in Sunday School, there was something sweet about it too.

Everyone went back to Lauryn's house after church for pot roast and mashed potatoes made by her mother, who was already jumping right into her new role as resident chef. Lauryn had never known her mother could cook like this. Growing up, her mother had always wanted to go out to eat on Sunday afternoons.

Plans were made to send her mother back to Florida to take care of the business of moving permanently to New York. And to Logan's disappointment, plans were made for her return to Utah.

She would go back for her junior year, then she hoped to come back to New York to find a summer job. As for Brody, well, it appeared he was moving permanently out of the picture. Logan hadn't answered his messages or even mentioned his name in over two weeks. Logan was returning home a changed young woman, filled with new goals and bigger dreams.

"Mrs. Alexander," Jace said, leaning back in his chair. "That was the best meal I've had in weeks."

"Thank you, Jace," Lauryn's mom answered proudly. "I have a nice apple cobbler in the oven. Would anyone like some?"

"I'll help you dish it up," Logan offered. She helped gather up plates and carry them to the sink.

Lauryn was a little surprised at how well her mother and Logan were getting along. She'd anticipated a bit of animosity, but there was none. She was so relieved.

"Thank you, dear." Lauryn's mother accepted her help with gratitude.

"So," Chloe said, leaning forward in her chair. "What's going on with you two?" She waggled her finger at Lauryn and Jace, who were sitting next to each other on the love seat.

"Gee, Chloe," Emma said. "Cut right to the chase, would ya?"

"Sorry, but my plane leaves in a few hours. I need to know before I go."

"Well," Lauryn said, looking at Jace. "I'm not sure what to say."

"First of all," Jace said as he put his arm across Lauryn's shoulders, "I'm moving here to Manhattan to help Lauryn set up her business. I'll also be doing consulting work."

Lauryn looked at Cooper and said, "Is there anything you'd like to add to that announcement?"

Cooper wiped his mouth with his napkin and said, "It's not official yet, but I will be joining Lauryn as her assistant."

The group erupted in congratulations and cheers.

"Of course, once we get established, Cooper will become a partner in the business. Because eventually, I won't want to work full time."

"Why?" Emma asked.

"Because I'll want to devote time to my husband and family."

"Your husband . . ." Emma started, then the realization dawned on her. She looked at Jace. "Are you two—"

"Getting married?" Lauryn finished for her. "Yes! Jace asked me last night."

Between the celebratory screams from her friends and Cooper's hyperventilating, the noise nearly raised the roof. Everyone joined in the hugs and congratulations.

"I'm coming to New York more often," Jocelyn said. "I've had more excitement in the last three days than I've had in the last three years!"

"Not to mention meeting Vanessa Cates!" Andrea exclaimed. "I was so surprised to find out how down-to-earth she is."

"I know," Chloe agreed. "How about when she invited all of us to the Academy Awards if she gets nominated."

"That's how she is," Logan said. "She's the type who will sit and eat pizza and drink soda with you and then burp right in front of you."

"You know, Lauryn," Emma said thoughtfully. "It seems as though once you got the Butterfly Box, all these great things started happening. Talk about a good luck charm."

"It wasn't luck," Lauryn said. "It's a result of your faith and prayers . . . and a lot of hard work. I never could have done any of this without all of you." She felt a catch in her throat as she realized that for the moment, everything in her life was just as she'd dreamed it would be.

* * *

Monday morning, Lauryn slept late. The roller-coaster events of the past week had nearly leveled her.

Lounging in bed, she mulled over the events in her mind, reliving the thrill of her first fashion show, the excitement of having it well-received, and the anticipation of everything to come.

Whoever said that it was always darkest before the dawn was right. For a while there, she didn't think it could get any darker;

then suddenly, the light flickered, then burst into flames as everything miraculously fell into place.

There was no other explanation for it but receiving help from her Father in Heaven. Her prayers had seemed in vain at times, but now she realized that they hadn't been. She'd learned that a person could never stop praying, especially when it seemed like God wasn't listening, because that was when He listened the most. She was proof of that.

She shut her eyes and offered a silent prayer of thanks. She never wanted to relive the last two weeks of her life, but she was so very grateful for them.

Glancing over at the clock, she decided it was time to get up. She'd never slept in until noon, and she wasn't about to start. Besides, Jace was coming over to take her to lunch so they could talk wedding and business, and she wanted to be dressed and ready when he arrived.

Logan was in the living room watching television when Lauryn stepped through the door from her bedroom.

"Glad to see you didn't die," Logan said when Lauryn joined her on the couch. "I was beginning to wonder."

"So was I. I felt like I was dead. Have I missed anything?"

"Those arrived while you were in bed." Logan pointed to a flower arrangement the size of her kitchen table.

"Good grief! Who in the world sent that?"

Logan shrugged. "I didn't look at the card. I've been dying to know, though."

Just as Lauryn suspected, the flowers turned out to be from Vanessa.

Darling Lauryn,

You were a hit! But I knew you would be. You're an incredible woman, and I'm glad we're friends. Let's go to lunch soon. I know a wonderful place in Paris. I'll call you.

Love, Vanessa

Lauryn shook her head. She couldn't deny it. Having Vanessa for a friend was outrageous. The woman was very generous.

"You can't go without me," Logan said after she read the card. "I hate that I have to go home. I want to stay here with you."

Logan was scheduled to fly back to Salt Lake the next day. Lauryn had to admit she was going to miss having her younger stepsister around. They had grown close. But with Lauryn's mom coming to live with her and school starting for Logan, there was no other choice.

"You can come again next summer. I promise." Lauryn gave Logan a hug.

"This has been like the best thing that has ever happened to me. I feel like a totally different person than when I came," Logan said. "Thank you."

"Hey, that's what sisters are for," Lauryn said. "Which reminds me, Jace and I haven't set the date yet, but I was wondering how you'd feel about being my maid of honor at the wedding."

Logan's mouth dropped open. "Are you kidding? What about your friends?"

"I want you," Lauryn said. "Besides, I could never choose just one of them. The others would feel so bad. So you'd be helping me out a lot if you said yes."

"Of course I will," Logan said. "Will I get a new dress?"

"I've already got some ideas."

"You are the best sister ever!" Logan gave Lauryn another big squeeze.

Lauryn's phone rang.

"I'm going to jump in the shower," Logan said.

Lauryn nodded as she answered the phone. "Hello?"

"Lauryn, dear, it's Jacqueline."

"It's so good to hear your voice. How are you?"

"Well, I'm still sad that you aren't coming back to work for me, but I would be lying if I didn't say you would be making a huge mistake if you did. I'm also having quite a laugh, and I thought you might also get a chuckle out of it."

"Out of what?"

"The fact that Laszlo Molnar was in the paper today."

"For what this time?"

"Tax evasion. Apparently he owes millions in unpaid taxes."

"No!"

"Yes," Jacqueline said with a chuckle. "I know it's mean-spirited, but you have to admit, the man deserves it. The way he treats people and conducts business, it's no wonder it all finally caught up with him. I'm so glad you got out when you did."

"Wow, he could be in some serious trouble."

"We're talking jail time," Jacqueline told her. "But listen, I really just wanted to check on you and see how you're doing. I was worried about you Saturday. Have you recovered?"

"I feel great and very blessed. Jacqueline, I want to thank you for giving me a chance in this business. You have been an incredible mentor, and I hope you know that I will be asking for your advice every step of the way. In fact, you're probably going to get very sick of me!"

"Darling, let me tell you, I'll always be there for you. I never had the privilege of marrying or having children. You are the closest thing to a daughter I'll ever have. How could I want anything more for you than to be successful? I am so proud of you."

"Thank you, Jacqueline."

"And you'll still do a few designs for me now and then?"

"Of course," Lauryn promised.

"In fact, I could use your help on the designs for this movie I'm doing. I think a few of your gowns would be incredible on Nicole."

The thought of designing a gown for someone as elegant as Nicole Kidman was a thrill. "I'd love to help."

"I'll have my assistant check my schedule and give you a call so we can get together soon."

They said good-bye, and Lauryn floated into her bedroom to make her bed and get ready for the day. Life was unbelievably perfect right now.

She pulled the sheets tight on the bed and fluffed the pillows. Then she stopped when her eyes caught the Butterfly Box reflecting the late morning sun onto the wall in tiny sparkles. Almost involuntarily, Lauryn fell to her knees at the side of her bed. With her hands clasped and her head bent, she shut her eyes and poured out her gratitude. Even though the words were inadequate, she needed to express them. She'd always been taught that if she put the Lord first and was obedient, He would bless her with the righteous desires of her heart.

With tears streaming down her face, she thanked the Lord for the faith and prayers of her friends, for guiding her choices, for guiding her future, and for sending her the most amazing man to share it with.

Lauryn finished her prayer just as a knock came at the door.

Glancing at the time, she realized it was probably Jace.

Completely forgetting that she was still in her pajamas and that her hair was smashed on one side in a frizzed-out ponytail, she jumped up from the bed and raced to let him in.

Lauryn swung open the door and felt her heart melt at his dimpled smile.

"Hey, beautiful—" He looked at her with alarm. "You've been crying. What's wrong? Are you okay?"

"I'm great."

"Are you sure?"

"I'm sure. These are tears of joy."

"I'm glad. Those are the only kind of tears I ever want you to cry."

He gave her a hug and held her close.

Lauryn gave a contented sigh. "How have I managed to survive without you in my life?" she asked.

"I was wondering the same thing on my way over."

"Sorry I'm not ready. One day out of a job and already I've turned into a sloth."

"You're a very beautiful sloth. Besides, I'm unemployed, too, and I intend to take advantage of being jobless. That will change soon enough, and we'll be working our tails off to make your new business an enormous success."

"I like that," she said. "What do you have in mind?"

"Why don't we pack a lunch and go to Central Park for a picnic."

"That sounds wonderful," she exclaimed. "I would love to kick off my shoes and relax in the sunshine."

"Good. Maybe later we can find an arcade and play a few rounds of pinball."

She raised her eyebrows and smiled. "I like that idea. You sure you're up to being beat?"

One side of his mouth lifted in a smile. "I'll take my chances."

"And can we go out for Chinese tonight? Since my fortune came true, I need to get a new one."

He laughed. "What did it say again?"

"It said, 'You will find your future in your past.'"

"It really did come true. But I don't think it has anything to do with a fortune cookie. I think Heavenly Father played a pretty big role in bringing us together."

She nodded. "And I thank Him several times a day for doing so."

"I love you, Lauryn," Jace said.

"I love you, too," she replied.

About the Author

In the fourth grade, Michele Ashman Bell was considered a daydreamer by her teacher and was told on her report card that, "She has a vivid imagination and would probably do well with creative writing." Her imagination, combined with a passion for reading, has enabled Michele to live up to her teacher's prediction. She loves writing books, especially those that inspire and edify while entertaining.

Michele grew up in St. George, Utah, where she met her husband at Dixie College before they both served missions—his to Pennsylvania and hers to Frankfurt, Germany; and San Jose, California. Seven months after they returned they were married, and are now the proud parents of four children: Weston, Kendyl, Andrea, and Rachel.

A favorite pastime of Michele's is supporting her children in all of their activities, traveling both in and outside the United States with her husband and family, and doing research for her books. She also recently became scuba certified. Aside from being a busy wife and mother, Michele is an aerobics instructor at the Life Centre Athletic Club near her home, and she currently teaches in the Relief Society and is the Activity Day Leader.

Michele is the best-selling author of several books and a Christmas booklet and has also written children's stories for the *Friend* magazine.

If you would like to be updated on Michele's newest releases or correspond with her, please send an e-mail to info@covenant-lds.com. You may also write to her in care of Covenant Communications, P.O. Box 416, American Fork, UT 84003-0416.

Enter to win a formal gow

Beautifully Mode

Win a dress valued up to $500 from BeautifullyModest.com.

OFFICIAL ENTRY FORM (By submitting an entry form, you acknowledge that you have read and understand the official rules.)

Name: _____ Age: _____

Address: _____

City/State: _____ Zip: _____

Phone Number: _____

E-mail: _____

Would you like to receive either of these magazines? ☐ Bridal AND/OR ☐ Formal

To enter fill out the information requested above and mail entries postmarked by December 31, 2008 to
Gown Giveaway: BeautifullyModest at 575 University Parkway #F111, Orem, Utah 84097

No purchase necessary, a purchase does not increase chance of winning. Void where prohibited. Must be legal US resident 13 years or older as of 12/31/08 to enter. Email GownGiveaway@gmail.com for official rules and entry forms. Sweepstakes begins on 5/01/08 and ends on 12/31/08. Sponsor: BeautifullyModest.com, 575 University Parkway, Orem UT 84097